THE
BIG
SCORE

ALSO BY MICHAEL KILIAN

The Valkyrie Project
Northern Exposure
Blood of the Czars
By Order of the President
Dance on a Sinking Ship
Looker
The Last Virginia Gentleman

THE
BIG
SCORE

MICHAEL KILIAN

ST. MARTIN'S PRESS
NEW YORK

For Eric and Colin

This is a work of fiction. Although reference is made to several noted figures of the past and present, all of the characters in this book are fictional and are not in any way based on any actual person, living or dead, nor is this story based on any actual event, either in Chicago or anywhere else.

Design by Sara Stemen

Library of Congress Cataloging-in-Publication Data

Kilian, Michael
    The big score / Michael Kilian.
       p.   cm.
    "A Thomas Dunne book."
    ISBN 0-312-09925-8
    1. Architects—Illinois—Chicago—Fiction. 2. Family—Illinois—Chicago—Fiction. 3. Men—Illinois—Chicago—Fiction. 4. Chicago (Ill.)—Fiction. I. Title.
PS3561.I368B3   1993
813'.54—dc20   93-11466
                                               CIP

First edition: October 1993

10 9 8 7 6 5 4 3 2 1

ACKNOWLEDGMENTS

THOUGH THE PEOPLE and events are fictional, the background material for this novel comes from knowledge I have gained from a thirty-three-year career in print and broadcast journalism in Chicago and other cities, covering fields as diverse as police and politics, fashion and society, and art and architecture. A number of individuals were extremely helpful in adding to that knowledge over the years, including such *Chicago Tribune* colleagues as George Tagge, Jack Fuller, Dick Ciccone, Lois Wille, Jim Coates, Lisa Anderson, Paul Gapp, Bill Rectenwald, Joe Morang, Eleanor Page, Ed Schreiber, and, of course, Mike Royko.

My education in newspapering and the ways of Chicago was particularly blessed by having once had A. A. Dornfeld of the City News Bureau of Chicago as a mentor.

I am also extremely grateful to a number of other important and knowledgeable Chicagoans I've been pleased to count as friends, including Nancy and Tom Moffett, Paula and Wayne Whalen, June and Marvin Rosner, Connie Fletcher, Mary McDonald, Jim Ruddle, Megan McKinney, Nancy Jennings, Victor Skrebneski, Dave Gilbert, and Frank Sullivan.

I'd like to thank J. Carter Brown, former director of the National Gallery of Art, Sue Ann Prince of the National Portrait Gallery, and Elizabeth Wilson of the Pierpont Morgan Library for adding so considerably to my knowledge of art.

To my agent, Dominick Abel, and my editors, Tom Dunne, Ruth Cavin, and Reagan Arthur, I extend deep appreciation.

I owe a special debt to my father, D. Frederick Kilian, who first suggested I try my hand at newspapering in Chicago, and I am grateful to my wife, Pamela, and sons, Eric and Colin, as only they can know.

CHAPTER

1

IT WAS EARLY to be seeing a sailboat—still more night than morning, the pale first light all in the east behind the dunes. As the dawn's glow increased, it made the boat's sails starkly bright against the implacable darkness to the west, from which the craft apparently had come. Relentlessly the boat moved nearer still, its sailcloth fluttering and flaring pink as the sun finally lifted into the sky. The western gloom began to yield, revealing the sharp line of the watery horizon and the full breadth of Lake Michigan, which was perfectly empty, except for the boat.

The fisherman, who had set up his small encampment on the breakwater shortly after midnight in the vain hope of returning with a coho salmon or two, was irritated by the sailboat's presence. When it had first appeared as a vague, gray, forbidding glimmer in the false dawn, it had frightened him. Then, when he had finally come to realize what it was, he had been oddly comforted, glad of its company, welcoming the interruption it made in his long, lonely, fishless vigil. In its leisurely way, it seemed headed directly for him. He called to it, expecting an equally cheerful reply, but received none—heard nothing at all. For a time he ignored the boat, busying himself with checking his bait and recasting his line.

But it was still there, edging ever closer, swinging in slow, idle, partial circles from right to left and back again, under way but not truly sailing. The breeze was very light, but constant. It had been out of the southwest all night, warming the air but bringing only a slight, rhythmic slosh of water against the breakwater. Except for the occasional scree of a seagull and the tiny clank of the boat's rigging, there was no other sound.

Setting down his rod, the fisherman stood, wincing at the ache in his legs and back. He called out again, more sharply. There

1

was no answer. He could see no one at the helm or in the boat's cockpit. He reassured himself with a new thought: The boat must have come loose from its mooring in some distant harbor and been blown across the lake. But his unease returned when it occurred to him that no one would have left a boat tied up with its sails fully rigged and cleated. The mainsheet was taut, but the boom and tiller appeared to be caught up in tangled lines, accounting for the craft's erratic behavior in the water.

He realized then that he could be looking at death, or a sign of it, that whoever had been aboard might well have fallen over the side, drowning unheard and unseen in the night's vast darkness. The fisherman could make out the letters and numbers at the bow clearly enough to note an Illinois registration. The straight-line distance from the Grand Pier, Michigan, breakwater where he stood to Chicago across the lake was nearly forty miles, a long way to travel in a single night. He stepped back from the edge.

There had been no storm, no heavy winds, nothing to overwhelm a helmsman or cause sudden distress. One could have crossed the lake in a tiny outboard that night, if one had gasoline and courage enough. Whoever had been aboard probably had been drinking. It happened all the time.

The boat's northeasterly course continued to bring it nearer, but was taking it farther along the breakwater. The fisherman thought of going for help, but it was a long walk to the harbormaster's office, and he wasn't sure anyone would be there this early. Grand Pier was not a busy port, even at the height of the summer boating season.

He began moving along the breakwater, keeping pace with the boat. It was large enough for a comfortable crossing, thirty feet or more, a cruising sloop that might sleep six. He called to it again, more loudly than was probably necessary, hoping that someone might somehow be below, asleep.

Then, as the boat shifted slightly away from the wind for a moment, he was able to see down into the cockpit. There were several dripping lines of rustlike red running down the side of the seat by the helm. The water sloshing thinly in the bottom was a paler red.

At last the boat bumped against the breakwater. The bow swung away and then the craft bumped again on the beam. A jib sheet was hanging over the side by the starboard maststay. The fisherman grabbed up the rope, pulling back, and tied it tightly around one of the rusty stanchions of the railing that ran along the center of the breakwater out to its end. Standing up, he could see into the shadowy cabin, could see the feet splayed at the entrance way.

The left foot was in a dark-brown, white-soled boating shoe. The other was bare. The legs were tan. The sole of the unclad foot was white, like boiled fish meat. They were small feet, women's feet.

After rechecking the knot he had tied at the stanchion, the fisherman clambered clumsily down into the cockpit. He was a heavyset man, and caused the craft to rock sharply. Steadying himself, he sat down on a seat, the pink water in the bottom slapping against his boots. Gathering his courage, he peered into the cabin.

The body was indeed that of a young woman. She wore khaki Bermuda shorts and a white blouse that was all dark and dirty at the back. The fisherman took a deep breath and tried to stop trembling. He had handled drowning victims before. This was different—scary. With a grunt, he leaned over, grasping the girl's ankles, and pulled, hard. Her belt caught briefly on the cabin steps, then slipped free, and she came up to him, her bottom high.

Her blouse had been pulled out of her shorts and was loose. There were two holes in the back of the garment, surrounded by merging crimson circles. Heaving again, he got her into the cockpit, still lying on her stomach. She was quite slender, and had very fine light brown hair. Her arms were extended over her head, and her hands were tightly clutching a curled and slightly crumpled heavy piece of paper or cardboard. The fisherman ignored that and turned her over, startled by her large, light-blue eyes—that they were so dead, that they were staring at him. Putting his hand gently to her cold cheek, he turned her face away. She was in her twenties, maybe even thirty, and very attractive.

The front of her blouse was bloody, too, but had been pulled open and was missing buttons. She wore no brassiere. Her small breasts were stained a shiny red, as was her belly beneath. There were two larger, more ragged holes in her chest—one just above her stomach, the other torn through her right breast. The blood looked dry.

He felt sick. He was breathing very heavily, making a loud noise with it. Closing his eyes, he sat back a moment, making his diaphragm and stomach relax, wondering stupidly what next he should do. Looking at her again, studying the clear-cut line of her beautiful young face, he felt very angry at whoever had done this. Then he gently took the thick paper from her hands.

It was actually something else—a painting. The fisherman had never seen one out of its frame before. It was a dark painting—oil, he guessed—made all the darker by the blood smeared over its center. It was a strange sort of painting, what he supposed was modern art, but of a kind that made clear what it was about. A crowded street. Despite the smears, he could make out the figures of the people. Men in top hats. Women in furs. All hurrying toward a high, brightly lighted building in the background, colored as red as her blood. It rose above them into a stark, black sky. In the foreground, a woman in a long red coat, low-cut pink dress, and white high-heeled shoes stood watching them, a slash of a smile on her face.

The painting had been disfigured by two holes to either side of the woman in high heels. The girl must have been holding it to her chest when she was shot. There were small scratches on it also. He guessed they might have been made by her—maybe in the pain of her last throes of dying.

With a shudder, the fisherman tossed the painting back into the cabin. A small chugging trawler was moving along the water to the south, heading out into the lake. He looked at his watch, and then at the sticky redness he'd gotten on his thumbs and fingers. Wiping it off on his pants, he turned and heaved himself back up onto the breakwater. Stumbling, he got to his feet and started back toward the shore, moving as fast as his bulk and age would permit.

When possible, Matthias Curland always took a window seat when flying. The view from on high never bored him, even when he was flying over the featureless sea or, as now, the flat checkerboard plains of the American Midwest. It gave him the truest sense of where he was, and put man and his works in proper perspective.

The farmland, green and yellow in the late spring, slid relentlessly by. Then, in a sudden magical moment, it began to give way to the cerulean blue curve of the Lake Michigan shore. The juxtaposed colors of earth and water and angle of line offered the prospect of an interesting painting—two-dimensional shapes rendered three-dimensional by the angle of perspective. But the aircraft moved on over the lake and the picture vanished, as if erased, his window showing only the merging blues of hazy sky and water. Curland straightened in his seat, looking at his watch. He drank the last of his coffee and folded the drop table back into its recess, politely handing the empty cup to a passing stewardess. He leaned back, calm and patient, his abiding melancholy receding like an ebbing tide. It would return, inexorably, but for now, he was almost content.

Here in economy class, his Chicago-bound flight was crowded with businessmen, wearing the ubiquitous dark, drab suits that served as the uniforms of corporate slaves. These were men traveling not where they desired but where they were sent.

Matthias was dressed casually—an old navy blazer, a light-blue button-down shirt open at the collar, gray flannels, and black English loafers, worn at the edges. A tall, slender man not yet forty, with long, elegant hands, narrow nose, thin lips, and patrician face, he had the easy poise and reflexive courtesy of the kind of well-bred person Oscar Wilde had in mind when he said, "A gentleman never insults—except on purpose." Two years in the Mediterranean sun had deeply tanned and lined his skin, bleaching his graying hair back to something near the blondness that, along with their blue-gray eyes, was a common trait of his German-American family.

A woman had once told him he looked rich. He'd never really been that. His grandfather had been rich, of course. For his time, fabulously rich. Matthias had grown up in the old gentleman's house in Lake Forest, one of those great stone mansions that clung to the tops of the bluffs above the shoreline like miniature baronies, but after his grandfather had died, leaving most of his money to his private foundation and favored charities, Matthias's parents' fortunes had rapidly diminished. Matthias had been compelled to go through life as an ordinary man—just another architect struggling to pay his bills. When he'd finally managed to change his life, it had not been to become rich, but to become poor.

Hoping initially to become a painter, Matthias had attended the Pennsylvania Academy of the Fine Arts in Philadelphia. Then he'd switched to the Illinois Institute of Technology, where his father had studied architecture. Matthias's classmates had included a lot of people whose grandfathers had been steelworkers and subway motormen. Most had become far more successful than he had ever managed, even when the family architectual firm was prospering.

For the last two years, Matthias had been living largely on the bum, attempting—pretending—to be the painter he had always dreamed of becoming. He had had to borrow the money to make this flight. He hadn't the slightest notion of how he was going to pay it back.

He leaned close to the window again, watching intently as the Chicago skyline appeared in the distance ahead, the tiny toy buildings standing like little battlements before the following sweep of hazy city.

Matthias loved cities. Even in his sunny exile in the south of France, he had chosen to live in the crowded bustle of Cannes. Though he was returning reluctantly, he considered Chicago very special, almost as special as Paris. New York was really only Manhattan, a very small place really, crowded in on itself, its buildings all slabbed together, stubbornly ignoring the enormous world around it. Los Angeles resembled the scattered contents of an upended toybox. Washington was an insulated, prettified federal park, bordered by slum—except for its monuments and government buildings, an architectual void.

Chicago was a true capital, queen city of America's emerald inland seas and master of its sprawling midwestern region. It had a full sense of itself, a view of itself. Its buildings stood as individuals. There was a mightiness to them, as if they had thrust themselves out of the earth.

The city's three principal towers stuck up above the rest—the dark domino of the Hancock Center, the thin white pencil that was the Standard Oil Building, the gray-black bound shafts of Sears Tower which was now being challenged for the title of tallest in the world by an egomaniac billionaire in New York who had plans for a slightly higher pile of steel and concrete, erected on some land along the Hudson River once owned by the now-long-broke Donald Trump, who had hoped to have his own name on such a monument.

As the aircraft thrummed nearer to the shore, Matthias pressed his forehead against the window, straining his eyes. The air was clear enough along the city's lakefront for him to make out his own small contribution to the Chicago skyline—a narrow, green triangular-shaped tower facing Lincoln Park just to the north of the Gold Coast. The developer had given him a very free hand in the design, and the building had won a very prestigious architectual award. The developer had gone bankrupt.

Matthias had been an architect for seven years in Chicago. He had moved to New York because the woman he had married was from there and desired it. When they had eventually divorced, he had escaped not only her but his profession and past life. He became "a painter"—in Paris, Cannes, Nice, and Cap Ferrat—supporting himself as best he could, sometimes starving, often sponging, but managing somehow to remain "a painter," resembling Paul Gauguin in many ways, though not in talent.

Now he didn't know what he was—only where. He was home, the last place he had thought he wanted to be.

Landing only twenty-five minutes late, the plane lumbered to its gate with many pauses. Before it came to a stop, one of the businessmen leapt up to reach for one of the overhead bins, and others followed suit, grappling for briefcases and garment bags, every gained minute somehow vital. Matthias remained relaxed in his seat until the aisle was clear.

He strolled through the bizarre, tubular high-tech architecture of O'Hare's redesigned interior corridors, liking the light, airy, friendly feeling they gave, but finding a lot of the touches obtrusive and artificial. He arrived at the luggage carousel to find his two bags already there. He bought both of the Chicago papers, then stood by one of the car rental counters, waiting, watching the down escalator from the main level above. He wanted to smoke his pipe, but a sign sternly forbade it.

His brother Christian had promised to meet his plane, but of course had not. Matthias waited nearly half an hour, out of courtesy, paying Christian the respect of believing in his good intentions. Finally he surrendered to the obvious, gathering his belongings and heading for the taxi line.

His driver was a friendly black man who began talking about sporting contests Matthias knew nothing about. He kept up a conversation as best he could but, after a few minutes, allowed it to lapse and turned to his newspapers.

Both the *Tribune* and the *Sun-Times* had front-page stories about someone named Peter Poe offering to buy the White Sox baseball team. The articles included commentary to the effect that it was doubtful the league would permit such a purchase by a man who owned a casino in Indiana and gambling riverboats on the Mississippi, even if he divested himself of these properties. What caught Matthias's attention most was a paragraph noting that, the year before, Poe had bought Cabrini Green, a crime-and vermin-infested complex of crumbling high-rise public housing on the Near North Side that had been erected in the less than visionary 1950s as a daft, utopian answer to slums.

When Matthias had left Chicago, gentrification had been spreading west from the Gold Coast and Lincoln Park areas into what had been an abysmal black ghetto. Cabrini Green lay not far from the North Branch of the Chicago River. He supposed the man might have made a shrewd investment. There were nightclubs and restaurants now on Clybourn Avenue, not far away from the project.

"Who is Peter Poe?" he asked.

"You don't know Peter Poe?" said the driver, incredulous. "He's Mr. Chicago. Shit, he's gonna own the whole fuckin' town before he's through. He's the guy who made legalized gambling such a big deal over in Indiana. He's got a big casino in Michigan City. He's got buildings all over town—one of the biggest yachts on Lake Michigan."

"Sorry," Matthias said. "I've been away."

"You must have been far away, man. He's on the news like every night."

"I'll have to watch the news then."

The driver turned the conversation to sports again, launching into a monologue about the deplorable state of the White Sox ball team. Matthias tried to remember the last time he had looked at the major league standings. As the driver talked, he contented himself with gazing out the windshield at the distant downtown towers. There were a few he'd not seen before.

Christian Curland opened the door of the old brick house on Schiller Street before Matthias could ring the bell but, characteristically, not in time to help bring the bags from the curb. Their grandfather, the original owner of the house, had left it to their mother as an in-town residence, but the two brothers had taken it over after college, sharing it until Matthias had married. When Matthias and his wife had gone back East, Christian had moved back in again. A succession of women had lived in it with him, according to letters Matthias had received from his sister. He wondered if one was there now.

"At last," said Christian, a glass in hand, his uncombed dark hair falling over his brow. "I shall forebear from reference to the prodigal."

8

Matthias set his luggage down carefully on the parquet floor of the foyer, which badly needed polishing.

"You weren't at the airport," he said.

"Didn't you get my message, big brother? I asked them to page you. Thought I did, anyway. Couldn't possibly drive. Not in this incandescent sunlight. Grandmother of hangovers. Terrible night. Well, wonderful night, but a terrible morning. Just now getting well."

There was tomato juice in the expensive crystal glass—and a lot of something else.

For a moment, Christian looked as if he might actually give his returning brother a hug, but he thought better of it, perhaps fearing he might spill the precious fluid in his glass. Matthias followed him into the gloomy living room, glancing at the paintings and fixtures and surprised to find them still there. Except for a favorite nude he had painted and a couple of prints, the contents of the house came mostly from old family holdings, to which Christian could make some claim.

Drawn drapes kept the room dark, but for a thin shaft of light slashing across the carpet from between the curtains. Matthias took a seat on the couch out of its reach, lighting his pipe and puffing on it deeply. Christian slumped into a large armchair opposite. Time and drink had not ruined his attractiveness. Rather, they seemed to have enhanced him, making him look worldly, wiser, more masculine. His dark hair was a striking anomoly. No one else in the family had it. He made jokes about being a bastard. It forestalled gossip implying more seriously the same thing.

"Drink, big brother?"

"Some coffee, later."

"Still off the sauce, Matthias? After all you've been through?"

"You might try giving it a rest yourself sometime."

"Instant coffee's all I have," said Christian, retreating from the subject. "Have to make it yourself, I'm afraid. Except for the cleaning woman, haven't any help."

A part-time cleaning woman is all Matthias and his wife had ever employed, though he suspected she would have been delighted to have live-in servants to wait upon her.

"You've no companion?"

"Not in residence. They get in the way of my work. You stopped in New York, to see your ex-wife?"

"I saw her briefly. It wasn't a very successful reunion."

"Hillary's still living in Westchester?"

Matthias nodded. "It's all she ever wanted. Her new husband's an advertising man. He likes that life."

"Advertising. How middle class."

Unlike Matthias, Christian clung to the notion that he was an aristocrat. Snobbery was part of his image of that.

"At least he earns a living, which is more than I've been able to say," said Matthias.

"But, art, big brother. You've had art."

"I've sold three paintings this year. For two thousand dollars each."

"Not bad, big brother."

"They were nudes—big blondes, à la Veronese—for an Arab. For his yacht."

"Paint some more. We could use the money."

Christian looked into his glass as if something important were hidden in the tomato juice. Then he drank, keeping his eyes from his brother.

"Have you actually picked up a brush since I left?" Matthias asked.

"Actually have, big brother. Done a portrait or two, and a few other things. Still some Lake Shore Drive ladies who like my work."

He actually dared use this word, though the "work" these ladies liked had little to do with Christian's painting. They paid him retainers for "sittings" that sometimes lasted for weeks and months, though they were seldom dissatisfied.

"Just how much money could *we* use?" Matthias said.

Christian took a very deep breath and then sighed. "The Curland family is close to stony broke, big brother. Do you want all the gory details now, or can we wait until tonight? We're having dinner at the Lake Forest house. Annelise will be there. She'll tell you everything, rest assured."

"Tonight."

"Mother died four days ago, Matthias."

"I came as soon as I was able."

"You could have stopped in New York on the way back to France."

There was a painting of their mother over the fireplace—a brilliant portrait, managing to depict her in all her beauty, elegance, and dignity, without masking the meanness and madness.

Christian had done it when he was only twenty-two, still a student at the Chicago Art Institute, where his paintings had been the centerpieces of annual student shows.

"*If* I go back," Matthias said. "I have some doubts."

"What?" Christian was so startled he spilled some of his drink.

"Mother's dying—my having to come home like this—I took it as something of a message, a sign. I think I've been wasting my time. I wanted to prove something to myself. It wasn't what I had in mind, but I did."

"You're going to stay on here in Chicago?"

"It's the last thing I want to do. But Cannes, Paris. *Probablement, c'est finis. Rien de plus de la peinture.*"

"You're sure?"

"Pretty sure. Sure enough."

"What will you do?"

"I wish I knew."

"Son of a bloody bitch." They looked at each other for a long moment without speaking. Then Christian downed the rest of his drink and set down his glass. His hand shook slightly as he did so.

"Annelise didn't think you were ever coming back," he said. "Not even for Mother's funeral."

Annelise was their sister. She raised giant schnauzers in Barrington, in Lake County.

"When is it?"

"Tomorrow morning. In Lake Forest. She was cremated. We're to scatter the ashes in the lake. If you haven't a dark suit, you can borrow one of mine."

Zany Rawlings was not a chump. His old Chicago cop friends in the Area Six burglary detail had told him he was taking a chump job when he'd quit the department five years short of twenty-year retirement to hire on as police chief of Grand Pier, but he could smell the sour grapes when they said it. His pay was barely half what he made as a detective in the city, but his wife ran a beach shop that brought in a lot of money in the summer, and the job was as good as retirement. Crime in the old resort ran to fights on the beach, drunk and disorderlies in the town's five bars and two Bohemian restaurants, the occasional burglary of an unoccupied summer house, and speeding on the highway that led out to the interstate. They'd only once had a problem with drugs, and that had involved a marijuana ring, some college dropouts who'd turned a pastime into a business. Zany and the local district attorney had thoroughly shut it down.

Zany had six good men and two even more capable women working on his three-car force, leaving him plenty of time for reading, fishing, messing with his home computer, and swapping lies with the old-timers on the outsize pier from which the town derived its name. His daughter was finishing college and his son already had. His wife was happy running her souvenir, newspaper, and beach supplies store. Life was good.

At least, it had been until the sailboat with the dead girl in it had turned up that morning. Zany had been sitting in his kitchen, drinking coffee and reading a new Sara Paretsky mystery when his sergeant had rung up from the harbor. Unfortunately, Zany had just finished breakfast.

When he'd first joined the Chicago cops, they'd tried to call him Cowboy Rawlings. His first name was Zane, like the western novelist Zane Grey, and, except for his four years at the university in Laramie, he'd spent the first twenty-three years of his life in and around Meade, Wyoming. But "cowboy" didn't fit. He'd ridden a horse only twice in his life, disliking it more the second time than the first. His jobs as a young man back home had included work as a reporter on the weekly newspaper, as a dynamiter in the nearby strip mines, and as a cop—acting chief of the Meade police force for three months when he was the only policeman on the payroll. He'd even spent a night in the town jail once, after too enthusiastic a payday carouse.

They'd stuck the name Zany on him when they could think of nothing more appropriate. He was six foot four inches tall and wore clothes that always seemed somehow too small for him, his belt line always sagging below his large belly. He had a beard and a habit of rapidly blinking his pale-blue eyes whenever he was doing serious thinking. The effect was magnified by his glasses, which gave him the look of an eccentric professor. He read books constantly and could work magic with computers. For all his intelligence, he had been a careless and forgetful cop. He'd frequently misplaced his service revolver, and once had inadvertently killed an electric typewriter getting his gun out of a desk drawer.

Like many who had grown up surrounded by mountains and arid plains, he passionately loved the water. Lake Michigan, to him, was one of God's most magnificent creations.

Now it had betrayed him.

He gave the girl's body only the most cursory visual examination, quickly stepping back to let the ambulance attendants remove it. His sergeant, George Hejmal, had taken a whole roll of photographs, and Zany could examine those later, when he was at more distance from a meal.

The boat that had come so far to reach his shore was named *Hillary*. There were six bullet holes in it. Two had gone through the girl's back, exiting from her lower chest and digging into the flooring of the cabin. Two others had struck the bulkhead to the right of the doorway. The remaining two had gone through the cabin roof. The angle of every one of them made it clear they'd been fired obliquely from above, as if from a bridge; another, higher boat; or even a low-flying aircraft. His men had been able to dig out most of them, including the two that had killed the girl. They were .38 specials, the same caliber that had been standard police issue until big departments like Chicago's had begun using 15-shot, 9mm automatics.

The painting that had fallen out of her clothes interested Zany even more. Something that had escaped the notice of his patrolmen had been immediately obvious to him. The bloodstains and bullet holes that so marred the unrolled canvas were mirror duplicates of those on the body. There was a dented crease near the bottom of the painting that coincided with the waistline of her shorts. She had apparently had it wrapped around her beneath her blouse when she had been shot.

He had Hejmal take a number of photos of the painting as well, front and back, then put it in his safe upon returning to his office. Zany knew a little about art. He had gone to see a Frederic Remington exhibition at the Art Institute shortly after moving to the city and had gone back on days off regularly after that. He had seen a number of works done in the peculiar style of the bloody painting in the boat. European mostly, done before World War I, or in the 1920s.

Zany called the county prosecutor, Douglas Moran, and then the Michigan State Police investigations unit, making it as clear as possible that he was simply following standard procedure in informing them of the crime, but was definitely not inviting them to come in and take over the investigation. He could have turned primary jurisdiction over to them, of course, and returned to his reading and fishing. But the county prosecutor—a man who loved publicity so much he had once posed for news photographers helping Zany's people shoo late-night neckers off the beach—would never have permitted that. Local authority would enforce the local laws—those concerning homicide as well as moral turpitude.

The State Police detectives would be a good hour getting to Grand Pier. Prosecutor Moran was there in minutes and was about to start rummaging about the boat until Zany suggested that he would be the best man to deal with the reporters who would descend upon the scene shortly. Moran readily agreed. Zany gave him enough information to provide a sound bite for the local television, then went back to his office, and to serious work.

The boat was easy to trace, requiring only a phone call to the Chicago police marine unit. It was registered under the name of a Dr. Richard Meyerson, who said he hadn't used it since the previous weekend and didn't understand why it wasn't still in its slip in Chicago's Burnham Harbor. He seemed genuinely astonished to hear that it was now at Grand Pier, Michigan, and was stunned speechless when Zany told him about the murdered girl. When asked to come out to Grand Pier as soon as possible, he became quite indignant, complaining he was an oral surgeon very busy with patients. He had done nothing wrong, and demanded that the boat be brought back to him at once. After Zany threatened to send Chicago police to pick him up—a rather farfetched prospect, actually—the dentist reluctantly agreed to come out that afternoon.

He arrived a little after three. He made a positive identification of the boat but, during questioning by Zany and two men from the State Police, said he knew nothing about any girl and was exceedingly upset when Zany made him come with them to the hospital to look at the body. Not many bullet holes in molars.

After the State Police investigators completed the examination they'd insisted upon, making the search for fingerprints that Zany had neglected to do, Zany also made the dentist look carefully through the boat to see if anything had been taken—or added. There was nothing new, and very little out of place. All that was missing was gasoline. He said that, as usual, he had refilled the boat's tank before tying it up for the week. Now it was bone dry.

The dentist said he knew nothing about the painting, and showed little interest in it. He demanded to know who would repair the bullet damage to the boat, and was furious when Zany told him it would have to be impounded for the time being as evidence.

Zany had the man make out an official statement detailing where he had been the night before—dinner at Eli's, poker with buddies. Then he sent him on his unhappy way back to the city.

After the State Police detectives finally left, pointedly asking Zany to keep them informed of every development, he called Chicago police headquarters at 11th and State to see if they had any missing persons matching the girl's description—they didn't—and to ask if they'd mind checking out the dentist's statement. He sent Hejmal up to St. Joseph to get the photographs developed and printed overnight.

After that, he didn't know what to do—except think. He had a couple of beers while he did that, sitting on the screened-in porch of his house on the bluff, staring at the lake.

After lunch, a shower, and a long nap to dispel his remaining jet lag, Matthias went for a walk through the Gold Coast, his old neighborhood, hoping the remembered sights would help shake off some of the sadness that had been clinging to him for days. He was pleased at least to find so many of the old houses still surviving and the Edwardian atmosphere of the genteel district little diminished. There were some new high-rises encroaching here and there, but not near enough to his house to matter.

His stroll took him down Lake Shore Drive, his spirits refreshed by the lake breeze and the sweeping view south to the Drake Hotel and the new, tall buildings along Michigan Avenue beyond. There was no such prospect in New York City. To fully appreciate the towers of Manhattan, one had to stand in a cemetery near the East River in Queens, and even then they seemed a jumble.

When he'd lived in Chicago, he'd often taken this walk in the evening with his wife—and, discreetly, with another woman. She was still in the city. The thought troubled him, and he tried to put it out of his mind.

His brother stayed away all afternoon, returning with only time enough to change for dinner. Matthias drove, as Christian had apparently continued drinking through the afternoon, and even now had brought along a vodka martini for the car—a Jaguar sedan. They took the Edens Expressway because they were late, though Matthias would have preferred the slower route up Sheridan Road, which wound along the lake through the North Shore suburbs. He didn't mind being late.

"Rather a nice car, for a family going stony broke," he said.

"It's not mine. It belongs to a client."

"Client?"

"A woman whose portrait I'm painting." There was a clink of ice in Christian's glass. "Winnetka lady. Very pretty."

"And over forty, no doubt."

"Over fifty, actually. A lady in full bloom."

The prospect of more such conversation made Matthias now feel like hurrying. He moved their speed up to ten miles an hour over the limit and kept it there, threading the long car through the evening traffic. Expressways were easy after the roads he'd driven in France, roads like Monaco's Moyen Corniche, the cliff road where Grace Kelly had died on a hairpin turn.

Matthias had left a woman back there on the Côte d'Azur. She was named Marie-Claire, and she was married to someone else. Matthias had lived with her for eight months, until her husband had returned from an extended stay in Asia. He still saw her from time to time. He was very fond of her, though she drank too much.

He shouldn't hector Christian about his "clients."

"Was it bad, at the end? When Mother died?"

"Not for her, I don't suppose. She'd been dying ever since the stroke, inch by inch. The doctor called it a blessing."

"Did you have to have her cremated?"

"That was her wish—after her legs were amputated. Loss of circulation after the stroke, don't you know. Gangrene. Nasty business, all of it."

Christian sipped from his drink again. Matthias wondered if his brother was always this way now, or if he was just responding to the dreadful stress of family loss and grief and the return of his old rival, big brother Matthias.

"All right," Matthias said. "Tell me how bad it is. I don't want to wait for Annelise."

"The money."

"The lack of it."

"Well, big brother, Father is truly on his ass. He's gone through everything. He took out two mortgages on the Lake Forest house and is behind on the payments. If it weren't such a monstrous thing to sell, the mortgage holder, whoever it is, would be foreclosing now. The house on Astor is still unencumbered, but it's badly in need of repairs, and I think a new furnace. Froze a bit last winter."

"What did he spend it on?"

"Anything and everything that entered his mind. God, he's still buying rare books."

"Did he pay Mother's medical bills?"

Christian drank again. "They were taken care of."

"What about the firm?"

"The firm. Curland and Associates. Architects extraordinaire. The firm is infirm, big brother. Father hasn't been to the office in more than a year. Henderson's long gone. Our young genius took a job in Miami, where they're still building buildings. He finished that shopping mall job, though. Hideous thing. He hired two college graduates from IIT. One of them is still with us, though he's looking. The other comes around from time to time, in the vain hope, I think, of back pay. We had to move the office to cheaper quarters, one of those 'historic' Louis Sullivan–era buildings in the south Loop that's always looking for tenants. I'm not sure how much longer they'll want to keep us. Something about rent. This recession hit Chicago rather bad."

"No clients?"

"Not recently."

"Why didn't you tell me?"

"You've had enough problems. Especially with money."

Even coming from his brother, the observation embarrassed Matthias.

"And Grandfather's museum?" he asked.

Christian finished his drink, then took a pint bottle of vodka from the glove compartment and poured some into his glass.

"It's all right? The museum?" Matthias asked again.

"Yes, yes. Just as Grandfather left it, God damn it to hell," he said. "Every dusty painting in its place, just as his lunatic will commanded. But think of it, all those paintings. If we sold just one or two this nightmare would be over. There's a Schonfeld in there that must be worth two million."

"You know we can't touch it."

"It's just a will. There are lawyers. There are judges. This is Chicago, big brother."

"We've been through this, many times."

"I only open the museum to the public by appointment now. Saves on expenses. The tax people will doubtless be on us one

17

day for that. Jill Langley left us, you know. Took a job at Larry Train's gallery for twice the salary."

"She wrote me about it."

"You and Jill were writing?"

"For a while. We stopped."

"She was in love with you."

"I know." Matthias didn't want to talk about that. Not at all. "Did you keep my sailboat?"

"So to speak. I leased it to someone with an option to buy. You'll have a chance to get it back at the end of the year. Otherwise, it's his if he wants to pay for it. I told him I'd want twenty thousand, which is a lot for a boat that old. I let him register it under his name."

"Was that necessary?"

"You said I should do it if I thought it was."

"Did he change the boat's name?"

"No, it's still the *Hillary*. I think he likes the nice Waspy sound of it. He's a dentist. Named Meyerson."

Christian had a number of disagreeable qualities, and his lingering anti-Semitism was one of them.

"Jill wasn't very happy about my leasing the boat," Christian said.

"I told her she could use it whenever she wanted."

"She was with you when you won the Mackinac race, wasn't she?"

"It wasn't the Mackinac. It was the Chicago to Menominee."

"There's the girl you should have married, big brother. Jill wouldn't have made you move to New York. You would have stayed here and prospered. We'd all have been a lot happier. Especially Jill. She was really quite nuts about you."

"I was married when Jill came along."

"You haven't been for two years."

"Did you invite her to the funeral?"

"I . . . no. That would really be cruel, wouldn't it? After the way you treated her."

"Shut up, Chris."

"Sally Phillips is still in town."

Dark hair. Skin the color of the purest ivory. Prussian blue eyes. A kiss outside the Drake Hotel by Oak Street beach on a cold winter night. It was the last time Matthias had seen her. She'd been married, too.

18

"I'm not surprised. Her husband's one of the richest men in Chicago."

"They're divorced now."

They were nearing the Glencoe exit. Almost there.

"Divorced."

"Do you want to hear about it?"

"No."

Ignoring FAA regulations, Peter Poe dropped his helicopter down low over the water once they were above Lake Michigan, tilting the aircraft to a steeper forward angle and increasing his speed to near maximum as he turned onto a course for the south. It was a calm night with an early moon, and the water's surface shimmered all the way to the eastern horizon.

Poe excelled as a pilot, just as he excelled at everything he set his mind and hand to. He was certificated to fly jets, choppers, multiengine aircraft, and carry passengers for hire—an amusing idea for a man believed to have $1.2 billion in assets.

He flew relaxed, his hand loosely holding the control column, his mind on the next day. It would be a busy one—endless phone calls, meetings, important social engagements—like every day of the year, every day of his life. He had promised his wife, Diandra, a holiday at their country place on the shore of Wisconsin's Lake Geneva. He had come up to join her the night before but had become edgy and irritable and impatient to get back to the city. He'd insisted on their returning now. There was a very major party on Lake Shore Drive the following night, and he wanted Diandra in attendance. She was a spectacular-looking woman, a good five inches taller than he and magazine-cover beautiful. He always felt uncomfortable without her, as uncomfortable as he'd be without his $2,000 Gieves and Hawkes suits and Piaget watch. He took her everywhere, even to businessmen's luncheon club meetings.

She was in the passenger compartment behind him, along with Poe's former Bears tackle bodyguard, Lenny Krasowski, reading some book by a small cabin light.

Poe had followed a course southeast from his Lake Geneva house, crossing the Lake Michigan shoreline just north of Waukegan. The night was clear enough for him to pick up the distant lights of downtown Chicago.

The silhouette of a two-masted sailboat—a yawl or ketch; Poe could never remember which was which—appeared dead ahead. He swung the helicopter off to the left, not wanting to startle the occupants with too close a pass at such a low altitude. He studied the boat as he flew by, admiring its size and gracefulness. Poe owned one of the largest motor yachts on the Great Lakes, but it was beginning to bore him. It was time he got himself a big sailboat. Donald Trump never had a sailboat. Ted Turner did, and had once won the America's Cup.

Poe would see about acquiring a boat that week. He would pay cash. The interest on his capital debt was costing him some $35 million more a year than his various enterprises were taking in, but he'd not let that become a problem. It was other people's money. He'd built his entire empire with other people's money. There was more to be had.

They were skimming alongside the Outer Drive now—tiny headlights moving to their right, high-rise apartment buildings dotted with lighted windows standing invitingly beyond the dark greensward of Lincoln Park. Ahead, the tower of the Hancock Center, a band of light shining eerily around its top, stood like a sentinel, guarding the Gold Coast.

Poe steered left, gaining altitude, until he could see Lake Point Tower and the long rectangle of Meigs Field, the city's lakefront airport, popular with fliers and air commuters, disliked by most everyone else as an infringement on the holy lake shore. Then he clicked on his microphone, reporting his position and approach plan to Meigs' tower. A friendly voice responded. Poe used the field so frequently his call letters were almost as well known as his name.

As he neared the airport, its flashing strobe lights visible at the end of the runway, he slowed the helicopter and hovered a moment, taking in the jutting mass of buildings that filled the city center. Only one of the tallest there was his, an office-apartment tower on Michigan Avenue. It was distinctive, the red cupola on top brilliantly floodlit, glowing in the night skyline like an ember, but it was far from dominating. No one building dominated the Chicago skyline anymore.

Poe came down along the center of the runway, then fluttered right, bringing the craft to rest just short of the terminal. He killed the chopper's powerful turbo engine and sat back, stretching his arms and fingers as the big rotor blades whined and shuddered to a stop.

His secretary, Mango Bellini, was waiting for him on the tarmac, her long dark hair whipped about by the turbulence from the rotor blade. Behind her was one of Poe's trademark red stretch limousines, with waiting chauffeur.

"Hi, boss," she said as he stepped out.

"Everything all right?"

"Sure. Why not?"

Poe nodded. Diandra said nothing to the woman. Inside the small terminal building, Poe stopped at the general aviation counter to sign the log book.

"Nice trip, Mr. Poe?" said the man behind the counter.

"Fine, Jimmy," said Poe, who had made a point of learning the man's name. He smiled. Poe had an M.O., a trademark—rare for a major money man. He was a nice guy. He treated everyone like a pal, whenever possible, using first names.

"Did you make a flight last night?"

"Yeah. Went up to Lake Geneva. It's in the logs. What about it?"

"Did you have some trouble or something?"

"Trouble?"

"Someone reported a chopper down low over the lake. We thought it might be you, in trouble."

"No trouble, Jimmy. I just take awhile to get to altitude sometimes."

"Gotta be careful, Mr. Poe. The boaters complain sometimes."

Poe smiled again. "Good night, Jimmy."

"Good night, Mr. Poe."

Poe's chauffeur had the stretch's engine running. Krasowski loaded their few bags in the trunk, then took his seat beside the driver. Mango took one of the jump seats. Diandra sat beside Poe in the rear, saying nothing, looking tired, or at least unhappy. She had really wanted to stay at Lake Geneva.

"Poe Place first," said Poe. "Then take Mango home."

"Yes, boss."

Mango gave him a dark look. She had probably figured on coming back to Poe's penthouse with him—for some late work. Mango's birth certificate name was Rose Scalzetti, but she had assumed the Mango Bellini when she had begun her not-too-successful career as a saloon singer, taking the name after a cocktail she'd been served in a celebrity haunt she liked in New York.

Mango wasn't much of a singer, but customers liked to look

at her. Poe had hired her for a six-week run in the lounge of a casino he used to own in Atlantic City as a favor to the man to whom she had then belonged. After a week, he'd promoted her to his personal staff and quite different duties. He'd continued to promote her. The simple title "secretary" was grossly inadequate for the role she now played in his life and business affairs. The man she'd belonged to hadn't much liked any of this, but he was no longer around to complain.

She was bright, as smart as she was good-looking. A little broad in the behind, maybe, but the rest of her was wonderful— showgirl legs, a trim waist, good shoulders, and spectacular breasts that had been mostly responsible for what success she had enjoyed as a professional singer. She had olive skin that tanned when she walked under a street lamp, enormous dark eyes, and thick, black curly hair she wore down to her back. If she had been a call girl—and she insisted she had never been that—she could have made herself rich.

Working for Poe, she was getting a lot richer.

Mango had once been into cocaine and all-day booze, like so many in her trade, but Poe had had no difficulty in persuading her to give up both, after telling her her job depended on it. His wife, however, was beginning to drink a little early in the day and a little long into the night. It bothered him.

Diandra was an altogether different kind of lady, indeed, a real lady, a graduate of Michigan State who had planned on a career in advertising until someone had turned her to modeling. She was nearly six feet tall and thin as a pole, but coolly, classically beautiful. Her eyes were an odd blue-gray color that sometimes seemed hazel and sometimes pale green, in any case complement- ing her flame-colored hair. She didn't always photograph well, though she'd been much prized in the fashion industry as a runway model. He'd met her at a fashion show at one of his hotels. They were married within six months. She'd refused him at first, returning all his presents. Then, mysteriously, just as he was giving up on her, she'd accepted. Poe hadn't yet figured what it was about him that finally attracted her. He let her model from time to time, mostly at society, ladies-who-lunch charity fashion shows. She was much in demand for these, though the city's social elite had yet to invite her to join any of their exclusive boards and benefit committees.

Diandra didn't like Mango, but had come to accept her. They had learned to stay out of each other's way.

Mango lighted a cigarette. Poe hadn't been able to get her off those.

"Did you get the newspapers?"

Krasowski handed copies of the *Tribune* and the *Sun-Times* through the open divider. They were early editions of the next day's papers.

Poe thanked him and quickly skimmed through them, the *Tribune* main news and metropolitan sections first, then the *Times*. He read only the headlines, and was done by the time the stretch reached Michigan Avenue. There was no news of any great consequence.

There were only four of them for dinner at the Lake Forest house—Matthias and Christian, their sister Annelise, and her husband Paul, a suburban banker and Presbyterian elder who had long disapproved of the way the Curlands lived and squandered their money. Paul was an essentially nice man, who suffered Annelise's dominating manner with some dignity and, in his straitlaced, dour way, seemed to love her deeply. But he was an improbable mate for the bluff, outspoken, often boistrous Annelise. The marriage only made sense when you considered their mutual fondness for dogs.

The men were in black tie, Annelise in a long black gown. It had long been a family idiosyncracy to dress for dinner when at the Lake Forest house, a custom largely unknown to their generation even among their truly rich neighbors. Their father had insisted upon it for this unhappy reunion, though in the end he never came to the table, remaining in the sanctuary of the library.

At table, the conversation was surprisingly cheerful at first, carried along mostly by Christian, who was full of ribald, gossipy anecdotes about social life in Chicago during Matthias's absence. They did not talk about their mother, and the subject of money was not once broached, though clearly it was the only one that interested Paul.

He was far fonder of dogs than he was of Matthias and Christian. The former he considered a feckless intellectual dreamer, the latter, a self-indulgent hedonist; the both of them useless, unproductive sinners woefully in need of redemption. Paul sat morosely through Christian's breezy discourse, looking pained during Christian's more salacious stories.

The wine, which Matthias declined and Annelise and Paul barely touched, took its toll of Christian, and the stories became vague and then incoherent. At length, Christian abruptly stopped talking and stared bleakly at his dessert plate. Matthias feared he might topple over were he to lean back in his chair.

Annelise pushed back her own. She had the family blond hair and ice-gray eyes and, like her brothers, was quite tall. She might have been a strikingly lovely woman, had she worked at it, but after she had safely married Paul, she had lost all interest in that. Life was all dogs, horses, her country place in Barrington, and her two children. Her years spent daily in the midwestern outdoors left their mark. She didn't care.

"All right, Matt, let's get it over with," she said, and rose. "Time for the lion's den."

Annelise led the way, pushing open the door of the library. Their father had changed into a dinner jacket, but was in the same corner leather chair where Matthias had found him upon arriving.

"Well, Father," she said, with booming voice, for his hearing was failing badly. "You've done it again."

The balding, white-haired old man, sitting bent over a large book, looked up and smiled. He had a very charming, ingratiating smile, as effective with the ladies as Christian's, and he used it reflexively for every occasion, sparing himself the effort of working up a more appropriate expression.

"What? What have I done?"

"Missed dinner," said Annelise, towering over him as she came to his side. She looked disapprovingly at the large glass of brandy on the lamp table. "Do you ever eat?"

"Oh, yes. Had lunch. I'm fine, fine." He sneaked a glance at the page before him, as if trying to gobble up a few more words. "Sorry about dinner. Got distracted. Lost all sense of time. But I'm fine."

He began to cough. There was a cigarette smoldering in the ashtray. His doctor had forbidden smoking and drinking.

The cough consumed him, shaking his bent, fragile body. They all waited for it to pass, none more impatiently than he.

"Are you all right?" Matthias said finally.

"Fine, fine," said his father, sputtering. "Good to have you home, Matthias. Sorry your mother's not here."

Brother and sister exchanged a look. Annelise shook her head.

"Sorry to disturb you, Father. Matt and I are going to have a little talk now. Don't stay up too late." She leaned to kiss him.

"Of course not." He flashed the ladies' man smile again, then greedily returned to his book.

Matthias put his hand on his father's shoulder, but the old man paid him no further mind.

"Shouldn't we put him to bed?" Matthias said, as Annelise closed the door behind them. They walked slowly down the hall.

"The housekeeper will do that in the morning," she said. "He'll still be in that chair. We've put him to bed a hundred times, but he's always in that damned chair in the morning."

Matthias frowned.

"He can be quite competent, when he needs to be," Annelise continued. "He still drives, you know. Takes that big car into the village, goes to the bank. Buys liquor when we try to keep it from him. Buys things. Bought a pewter chess set last week. We try to return things when he's forgotten about them, but you don't always get your money back."

"Does he show any interest in architecture?"

"About as much as Christian. About as much as Paul. About as much as my dogs."

"Christian said he hasn't been to the office. Not in months."

"He used to make quite a thing of it. Three-piece suit. Club tie. Briefcase. But all he'd do there was sit in his office and read books."

"He's seventy-five years old."

She sighed wearily. "Let's go out on the terrace."

They went through the huge sitting room, passing through the French doors to the warm night air outside. The moon glittered on the lake. Little waves splashed quietly at the foot of the bluff below.

"God, I'm a coward," she said. "I try to bring up money, and he just cringes, as if I were hitting him or calling him vile names."

As Matthias thought upon it, Annelise was the only member of the family who still had any money. Their maternal grandfather, Karl Albrecht, had settled $1 million on each of his three grandchildren. Matthias had put most of his back into the family architecture firm. Christian had spent his with astonishing swiftness. Annelise had put her money into sound investments and into her kennels, which had prospered.

Matthias leaned forward against the railing, gazing unhappily out over the lake. He felt like a ghost, revisiting his own life.

"I'd forgotten this view," he said. "It could be the ocean."

"You're damned lucky it's still here for you." She spoke quietly and matter-of-factly, but he could sense her bitterness. "Did you know Father bought land in Utah? Damned dry desert. He saw pictures in *National Geographic* and thought it would be nice to own some of it. And there's a Rolls-Royce in the garage."

"What? Those damned things cost a fortune."

"It's quite used. Barely runs. He called it a wonderful bargain. Said he bought it for Mother. For when she got well. Dear God. To think he was once a forest preserve trustee and president of the German-American Society."

Their father had attained those positions mostly because their grandfather had held them before him, but he couldn't have served in them now. Matthias shook his head. He'd been doing that all night.

"Did Chris fill you in on the particulars, on the way things stand?"

"Yes. He didn't explain how he's kept things going, though."

"He makes some money with his portraits. His women customers are very generous, don't you know. And I think he gambles."

"Gamblers tend to lose."

"Especially those who drink at the same time. He tried to quit this year. Stopped in January, for a fact. But he's been nipping at it lately. And this weekend, God, it's been just like the old days. I don't hold out much hope for Christian."

Matthias caught himself as he began to shake his head again.

"In any event, Matt, I think we're at a dead end. If we sold this place and your house on Schiller Street—if we sold everything else, the furniture, that goddamn vulgar car, cancelled father's club memberships—I think we'd have enough left over after paying off all the debts to get an apartment for him and keep him comfortable. In one of those residences, for people like him. That's what Paul has been pleading with me to do. He thinks we should go to court and have Father declared incompetent and then sell everything. I begin to think he's right. And it can't be much longer before we have no other choice. Christian insists it won't come to that, but I can only presume that's vodka talking."

Matthias said nothing. He listened to the breeze in the tree leaves above. Their grandfather had had this house built as an anniversary present for his wife. Their father, a young man then, had been its architect. Big houses like this had been his specialty. No one built them anymore. No one wanted them.

"You're wondering why I haven't contributed anything," she said. "Why I haven't thrown any of my money down this toilet."

"No, I wasn't. Actually I was thinking about the dances they used to have out here."

He had danced with his wife on this terrace, and with Sally, and with others. With each, it had been a lovely moment.

"Well, I'm not going to do it," Annelise said. "And I don't want you to give up another penny. I want you to go back to France and your painting. If you sell your house—and it's costing Chris a lot to keep it up—I want you to use the money to live on until your paintings catch on."

He shook his head. "My paintings."

"The three of us can work on Father together. Get him to understand. If he won't go into one of those residences, well, I'll make a room for him at my place. We'll find a way for him to keep some of his books. That's all he needs, except for brandy and cigarettes."

"It would kill him to lose this house."

"He doesn't have much longer anyway, not with his stubborn habits."

Matthias smiled gently, hoping she wouldn't misunderstand what he was about to say. "If we did all that, it would be the end of things for you socially. The *Social Register* and all that. They'd find out. They'd drop you."

They stared at each other. Their faces were so much alike, it was the same as looking into mirrors.

"Matthias, I don't really give a shit. Do you?"

"If you care, you shouldn't be in there. Isn't that what they say?"

"That wife of yours sure as hell liked being there."

"She's no longer my wife."

"Christian cares about all that, the goddamned snob. Being dropped from everything would do him good. Make me feel damned good." She turned away. "I have to get some sleep, Matthias. Tomorrow starts bloody early."

"Annelise. Would it help if I came back for good, to try to get the firm going again?"

She hesitated. "I thought you hated that. What did you use to say? 'Form doesn't follow function in Chicago, it follows money.' "

"Money is what we need."

"To be brutally frank, brother dear, I think it's much too late for that. Chicago's still got a lot of money around, but the town is run by people like that wretched Peter Poe. Have you seen that monstrosity of his on Michigan Avenue? That's the kind of trash they're putting up these days. They won't want an aesthete like you. What would you design, houses? They're tearing down the houses Father designed right and left. Go back to France. Go back to painting. Think of yourself. Be a little selfish. Everyone else is. All this will take care of itself."

"I'm not sure it will."

"It will. Paul will see to it." She took his hand. Hers was rough and calloused. "I think you're a wonderful painter, Matthias. Don't waste it. Don't throw it all away like Christian." She kissed his cheek with a brush of lips. "Good night." She was gone with a rustle of gown. He was alone with the moonlight. He felt like a drink, but he let the moment pass. He began to walk the long, wide terrace, thinking about his family, and how it had come to own such a terrace.

The Curlands had mostly been farmers—in Germany, and in Michigan, where they had settled in the 1840s. Matthias's father's father had been the first Curland to attend college.

The Albrechts were different—"special." Not "better," but different. Bold people who had gone through life snatching up whatever they wanted. The first in America, Gottfried Albrecht, had been a Prussian-born lieutenant of Hussars serving with the British army in the American Revolution. After the Battle of Monmouth, he had taken most of his squadron of cavalry with him over to the American side.

After the war, he settled in Pennsylvania. His son Johannes moved west into Ohio, establishing a small shipping line on Lake Erie. Johannes's eldest son Rheinhard had taken the shipping line to the burgeoning little town of Chicago, buying land to the north of the river and selling it off in small parcels to the German settlers who followed. He started a brewery, a building firm, a ship chandler's company, and a cooperage and lumber business.

Rheinhard's son Manfred was the richest and the worst Albrecht. He expanded the family holdings into railroads and financial trading. Ruthless and compulsively greedy, he prospered in panics that ruined thousands of others, emerging one of the wealthiest men in the city in the Gilded Age of the robber barons. Socially ambitious, he had adopted the Anglophile ways of Chicago's social elite, marrying his daughter off to a knighted Englishman and sending his only son, Karl, to Harvard. Manfred's death from a heart attack suffered in a brothel in the Levee District had caused a minor scandal.

His son Karl, Matthias's grandfather, had been the best Albrecht. From Harvard, he'd gone to Paris to study painting and then to Leipzig to learn architecture. When World War I broke out, he returned to America, enlisting as a private soldier and suffering severe wounds at Belleau Wood inflicted by his ancestral countrymen.

The physical and moral carnage of the war appalled him, and he'd dedicated the rest of his years to efforts on behalf of civilization. Liquidating most of the family holdings, he'd built a settlement house and an orphanage, and donated large tracts of land for parks and forest preserve. He'd begun collecting art before the war, and renewed his acquisition with much passion afterward, building a small museum on the Near North Side. Prohibition and the Depression put the brewery and what remained of the family companies out of business, though the architecture firm Karl founded in the 1920s survived and flourished. He'd died a still wealthy man, not counting the value of the museum and its extraordinary painting collection.

His daughter and only child, Hannah Albrecht, married a young associate in the firm, Rudolph Curland. Leaving the museum to her care and the architecture firm to Rudolph's, Karl had gone to his grave content that these most beloved of his creations would endure. Especially his museum, which he'd left to a small foundation he'd established, to be administered by a board made up of his daughter Hannah, his son-in-law Rudolph, and his grandsons Matthias and Christian, who had pleased him by studying art and architecture as he had done. Annelise had shown no interest in the place.

The art museum, still called the Albrecht Collection but also listed in the tourist guides as the German Museum, had an endowment, but its investments had been poorly handled and the interest was failing to meet expenses. When this happened to some museums, parts of collections were sold off to raise funds—often at great profit. But under the terms of Karl's will, no painting in the collection was to be sold. Should the museum be forced to close for any reason, or the collection tampered with, everything was to be donated to the Art Institute of Chicago.

If Christian was correct, the architecture firm could be out of business in the morning.

Matthias leaned against the railing, inhaling deeply of the scented warmth of the night air, tilting back his head to stare at the moon. On just such a night, far too many years before, he'd proposed marriage on this spot to Sally Phillips. He'd been very young and worth at most $50,000. She was being romanced by a man much older who was worth a hundred times that. With a kiss and much sadness, she'd turned Matthias down.

If his grandfather hadn't been so eccentric, hadn't become so obsessed with his museum, hadn't put all his money into it, the Curlands would have been spared all these problems. He'd be a different person. He'd be rich.

He'd tried to be an ordinary man. He'd failed at that as he had so much else. But to live according to the trivial tribal rituals of the rich, and think that was special, was a ridiculous illusion. Special was different. Perhaps that was why his grandfather had done what he'd done.

Jill Langley had thought that. Jill would have married him rich or poor, had wanted to, but it was much too late to think about that now.

Lighting his pipe, he paced the terrace some more, then stopped to lean back against the railing and look up at the great house, pondering ghosts, imagining who might be behind those windows if he could travel back in time. He thought of his grandfather, standing at the window of his dressing room in the morning, gazing out at the lake, as if it were one of his possessions or, at least, one of the public institutions in his beneficent charge.

His own father had designed this house, approved every brick and cornice.

Matthias found guilt in these thoughts. Annelise and Christian had made one thing perfectly clear. It was now up to him. If this house and all it represented was to be saved, he alone would have to do it. Annelise didn't care and Christian was incapable. If Matthias refused to make the effort, and allowed this house and the history it embodied to vanish from the family's present life and future, the deed would be his, and it would be a deed, a conscious act. This was not something from which he could walk away, as he had from so much. Walking away would be a conscious, deliberate, painfully consequential decision, and the blame and guilt for the consequences would be his.

He would be undoing work—the labor of generations. Except for the museum and a few commemorative placques in public places, the house was all that testified to the achievements of two centuries of Albrechts. A little labor and effort on his part was all that was required to save it. Too many of the great families of this city had diminished to descendants who just didn't give a damn, who let everything slip away.

It wasn't too late. He'd called his mother's death a sign, and perhaps it was—a summons, come just in time.

But how to do it? Art was no answer—not his, not any of the sacrosanct paintings in his grandfather's museum. He was no good at investments and finance, his great-grandfather's game. None of them was.

It had to be architecture. Chicago had made many an architect rich, many more poor, even bankrupt. The trend in this lingering recession was to the latter. He'd heard that Skidmore, Owings and Merrill, the city's largest architectual firm, had laid off something like half its staff at the depths of the economic troubles, and since then had hired few back.

He had at least to try. Something might turn up. That was his brother's motto for life. Sometimes it did.

Upon arriving home, Diandra went immediately to bed—in her own room. The separate sleeping chambers had been Poe's requirement. He'd broached the idea early in their engagement, almost as a condition of marriage, but she'd raised no objection, though she'd seemed curious, as she still was about his peculiarities and idiosyncrasies. The arrangement was not intended as a limitation on sex. He took that when he wished, which was often enough. Rather, as with everything else in his life, it was a matter of his convenience. He did business at all hours of the day and night, and there were occasions when he wished sex with someone else and did not want to waste time leaving his apartment.

Diandra's bedroom suite was on the top floor of the Poe Place penthouse, looking north over the Gold Coast and up the lake shore. His was on the main floor, opposite his study and just down the hall from the wide gallery that opened onto his south terrace. It was to the study he went first.

Poe had a half-dozen people to answer his phones for him. For his most private line, however, he used an answering machine that required a computer code to access and activate. He settled behind his desk, punched the requisite buttons on the desk console, and leaned back in his $10,000 Italian leather swivel chair to listen.

There were calls from his accountant, a business associate in Michigan City, and the governor of Indiana, among some dozen messages. These could wait until the morning. Another call troubled him. He jotted a brief notation, then used the same ultra-private line to dial a number.

He let it ring some nine times, irritated that he was being made to wait in this manner, then terminated the call and placed another, taking the number from a directory in his desktop computer.

This call was answered after just three rings. A soft, male voice came on the line.

"Mr. Train, please," said Poe.

"Who?"

"Laurence Train."

"What makes you think he's here?"

"Please. Mr. Train."

"Who's calling?"

"He'll know."

The line went silent, for longer than pleased Poe. Finally, Train's nasal, high-pitched, overeducated, and affectedly Eastern voice filled Poe's ear.

"What do you want, Peter?" he said abjectly.

"You called me, Larry."

"Yes, I did. I got a little nervous about something. But it can wait."

"I don't like to wait."

"I left my other number."

"I tried it. No one answered."

"How on earth did you get this number?"

"You called me, Larry. What do you want?"

"One of the paintings is missing. One of the Kirchners. *The Red Tower*. The one you liked so much."

Poe drummed his fingers a moment. "Missing from where?"

"From the gallery. I had two cheaper paintings plus the Kirchner set aside in a box for you. It's gone."

"Gone."

"That girl, Jill Langley, she's sometimes there on weekends. I thought she might have taken the box to deliver it to you—it was marked for your yacht—just to do that little extra. She always stays late, don't you know, doing the extra. But I can't find her. You might want to check your yacht, in case she did bring it there."

"You should never have hired that girl, Larry."

"It wouldn't do to have her at the German Museum now, would it? Under the circumstances? We talked about this. It was a good idea—get her out of the museum, keep an eye on her."

"Which you failed to do, apparently."

"I'm sure she'll turn up. It'll be all right. But I thought you'd want to know."

"You make too many mistakes, Larry."

"I do my best, Peter." Train sounded nervous.

"Do better."

Poe hung up before Train could speak again. He sat very still, then began drumming his fingers again. At length, he hit a button on his desk console that automatically dialed another number. Mango answered on the fourth ring. She sounded a little nervous, too.

"Is something wrong, Peter? I just left you."

"I have some work for the guys," Poe said. "There's a girl who works for Larry Train. Her name's Jill Langley."

"Jill Langley. Yes."

"Do you know her?"

"Talk to her on the phone sometimes, when I call over there. What's wrong?"

"Probably nothing. She's missing. I want to know where she is. There's a painting missing from Train's gallery. One of those that was supposed to go to me. She may have it. One of the special ones. *The Red Tower,* by a guy named Kirchner."

"I remember it. I asked you if it was supposed to be New York. You said it was a picture of Berlin or something. How would she get her hands on it?"

"Train isn't sure. It may be on the boat. She may have brought it there, trying to be helpful. Have the boys check it out. If it's not there, I want it found. The girl, too."

"I'll get them right on it. Anything else, Peter?"

"No."

"You want me to come over?"

"Not tonight."

"What about the—the thing tomorrow?"

"I thought it over. I still want you to go through with it. I want to get started with this."

"All right." She paused. He wondered if that was an indication of uncertainty. "I'll get it done. I'm ready now. I can pull it off."

"We could use somebody else."

"No one you can trust. Not like me."

"Okay. Don't fuck it up."

"You're so goddamned encouraging."

"I love you, babe."

"I love you, too, Peter. I wish I could be with you."

"Time enough for that. Good night, Mango."

"Good night."

He hit a button, ending the call, then leaned back, swiveling the chair to look out the window at the yellow-orange lights of the city streets, stretching off to infinity. Then he went to his bar and poured himself half a glass of extremely expensive scotch, adding four rounded ice cubes from a dispensing machine he had had built into his bar. He took the drink across to his bedroom. After removing all his clothes in his dressing area, he went to his bed and sat sipping the drink, gazing out the floor-to-ceiling window. He did not feel content. After gulping down the drink, he set down the empty glass and went out into the hall to the small elevator that served all three floors of the penthouse.

Diandra was in bed, reading. He looked at the cover: Somerset Maugham's *Moon and Sixpence.* He'd never read it.

He continued to stare at the book, until she put it down, noting his nakedness.

"Now?" she said, without hostility, but also without any discernible enthusiasm.

He nodded.

She put the book on her night table, and then her glasses. Hesitating a moment, she then threw back the bed covers and pulled off her nightgown, spreading her long legs slightly.

In rather a short time, Poe was finished. He held her body tightly a moment, motionless, then pulled back.

"Are you happy now?" she said. Her voice was soft and musical, and always under perfect control. She could speak to him in this gentle, kindly manner yet manage to keep affection out of every word.

"Yes."

"Good night, then."

"Good night, babe."

She went back to her book.

But he wasn't happy. Returning below, he made himself another drink and went to the long gallery, snapping on an overhead spotlight. It was focused on a large-scale architectual model of downtown Chicago and its buildings, complete with a greensward representing Grant Park. At the northwest corner of the model, on the edge of the city center, was a tall, thin tower, painted a bright crimson, standing higher than any of the other building representations. Unlike the others, it had not been yet built.

The spotlight was positioned to shine directly upon it. Because the rest of the gallery was in darkness, the red tower was reflected in the gallery's long window, though the city skyline and lakefront was clearly visible beyond. The effect was to superimpose the tower in the window over the actual skyline beyond.

But it was in the wrong place. Taking a large swallow of whiskey, Poe lifted the model building and set it down on the other side of the miniature cityscape, placing it on the flat rectangle that represented Meigs Field. It stood there firmly, rising above all else—the Hancock Center, the Sears Tower, everything.

Poe looked up. In moving the object on the table model, he caused its reflection in the window to shift to where it seemed to be rising from the actual lakefront airport. He went to the wall and turned a knob that redirected the spotlight to the tower's new position. It stood out sharply, dominating all else, like it was the commanding general, in front of the ranks, and every other structure in the city merely the army.

"If you pulled this off," Mango had said when he'd told her his idea, "it would be fucking amazing."

It would be more than that. If he could make this happen, he could make anything happen. And everyone in the city—everyone in the whole goddamn world—would know that he could make anything happen.

He sipped once more. Now he felt content.

CHAPTER

2

THE SERVICE FOR Hannah Curland was held on the back lawn of the Lake Forest house, the chairs for the two dozen or so family members, friends, and acquaintances arranged just below the terrace wall, facing toward the lake. Both the Curlands and Albrechts had long been at least nominal Presbyterians, and the minister from the local church had been asked to officiate, a token gesture to accommodate whatever spiritual belief Hannah may have harbored, though little was suspected. The minister was a surprisingly young man—one Matthias's mother had hardly known. He read, in somewhat timorous voice, from appropriate passages of the King James Bible, then recounted the deceased's fondness for flower gardens and animals and her love for church and husband and children—portraying a woman who had pitifully little in common with the once-wild North Shore party girl whose eventual loss of beauty to age and dissolution had driven her to fits of hysteria, numerous infidelities, and a penchant for terrorizing everyone in her family. She had been a quite popular person in the community, but that had to do with charm, not goodness—and she'd used her charm like money, paying it out for what she wanted. Her intolerable behavior as an old woman was part of what had driven Matthias to acquiesce to his wife's demands to move away to the East, and from there to his exile in France.

He had forcefully emptied his mind of all these dreadful memories and thoughts of his mother—even during the late hours of the previous night, when he had relentlessly paced the terrace like some solitary, sentimental ghost. Now they came rushing back, uninvited. He sought distraction by glancing over his shoulder at the mourners in the chairs behind him, wondering if Jill Langley might have come to the service. Christian had been so sure that she wouldn't, but Matthias felt somehow that she would be there.

She wasn't. Instead, he was startled by the sight of Sally Phillips in the last row. She was a little thin and careworn, but still had the same sleek, dark-haired, neatly turned out beauty he had remembered, sometimes even when lying in another woman's arms.

She quickly caught his eye and gave him a quick glimmer of a sympathetic smile. He looked away, regretted that rudeness, and, attempting amiability, turned back, but found her then gazing fixedly past him at the young minister.

Christian came up, a drink in his hand. "I see you've noticed Sally."

"Hard not to," Matthias said.

"Jill's not here."

"You said you didn't invite her."

Christian gave him a strange look, then moved away.

After the service, as well-wishers filed inside, Sally lingered on the terrace. Matthias took that as invitation. He approached her slowly, giving her opportunity to evade him. She didn't use it.

"Hello, Matthias," she said softly. "I'm so sorry."

"We're all calling it a blessing."

"I liked her. We got on well."

"You were fortunate."

Seen close up, though perfectly groomed and very carefully dressed, Sally did not look her best. The youthful freshness had faded and her beauty turned fragile, almost brittle. There were small lines at the corners of her eyes and mouth. He wondered which had been worse, her divorce, or marriage.

"You're still living in France?"

"So to speak," he said. "I don't know when I'll be going back."

"Then you'll be here for a while?"

"For a while. Family business to attend to."

She smiled, pleased. "Are you staying here in Lake Forest?"

"In the city. We still have the house on Schiller Street, for the moment."

Her silence indicated she knew all about his family's financial predicament. All of Chicago must.

"I live in town myself," she said. "I have a little apartment, and a job. I run a little shop in Water Tower Place."

"Are you all right?"

"Yes. Well, I'm managing. I have to work."

She said this so distastefully it amused him. But he was concerned about her, and curious. Her ex-husband must have caught her in some indefensibly compromising circumstance, or else gotten his hands on a corrupt divorce court judge. Perhaps both. The latter had always been easy in Illinois.

Matthias noticed that a few people were waiting to speak to him. Beyond them, Christian, bloody Mary still in hand, stood with Annelise by the terrace railing. His sister held the silver urn containing their mother's ashes.

"I'd like to talk to you," he said to Sally. "Can you wait?"

"For a little. I left my daughter with a sitter. It's a long train ride back."

"I'll drive you."

He said that on impulse. It would mean taking his father's ridiculous Rolls-Royce, as he wanted nothing further to do with the Jaguar on loan to Christian from his middle-age amour. He'd have to be very careful with the Rolls. The car, and much else, might yet have to be sold.

"That would be very nice. Thank you, Matthias."

"Give me a few minutes." He nodded toward his brother and sister. "We have a ceremony to perform."

She turned and saw the urn. "Are you going to a cemetery?"

"No. Just down to the bottom of the bluff. To the water's edge."

"Was that her wish?"

"Her wish was to live forever, as a beautiful girl. No. This is our decision. This bit of shoreline was her favorite place. We'll scatter her ashes on the rocks; make her part of the lake." He paused. "It's not as if she's vanishing without a trace. She'll remain behind, in that portrait Chris did of her."

"The one that was in your Schiller Street house?"

"Yes. It's still there."

"It's a lovely painting."

"It's ingenious." He touched her shoulder. "Go get a drink, or something to eat. This won't take long."

The old log steps cut into the side of the bluff had not been well maintained and the trail was dangerous in places. Hannah's three grown children left their frail, elderly father to cope as best he could with the funeral guests in the house and made the precarious descent on their own. Annelise, leading the way, managed it

38

best. Matthias, carrying the urn, followed at a slower pace. Christian, stumbling several times, was last. They had to wait for him after reaching the shoreline rocks.

The waves were gentle, sloshing between the bigger stones, but not over them. There was little wind. When Christian, clutching a nearly empty glass, finally joined them, Matthias stepped up onto a large rock that extended farther out into the water than the others. Carefully he removed the lid from the urn.

"Not all of it," said Annelise.

"What?"

"Don't put all the ashes in the lake," she said. "Leave some in the urn."

"That's like cutting her in half," Christian said.

"No, it's not," said his sister. "Part of her should be here. But there should be something left to bury."

"What about her legs?" said Christian. "Maybe they still have them in the body parts bin at the hospital."

"Shut up!" said Annelise. For an instant, Matthias thought she was going to hit him.

They stood in awkward silence for a moment. Matthias could think of nothing ceremonial to say. The minister had uttered all the ritual words. The three children had their private thoughts, none that should be given voice. Ultimately Matthias found a trace or two of remembered love for his mother in the turmoil inside him. Perhaps that would suffice. Leaning forward, extending the urn over the blue-green slosh, he slowly tilted it. The ash fell in a spray, a thin spatter on the water's surface, quickly gone.

Matthias straightened the vessel, then peered inside it. He'd poured out about two-thirds of its contents. There was a tiny triangle of bone in the ash at the bottom. Swiftly he replaced the lid.

Annelise, to his surprise, was crying.

As Matthias stepped down, Christian hopped up in his place. He lifted his glass to the hazy sky, then emptied its meager contents with a tiny splash.

"Sacrifice," he said.

The old Rolls's engine made an objectionable clatter but chugged along unfalteringly. As the day was warm and he wished to experience his reclaimed surroundings as fully as possible, Matthias had put the top down. He drove rather slowly, not wanting the wind to snatch away their words. He wanted to talk to Sally

very much. He wasn't sure when there would be another opportunity. She'd been his first love. Whatever had happened to
her—to them—that fact endured. It wasn't love he felt now.
Simply loyalty, and regret. It sufficed for a bond, for some kind
of reconciliation.

They were following the weaving course of Sheridan Road as
it wound through the ravines and bluffs of Highland Park and
Winnetka. It would take them a good hour or more to reach
Sally's apartment building.

She leaned back in the weathered leather seat, tilting her face
toward the sky and stretching out her arms.

"How many times did we make this drive, you and I?" she
said.

"The last one wasn't my favorite."

"Nor mine. Now that I've had a few years to think about it."

She straightened. The passing trees loomed large overhead,
reaching down as if wanting to touch them. They were very old.
He wondered if any had been growing before there had been
houses here.

"So you're divorced," he said.

She waited a long time before answering. "It happens," she
said. "It was for the best."

For all her studied manners and carefully elegant dress, Sally
was very much a girl of the middle class, the suburban commut-
ing class. Her father had been an executive with a wall coverings
manufacturing company, pushed into increasingly responsible
and better-paying positions more by his wife's ambitions than
any of his own. Sally had been born on the North Side of Chicago and spent her early childhood in Lincolnwood. A fortuitous
promotion had enabled her father to move his family to an
address in West Lake Forest when she was fourteen, and her
mother had taken over from there, getting Sally into a good
private school and pushing her into relationships with likely
young men whose social backgrounds the mother had carefully
scouted.

Because of the Curlands' high profile in Chicago cultural and
civic affairs, the mother was initially thrilled when Matthias and
Sally had begun dating. She carried on as if Karl Albrecht's big
house on the lake was some feudal manor and Matthias a noble
who went with it. But she had investigated the Curlands as she
had all her daughter's young men, and had been thunderstruck
to learn how little money they had outside of what was tied up

in the museum, and how much Matthias's father owed. After that, she began obstructing the relationship's progress in all manner of unpleasant ways, neglecting to take Matthias's telephone messages and committing Sally to social engagements that interfered with their dating.

Acquiring the allure of something forbidden, their romance had only flourished. Sally had already lost her virginity to one of her mother's eligible young finds by the time she'd begun dating Matthias, but she gave herself to Matthias with all the flushed innocence and awkward passion of a virgin. Glancing at her now, he thought of the first time she had opened her blouse to him, in the seat of an open car much like this.

For all that, her marriage to someone like her ex-husband was inevitable. Though divorced and much older than was considered suitable, he was everything else her mother had desired—rich, well connected, a member of the Chicago and Casino clubs, active enough in Republican politics to know the governor and be recognized by name by the president at fund-raising dinners, a man mentioned frequently in both the society pages and the business pages.

"I'm sorry."

"Are you?" It was a rebuke.

"This isn't how you should have ended up."

Sally frowned, then sighed. She rubbed her temples with the heels of her hands, then glanced about, as if there was some way she might escape this situation. Finally, folding her arms, she fixed her gaze forward out the windshield. "I should never have married him. If it weren't for having my daughter, I'd hate my mother for pushing me into it. I suppose I do anyway."

"Did he give you that bad a time?"

"Yes."

"Did he get violent? I was worried about that, from what I know about him."

"Sometimes."

"That's why you left him."

"I didn't leave him, Matt. He threw me out. I gave him cause. You might as well know everything. I had an affair."

He thought upon the women in his own life. "In this day and age, that ought to be a forgivable offense."

"Would you forgive me, Matt?"

"What do you mean?"

"It was with your brother Christian."

41

Matthias's hands jerked on the steering wheel, causing him to veer toward the curb until he snapped the car back on course. He took a deep breath, steadying himself.

"You weren't here," she said. "You were a million miles away." She started to say something else, but her voice caught and then broke. She began sobbing.

For a long while, there were no more words between them. He could think of nothing adequate or useful to say—not to her, not to himself. Who hadn't Christian slept with? Their mother? Annelise? Hillary? Christian had made several passes at her. He'd gone after Jill, too, though she'd firmly rejected him.

"How did he treat you?" he asked.

"My husband?"

"Christian."

"He was very kind. I think that's how it happened in the first place."

"He's manic-depressive, you know. It goes with creativity. Vincent Van Gogh."

"There's no need to trash Christian like that."

"No?"

"Van Gogh's whole family was like that, after all. It runs in families."

It was true. The remark was very pointed, and deeply wounding.

She fired another shot. "You weren't very faithful to your own wife, were you? Christian told me about you and that girl who worked for you."

Christian. He never passed up an opportunity to seize advantage. No wonder Sally hadn't felt disloyal.

"Is it over?" he asked.

"Christian's still my friend."

"Is it over now?"

"Yes. Now."

She was staring at him. He tried turning on the car radio, but it didn't work.

The road wound on through less pretentious suburbs, passing through a section of Evanston lined with brick apartment houses, then following a curve of the shoreline into the northern districts of the city and turning ultimately onto the Outer Drive.

Sailboats dotted the lake horizon to their left. The crowded playing fields and picnic grounds of Lincoln Park stretched away to their right. Passing Belmont Harbor, he caught sight of a slim green tower nestled among a huddle of larger, cruder structures.

"There's your building," she said, so softly he could barely hear her.

"I'm amazed it's still there," he said. "I half expected some big new condo with lots of balconies to be sitting in its place."

"Yours is the most beautiful building in Chicago," she said. "It ought to be set out here on the lake, where everybody could see it."

"That's the last thing I'd want," he said. "No damned buildings on the lakeshore. This is Chicago, not Miami."

His words came out sharply, sounding too much like a rebuke. She turned away. They were rapidly approaching the Gold Coast. She lived in the west part of it, over near Dearborn Street. With so little traffic, they would be there soon.

He took her hand.

"It's all right," he said.

"What's all right?" She was hurt and angry.

He curved his fingers tightly around her palm. "Everything. Everything will be all right."

How could he know that? He'd been with her less than two hours after an absence of years. She might be about to lose her job. Her child might be seriously ill. Her ex-husband might be plotting to ruin her life. When they'd parted, Matthias had promised his woman in France that he would return. What was he doing?

They were approaching the North Avenue exit. He took his hand from Sally's and returned it to the steering wheel.

"Have you come back for good?" she asked. There was a plaintive tone to her voice.

"I'm not really sure. I'll be here for a while, perhaps a long while. The family affairs are a mess. There's a lot to put back in order, especially at my father's firm."

Earlier he would have said "my firm."

"Do you think you'll go back to being an architect?"

At their slower speed, moving along the busy street, Matthias noticed that people stared at his car. "I'll do whatever has to be done."

His answer didn't satisfy her.

"You wanted so badly to be an artist," she said. "A painter. Like Christian."

"The kind of painter Christian could be. Not the kind he is."

"Did you succeed?"

He'd never lied to her before, not really. "No."

Her apartment building was old and small, but had an awning and a doorman. She was at least keeping up appearances. Matthias pulled into an open space next to a fire hydrant. He wouldn't be able to accept an invitation to come upstairs parked there, not that he was prepared for that.

He got out and went around to her side, gently opening the door and taking her hand to help her out.

"Do you think you might be free tonight?" she asked.

"I don't know. I'll have to check with Annelise."

"There's a party at Bitsie Symms's. I don't think you know her. She's become quite the big deal around town, very social. In *Town & Country* and *W* magazine all the time. It's supposed to be quite a big party. The mayor may even come."

"I'd forgotten about such parties."

"I go to them all the time."

He wondered why. Old habits? Augmenting an otherwise meager diet? Looking for a husband? He felt so sorry for her.

She took an old calling card from her purse and a pen, hastily putting down her telephone number. "Call me."

"All right."

She leaned forward, hesitated, then kissed his cheek. He put his hand on her shoulder, then dropped it as she stepped back.

"It's so good to see you again," she said. "I was so sad this morning. I feel lots better now."

She gave him a wisp of a smile, then turned. As she disappeared into her lobby, Matthias wondered if he could get away with smashing his brother in the face.

Peter Poe had his breakfast on the terrace of his penthouse facing Lake Michigan. He'd sent his man Krasowski out early to fetch some yachting magazines from the newsstand at the Drake Hotel, and looked through them while he ate. Then he had a telephone brought to him and got busy.

Poe had three lawyers on retainer. One, with solid experience in criminal law, was in Indiana, his principal function that of keeping every aspect of Poe's casino operations—on the surface, at least—within the bounds of state and federal law. The second was a stuffy and well-pedigreed old fellow who was a senior partner at one of Chicago's more decrepit if eminently respectable law firms. Poe used him mostly as his front man when

44

dealing with the city's elite, and liked to have him at his side at the press conferences he called to announce new projects.

Poe's third and principal attorney, Bill Yeats, was a tax and money man who knew Chicago's power structure inside out— knew it the way the city's garbagemen knew all its alleys and gangways. He worked mostly for Poe now, and had become one of his most trusted advisers. Poe trusted him mostly because he had so thoroughly bought him. Yeats's considerable retainer included a small percentage of Poe's casino receipts.

Yeats's office was just up the street, on one of the lower floors of the Hancock Center. His apartment, a large, sprawling place, was on one of the higher residential floors of the same building. He was usually to be found in one or the other on most mornings, as Poe liked him on hand in case he worked up an idea during the night. He summoned Yeats now for just that reason. The lawyer was at Poe's penthouse in eleven minutes. Poe timed him.

Yeats had thinning, pale-red hair and a slight paunch; and had put the Southwest Side Irish-Catholic parish of his childhood far behind him. He was in summer Sunday morning clothes, including a light-blue Lacoste polo shirt, a navy blazer, lightweight gray flannels, gray socks, and Sperry Topsider boating shoes. He wore half-glasses, which, perhaps calculatedly, gave him the look of an erudite WASP.

As requested, he had brought what he and Poe simply referred to as *The Book*. It was an inexpensive ledger of the kind commonplace in office supply stores before the age of computers. It contained not a single word. Its entries consisted entirely of numbers and dollar amounts, identified only by the page line they occupied. The first set of two columns, for example, represented the reported and actual monthly receipts from Poe's casino in Michigan City. Another set was for his gambling riverboats operating out of Dubuque, Iowa. Sometimes the parallel columns of figures were exactly the same. Whether they were or not depended on the final entry on each page—indicating whether Poe's various operations were showing an overall profit after payment on his huge debts or a loss. For the last five months, this bottom line had indicated loss.

"I want to buy a boat," said Poe, after his housekeeper had poured Yeats some coffee and gone back to her kitchen.

"You already have a boat," Yeats said. "One of the biggest on Lake Michigan."

"I mean a sailboat. A big one, with two masts." Poe turned one of the yachting magazines toward Yeats, laying his index finger on a quarter page advertisement for a black-hulled sixty-five-foot ketch that was listed for $305,000.

"You want to sell the one you have now? It's a rough market for big tubs like that. The banks are still stuck with that one of Donald Trump's."

"The day I sell the *Queen P* is the day I'm washed up. No, I want a second boat."

"For down in Florida or something?"

"No. For here."

"Why?"

"All the big players in the yacht club own sailboats. Including you."

"Most of them race."

"I know. I want to race. Like Ted Turner."

"Peter. You've got to know something about sailing."

"No, I don't. I'll hire somebody who does to race it for me. Maybe I'll have him teach me."

Yeats tapped his foot, his only sign of exasperation. He had planned to devote the next week to persuading Poe to drop his plans for trying to buy the White Sox. Now this.

"You can't write off two boats; only one. And even that's hard nowadays."

"I want to buy a sailboat, with two masts. There are some others in here for even less. Two hundred large. Maybe two fifty."

Yeats shook his head.

"These are cruising boats, Peter. Too slow for racing. If you want to race, get a sloop rig."

"Two masts?"

"Just one. But they're fast. Here's one. A fifty-one-footer, built for racing. Perfect. And only $145,000. The commodore of my yacht club has one a lot like it."

Poe stared at Yeats, expressionless, reminding the lawyer of a lion studying something he might want to eat.

"One mast. And it's small."

"It would be a gentleman's boat, Peter. The America's Cup racers are sloop-rigged, after all. And the accommodations would be ample for a small party. This one has two private staterooms."

More silence.

"Do you want me to find one like this for you?" Yeats said. "Is that why you called me over? To help you buy a boat?"

"One of the reasons," Poe said quietly, but sounding friendly—Peter Poe, the "nice guy" billionaire once again. "You know sailboats. Find one. Big but fast. I want to sign a purchase agreement this week. And I want to enter it in a race this summer."

"This summer?"

"Yes. Maybe the Mackinac."

"The Mac? That's very big league, Peter. And I don't think you'd be able to get a crew put together and trained in time. Do you plan to be aboard?"

"Yes. I want to be in the picture at the finish."

"They won't take your picture unless you win."

"That's right, Bill. I want to win. I'd like to be in the papers as a big winner at something this summer."

"You might be able to get into the Chicago–Menominee. That's up the lake, around the Door County peninsula, and across Green Bay. It's a rough race, but not so many top skippers. Not so many boats. In late July."

"Do it."

"You want me for your skipper?"

"No. You have your own boat."

Yeats shrugged. When Poe said nothing more, he started to reach for his briefcase, which contained *The Book*.

"Get it out, Bill. I want to know if I can buy this thing for cash."

"Not if you're going to press on with this White Sox thing," he said, opening the case. "My fees alone could run you as much as a boat."

"I have no intention of buying the White Sox."

Yeats blinked. "What do you mean? You've been all over the TV news this week acting like you already own them."

Poe looked at him as if he were an utter fool. "Everyone thinks I'm all set to buy the Sox, that I've got the money to buy the Sox, the Cubs, the Bulls, anything I want. The *Trib* had an editorial comparing my fortune to old A. N. Pritzker's. They're wondering where I'm going to stop. Right?"

"Yes."

"That's all I wanted out of this. Now I can go to the bank on the Cabrini Green deal. They'll open their vault and hand me a wheelbarrow. Right?"

"Which bank? Continental Illinois? First National? They're not in a mood to hand anyone a wheelbarrow with this recession. Maybe a small shovel. Maybe a spoon."

"The new bank. Inland Empire. They're not as big, but they're players, and they've got a Japanese connection. They see me on a roll. They want to get the city moving again. They want to be a part of it. We'll score. It means a lot of their eggs in my basket, but I'm the only action in town right now."

It was a correct assessment.

"I was going to talk to you about them," Yeats said. "If Continental or the First turned you down."

"Bill," Poe said with an amiable smile. "That's bullshit."

Yeats looked at his Sperry Topsiders. They were brand new. He wore a very old pair when he was actually on his boat.

"What I want to know is this, Bill. Will Inland Empire want my casino or the riverboats for collateral? Everything else I've got is leveraged."

"Sure they will. They may be players, but they're bankers."

"All right," said Poe, nodding to *The Book*. "Starting now, I'm putting everything into the till. One set of figures."

"Everything?"

"Every two-dollar chip."

"For how long?"

"Until I say otherwise."

"What about all your debt service?"

"I'll take care of it."

"How?"

"You don't need to know that."

"What about Bobby Mann?"

Mann was Poe's casino manager. Poe had hired him at the request of some of the investors who had backed his Indiana operations. Mann had managed a casino in Atlantic City. He scared Yeats more than anyone in Poe's organization, more than Poe himself sometimes.

"I'll deal with him."

"And your partners?"

"They're silent partners."

"They won't stay that way."

"They will if they think the IRS is sniffing around. I know somebody in the U.S. Attorney's office. I'll have him give me a call—when I'm out at the casino. Or send an official letter. That should keep my partners very quiet for a while."

"You say you can take care of the shortfalls?"

"Don't worry about it."

"And you still want to buy a boat?"

"I'll have the money," said Poe. "You just get me the boat."

"Whatever you say." Yeats stood up. He started to put the ledger back into his briefcase.

"No," said Poe. "Leave that."

"I've always had that."

"Things change, Bill. After we've got a deal on Cabrini Green, we'll start a new system."

Yeats frowned. "Somehow I don't think I know all that's going on here."

"You're a perceptive guy."

"If you can't trust your lawyer, who can you trust?" Yeats said. He smiled, to show it was a joke.

Poe didn't smile. "If I didn't trust you, Bill, you wouldn't be here."

He walked his guest to the penthouse elevator.

"Have a nice day," he said, as the doors opened. "Why don't you go sailing? Maybe you'll run across a nice boat for me."

"With this recession, it shouldn't be a problem."

"I don't like problems, Bill." The words were his farewell.

After the doors closed, Poe went into his study and made a phone call to Mango Bellini. It rang four times, and he began to get angry. Finally she answered.

"This is the third time I've called you this morning," Poe said. "Why didn't you answer my messages?"

"I just walked in, Peter. The phone was ringing as I was opening the door. Honest. I'm sorry."

"Where were you?"

"In church. At mass. He was there. He always goes to mass when he's getting itchy. I guess it cleans the slate. Makes room for new sin."

"Wasn't that a little risky?"

"It's a big church. I came late. Sat in the back. Left before it was over. It felt right, Peter. I think he'll be coming out to play tonight."

"You sound a little nervous. Are you sure you're up to this?"

"I'm not nervous. Just getting psyched up."

"Anything from our guys?"

"There were some paintings on your yacht, but not the one you're looking for."

"And the girl? Jill Langley?"

She paused to cough. He'd have to get her off cigarettes.

"Nothing yet," she said.

"Okay."

"Let me take care of this thing tonight."

"Okay, okay. Call me when it's over. We're going out tonight, but I'll be back by midnight."

"I'll call as soon as I can."

"Love you, babe. Stay cool. Don't let anything spook you."

He hung up the receiver just as Diandra came down the hall, barefoot and quiet, the breeze from the terrace fluffing her strawberry blond hair and billowing her long silken robe. She glanced at Poe and nodded—as if a wifely "good morning" and kiss and hug could be rendered in the simple shorthand of that gesture. Then she moved on to the terrace, pulling a chaise longue into the shade to protect her pale, clear skin. She'd kept all her model's habits, except avoidance of drink. She brought one with her—a fruit juice thinned by gin or vodka. Turning on the terrace stereo and tuning it to a classical music station, she waited until she had fully reclined on the chaise before taking her first sip. Then she closed her eyes, listening to the music.

Poe, watching her through his open study window, felt like going out and kicking over a chair just to shatter her tranquil moment. Tranquility was the one quality of life that had eluded him, and it angered him that she could arrange it for herself with such ease.

Instead, he turned again to his phone. He made several calls but could not find Laurence Train anywhere. This displeased him immensely. Poe liked to be able to reach people anywhere, anytime, like an angry god, not to be trifled with.

Zany Rawlings was in the middle of his breakfast—Polish sausage, scrambled eggs, hash browns, and a cold Bohemian beer—when Sergeant Hejmal showed up with the autopsy report from the hospital and the developed pictures from the film processors in St. Joseph. Zany gave them the briefest glance, pushed the remains of his breakfast away, and then led Hejmal out to his screened side porch, taking his beer and bringing one for his sergeant. Zany took a sip, stifled a burp, and then let his stomach settle before turning to the pictures again.

"Real pretty girl," he said.

"I checked missing persons again," said Hejmal, munching on one of Zany's sausages. "Michigan, Indiana, Illinois, Wisconsin. There's a bulletin on two girls from Indiana, but they're teenagers, and out of Laporte. Nothing out of Chicago."

"Someone's always missing in Chicago," Zany said.

"No girl like this."

Zany read through the autopsy report slowly. The angle of the bullets' paths indicated they had been fired from above and behind, but that much was already apparent from the bullet holes in the boat and the position the body had been in when the fisherman had found it. As Zany stopped to think about it, the shooter could have fired at her from almost anything—maybe even a bridge or a high seawall.

He read on. The girl had had at least one alcoholic drink before her death. She'd not eaten, nor had she had sexual intercourse. Her bowels and bladder were mostly empty.

Zany's stomach began rumbling again. He gave the report back to Hejmal.

"Send a copy of everything to Lansing," he said. "Give some of these pictures to the district attorney so he can give them out to the press, but cut off the messy part."

"Okay, Chief. Did the Coast Guard come up with anything yet?"

"Nope. Well, they had a couple of distress calls on the Illinois side, but nothing checked out. They told me that, running on the motor, with a following wind, the boat could easily have made it across the lake in six hours, maybe less. Maybe it happened on our side."

"Six hours from Chicago?"

"Yes."

"Hmmmm." The sound indicated that Hejmal's brain had shifted into neutral.

"I'm going to drive over there," Zany said. "I want you to run things here in town. If something turns up, you let me know, but don't blab it to Moran. I'll fill him in later."

"Are you going to take this to the Chicago cops?"

"I'm going to ask for their help. Have them check out this painting."

"Do you think it was stolen?"

"She made somebody mad."

"I wonder if it's worth a lot of money."

"Not now."

Ruth Anne Mazureski wondered if she really had reason to be worried. Jill Langley was one of three tenants in Ruth Anne's Old Town four-flat, all of whom were single women and most of whom kept odd hours, often spending Friday or Saturday nights elsewhere. Jill had once been like that, but her lifestyle had changed—something to do with a romance gone bad. Now, when she wasn't working late, Jill had taken to spending nearly every evening at home, sometimes joining Ruth Anne for a little television or a drink down at the bar on the corner, though usually holing up by herself—her stereo playing sad classical music until late in the night.

For most of the weekend now, there had been only silence. Ruth Anne had knocked at the door several times, once hearing the telephone ringing endlessly.

Jill might have had a reconciliation. She might have met someone new. She might be lying naked and raped and dead in some alley. Ruth Anne had no way of knowing.

The weekly grocery shopping had to be done. Often Jill and Ruth Anne went to the Treasure Island supermarket together. It made Ruth Anne a little sad, and increasingly uneasy, to be going alone now. Pulling a thin sweatshirt over her leotards, Ruth Anne set out at a brisk walk, cheered a little by the balmy weather. The supermarket was crowded, and it was nearly an hour later when she returned, struggling up the stairs with three fully laden shopping bags.

Jill's door was open, about an inch. After setting down her burden, Ruth Anne knocked on it loudly, finally pushing it open all the way and calling out Jill's name.

There was no answer. Stepping into the little foyer, Ruth Anne was stunned and bewildered by what she saw.

The living room was in chaotic disarray. The paintings on the wall had been taken down and cast aside. The rug had been pulled back. The kitchen was as bad, and the bedroom had been gone through as well. The bed covers had been pulled apart.

Ruth Anne started to look to see if any of Jill's clothing or jewelry might be missing, but fear began to overwhelm her. She fled from the apartment and ran down the stairs. When she'd left for the Treasure Island, she'd seen two men sitting in a car at the curb, one white, one black. She'd taken them for police. A lot of police were to be seen sitting in cars like that in Old Town, even on a Sunday afternoon.

They were gone.

Matthias Curland hated cocktail parties more than any other form of social congress. As a rule, they were about as festive and conducive to meaningful conversation as the Howard Street elevated during rush hour. The one aspect of "old money" upper-class life he truly did admire was that most such people abhorred these milling, swilling swarms, with all their rudeness and mindless chatter. Instead of "cocktail parties," they preferred smaller, more comfortable social occasions, where people could seat themselves or move freely about, enjoying their hosts' art and books and surroundings as pleasantly as if they were their own.

Paris had been like that—intellectual Paris, at least. So had the south of France, when film festivals weren't in season. He had met his French woman at such an affair. He had seen her on the topless beach at Cannes one afternoon while pausing during a stroll along La Croisette. She'd been nestled against the seawall, reading, and looked up, challenging him to move his gaze elsewhere. He'd walked on, only to encounter her again that evening at a party in a villa on a hill that looked onto the Tour de Mont Chevalier. This time she was standing near the open doors of a terrace, looking at a painting of bathers on the channel coast by the American artist Guy Pène Dubois. Matthias knew the work well enough to discuss its satirical point with her. That party had had perhaps fifty guests and the villa nearly as many rooms. As in so many scenes in Fellini films like *La Dolce Vita,* the party had progressed through them, chamber by chamber, through the night, ending at dawn on the rocky beach.

He'd taken the woman home by cab. As he recalled, she'd had to pay the fare.

That taxi ride through the streets of Cannes seemed a century ago. The one he took now with Sally was nothing so exotic— passing by the garish neon of liquor stores and bars and burger joints, the sidewalks filled with middle American couples heading for restaurants or Rush Street night spots. A hansom cab was stopped absurdly behind a wheezing city bus, the coachman a dopey-looking youth in top hat and tennis shoes. A stretch limousine began honking. America.

It was a warm night, and he'd left his father's eccentric old

Rolls parked on the street outside his Schiller Street house, hoping he and Sally might walk the few blocks to Bitsie Symms's apartment on East Lake Shore Drive. But Sally insisted on "arriving," which meant at the least a taxi. It occurred to Matthias that he didn't have much more money on him than he did that dreamy morning in Cannes.

There was no prospect of pleasant contemplation of books or paintings at Bitsie's. Her apartment was huge, occupying a high floor of an old between-the-world-wars residential stone tower with a view that reached up the lake shore to the city's northern limits and beyond. But she seemed to have invited half of Chicago, the loud, shoulder-to-shoulder crowd extending almost into the entrance hall.

"My ex-husband's supposed to be here," Sally said, taking a glass of champagne from a waiter, who was working the outskirts of the swarm. "I'm sorry. I should have told you."

"Should we leave?" Matthias said, declining a drink.

She frowned. "No."

They moved farther inside, Sally stopping almost at once to talk to a woman with dyed ash-blond hair and a tonnage of large jewelry. Many of the female guests seemed to have hair of the same color.

Matthias didn't recognize the woman, but he saw others he did. And many men—politicians, lawyers, corporate chairmen, society swells, local news anchors, union bosses, gallery owners, newspaper columnists, and an interior decorator or two. They were paunchier, grayer, and balder than when Matthias had seen them last, but otherwise unchanged. Another loathsome thing about cocktail parties was that they were gatherings of tribes—in New York, literary tribes and real estate tribes and arts tribes; in Washington, political and diplomatic tribes; in Los Angeles and Cannes, film tribes. In Chicago, there was only one tribe, and its chiefs, whatever their professional calling, moved through life largely together, with only death rearranging their ranks. Matthias's parents' Lake Forest friends would have had little interest in attending such an evening, but the people with real power and influence in the city apparently found it obligatory. Matthias even saw an architect he'd gone to school with, a well-connected fellow whose big, important firm specialized in massive high-rise buildings.

Matthias turned away from him. There was only one architect in the city he would have been happy to talk to in his present embarrassing circumstance—the legendary genius Harry Weese—and he was not there.

Sally found more friends. Before she could drag Matthias into introductions, he slipped aside, moving through the crowd toward an adjoining room that seemed less populated. A few people waved to him as he passed, some expressing great surprise to see him, but he kept going, resolutely steering for the sanctuary of the uncrowded room. In it, he found a couple whispering together on a small settee, their coy, surreptitious manner suggesting they might be married to other people. In a corner, three men in dark business suits were volubly arguing about some point of commerce. By the unused fireplace, an exceedingly tall and slender woman was actually studying a painting.

It was of a violently scrawled, grinning, skull-like human head, supported by a sticklike body. The highly textured background was purple and black. Matthias recognized the artist, but for some reason could not think of his name.

The woman was far more compelling than the deathly image on the canvas, her ethereal beauty antithetical to the message of the grinning visage.

Perhaps not. Perhaps they were just two sides of the same thing. "Beauty is the scent of roses," F. Scott Fitzgerald had written, "and the death of roses." Implicit in every lovely face was decay and rot. A grinning skull lurked behind the most beautific countenance. His mother had been beautiful.

Matthias stepped closer. The woman's thinness was extraordinary, yet nothing at all like the neurotic, skeletal, anorexic emaciation common to so many clinging desperately to self-images of aristocracy and youth. Rather, her long, graceful, pale-skinned body spoke of weight and health in a state of perfect control, as perfect as her careful and understated makeup and well-combed and brushed strawberry-blond hair.

She was as tall as he was—a little taller even in the satin black high-heeled pumps she wore with her simple but elegant black lace cocktail dress. She wore a plain gold bracelet and a thinner gold necklace at the base of her long, slender neck. As he came beside her, there was the faint, delicate scent of fresh flowers—a marked contrast to the heavy, cloying clouds of expensive perfume that hung with the cigarette smoke throughout the other room.

She looked at him, and he saw that she had wide, light-blue eyes. He saw also an exception to her perfection—tiny lines implying weariness and worry, a few faint furrows on her brow. She was in her thirties, though he could not tell how much younger than he.

"It's very ugly," he said, nodding to the painting. "Like an angry child's scrawl."

"Jean Dubuffet," she said, matter-of-factly. The silkiness and clarity of her low, soft voice struck him as much as her beauty. It was like a summer evening breeze.

"I was trying to remember who it was," Matthias said. "Dubuffet. Of course."

"I'm no expert," she said. "I was just looking through an old Art Institute catalog this week. The 'High and Low' show? It had a lot of Dubuffet stuff in it."

"He was a caricaturist and an existentialist," Matthias said. "He liked to disturb."

"He succeeded, didn't he?"

Matthias looked about the room again. In addition to the Dubuffet, there was a René Magritte drawing on the walls.

"I never met our hostess," he said. "But she's certainly acquired a lot of art."

"Three husbands' worth," said the woman. She turned to Matthias, her cool blue eyes assessing him. Giving him a careful smile, she extended her hand.

"I'm Diandra," she said.

"Matthias. Matthias Curland."

Just as he took her hand he felt another on his shoulder. It was Sally, looking earnest.

"Come on," she said. "Bitsie wants to meet you." She nodded politely to the strawberry blonde, who turned aside.

Matthias let himself be tugged away. Bumping through the crowd, he found himself hauled into a circle of people gathered around a luminescent, golden presence.

As they used to say in New York, Bitsie Symms was a woman somewhere between forty and death. Instead of ash blond, her hair was shiny bright, almost matching the circus yellow of her gaudy, low-cut dress. It was all wrong for the olive color of her skin, which seemed stretched unnaturally taut over her bony face, as smooth as Saran-Wrap over a bowl of leftovers. She had enormous breasts, set unusually high. They seemed on the verge of falling out of her bodice. At the base of her cleavage was an enormous gold and diamond pin in the shape of a rising sun, the whole effect—he supposed—meant to distract from close inspection of her face. Her large, dark, almost black eyes were intent with the task of watching others look at her.

"Bitsie," said Sally, clinging to Matthias's arm. "This is Matthias Curland."

Mrs. Symms, discarding the others around her, swept forward, taking Matthias's right hand in both of hers and clasping it up toward her bosom. "My dear Matthias. How absolutely wonderful you could come. I've been hearing so much about you."

She had a peculiar inflection, her accent obviously one of her own confection, completely cleansed of the broad, nasal speech of most native Chicagoans.

Dropping her left hand, she thrust her right forward toward his mouth, making it seem as if he had set about kissing it. In hastily remembered correct Prussian fashion, he bowed his head over her hand but did not touch his lips to it. Finally she released him.

"I was so sorry to hear about your dear mother," Mrs. Symms said. "Such a sweet person. So active in the arts."

The only art Matthias's mother had shown any serious interest in had been portraits of herself. Mrs. Symms could not know this, however. Matthias had not even heard of this woman until that afternoon. He wondered if Sally had called her before the party.

Mrs. Symms picked up on his blank stare. "You are Matthias Curland of the Lake Forest Curlands, aren't you? The famous architect? The museum director? The painter? The yachtsman?"

"Yes, I . . . my father lives in Lake Forest."

"Well, there you are. And here you are, the star of our party! Now come with me. There's someone you must meet, because he's been looking for an architect!" She squealed and giggled. "Isn't that a wonderful coincidence? He was just telling me he wanted the very best architect in the world, and that would just have to mean a Chicago architect, because Chicago has always had the best architects in the world."

Matthias felt hot and flushed, hoping his acute embarrassment did not show. He saw the tall strawberry blonde moving sedately by, oblivious of the din and press of people, as if she were at the apartment on some quiet purpose of her own.

She vanished. Bitsie Symms had taken his arm and was lugging him along, Sally tagging after. The party guests swiftly cleared a path for them as the hostess pushed ahead, passing into yet another room and coming to a halt before a small circle of men standing by huge windows looking out onto the lake. Among them were two politicians he remembered from the old days. Another one there was Sally's *Social Register* lout of an ex-husband, who turned and left as soon as he saw them.

In the midst of this circle, presiding over it as Bitsie Symms had the crowd in the main room, was a short, well-scrubbed man in the most perfectly tailored suit Matthias had ever seen. He was a little stocky, with broad shoulders and a short neck, but the expensive material of suit and shirt fit without a wrinkle or bulge. The man's very British striped rep tie was knotted precisely and his graying, wiry hair cut and trimmed like a piece of sculpture. He had wide cheekbones and large ears, a strong, square chin and firm mouth. His most dominant and dominating features, though, were his almost turquoise blue eyes. They were as calculating as Mrs. Symms's, but also penetrating, arresting. One didn't want to look into them for long.

His hands and feet were small. Glancing down, Matthias noted expensive-looking oxfords as highly polished as a British guardsman's boots.

"Peter!" said Mrs. Symms, pulling Matthias forward. "Look what I've found for you! The best architect in Chicago! Christian Curland's brother!"

Never in all his life had Matthias thought that the occasion might arise where he'd want to strike a woman. It was the second time that day he had had a violent impulse. It would take a lot of solitary sorting out to determine where that compulsion was coming from. It couldn't be just that he was back in this big, brawling, violent city.

"I'm Matthias Curland. I used to be an architect here, years ago."

The man's grip was firm, but careful. The turquoise eyes flickered over Matthias, taking in the casually worn blue blazer, gray flannels, rumpled gray-and-white striped shirt and old navy-blue dotted tie, and then returning to the face, gazing into Matthias's eyes as directly as he could manage from his lesser height. Matthias felt like an object about to be purchased in a store.

"Peter Poe," said the other.

"You're the man who's going to buy the baseball team."

"Maybe, maybe. What buildings are yours?"

"Sorry?"

"Buildings. You're an architect. What have you designed?"

"Nothing of consequence."

Sally was standing just behind Matthias. "He won an international prize," she said.

"Really?" said Poe. "What for?"

"An apartment building up by Lincoln Park."

Like a ship's captain moving about his own bridge, Poe went to the window, two other men moving out of his way.

"Show me," Poe said.

"You can't really see it from here," Matthias said, going to the man's side. "The buildings on the drive screen the view. It's near the zoo. It's a tapered column with a triangular base—a pyramid, actually, but it's so elongated you don't quite notice the incline. There's a glass curtain wall on the side facing the park."

"Kind of green."

"A green tint, yes."

"I know that building. The Halsman something."

"Halsman Tower."

"Yeah. Halsman Tower. The guy went belly up, didn't he? A shopping center or something that got mixed up in the savings and loan thing."

"It was a bank, actually. It pulled out of its commitment at the last minute. Because of the savings and loan problem, it got very cautious about money."

"Bankers are a pain in the ass." Poe caught himself. The chairman of one of the Loop's biggest banks was standing nearby. "I know your building real well. I always wondered who did it. Nobody who ever worked for me could design anything like that."

He continued looking out the window, as if he could see Matthias's building through the other structures.

"You know, I bought Cabrini Green," Poe said, turning back to Matthias. He glanced sharply at Bitsie, a dismissal. She caught the signal and began talking briskly to Sally and the others, drawing them away.

"So I understand," said Matthias. "What's going to happen to all those people who live there?"

"Most of them are out of there. I'll have them all out by July first. It's a blessing for them, believe me. A blessing. The city's got a relocation program for them. Rent subsidies. Some low-rise housing projects on the West Side. They'll be all right. I take care of people. I'm not like those guys in New York. I don't give people a hard time."

Matthias didn't know what to say.

"I own a lot of land around the North Branch of the river there," Poe continued. "I want to do something big with it."

"The high-rise projects at Cabrini," Matthias said. "They're not salvageable."

"No way. Gotta go. The concrete must be soaked through with urine. And blood. No, I'm clearing the whole area, starting July one."

Matthias wanted to ask what he was putting up in the project's place, but the conversation was beginning to make him nervous. Poe was friendly enough, very much under control, but there was something thuggish about him, something in the set of his shoulders, in the cast of his eyes.

The tall strawberry blonde came up to Poe quietly and stood at his side. Poe glanced up at her, then put his arm around her, possessively pulling her a little closer.

"This is my wife, Diandra. This is Matthias Curland. He designs world-famous buildings."

"We just met," Matthias said. Of all the men at the party he would have picked as her husband, Poe would have been the last he'd have guessed. Though perhaps not. They were probably the two most impecably groomed people there. Matthias wondered if Poe was as attentive to the details of her dress as he was to his own, though perhaps it was she who saw to his.

Poe's eyes were showing uncertainty—possibly unhappiness.

"We met just a few minutes ago, in the other room," Mrs. Poe said. "We were looking at a painting."

"My wife loves paintings," Poe said. "She helps me with my collection."

She was staring at Matthias. The three of them stood uncomfortably for a moment, not speaking.

"Mr. Curland," said Poe. His voice was full of authority, like a corporate CEO wrapping up a meeting. "I'd like to talk to you some more. Can you come to dinner this week?"

"This week?"

"Tomorrow night. Diandra, are we doing anything important tomorrow?"

"Everything you do is important, Peter." Her clear, soft, perfectly measured voice had the tiniest edge of sarcasm to it. Matthias wondered if Poe noticed.

"Whatever we have going, it can wait. Mr. Curland, come to dinner. Tomorrow night. Eight o'clock."

He seemed to be giving Matthias no choice. "Well, I am free.

Yes. Thank you very much." Matthias at once wished he could take the words back, but as much as he was repelled and made apprehensive by this man, he was intensely curious.

"You know my building on Michigan Avenue, Poe Place, the one with the red top?"

"I can find it."

Poe reached forward to shake hands again. "Good. Excuse us now. I better see if the mayor's here. Need some words with him. You can't do business in this town without politicians."

As they began to move away, Diandra took Matthias's hand briefly in hers. "Good night, Mr. Curland." Her touch was cool. Her hands were long and beautiful, just like the rest of her. The vague scent of fresh flowers lingered after she had gone.

Donald O'Rourke, father of eight, regular at mass, the most important man in his community—a wealthy real estate and insurance broker who had worked his way through the Democratic organization from state representative, to alderman, to ward committeeman, to president of the Chicago Park District— left his large, comfortable home in one of the most prosperous middle-class neighborhoods on the Northwest Side to attend a political meeting. His wife, Mary, was a long-suffering political wife who understood that such meetings, even on Sunday evenings, were as much a fixture of his life as going to the supermarket was of hers. She didn't ask where the meeting was or what it was about; only when he would return. All he said was "Not too late."

There was such a meeting, down at the south end of the ward, and O'Rourke actually went to it, staying less than an hour, making a big show of taking a couple of precinct captains who were with Streets and Sanitation out for some frosty cold ones.

That's all he had—one beer, with a couple of shots. He was a big, white-haired, pink-faced Irishman, with a little too much gut and a heart problem that made his doctor nervous. The doctor allowed him a beer or two a day, but would not have approved of the two shots. O'Rourke needed them. He always did when he did this. Liquor got him stirring, kept up his nerve.

He'd picked up his philandering habit with the bimbos down in Springfield when he'd been in the legislature, and it had proved more addictive than beers-and-shots or the three to four packs of cigarettes he had smoked until his doctor had started treating him like a war criminal.

Venereal disease had worried him a little, and the new AIDS thing a lot, but he always took precautions and nothing had showed up in the frequent physical examinations he now underwent because of his heart. He had long since stopped worrying about the coppers. The license plate on his station wagon bore his ward number and his initials, "DOR." No beat patrolman or vice dick was going to mess with that. It was a quick way to end up working the midnight watch in Hegwisch, or patrolling the river docks in January.

If his wife Mary held any suspicions, she'd never even hinted as much, and O'Rourke had never done anything to encourage them, or to provide a private investigator anything to work with—no hotels, no credit cards, no phone calls to escort services, no bimbo on the payroll who might squawk later if she didn't get a promotion or a raise. Everything in the car. As for the risk of getting rolled and dumped upside-down in a back alley garbage can, well, he didn't use alleys. He had his own spot, one he'd picked carefully, the same way he picked his girls. And if worse came to worse, he had a .44 Magnum with a four-inch barrel underneath his car seat.

The summer evening was fully dark now. O'Rourke knew his city, had learned it precinct by precinct, and was as fully informed about the ebb and flow of vice activity on its night streets as a general keeping tabs on enemy troop movements. Old Town was too hot now. Local businesses had complained about an excess of streetwalkers, and the cops were cleaning up. The Clark and Diversey area was too full of weirdos. O'Rourke chose a section of Uptown where the Yuppies with their gentrification had been pushing the junkies and sleazos out, but where a stretch of Broadway was still in business.

The hellish orange glare of the sodium vapor streetlights illuminated the girls along the sidewalk like packages in a supermarket. He drove by slowly, browsing like a shopper, taking note of the choicer lovelies and sorting them into possibles and forget-its. He took a turn around the block, speeding by the Yuppie townhouses on the side streets, then came up Broadway again, again slowly, making his pick.

She was tall, with fantastic legs and big knockers. She wore dark glasses and her long blond hair was probably a wig, but he could see she was a real looker, easily the best-looking girl he had seen on the street in a couple of years. She had seen him coming and pushed another girl out of the way to step off the curb as he approached, smiling at him like she was a little kid and he was Santa Claus. He smiled back but kept on going, following his usual procedure of making one more circuit of the block to check for cops or any other sign of trouble.

There was none. As he approached on his final pass, he saw that the other chippie, a black girl also in a blond wig, was hassling the one with the great legs and tits. There was a quick way to end that. He slammed on the brakes in front of them and nodded for the one in sunglasses to get in. She did so like someone coming in out of a downpour.

"Thanks," she said. "I don't think that lady likes me."

"I like you."

"You should. It's not often you find a girl like me on the street."

They drove on through an intersection. She looked even more terrific close up. He couldn't have done better if he had picked up a contestant in a beauty contest.

"Why is that?" he said.

"What?"

"Why are you on this street?"

She gave him an enormous smile. He had never seen such good teeth on a hooker. "The man who pays the rent on my apartment tossed me out on my ass. I need some money, quick."

"How much?"

She folded her arms beneath her big breasts, pushing them up and almost out of her halter top. "Two."

"Two? This isn't Michigan Avenue."

"It doesn't have to be quick."

There was something about her voice. She didn't sound like a hooker. But then, she didn't sound like any lady cop he'd ever met, either. It took him another block to figure it out. She didn't have a Chicago accent. But that was all right. Hookers moved around. She might be someone out of Las Vegas or Miami.

"I only have time for quick," he said.

"Okay. One. I like you. You don't look like a creep. But it doesn't have to be too quick."

He went on another block, saying nothing.

"Something wrong?"

"Are you wearing any underwear?" he said a little uncomfortably.

"Why?"

"If you are, take it off."

"My panties?"

"Yes."

She studied him. "You think I'm a cop?"

"I like to be sure of things."

"I'm not wearing any panties." She wriggled in the seat and pulled her skirt up.

"You sure as hell aren't."

The skirt came quickly down again. "I like to be sure of things, too. Open your fly. I want to see who I'm doing business with."

He smiled to himself. No lady cop would expose herself on decoy duty, but many male officers would have no such compunctions. This was Chicago, not Evanston.

"You do it."

She leaned over and unzipped his fly, pulling his penis out gently and rolling it slowly between her hands. It quickly began to swell.

"Mmmmm," she said. "I'm going to like doing business with you."

It was going to be a good night. O'Rourke turned at the next corner and headed east.

"Where are we going?" she said.

"I know a place. We can be real discreet."

"In the car?"

"Yeah. In the car. In the back. Plenty of room."

"But where? In some alley? Under the 'El'?"

He wondered if she had ever worked any street before. Probably just bars and hotels. "I know a place where no one will bother us. In the park."

"In the park? It's full of creeps and muggers."

He wanted to see her eyes behind those dark glasses, but he wanted something else a lot more urgently.

"I own the park," he said. He laughed. "I've got a good place. There's a fence around it no one can get in. I've got a key to the lock."

"I've got a better idea," she said. "I've got a room, a nice big, soft bed."

"I thought you said you were thrown out?"

"I was. I've got a hotel room. I took it for the weekend. It's not bad. Not a flop. And it's near the park."

"No, thanks," he said. "I get nervous in hotel rooms."

"I won't make you nervous. I'll make you happy. I've got a

bottle of Wild Turkey. A bed's better. I can do more things for you. I can do really great things—in a bed."

For a moment, the idea tantalized him. But he'd always stuck to his rule and it had never failed him.

"We'll go to the park."

They were nearing Lake Shore Drive. She had let go of him. She seemed to be thinking about something, hard.

"How would you like some company?" she asked.

"I've got company."

"I mean another girl. The one who was with me on Broadway. Let's go back and get her."

"What for?"

"I jumped her turf. They're not going to make me feel very welcome if I try to work there again."

"So work somewhere else."

"Come on. I don't want to get my ass in a jam. Her pimp might be a knife artist or something."

"No, thanks."

"Please? It won't cost you anything. I'll cut her in for half of the one. That's what she works for."

"I'm not interested in that girl."

"Oh, she'll make you interested. That lady knows things. Have you ever done a twofer before?"

He stopped to think. He never had.

"I'll put it this way," she said. "If you don't go back and get her, you can fucking forget me."

His erection was so hard it was almost touching the steering wheel. It was getting late.

"All right," he said. "You work it out with her."

The black girl was surprised to see them return, but simply shrugged when the blonde in sunglasses made the proposition. The second girl hopped in the back. She smelled a little of sweat.

"We're going to the park," said the blonde in sunglasses. "It's back-to-nature night."

Mango Bellini had worked it all out, just the right hotel, a room right off the elevator, paid for in advance with cash, enough benzedrine in the Wild Turkey to give the old bastard's heart a stiff jolt and make him sick. Then she'd run downstairs, complain to the desk clerk that her john had gone bad on her, and disappear into the night. After that, a quick stop at a pay phone to call

911 for the paramedics, and then a call to the city news bureau with a hot tip. They'd check it out and hit pay dirt. It would be in the morning papers. The chairman of the Park District stricken in a hotel room he'd gone to with a big blond chippie. If he should kick from the bad heart, too bad. Either way, there'd be a big vacancy in the city power structure.

But the son of a bitch had fucked it all up, and now she was part of a half-assed menage à trois headed for some storage yard in the middle of Lincoln Park. Her idea in picking up the black girl was to get her and O'Rourke having at it in the back of the car while she slipped away and tipped the cops to someone breaking into Park District property.

She realized now that was stupid. What was she going to do, flag down a squad car? How far would she have to run to get to a phone? Who would see her?

He had seen her. If they had made it to the hotel room, it would be logical for her to get scared and split if he had an attack, or simply passed out. But if she ran off from the park scene and the cops showed up soon after, he'd know he'd been set up. And he'd sure as hell try to find out why, and by whom.

Her mind raced, but came up with no answer. Once in the park, he turned onto an old bridle path and killed the car's lights. At length they came to a big chain-link fence, with a high gate. He opened the padlock, swung open the gate, drove inside, then closed and locked it again, dropping the keys into his pocket. He stood listening a moment, then got back in the car and drove it around behind a big parked truck.

He wasn't satisfied with Mango's hand work. He wanted a blow—and with a condom on. She did her best, hating the taste of the latex and the smell of his crotch. The other girl had taken off her clothes and was reaching to unbutton his shirt.

Mango was kneeling on the floor of the front seat. She pushed herself upright, her hand inadvertently slipping between his legs to beneath the seat. She felt the hard, cold sculpted metal of the heavy object there and knew instantly what it was. She knew then what she was going to do, what she had to do.

"You ready, honey?" she said. "Really ready?"

"Oh, yes. Come on."

The backseat was already down when he'd first picked her up. The black girl was crouching on the platform it made folded in place.

"Get in back, honey," Mango said, "and let her have a turn. Then I'll finish you off in a way you'll never forget."

He muttered something happily, then, with his pants still down, snapped open the door and lurched around into the back.

He'd left the front door open, which kept the overhead light on. Mango reached and shut it. The black girl, her wig slipping sideways, climbed on top of him and began bouncing up and down, as practiced at her task as an auto worker on a production line. The leather of the folded-over seat began squeaking in time.

Mango couldn't wait a second longer. Seize the moment. Get it done. It had to be done. Get it over. Do it!

She pulled out the big revolver, holding it in both hands as she raised it over the seat and leveled the short barrel at the back of the black girl's head. The sharp, ringing volume of the explosion in the enclosed car surprised Mango. There was smoke, and an acrid smell. The black hooker's head flopped and she went flying, her lower body heaving onto O'Rourke's face. He was making frantic noises that were not words, flailing and struggling to get out from underneath her.

Mango had no clear shot. She just kept firing at them both till the gun was empty.

He was quiet. Neither of them moved. Mango said a prayer for herself. They were both worthless people, both whores.

She had to move quickly. Sliding out the door, she went to the back and shoved the girl's bloody body off of his. Wallet. Robbery. She got the desired object out of his coat breast pocket easily, but had to rip back a pants pocket to get at his keys. God, the smell. Both their bodies had been opened up. She stepped back to run, then caught herself. Fingerprints. She grabbed up the black girl's skirt and began wiping the door handles. She didn't think she'd touched the steering wheel, but wiped that, too. Then to the fence. The padlock fell to the ground after she unlocked it. After retrieving it, she wiped it clean and dropped it back to the dirt.

There were bushes just across the little lane they'd taken to this place. Gun and wallet in hand, she darted through them into a small clearing. She could see car lights ahead, moving down the Inner Drive, but there were no sirens. No one was near. She scrubbed the gun with the skirt. After taking the money from the wallet, she cleaned that, too—and the keys, carefully, one by one.

Then she gathered everything up in the skirt and threw the bundle back into the brush.

After removing her shoes, she began to run. Her upper thighs were moist, oily. She realized it wasn't sweat. She almost laughed at herself. She'd had an orgasm. It had happened before like this.

Keeping to the dark, she proceeded south through the park, working her way closer to its western edge. Passing one streetlight, she saw that she had blood on the inside of her hand and arm. A quick thought. Into the darkness again. She removed her halter top and, crouching half nude, rubbed off the smears. Turning the halter inside out, stretching it far so that nothing would come off on her face, she put it back on. There was nothing for anyone to notice. At least not at night.

It was a long walk to the hotel where she'd taken the room, but the desk clerk would hardly worry about the hour.

She'd left nothing in the room but a small, cheap overnight bag and the doctored whiskey. There was a change of clothes in the bag—longer skirt, a clean blouse, more sedate heels. She put them on quickly, then gathered up the rest of her things.

"Checking out," she said to the clerk, who was reading the *Sun-Times.* She slid a twenty toward him with the room key, a tip for his indifference.

He glanced at the wall clock beside him.

"Slow night," she said, and strolled out the door.

After leaving Bitsie Symms's party, Matthias and Sally walked along the Drive, following it around the curve of the shore to where they had a view of the man-made peninsula of Olive Park and the filtration plant and the long, antique hulk of Navy Pier beyond. There were a number of boats out on the water, their riding lights twinkling in the mist, making him think of his own sailboat and how much he'd like to be on it, out on this gentle inland sea with all the others. The night haze and the reflected glow of the city obscured most of the stars, but Matthias could see Venus shining brightly and the curving slice of the emerging moon. Sally clung to his arm, walking slowly and close.

"I think you impressed him," she said.

"Who, the mighty Mr. Poe?"

"Yes. You could tell by the way he looked at you. He was making a judgment."

Matthias made no comment.

"He puts up buildings," she said.

"It's a nice hobby."

"And now he's invited us to dinner."

The invitation, he was sure, had been extended solely to him, but he'd be happy to arrange Sally's inclusion, as she seemed so keen on it.

"What are you thinking, Matthias?"

"Nothing, really. I'm just trying to get used to being back in Chicago. A few days ago, I was sitting on the beach at Cap Ferrat, and Chicago might as well have been on another planet. I still can't quite believe I'm here."

"Well, I can." She gave his arm a little squeeze.

They turned west again at Walton Street, heading toward the lights of the Drake Hotel. He let memories of their last meeting there come and go without comment.

But that recollection was followed by others. Reaching Michigan Avenue, they crossed and turned south, passing by the very English Gothic revival façade of the Fourth Presbyterian Church, a very social house of worship that his mother had liked to attend on Christmas Eve and Easter. Next to the main building, enclosed by the church buildings and a medieval arcade of carved Bedford stone, was a quiet, grassy courtyard with a handsome fountain in the center. It served as an open-air sanctuary. When one stepped into it, the noise from the traffic on the nearby boulevard seemed to fade away. One could imagine madrigals coming from the stained glass windows.

Sally put her head against his shoulder, but this was not the place for that. The memories this churchyard held for him were of Hillary, the woman who had once been his wife, and Jill. He had kissed them both in this enclosure. He and Hillary had been married in the church whose spire loomed overhead. Gently he pulled Sally away, back out onto the street.

But she was bent on nostalgia, and more. Turning another corner, they went by the old Tremont Hotel. At the short alley beside it, Sally stopped, then led him within.

"Do you remember?" she said.

He looked at her blankly.

"A zillion years ago," she said. "A bright sunny day. You'd taken me to the movies and we went walking afterward. You pulled me in here and said, 'Sally in our alley,' and kissed me."

He remembered the poem: "Of all the girls that are so smart, there's none like pretty Sally. She is the darling of my heart, and she lives in our alley."

He repeated the lines aloud. Sally gazed up at him, looking absurdly happy. She closed her eyes. He hesitated, then kissed her softly. She pulled herself tightly up against him, and the kiss became quite something more. He still cared for this woman. He'd felt deprived, cheated, when her mother had plucked her from him and pushed her into her marriage. Now Sally was being handed back to him, as if on a golden plate. Another sign?

Sally at last relented, relaxed her hold, and stepped back, her eyes merry.

"I told my baby-sitter I'd be home rather late," she said.

He knew what to say, but didn't.

"It's not late," she said.

"No, it's not."

"I'd like a nightcap."

He glanced at the canopy of the Tremont's bar, Crickett's. In his day, it had been the hangout of the town's most glamorous society divorcées.

"Here?" he said.

"No. Let's go to your house."

They took a taxi. He had trouble finding the key to his door.

"I've been living in the past," she said. "I forgot that Christian lives here now."

His key came to hand. "Not really. He keeps his clothes here, but he seems to spend most of his time elsewhere. He's staying on the North Shore tonight."

"Lucky us."

He turned on some lights, leading Sally on into the small library, where Christian had established an ample bar. He poured her a brandy and himself a Diet Coke. As he handed her the cognac, he noticed she was staring with astonished fascination at a picture above his desk. It was of a naked, red-haired woman slouched in a chair. Her body was sprawled in the most open, wanton fashion, her lushly exposed pubic area the focal point of the piece, but the look on her face was hard, and a little frightened. A woman who had learned all the secrets of life, and didn't like them.

"What an extraordinary painting," Sally said uncomfortably.

"It's not a painting, it's a print," he said. "The original is in a museum in Berlin."

"Don't you think it's kind of lurid?"

"The artist was Egon Schiele. Austrian, but a very Dostoyevskian character. He went to prison, some say unjustly, for rape

70

and kidnapping when he was twenty-two. Then he was a soldier in World War I, and somehow survived that, only to die in the flu epidemic of 1918. He was twenty-eight. After his death, he became very famous."

"He must have been very unhappy."

"This woman was his mistress. As you can see, he knew her very well. He knew what she knew."

Sally shuddered. "I wish you'd left it in the closet. Let's go into another room."

He smiled in resignation and took her back to the living room, where another new picture was hung.

"This is a wonderful painting," she said, going up close to it. "And it is a painting, isn't it? Not a print?"

"Yes. Finished this year."

"That man on the beach, in the white pants and blazer. That's you!"

That fact was inconsequential. It was a handsome piece of work, done in the century-old style of a John Singer Sargent or Thomas Eakins. The male figure who was its focal point was standing on a narrow rocky beach, staring in total absorption across dark blue-green Mediterranean waters at a distant fiery sunset almost volcanic in its intensity. Small, jagged mountains ringed the background. All about the man, young women in white summer dresses sat upon the rocks, their gaze following his, all of their faces tinged with the flaming sun's rosy glow. All were utterly rapt, as if witnessing the birth of the world—or the death.

"It's the south of France," Matthias said. "The coastline up from Cannes. At least it's supposed to be. The mountains aren't quite right."

"It's just fantastic," she said, turning to him excitedly. "You see, you're a wonderful artist! A truly great artist!"

"Christian painted it, not me," Matthias said, taking a sip of his soft drink.

Flustered, as if she'd just broken something, she looked away, unable to find words with which to rescue herself.

"He's never been to the south of France," Matthias continued. "He did this from a photograph I sent him. And his own imagination."

The evening's mood had been blown away as if by a sudden gust of wind. Sally appeared desperate to restore it. She set down her glass, then took his and put it aside as well.

"You're both wonderful artists," she said, and moved to kiss him again before he could speak, pressing her pelvis urgently against his. He responded as she wished.

Afterward, he raised her from the floor and turned off the lights. They sat on the couch in the near darkness and quietly finished their drinks, their naked bodies softly touching. He feared what she might say, what she might ask of him. He wasn't ready for the answer.

"I have to go," she said finally. "I'll see you tomorrow?"

"Yes."

He'd let it all happen. From the moment a few days before when he'd received the telegram from Annelise about his mother's death to this scene of passionate surrender, he'd let himself be swept back into his past as helplessly as a boat torn from its moorings in a strong-running tide. He was back in Chicago, wedged fast in his old life. Now he had to make something of it, as he'd failed to do before.

Peter and Diandra Poe returned home late. He had stayed at Bitsie Symms's party long after he was tired of it, only because Bitsie insisted that the mayor would be there. The man did show, but only just, making of the gathering merely another stop on a round of evening events—a couple of wakes, a charity fundraiser, a Hyde Park PTA celebration marking the end of the first year of a new integrated experimental school, an Italian-American dinner dance—all routine appearances in the daily life of a mayor who intended to stay in office a very long time. Bitsie's party was just a drop-by. The mayor greeted her, shook a few hands, sipped a small amount of soft drink, and made a few halting remarks about the Gold Coast Garden Festival that was the ostensible reason for the gathering. Then he and his two ubiquitous aides were gone.

Poe had hoped for at least a few minutes of private conversation, but the mayor had done no more than nod to him. In a few weeks, Poe would make an official call on his honor at his City Hall office to make an official presentation of his plans for Cabrini Green. That was not enough. He needed a one-on-one, a chance to bounce a few shots off the man and watch him respond without the guidance of his close advisers or some panel of experts. Poe was going to have to move the mayor's office a long way on this one, and the first steps were going to be hard. What City Hall had in mind was a sort of Cabrini Green for Yuppies, a mix of midlevel high-rises and townhouses like those of the Carl Sandburg Village project east of Old Town that the great wheeler-dealer developer Arthur Rubloff had put up in the 1950s as—ha-ha—moderate-income housing. Sandburg had quickly turned into some of the most desirable real estate on the Near North Side and had pushed away the slums. That's what the Hall wanted Poe to do, provide an anchor to help other developers to clear out the slums and old warehouses all the way west to the North Branch of the Chicago River.

That's not what Poe had in mind. He wasn't going to let the mayor in on his real plans, but when he moved, he didn't want the man in the way.

Normally, Poe would end the night checking the calls to his private line and making a few of his own, ringing up Mango or Yeats or another of his close associates to talk about his plans for the next day. He had a lot of other deals cooking, and some work to do on those.

Instead, he sat in a funk on the long couch of the penthouse's cavernous living room, glowering at the opposite wall.

Diandra had gone into the kitchen for something. She returned and stood in front of him, towering above his head. No wonder kings used thrones.

"Would you like me to stay up with you?" she asked.

He sighed. "No thanks, babe. Get some sleep."

"I'm going to read awhile. Good night, Peter." She walked away, her high heels clicking elegantly on the polished marble floor.

Poe stared for a long time at a painting directly opposite. It looked like spilled spaghetti but it had been valued at $150,000. Poe didn't understand the collectors who treated this stuff like the ultimate form of hard currency, but he was happy to take their cash money. He'd made a lot of money buying and selling art. Lately he'd mostly been selling it.

A sound caught his attention, a distinctive, purring musical ring from down the hall. He became fully alert and looked at his Piaget. Mango.

He got to the phone before the answering machine activated. It was her, all right, sounding higher than a jetliner.

"I did it, Peter! I did it!"

"Ease up, lady," he said, keeping his voice low. "What the hell are you on?"

"I had a couple of stiff ones. That's all, just a couple of belts. I needed them. Jeez, I'm flying. Wooooeee!"

"I said ease up!"

"It's done, Peter. He's finito."

"No problems?"

"I took care of everything. Read your morning paper."

"Okay."

"I feel terrific."

Poe wondered if she had fucked the chump. "Okay, okay. Cool off and get some sleep. Be here first thing in the morning. Here, not the office."

"I'll be there."

"And knock off the booze."

"Yes, sir."

"Good night, Mango. And thanks."

"Thanks? Just thanks? Like I ran an errand for you?"

"More than thanks. I love you, babe. I owe you large."

"Thanks." She hung up.

He trusted that woman more than anyone else in the world, but there were times when he wondered if he really even knew her.

CHAPTER

3

POE HAD HIS Monday morning coffee and bran muffins brought to his study along with the *Tribune* and *Sun-Times,* waiting until his valet had left before turning to the papers, not wanting to seem too anxiously interested.

There was nothing about Park District President O'Rourke on either front page. He turned on WBBM all-news radio just in time to catch the CBS network roundup on the hour. The president had returned from Camp David to announce a minor reshuffling of his cabinet. There was more trouble in the Mideast that would play hell with oil prices. There'd been rioting in Mexico City again. Some aging rock star had died of a drug overdose. Nothing about Chicago.

Poe's coffee was a little too hot to drink. He took a muffin and buttered it carefully, all over, as was his habit, then sat munching it as he began turning the pages of the *Tribune.* In the tall buildings all around him, people were doing the same thing, starting their day, their week, the rest of their lives. He wondered how many could exert as much control over the events that would confront them as could he, how many had as clear a sight of where they were going, of what they wanted to happen. The mayor was probably having his breakfast now. Poe wondered if his thoughts went much beyond the next city council meeting.

The *Trib* had nothing at all about O'Rourke—not in the front news section, not in Metro, not on the obituary page. Not a goddamn word. The same for the *Sun-Times.* Poe leaned back in his chair and swiveled toward the windows facing the lake and the morning sun. Maybe the stuff Mango had put in the whiskey hadn't fazed the guy; he'd just gotten up and gone home. Maybe the papers had just dismissed the tip as a crank call. Maybe the mayor had found out about the story early and shut it down.

But that was all right. The mayor was the only one whom Poe wanted to know about the secret life of the Park District boss. The mayor tolerated a lot in his city. He had to if he was going to stay on top. You didn't run this town by giving orders. You put together deals—on everything—and gave everyone his cut. Even the stupid Gold Coast Garden Festival was a deal. The rich bitches got a chance to show off their houses and themselves and raise a little money for their charities, and the next time the mayor wanted something from their husbands, he got it.

What the mayor could not abide was fooling around. He'd been brought up to believe that the family was holy, that wives and mothers were to be worshipped like the Virgin Mary, that cheating on them was the worst kind of sin. All of those in his inner circle were family men, many of them from the mayor's own neighborhood. There was not a single divorced person in the upper echelons of the administration. Poe had researched that point well. If the man in charge of the city's parks and playgrounds was caught with a hooker in a sleazy hotel, that should be it for him. "Finito," as Mango had put it.

So what had happened? Mango had said "I did it!" So what gived?

Just then, the radio station came to the end of a series of commercials and went into local news. The first story made Poe spill his coffee. The instant the announcer went on to the next Poe clicked off the radio and hit the button on his phone that automatically dialed Mango's number. He cut her off before she could say three words.

"Shut up," he said. "Get dressed and go to my boat and stay there. Don't call anybody."

"But, Peter . . ."

"Shut up! I've got meetings this morning. And a lunch."

"I know. I made the arrangements."

"God damn it, Mango. I said shut up. Go to the boat. I'll be there right after lunch. Two-thirty. We'll deal with this then. Now do what I say."

He hung up. The bodies must have been discovered after whatever early hour the late editions of both papers had gone to press. Otherwise, it would have been all over the front pages.

What a way to kick, shot full of holes with a hooker on top of you. Poe wondered if the guy had gotten any pleasure out of it before Mango had done her number. He found himself trembling a little—with fear, but also excitement, a weird thrill at having put something like that in motion. He'd reached out and, zap, a man was dead. He hadn't ordered him dead. He hadn't wanted him dead. He was going to make damn sure Mango hadn't gone cuckoo on him. But there it was. God. He felt like a Mafioso.

Matthias entered the offices of Curland and Associates feeling something of an intruder. He'd never been in this antique office building before, and had been a little disturbed by the quality of neighbors whose doors he had passed coming down the hall—a strange, obviously leftist political committee opposed to American imperialism; a divorce lawyer without partners or, apparently, many clients; the world headquarters of some psychic religious order; a massage therapist.

Martha Heller, the now-elderly woman who had been his father's secretary for as long as Matthias could remember, was at her desk, a cup of coffee and a Barbara Cartland romance novel on the worn blotter in front of her. He'd telephoned to tell her he was coming, so she welcomed him matter-of-factly. She probably would have done so had he walked in the door after so many years without any warning. She stood up and shook his hand.

"You look well, Mr. Curland."

"You, too, Martha."

"Things have changed since you left."

"I see."

"Can I run downstairs and get you some coffee?"

The woman probably hadn't run anywhere in twenty years. "No thanks, Martha. I just want to look through things, see how things stand."

"Business has been a little slow, Mr. Curland."

Indeed. The firm had once employed more than thirty people.

"So I understand."

"The new associate is out job-hunting."

He wondered why she wasn't. "I don't blame him."

She stepped around from behind her desk. She had something personal to say. "I must apologize for not coming to the services yesterday, Mr. Curland."

"That's quite all right."

"I didn't think she'd have wanted me there."

Martha was in her sixties. In earlier years, she'd been attractive. Matthias had always harbored curious suspicions about her and his father.

"To be frank," she said, "I didn't approve of her."

"That's quite all right, too."

"Thank you, Mr. Curland." She seated herself, sat with hands folded for a moment, then picked up her book.

There were only three rooms in this dingy office suite—Matthias's father's office, the one used by the associate, and the large reception room where Martha had her desk. Because there were offices, there was still a firm. Otherwise, it didn't exist.

On a table at one end of the reception area was a scale model of the small shopping mall that had been the firm's last major project—an assemblage of elongated blocks without design frills of any sort. This cleanliness of line was a Matthias Curland trademark, but not many developers had been fond of it. On the walls of the reception room were a number of dusty, framed sketches of other buildings Matthias had done—the Halsman Tower the most prominent. In his father's office, the pictures on the wall were of the father's work. Nearly all were photographs or sketched designs of large houses, looking very much alike. Frank Lloyd Wright, not to speak of Harry Weese, would have been appalled by all of them—neo-classical monsters, every house someone's personal temple.

On his father's enormous old desk was a silver-framed photograph of Matthias's mother. It had been taken when she was in her late forties, and still in retention of much of her beauty. There was a vacant, dreamy look to her eyes, as if her thoughts had been miles away when the picture had been snapped. It was ironic that Matthias's father would have chosen this particular photo for his desk. It was obvious to Matthias, and should have been to his father, that she'd been thinking of someone else.

If this became his desk, would he have a picture of Sally Phillips in that spot? She'd called him at home in the morning, to tell him she loved him. He'd told her the same, hesitantly, but he'd said the words. He wondered how long it would be before he knew whether they were true. They certainly had been, once.

But how would he explain this to Jill?

It was time to get to work. Matthias went through the firm's most current files, finding matters to be more or less as Christian had described them. There was no current business, not even any letters inviting Curland and Associates to make a bid.

There was a locked, reinforced steel cabinet in the corner, which had always served as the office safe. Matthias had asked his brother for the combination, but Christian, reached in Lake

Forest and hopelessly hung over, said he couldn't remember it. Martha could, of course. She had it open in a minute.

The drawers were largely empty. The uppermost one, however, contained what he was looking for: the company books. To his surprise, Matthias found his parents' household ledgers in there as well, stuck carelessly under a few old copies of *Inland Architect* magazine.

Most households, and certainly most businesses, kept such records in computer files these days, but his father had distrusted such devices, fearing a breakdown might erase things. Matthias had bought one for the office the year before he'd moved to New York. It had probably been removed immediately after.

He looked through both sets of books carefully, and then again, and then again. The numbers were not complete. There were some contradictory and confusing entries. But the bottom line was comprehensible enough, and startling.

Matthias got up and went through the files again—all of them.

"Martha," he said.

She came to the door, paperback novel in hand.

"I can't find the income tax returns. Not the state, not the federal."

"Oh, I think your brother has those."

"He does? Why?"

"He keeps them in a safe deposit box. I think that's what he said."

Matthias stood a moment, rubbing his chin. "Is Harold Steiner still the family lawyer?"

"Oh, no. He died. More than a year ago."

"Well, who's handling my mother's will?"

"I not quite sure, Mr. Curland. Some friend of your sister's husband."

"Thank you, Martha."

After she went back to her desk, he quietly shut the door, then went to the phone. It took the family housekeeper nearly ten minutes to rouse Christian from his sleep and bed again.

"What's the problem, big brother? I thought you and I had our conversation for the day."

"I've been looking through the books down here. I have some questions."

"I'm sure you do. For an architect, you were always abysmal at math."

79

"I'd like your help."

"I'm up here, in far off Lake Forest, barely able to stand."

"I'm serious about this, Christian. I'd appreciate it if you'd come down here. There's something that worries me."

"There's nothing to worry about, big brother. The funeral's over. Why don't you just go back to your sunny Mediterranean paradise and let me go back to bed."

"If you can't drive, take the train. But get down here. I'll meet you for lunch, at my old club."

"The Arts Club? I'm not sure we've paid the dues."

"We have. It's in the books. I just looked. I'll meet you at twelve-thirty."

"Well, all right. Do they make a good bloody Mary there?

"Hey, Zany, what're you doing here? Nice day like today, you should be on the beach."

Lieutenant Frank Baldessari of Area Six homicide still wore purple double-knit suits, just as he had when he'd been a detective sergeant. He entered his office as breezily as something blown in by the wind and thumped down in his chair, somehow managing not to spill the cup of coffee in his hand. Up went his feet on his desk, into his mouth went a Marlboro, and, zingo, there he was just as Zany remembered him—hairline receding a little more, maybe, eyes even more like deep caves, but the same guy as always, picture perfect.

"It's busy on my beach these days, Frank," Zany said. "I got a homicide."

"Homicide? No shit. What happened, some fisherman pop his old lady with a coho?"

Zany opened the old metal briefcase he used to carry around in the years when he worked downstairs in burglary and took out one of the morgue photos of the dead girl from the sailboat. He'd brought two. Then he handed Frankie a typed copy of his report.

"Gunshot," he said. "Twice. Both through and through."

"Good-looking broad," Baldessari said. "What do you got? Boyfriend? Rapist?"

"I don't know what I've got. She washed up on my beach that way in a sailboat, a sailboat out of Chicago. Two days ago."

Baldessari dropped his feet to the floor and swiveled his chair back to sit square with his desk. He squinted at the photograph more closely, then began giving Zany's report a quick, cursory read.

"This dentist's story check out?" he said.

Zany nodded. "I had some help from a couple of guys in the Chicago Avenue District. There was a card game, all right. The dentist was a big loser. The boat was apparently stolen. The funny thing is that the padlock on the hatch cover wasn't broken, it was unlocked."

"Maybe picked? Cheap padlock?"

Zany shrugged.

"Well, what can we do for you, Zany? Or should I be calling you Chief Rawlings? We got a big fucking case working. I've got every man on it. Somebody whacked the president of the Park District and a black chippie last night while she was giving him some short time in the back of his car in Lincoln Park. Shot 'em both up like the St. Valentine's Day massacre. Practically every round was a twofer, you know? Through and through her, through and through him, a couple right through the floorboards into the ground. Fucking Magnum. We got the piece. Dumb perp left it behind."

"I heard the story on the radio. I know you're busy. I appreciate your taking the time to talk to me, Frank. What I need most is an ID on this girl in the sailboat."

"I'll run it through missing persons for you. Check with the other homicide areas. It'll take awhile. We really got our hands full here. You got any idea the girl was waxed on our side of the lake?"

"It's a good possibility. And the state line's what, twenty miles out? Could be your jurisdiction."

"I'll do what I can, Zany. I'll get the marine unit on it, too. Tell you what. I'll put a couple of guys on it from here. Maybe Mulroney and Stacek. You know them?"

"I know Mulroney."

"But you gotta give me a couple of days. We're not going to have time to go to the crapper until we turn up a lead on this park district thing. The guy was a friend of the mayor's. Had a lot of clout. And if you think we're busy, you should see the poor guys down in vice. Already they're getting screams from downtown to clean out all the hookers. Can you fucking imagine that? Chicago without whores?"

"Do you have anything at all?" Zany asked.

The lieutenant stubbed out his cigarette and got to his feet. "Yeah. We got it narrowed down to someone in the park between ten P.M. and midnight. Can you fucking imagine that? A criminal in Lincoln Park? Come on, I'll show you the shit we recovered from the scene."

He led Zany out to the squad room, where the victims' personal effects and other objects taken from the scene had been spread out over a long table. Except for the bloodstains, it could have been from a church rummage sale.

The lieutenant pointed to a collection of small photographs arrayed in a group. "From his wallet. He was a real family man. Look at all those kids. And this straight razor came out of her purse. If he hadn't gotten whacked with the Magnum, he might have ended up with his throat cut."

"Lucky guy," said Zany. He looked at the weapon. Even with the short barrel, it was one of the largest handguns he had ever seen.

"There's one funny thing," Baldessari said. "The car doors, the weapon, the guy's keys. They've all been wiped clean of prints. I never heard of a park mugger doing that."

"Do you think it was a professional hit?"

Baldessari shook his head. "The piece was his. And it's too messy. And he would have noticed if he'd been followed by another car. You kind of have to snake your way into that place where he was found. We did get one clean set of prints, though. From the leather seat, right beneath the steering wheel. What's weird is that they're the other way around from what you'd expect from somebody sitting in the seat. The fingers are pointing up, not down. Forensics thinks it was somebody giving him a hose job or a hand job. But they're not the black lady's."

"Another hooker?"

Baldessari shrugged. "Who the hell knows? Hey, Zany, you want to see the crime scene pictures? The back of that car looks like a butcher shop."

Zany's pronounced aversion to the sight of bloodshed had not been forgotten.

"Some other time," he said.

Downstairs in burglary, business was slower, and Detective Myron Plotnik, another old friend, had ample time to chat. He was a balding, chubby man with short-fingered hands and a fondness for fat cigars that he chewed upon nervously but never lighted. He held the unrolled painting Zany had given him without regard to the scene it depicted, as if it were merely a simple object, like a toaster or a candlestick, just another stolen item. He looked at the reverse side and even turned it upside down.

"Sure isn't worth much now, is it?" he said, handing it back to Zany. "You guys checked it for prints?"

Zany nodded. "It's got the victim's on it, and a couple of smudged prints we can't identify." Carefully he rolled it up and put it back in the big cardboard tube he'd brought with him.

"I don't know, Zany. We haven't had any art heists in Area Six, least not recently. But I'll check the computer."

He did so with some difficulty. Zany, who could operate computer systems the way safecrackers could open other people's safes, wanted to help, but resisted the impulse lest Plotnik think him pushy. Finally the detective called up the correct file and bright lines began filling the screen. Slowly he began to scroll through the information.

"Wait, here's one in Area Three," he said, peering closer at the screen. "No, this couldn't be it. This is a warehouse job."

"A warehouse full of paintings?"

"A truckful, anyway. You remember those things, Zany. They advertise them on TV. 'Original oil paintings,' only $29.95? They set up at Holiday Inns and like that for a weekend and sell paintings by the truckload. Only somebody jumped this trailer out in a cartage yard. Must have pissed them off plenty to find what they got. What do you think, can those paintings be original?"

"They'd have to be," Zany said. "No machine could turn out work that bad."

Plotnik scrolled the file some more, going all the way to the end, which didn't take very long.

"The only other recent one I got is in Area One," he said. "A burglary in Lake Point Tower. A painting by some guy named William de Kooning. Could that be it?"

"Willem de Kooning," Zany corrected. "I don't think so."

"Well, sorry I can't help you. Looks like you got a real weird one. It's a week for weird ones. We caught a burglary case in Old Town yesterday where the perps went through some broad's apartment the minute the landlord took off to go grocery shopping. Broad daylight. Sunday afternoon. Tore the whole goddamn place apart in less than an hour and apparently didn't take a thing. Not a fucking thing. She told us she thought the perps might be cops. Jeez. Old Town, you know. Flake city."

"Yeah," said Zany. "I really miss Chicago." He handed Plotnik a photo of his unidentified victim, the last he had with him. "This is the girl. Maybe somebody's seen her."

"I'll keep it in the file. Why don't you take that painting down to the Art Institute? If it's something worth stealing, maybe they've got a record of it or something. They've helped us before."

"I'll try that."

"I'll give them a call. Tell them it's for us. They can get a little snooty sometimes. Throw around words like Impressionist. I don't know shit from Impressionist. It's all just insurable goods to me. But if it is stolen, we'll hear about it sooner or later. You can't file an insurance claim on these things without a police burglary report."

"I remember."

"Sorry, Zany. You've been out there in the dunes so long I forget how much time you put in this place."

"I haven't forgotten a minute of it. I just wish I'd put more time in homicide."

"How long were you there? Wasn't long, was it?"

"About three weeks. Until my first murder."

"Well, now you got another. You gonna transfer out again?" He laughed.

"In the Grand Pier P.D.," said Zany, "the only transfer is out. But I'm sure as hell not coming back here."

Peter Poe owned four aldermen—bought and paid for. From time to time, he rented maybe a half-dozen others. Like any proud owner of expensive goods, he liked to show them off, and so this noon hour had three of them to lunch at his regular and very prominent table at Eli's—two of the bought-and-paid-fors and one of the rentals. Poe had learned long before that it was image that counted more than anything, that power perceived or imagined—power feared—was of far more consequence than power rawly exercised. If you fired off your guns, people could assess just how much damage you really were capable of inflicting; and how much ammunition you might have left. And if you missed—if your target survived—you were that much diminished.

The first Mayor Daley—Richard J.—won the national title of "Boss" because of his shoot-to-kill orders during the riots that broke out on the West Side in response to the assassination of

Martin Luther King and because of his cops' violent crackdown on the rioting antiwar protestors who had made such a mess of his 1968 Democratic National Convention. Both actions, taken in sputtering, self-defeating anger, had won him the respect of the neighborhoods. Except for a brief outburst of random violence by a few radical Weathermen, there never was a major riot in Chicago again, and Daley won his next mayoral by his biggest vote margin ever.

Out in the rest of the country, however, Daley the First's enemies not only survived, but flourished. The wounded Hubert Humphrey lost Illinois to Richard Nixon. In 1972 Daley not only failed to prevent George McGovern and his peace people from winning the nomination, but he and his entire Chicago delegation were thrown out of the Democratic convention. He wasn't accepted back until Jimmy Carter's 1976 lovefest, and four months later the mayor was dead.

What had really made Daley "Boss" was not cops' nightsticks but the fear of the potential of his power—the fear of ward heelers that he'd vise their precinct captains from their city jobs, the fear of judges that he'd dump them from the party retention slate, the fear of developers that he'd say no to a building permit or zoning amendment, the fear of rich ladies on the order of Bitsie Symms that the city might say no to their silly garden festival or whatever.

Daley's first elected successor, the tempestuous Jane Byrne, never understood that lesson and tried to rule the city like Catherine the Great, rolling heads every five minutes. She was out on a her kiester next election. All the other successors, including the present mayor, demonstrated they had learned the lesson well.

So had Poe. He'd been born in Chicago and had studied its politics carefully. After buying up all these guys, he'd never once given them a direct order, never once threatened them with reprisals. From time to time, when he'd wanted something, he'd let his desires be known, and they were usually fulfilled. Most of the time, he kept these fellows around just for show, just as he did the state legislators and county board members he owned. People presumed that if these characters were so obviously in his pocket, a lot of others must be, too. He encouraged a lot of grander beliefs by taking a lot of judges to lunch, sometimes even congressmen and the state's two U.S. Senators. He freely allowed people the use of his several Bears season tickets and loaned out his three trademark red stretch limos. He entertained lavishly.

85

The mayor had never come to one of his parties, but the governor had.

He'd never directly asked any of these people for anything. You kept your hole cards in the hole until the bets were called. But every time someone accepted one of Poe's kindnesses or favors, he carried away a message for all to note. Peter Poe could reach far.

To Mango, lawyer Yeats, and sometimes his wife, Diandra, Poe referred to the three aldermen he was lunching with as Larry, Curly, and Moe. Larry he had bought because he was close to a member of the mayor's inner circle, and some of what rubbed off the friend rubbed off on Larry. Curly was chairman of the zoning committee. Enough said. Poe had never had a problem with any of his projects. Moe, chairman of the city council committee on forestry, Poe only rented, but he would shortly be buying him up for good in a very big way. The development Poe was going to put up on the Cabrini Green site would require a lot of insurance. Moe's brother had an insurance agency. In return, Moe was going to give up his aldermanic seat and go on the Park District board, there to do as bidden.

Or was he? Poe had selected Moe because he was rentable and buyable and because he was a natural to fill the next vacancy on the park board, as President O'Rourke's sudden demise had just now provided. Moe had begun his career on the public payroll as a Parks Department playground instructor. He was a parks nut, out playing softball every Saturday even at his age, defending every blade of park grass like it was Concord Bridge. Moe had even stood up to his fellow council regulars and opposed expansion of the McCormick Place lakefront exhibition hall. He was an organization guy, but the Friends of the Parks and other liberal outfits loved him.

But Poe had begun to wonder. As he studied the man across the table at Eli's, it occurred to him that Moe might be the short form of Mope. For all his prominence, the fellow was really nothing more than a playground instructor with big, deep pockets. He was compliant because he was dumb. The enterprise Poe was embarked upon could afford no clumsiness. Moe had trouble handling his fork.

It would be days—maybe weeks—before the mayor would move on naming O'Rourke's successor. Poe had time to think well on this.

For the moment, all that was on the minds of those at Poe's table was the manner of O'Rourke's passing.

"Son of a bitch," said Larry. "I always knew that guy was going to get his prick in a ringer. Why the hell didn't he just grab some broad out of the office?"

"He thought hookers were safer," said Curly.

"Safer, shit," said Larry. "The guy took five slugs. Five slugs for a piece of ass. Why didn't he just get himself a 'niece' like that old fire commissioner—what was his name?—Bob Quinn?"

"He was the one who set off all the city air raid sirens when the Sox won the pennant in fifty-nine," Moe said.

"Fifty-eight," said Curly.

"Fifty-nine."

"Anyway, Quinn was a bachelor," Larry noted. "O'Rourke had eight kids. And a wife who knew from nieces."

"Didn't something like this happen to Matthew Danaher, what was he, county clerk?"

"Clerk of the Circuit Court," corrected Larry. "And that wasn't gunshots. That was booze and some broad in a hotel. His heart quit. They never found the girl. The old man Daley was mayor then. He got real disgusted. Danaher was like a son to him."

"And George Dunne," said Curly. "He got caught fucking around in the park. With two broadies."

Dunne's was the only name Poe recognized. He was an elder statesman of the party, and for years had been county board president and party chairman.

"Those weren't hookers," said Moe. "They were employees. And nothing happened to him. He retired honorably."

"They gave him the wink just because he was a nice old guy. With no wifey."

"It's the Republicans who do all the fucking around," said Moe. "My cousin's a watch commander in Area Six. He says the coppers call the Gold Coast 'whore heaven.' There are all those call girls and mistresses, servicing the commuters."

"And when they finally do get home to the suburbs, they swap wives," said Curly.

Poe smiled to himself. These men looked upon suburbanites as an alien species. He remembered a ward committeeman in the building department once telling him about the creepy feeling he got crossing the city line from Chicago into proper, respectable, tree-shaded Evanston.

"What are the police saying?" Poe asked. "They have any suspects?"

"What, on O'Rourke?" said Larry. "They'll never make a pinch. Never."

"They'll be bringing in all the whores," Curly said. He pronounced the word "whooores."

"And they'll all walk," Larry said. "I don't think it was any hooker, anyway. Maybe a pimp. More likely some creep in the park. They'll never find him."

"I don't know," Curly said. "The mayor's pretty pissed about this. I think he'll lean on the coppers to turn something up."

Poe made a mental note to have Moe check with his watch commander cousin for progress reports on the investigation. Glancing about the crowded dining room, he noticed a political columnist from the *Sun-Times* at a nearby table. Perhaps he'd write in his column that Poe was seen lunching with these three, all regarded as powers in the council. Every little bit helped.

The *Tribune*'s social reporter had already noted Poe's presence at Bitsie Symms's "party of the year" on the Overnight page. That would help for a different reason.

But it wouldn't help Mango.

Matthias didn't like most clubs, with all their tribal ritual and conformity. The several socially prominent clubs his parents had belonged to served principally as badges of what passed for aristocracy in this city built and made prosperous by hardworking immigrants. Matthias found these mossbound institutions as stifling and pointless as the archaic, class-ridden English lifestyle they aped.

The Arts Club was different. Founded in the 1920s, it had been a revolutionary force in the city's cultural history, providing a beachhead for the modern art and modern ideas that the wealthy few who for so many years had controlled the Art Institute had resisted like a foreign plague. For those stuffy reactionaries and their grand dame wives, the history of art stopped with the pretty flowers of Impressionism. Art had no other function for them than to enhance their own surroundings and provide a moral, uplifting influence on the masses who labored on their behalf. Art as truth, art as an expression of thought, of revelation, of rebellion, of fear and sexuality, was as dangerous a concept to them as trade union collective bargaining. They were the "moral force" that had sent police to confiscate Paul Chabas's innocent nude *September Morn* as an unlawful obscenity in 1912.

Even in the 1930s, Chicago's ruling families were supporting a "Sanity in Art" movement that had driven many of the city's finest young painters to New York and Europe. Those who had remained had found sanctuary in the Arts Club, which bravely exhibited their work no matter how controversial. It seemed inoffensively mainstream and circumspect now, but only because the mainstream had caught up with it. Matthias felt more comfortable here than any other place in the city, except for his own house.

Christian arrived late. Natty in blue blazer, white pants, striped Oxford shirt, and polka-dotted ascot, he seated himself so quietly Matthias almost didn't notice him.

"Drinking wine, big brother?"

"One small glass." Matthias pronounced each word emphatically.

"I'll have a small martini, then, very cold," Christian said to the waiter who scurried up behind him. "With a twist."

"I'm disturbed," Matthias said.

"It's been a disturbing couple of days."

"You told me that the family's on the brink of ruin," Matthias said. "That the firm's about to go out of business. Annelise wants to sell everything and put Father in some sort of home."

"Yes. That's what she and her loving husband Paul have been urging for some years now. I've always resisted."

"I've just been looking through the books, Christian."

"No need to do that. Everything's in order."

"They're disorderly as hell. I don't understand all the entries, but I understand enough. There's a lot of debt, but the loan payments on the Lake Forest house are only two months behind. The office rent's up to date. Martha's been paid. The associate's been paid. The dues here have been paid."

"You've always loved this club."

"Damn it, Chris! If I understand the entries in those books, Father—the family—owed nearly seven hundred thousand dollars last year. Now the debt's down to just over three hundred thousand."

"And this disturbs you?"

"It isn't what you said!"

"Perhaps I exaggerated a little."

"A little? Where did this money come from? The ledger entries don't make that at all clear. The firm hasn't had a new commission in more than a year."

"Are you suggesting I robbed a bank? Fleeced my portrait clients?"

"You've been in enough of their bedrooms."

"I shouldn't go on so about bedrooms, Matthias. I noticed the traces of your house guest when I stopped by to change clothes on the way here."

"If you bring that up again, Christian, I'll hit you. I'll smash every glass of gin you bring to your lips. And you know why."

"Merely raising a point of fairness, big brother. As for my friendship with Sally—which I gather is what prompts all this righteous anger—well, she wasn't exactly married to you when we had our little tryst, was she?"

The two sat motionless, like figures in a *tableau vivant,* Matthias's anger draining. He knew his brother's cleverness well. Christian's provocation was intended as a distraction. Matthias got back to the point.

"Where did the money come from?" he said finally, quietly.

The waiter brought Christian's drink. He accepted it with much gratitude and ceremony, postponing the inevitable.

"Where?"

"You wouldn't approve, Matthias."

"Who did you rob?"

"Peter Poe."

"What?"

"The money came from Peter Poe or, more precisely, from his casino in Indiana. Also a few parties on his yacht, gambling among the many amusements. I gamble. I know Annelise told you that. She hates it. It's my latest addiction. I started doing it out of desperation and now I do it for the sheer pleasure. And I'm many thousands of dollars ahead."

"As many as I found in the books?"

"Oh, much more than that. You know my taste in things. That Jaguar's mine. I bought it for cash. And, for the time being anyway, I've kept the wolves at bay. Father still has the house. For now."

"Why did you lie to me?"

"I didn't want you to be 'disturbed.' Not by the amount of the debt or by the way I've been paying it off. I thought you'd see Mother into the oven and then be off back to your life of abandon on the Côte d'Azur. It didn't seem to me that you'd cared much at all about our financial circumstances back here. So why bother you with what I was doing about them? You obviously didn't want to be involved, so why involve you?"

"When I left Chicago, the debts were paid and the firm was solvent. It had clients."

"Your clients, big brother. Not Father's. But I don't begrudge you your playing the prodigal. You have the right to live your own life. I'm just living mine. And may I point out, sir, that gambling is perfectly legal in Indiana now. I've paid income tax on every cent I've won. I resent your treating me like a war criminal."

"How did you win?"

"Playing *vingt-et-un,* roulette. Nothing so declassé as craps."

"Do you have proof? Of your winnings?"

"Of course. I'm well acquainted with the passionate curiosity of the IRS. I've saved every cash slip."

"Cash slip?"

"When you cash in your chips, you're issued a little receipt. One's supposed to save them for the IRS."

They studied each other.

"What happens when you begin to lose?" said Matthias.

"Lose? Horrible thought. Hasn't happened often. There are times when I've wondered if Mr. Poe hasn't been using me as some sort of shill, returning to Chicago with my pockets full of money as an encouragement to all my society friends to come out and join the fun."

"What if, perish the thought, you should start to lose now? Do you think we could cope with gambling debts on top of everything else?"

"I suppose I should have to become a truly serious portrait painter. I could do Mr. Poe's portrait, or his marvelous wife. I'd like that. He's already bought one of my pictures. Paid ten thousand dollars for it."

Matthias stared into Christian's bleary eyes, holding them steady. "I want you to stop gambling, Chris. Now. Never again."

"All right."

"I mean it."

"Entendu."

"I'm having dinner with the Poes tonight. He wants to talk to me about his Cabrini Green project."

Christian's expression became extremely serious. "Are you back to stay, Matthias? Are you coming back into the firm?"

"Tell me about Peter Poe."

"Well, he's quite a nice fellow, actually. Nice to absolutely everyone. Always doing people favors. Always doing something generous for the city. Unlike those piggy junk bond arrivistes in New York, there's nothing at all arrogant about him. No hauteur. The newspaper and television people love him. Of course, he's not exactly our sort."

"Will you for once give that garbage a rest? I'm an unemployed architect and an incompetent painter. You're one step removed from a gigilo. The only one of us worth a damn is Annelise. She takes care of animals."

"Would you care to order, sir?" said the waiter, who'd been hovering too near.

"Another martini," Christian said. "And he'd like another glass of wine."

"No, I wouldn't." The waiter left. "Where does Poe come from? Why haven't I heard of him before?"

"He comes from here, which is to say, the Northwest Side. What's that neighborhood? Five corners? Eight corners? He's Polish. I think he was born Poricki, or Poretski or something. In any event, his father—he was a construction worker, I believe— he died when Poe was a little boy and his mother moved the family back to Pittsburgh, where she came from. Poe went to some horrid little college, changed his name, and moved to Philadelphia. Did you know he tried to pass himself off as a descendant of Edgar Allan Poe? *Quelle absurdité.* Old Edgar never had any children, did he?"

"You seem to know quite a lot about Mr. Poe."

"Spend so much time in Indiana, don't you know. And I've come to know a few of his people. Everyone in town gossips about him."

"Where did he get his money?" The question embarrassed Matthias. It was the sort of thing his mother and her friends would ask, and probably had.

"He started out in Philadelphia real estate. Rehab, and some suburban townhouse developments. Did well enough to buy into one of those casinos in Atlantic City. Not exactly what you'd call old money."

"Christian . . ."

"I think he was frustrated there because Donald Trump—who was still rather flush in those days—monopolized all the attention. And the business. Three casinos to Mr. Poe's one. I think Mr. Poe is rather obsessed with Mr. Trump, bent on succeeding where Trump failed, and all of that. He went back to Philadelphia and built a big building or two, carried on as if he owned the place. The Main Line would have none of that. He worked up some scheme to put up the world's tallest building in Philadelphia. Can you imagine that? They cut him dead. Wouldn't allow anything an inch higher than the Mellon Bank Center."

Matthias found himself fascinated by every word. "Is he honest?"

Christian looked at him blankly. "You make a poor Diogenes, brother dear. He has an enchanting mistress, who is also his private secretary, with the extraordinary name of Mango Bellini. His wife is very beautiful—a fashion model of some sort—but it's a strange relationship." He slumped back in his chair as his second drink came, not speaking again until the waiter departed. "And that is all I know about Mr. Peter Poe."

"Why did he come back to Chicago? Why not New York?"

"New York is such a mess. You know that. And there's so much competition. Chicago is better pickings. It was probably ready for a man like him. The way he puts it is, 'You can do business here.' Sounds like a nice nineteenth-century municipal slogan, don't you think? And he certainly is doing business. He may even do business with you now, big brother. Think of that."

Zany was treated courteously enough by the Art Institute people, but not very swiftly. The museum staffers he initially talked to decided it would be best if he spoke with the institute's curator of twentieth-century European art, but the curator was in a meeting that took more than an hour to conclude. When it was over, he had to take an important phone call, and then make one. Finally he received Zany with much graciousness, only to refer him to an archivist Zany doubtless could have spoken to the minute he walked through the door.

"My God, what happened to it?" she asked, when Zany unrolled the painting.

"It was in an accident."

"An accident?"

"I guess it looks kind of gruesome, doesn't it? It was in a

boating accident. In Lake Michigan. That's how it ended up with my police department. As I explained to your curator, I think it's valuable. I'd like to find out who owns it."

She hesitated. "The people on the boat . . . ?"

"There was only one, and she's dead, I'm afraid." He didn't want to bring up murder. The archivist looked apprehensive enough as it was.

"The fact is, we haven't been able to identify the woman yet. I'm not actually sure she owned the painting. I thought it would help if we could find out who does."

"All right, Detective . . ."

"It's chief. I'm the chief of police out there. But just call me Zany. I mean, my name's Zane Rawlings. My father liked to read Zane Grey."

She looked as if she had never heard of Zane Grey. "I'll see what I can do, Mr. Rawlings."

She led him back into a large, well-lighted library.

"If it's in private ownership or been sold recently, I probably can't help you. But perhaps it came from one of the major collections. I don't recognize the painting, but it's definitely a Kirchner. Ernst Kirchner. His is a sad story, like so many artists'. He was one of the German painters condemned by the Nazis. He died in Switzerland just before World War Two. Committed suicide."

"Because the Nazis condemned him?"

"Because his paintings were condemned." She took a large book down from the shelves. "This one was done before World War One, I think, judging by the people's clothes."

Taking Zany back to a large table, she set down the book and began leafing carefully through the pages. There were half a dozen or so small pictures of paintings on each. The process reminded Zany of someone going through mug shots.

"Why, here it is. *Das Rot Turm. The Red Tower.*"

"Does it say who might own it?"

"Good heavens, it's the Albrecht Collection. It says they purchased it in 1933, but knowing the Albrecht, it's probably still there."

"What's the Albrecht?"

"The Albrecht Collection of German Art. It's here in Chicago. They call it the German Museum."

Zany had a vague recollection of the place from his Chicago

policeman days, but had always thought it was a private collection, not a public museum. He'd never been to it.

"Do you have the address?"

"Yes. It's on the Near North Side, near the river, where the old breweries used to be. But I'm not sure they're even open. It's a very strange place. It was founded by Karl Albrecht. He was a big patron of the arts in Chicago years ago, but something of an eccentric. He established this museum, but with the stipulation that the paintings were never to be sold or loaned or even moved from where he hung them. The place used to be open a couple days a week, but I think it's just by appointment now, if that. I was there once, but I don't recall seeing this painting, or any modernist paintings. Albrecht bought a lot of modern art, but he stored it all away. I don't think he liked it very much."

"Is Albrecht still alive?"

"Oh, no. He died years ago. His daughter died just this week. It was in the papers. There are some grandchildren. One of them lives in Chicago. Christian Curland. He's a painter. Does portraits, after a fashion."

Zany caught a hint of disapproval in the way she said the word portraits.

"Would you have his address, too?"

"I'll check."

Poe's motor yacht, the *Queen P,* was 116 feet long at the waterline—as considerable a vessel as some of the old excursion steamers that had been so common on the lake a century before. Normally, the *Queen P* carried an operating crew of five, plus stewards and other servants, but it was so automated and filled with advanced electronics that one person could operate it on the water alone. Sometimes, when in a perverse or reckless mood, Poe did that. He took as much pride in his skills as a mariner as he did in his ability to pilot airplanes and helicopters. He couldn't dock it entirely by himself, of course, but when done with his solitary cruises, he would lay off the harbor and sound the vessel's deafening boat horn to summon crew from dockside to come out to help him with the mooring ropes.

It embarrassed him that he had never learned how to handle a sailboat, but he was going to attend to that, starting that night.

Mango was on the after sundeck, sitting on the edge of a lounge chair and smoking a cigarette, swinging her leg, looking agitated. He nodded to her, but went directly up to the bridge, where the captain was waiting for him, having been told to have the *Queen* prepared to get under way that afternoon.

"Everything's ready, Mr. Poe," he said. The man had served as a second officer on cruise ships and had a pleasantly obsequious manner. "We were low on fuel but I've topped off the tanks. What's our destination?"

"I'm taking it out myself," Poe said. "I want everyone off the boat in five minutes, except Miss Bellini. Leave a couple of men on the dock to cast off the lines."

The captain hesitated only an instant. "Yes, sir."

Poe started toward the control console, then stopped.

"Wait a minute," Poe said. "Someone delivered some paintings to the boat from the Train art gallery over the weekend, when I was up at Lake Geneva. They're supposed to be in my cabin—in a flat wooden box. Did you see who it was? A girl, maybe?"

"No one delivered anything while I was on duty, sir. We shut down for a day, since you were going to be up at the lake. I gave the men some shore time. If one of the stewards was still aboard, he might have put it in your stateroom. Shall I call them up to the bridge?"

Poe frowned. "I'll ask them later. Right now, I want them off the boat, too. Everyone off. Get going. I want to get under way."

When all the crew were clear of the craft, Poe started the two powerful diesel engines, then went out onto the open-air port wing of the bridge, where there were auxiliary speed and steering controls. The *Queen P* was very new, and was equipped with a sideways-facing propellor amidships, set in a small tunnel that ran from side to side of the boat under the waterline. With that, he could swing the vessel out with ease.

"Prepare to cast off!" Poe shouted to the waiting deckhands.

He touched the engine lever, then paused and looked back to the deck where Mango was now standing at the rail. "Mango! Come up here!"

She gave him a questioning look, but flicked her cigarette into the water and turned for the companionway. In a moment, she was beside him.

"You know how to run this thing," Poe said. "Take it out."

"Peter. For God's sake."

"I taught you how. Do it." He leaned over the railing. "Cast off!"

Mango stepped to the controls and, looking over the side, gentled the huge craft into reverse a moment, to provide slack for the mooring lines. When the men had slipped them free and thrown the ropes onto the yacht's lower deck, she used the thrust of the amidships propellor to push the boat away from the dock, then backed slowly aft into the channel. Having got that right, she steered to starboard and eased the vessel into forward speed, heading for the open lake and sounding the horn in warning.

Poe stood leaning against the bulkhead, watching her every move. When they were past Navy Pier and clear of the breakwater, he came to her side and kissed her neck.

"I just wanted to see how your nerves are holding up," he said.

"I guess I'm all right," she said. "Today's kind of a downer."

"Did you have to do that? Shoot the poor son of a bitch?"

Mango said nothing.

"I didn't ask you to do that. Nothing like that."

She looked away, then walked into the enclosed portion of the bridge. He followed, seating himself at the helm, adjusting the throttles.

"Where are we going?" she asked, coming to stand beside him.

"I'm making for Michigan City. I want to put you on ice for a few days, just in case. You can stay on the boat if you want. I'll take a chopper back. Go make me a drink, a gin and tonic."

She responded obediently. When she returned, he nodded her to the seat at the bridge windows next to him, frowning when she lighted yet another cigarette.

"Why'd you do it, Mango?" he said quietly, which was not a good sign. He often lowered his voice when he was really angry. "I don't mind that the bastard kicked. I half expected it. A guy who's going to mess with booze and broads with a bad heart like that deserves what he gets. We figured on that. But that fucking bloodbath in the car. Why'd you do it, Mango? Why did you screw up?"

His eyes were on the open water ahead. Hers were fixed on him as she spoke.

"I didn't screw up. I had no choice, Peter. He wouldn't go to the hotel. He had that place in the park and he wouldn't go anywhere else."

"You could have called it off. We could have tried something else."

"You told me you had a timetable and we had to stick with it. I always do what you say, Peter. Always. I had him pick up that other girl because I thought I could use her to set him up. There was some reform alderman who got set up that way with a black hooker back in the seventies. Under the El tracks. Only the cops were in on that one and were waiting for him. By the time I could get to a phone, she might have finished with him."

She took a long drag of her cigarette. "So I did what I had to."

"Where did you get the gun?"

"It's his. It was under the front seat. It's perfect this way, Peter. Even if they turn the whole town upside down, all they'll find out is that he picked up two hookers on Broadway and one of them blew him away. I took all his money. I wiped off all the fingerprints. Nobody saw us. There's no connection with the hotel room I took. I didn't call the cops so there's no recording of my voice. It's perfect. That girl had a straight razor on her. The cops said so. She might have done him herself. This happens to Johns all the time in this city. This one just happens to be a big deal."

Poe glanced at her. She was wearing a tight-fitting knit dress and sandals. "Where's your stuff? Your wig and all that?"

"Down below. In my bag."

"Burn it. Everything. Use the barbecue grill on the sundeck. When we get out a little farther, we'll dump what doesn't get burned. This really makes me nervous, Mango."

"It'll be all right, Peter." She looked unhappy.

He pushed the *Queen P*'s throttles forward a little. When the Chicago skyline was a diminished presence behind them, he put the engines back into neutral. Mango was standing over the little grill. He watched her add more charcoal lighter. There was a roll of steamy smoke and then a burst of flame. Poe hurried down the companionway to the cabins below.

Unlocking his, a grand stateroom that might have been the bedroom of a deluxe suite in one of his hotels, he went to his special locker. The wooden box was there, the seals broken.

He opened it and took out a rectangular package wrapped in thick canvas. It contained two paintings. *The Red Tower* wasn't with them, just as Mango had said. Poe had been hoping that somehow it had been overlooked. He went through the wrappings again. Nothing.

Mango came into the stateroom. She had taken off her sandals and was barefoot. "You don't look very happy, Peter."

"I want that painting. How did this box get in here? If she was going to steal it, why did she bother to come here at all? Why did she leave these?"

"Maybe someone took it from her. Or took it from here after she was gone. You're sure there was no crew around?"

"This just doesn't make sense. Haven't those torpedoes of ours turned anything up on her?"

"Nothing. Nothing yet. They went through her apartment. Nothing."

"I don't like this, Mango. Why do I have to worry about this petty shit when I've got so much else on my mind?"

"I'll take care of it, Peter."

"This is small. Tiny. One lousy painting. I've got major deals going. I don't have time for this."

"I'll take care of it. Calm down."

"Well, don't fucking take care of it the way you took care of that goddamned O'Rourke!" He picked up one of the other paintings, a picture of food, partially peeled fruit. His hands were shaking. He rolled the canvas up and threw it against the wall. Then he kicked a chair. "Shit!"

She stepped away from him, then reached to her back to pull down the zipper of her dress, letting its front fall loose.

"Peter."

He turned. His face was flushed and his eyes a little wild. "Not now, Mango."

She came close to him again, pushing her breasts against his chest.

"You've got to calm down, Peter. Let me help you calm down."

"No. I want to burn this stuff, too. The box, and both these paintings. Then I'm going to call Train and tell him the girl never made it to the boat."

Christian had a date for the evening—as he put it, with a "prospective client"—in Oak Brook. From an upstairs window, Matthias watched with dread, disgust, and amazement as his brother whizzed the shiny Jaguar off down the narrow street, barely missing another car pulling out of a parking space. Alcoholics, he'd been told, ended up in jail, a mental institution, or an early grave if they didn't stop. Christian seemed bound toward his fate, whichever it was, with madcap zeal.

Matthias had a few hours remaining before he would have to

pick up Sally for dinner at the Poes'. After dressing, he wandered into the upstairs room he had once used as a sort of studio. It was much given over to his brother's work now, and for the storage of a few pieces of accumulated rummage, including a somewhat chipped and shabby wooden Indian he had bought long ago at some antique store in Wisconsin.

In the corner of the room, propped up on a table, was a painting he had started years before and never fully completed, a sailboat coursing into the wind, close-hauled in full heel with a curve of swell and spray in the foreground. It was badly flawed, though not in a technical sense. The water was deftly realistic. The hull gleamed brightly. The sails billowed perfectly with the wind. It was very pretty.

But it was idle, without point. No more than a handsome decoration for some suburban family room or beach house. Unlike Winslow Homer's *Breezing Up,* it conveyed no sense of the power of the sea, of the quickness of life in a sailor's hands in a small boat in high wind.

The doorbell rang downstairs. Matthias guessed it might be Sally, or his sister, stopping by on her way home from a visit downtown.

Instead, he found a rather huge, bearded, bespectacled man in an ill-fitting suit. He carried a cheap, metallic briefcase.

Matthias was not interested in life insurance, home improvement, or a new religious faith. He resented people who earned their living making intrusions.

"Mr. Curland? Christian Curland?"

"He's not home. And I'm afraid we don't accept door-to-door solicitations."

"I'm not selling anything, sir, or seeking donations. I'm with the police." The man took out a badge in a leather case. "The Grand Pier, Michigan, police. I'm Chief Rawlings. Zane Rawlings."

He had the habit of blinking, as if perpetually uncertain.

"Yes, well, I'm Christian's brother. There's not been an accident or something, has there? He just left here."

"No, not that I know of. It's about a painting. The Art Institute referred me to you. I mean, to your museum. I went out there, but it's all closed up."

"Yes. I'm afraid so. Won't you come in, Chief Rawlings."

Matthias accepted the man into the vestibule, but no farther.

"We had an incident out my way this weekend," Zany said. He

paused. As with the woman at the Art Institute, he was reluctant to broach the subject of murder, at least immediately. He wanted cooperation and recollection, not shock, or panic. He wished he had learned more about handling homicide cases—in his long-ago three weeks in that division.

"A boat washed up on our breakwater. It had been in, well, a pretty bad accident. We found a painting aboard. The Art Institute said it might belong to you, or your museum. They had a sort of catalog there that showed it had been bought by your museum in 1933."

Matthias smiled. "That's a bit before I was born. And I've been living out of the country for the last few years. I'm not sure I can help you."

"Well, I've got it right here. Would you mind taking a look at it for me?"

Matthias led the bearded policemen into the house's long dining room. Bay windows on the far end filled it with light, but he turned on an overhead electric chandelier as well. Zany set the briefcase on the table, then hesitated, noticing a large painting of a full-length nude on the wall opposite, above the sideboard.

"My wife would never let me have something like in the dining room, or anywhere in the house."

"My brother's a bachelor. Also an artist. He lives here most of the time. I'm just visiting, more or less."

"Did he paint that?"

"No. I did."

Zany opened the briefcase and carefully unrolled the picture, pressing down on two corners to keep it opened flat. Matthias studied it with some concern.

"Is that blood on there?"

"I'm afraid so. Yes."

"I can tell you it's by Ernst Kirchner."

"That's what the lady at the Art Institute said."

"It's hard to say if it could be one of ours. There are more than three hundred paintings in the collection, and this one looks pretty obscure. Nothing famous. There's a catalog here in the house, but it's only for the pictures on display. We display no modernist art. All of that's kept in a vault. I'd have to go out there and check the files."

"Could you, sir? It would be very helpful. You could have been burgled."

"I doubt that very much. The place is like the Bastille." Matthias looked at his watch. "This isn't very convenient."

"It's not convenient for me, either, sir. I drove a long way out here."

"All right. Let's take a look."

Zany was a little surprised by Matthias's unique old Rolls-Royce, and by his willingness to park it in the seedy-looking street outside the museum. It was a big stone mansion, darkened with age and grime. There were thick, cast-iron grates over all the windows, which were shuttered. Curland opened three locks to get inside, and then disconnected a burglar alarm in the foyer before proceeding any further. It would take an army commando team to break into this place.

Matthias led Zany into an office off the main exhibition chamber, snapping on a light switch. Unlike every other office Zany had ever been in, it contained no fluorescent fixtures, but three green-shaded desk lamps came on. There were two desks, both old and huge. The third lamp was on a long table, stacked with dusty-looking art books. A row of file cabinets lined the wall nearest the door.

"I really doubt we have it," Matthias said, going to a cabinet in the middle and stooping to open a drawer. He thumbed through the backs of the thick notebooks it contained. "My grandfather didn't like Kirchner, not in the end. Although he once tried to buy his painting *Street, Berlin,* before the Museum of Modern Art got hold of it."

"I don't understand. Why would he want to buy something he didn't like? As an investment?"

"Oh, no. My grandfather despised people who did that, who treated art as a form of stock shares. He just couldn't make up his mind about modern art. He had a long debate with himself about it. He was caught up in the emotionalism of modernism. Some of the paintings he bought absolutely terrified him, but they also fascinated him. In the end, he decided they expressed too much truth, that truth was really all about death. He decided art should be an antidote to truth. He was fairly old by then. He would never willingly destroy a work of art. I think he valued art more than he did a lot of human beings, but he took all his modernist things—anything that wasn't somehow warm and beautiful—and locked them all away in the vault downstairs. I'm

102

not sure what all is in there. I don't think I've been in it more than two dozen times in my entire life."

The policeman was looking at him with wary puzzlement. "How about the Kirchner painting?" he said finally.

"Yes, excuse me." Matthias took a huge, dusty, loose-leaf ring notebook from the file drawer and set it on the nearest desk, flipping through its pages quickly. Suddenly he stopped and stood frozen.

"I'm quite surprised," he said, laying a finger by a small photograph glued to the page. "There it is. *Das Rot Turm. The Red Tower.* Ernst Kirchner, 1913. It's in the vault. At least, it's supposed to be. You say you found your picture in a boat, after an accident?"

"Yes."

"I don't understand how that it could be. You're from Grand Pier, Michigan?"

" 'Have a grand time in Grand Pier.' That's what the highway sign says."

"But Mr. Rawlings. You might not believe this, but no one has ever stolen anything from this museum. It's never been broken into, the neighborhood notwithstanding. We've had problems with vandalism. Graffiti and the like. But no burglaries."

"Well, I can believe that. But here's the painting. Right in my hands."

Matthias stood up straight, his hand at his chin, his eyes on the canvas Zany was holding.

"I wonder if it could be a copy," he said.

"You mean a forgery?"

"No, a copy. People copy paintings all the time. Especially art students. I just wonder. Kirchner was fairly popular in some avant garde circles. But it couldn't have been copied here. It's one of the very strict provisions of my grandfather's will. No one was to be allowed to copy any of the paintings in the collection. And no photographs, except for those he had taken for our records. This copy would have had to have been done before he acquired it. Unless, of course, it's the original."

"Mr. Curland. Just a suggestion. Why don't we go down to your vault and look?"

"All right. I'm as curious as you are."

It took Matthias a long time to root out the combination to the vault's outer doors from the files, and an even longer time to make it work, but at last the lock's tumblers fell into place. He pulled open one of the doors, and they were greeted by a cool, moist, musty rush of air. Curland clicked on a light, and Zany saw that they were in a long storeroom, crowded with metal racks that were filled with paintings, each in a flat, narrow box. There were numbers on the boxes' corners and on the racks' frames beneath each painting. Matthias moved quickly to where the Kirchner work should be.

The slot was filled. There was a narrow box in the slot.

"Something's there," Matthias said.

"Can we take it out and look at it?" Zany asked.

"I rather hate to do it, but I guess we must."

There was a workroom just outside the vault. Matthias set the box on a bench, located a small pry bar, and began lifting the edges of the wood all around the perimeter. When it was sufficiently free, he gave it a tug and lifted. The painting inside was covered with some kind of treated cloth. Gently he lifted the picture out.

There was the street, the people in evening clothes, the woman in the red coat, the red tower in the distance.

"Das Rot Turm," Matthias said.

"Son of a bitch," said Zany. "Two of them."

"Well?"

"I guess maybe you're right. Maybe this is a copy." He looked at the canvas in his hands. What with the watermarks, bloodstains, and holes, it did seem a little cheap and shoddy. "I just wonder how it turned up in a boat on my breakwater."

"Paintings, copies—all sorts of things—turn up in the strangest places," Matthias said. "There's a folio of Shakespeare's in the Folger Library in Washington that they found in a barn in Sweden wrapped up in an old nineteenth-century lottery ticket." He picked up the picture from the boat, gently fingering the back of the canvas. "This is a little surprising, however. It's hard to tell with the condition it's in, but the canvas doesn't seem very old. Of course, someone might have sneaked a photograph of it. That happens all the time. But the original's been here in this vault for years. Very strange."

"Strange as hell."

"It was in an accident, you say?"

Zany hesitated. "Involving gunshots. More like murder."

"Murder?"

"Yes. A young woman."

"In Michigan?"

It occurred to Zany he ought to show the man a photograph of the victim—just in case, just on a hunch. But he had given the two copies he'd brought with him to the Chicago police.

"We're not really sure where it happened. The boat turned up at our harbor. It was pretty bloody."

"Sounds awful. I think I'd better put this back. My grandfather's will also stipulated that the vault paintings weren't to be disturbed. We try not to come in here too often."

Zany felt a little embarrassed, and bewildered. He thought he'd been onto a major art theft, but now he was back on square zero. He needed to think.

"Who was murdered?" Matthias asked, rewrapping the painting.

"We haven't identified the body yet. It was a woman. She was all alone on the boat. The painting was under her body."

"A woman?"

"Yeah. Young, late twenties, early thirties. Nice looking. You know someone like that? Somebody who's been missing?"

Matthias frowned. "Not offhand. This was in Grand Pier? You hear about these things in the Caribbean. But Lake Michigan?"

"The whole world's getting pretty dangerous."

Curland completed his work and went back into the vault. "Can I drop you anywhere?" he said, after he'd come out again and was closing the big doors. "I'm running quite late. But if it's nearby."

"Thank you. I'm at that Days Inn near the lake."

Peter Poe was still getting dressed for dinner when Matthias and Sally arrived at his Michigan Avenue penthouse. His wife, Diandra, received their guests in his place, explaining her husband had been over in Michigan City on business and had been delayed by a thunderstorm over Gary flying back in his helicopter. At first, Matthias thought she might be trying to impress them—he had met very few people in his life who flew about in their own helicopters—but she spoke so matter-of-factly and changed the subject so quickly that he decided she was simply relating an occurrence that routinely happened. Poe's wealth was so conspicuous he didn't need his wife to elaborate on it. Anyone who looked at the Chicago skyline was aware of Peter Poe's presence in the city.

In contrast to Sally's traditional little black cocktail dress, Diandra Poe wore a summery, floor-length gown of midnight blue, with a simple white top that left her shoulders bare. Matthias had no idea who the designer might be, but it was obviously extremely expensive. For their first few minutes there, Sally's eyes scarcely left it. Matthias's eyes, too, when Mrs. Poe walked. She moved more gracefully than any woman he had ever seen other than on a ballet stage. It had long perplexed Matthias that no artist had ever adequately captured the beauty of motion; damn few film directors, either. They were concerned with photographic composition, with framed scenes, not movement.

He was about to comment on this, but caught himself. Mrs. Poe might not appreciate a discussion of her walk.

They followed her through an enormous, highly contemporary living room and out to a long terrace with a view of the avenue and, over the tops of other buildings, the lake. It had turned turquoise in the evening light, the color of Poe's eyes. After drinks were ordered, Mrs. Poe lingered at the railing, gazing out over it like a pleased child.

"You design buildings, Mr. Curland," she said, turning to him after a moment. "What do you think of this one?"

He worded his reply carefully, seeking a useful euphemism. When fellow artists were unimpressed with his paintings, which was often, they would say things like "Matthias, it's your best work yet."

"It's very powerful," he said, "but it suffers from its companions."

"Excuse me?"

"It has too many neighbors. There are too many buildings on Michigan Avenue. Too many near the lake. A tall, tough building like this should really stand by itself, on its own. Like Lake Point Tower over there."

"Oh, yes. I love that building. I love to watch the light move on it around sundown."

"It's based on a design by Mies van der Rohe, one he did back in 1921, if you can believe it. It was pure fantasy then. They didn't have the construction materials or the air conditioning and high-speed elevators a structure like that requires. They had to wait until after World War Two for all that to be invented. By then Mies was designing his famous glass boxes. Lake Point Tower was the work of some of his young protegés. The only thing wrong with it is that it's too close to the lake. It's the only building they've allowed east of Lake Shore Drive. I've always been afraid developers would try to use it as a precedent to put their own buildings on the shoreline, like Miami Beach. The open waterfront is what makes Chicago unique. It's sacred ground. If they allowed development on it, the city would just be another Milwaukee, or Cleveland."

"I'm glad Peter didn't buy it. He'd probably put a big red 'P' on the side."

"Well, I love your husband's building, Diandra," Sally said. "Everyone does. At Crickett's last week, the girls were talking about how much it's added to Michigan Avenue. It's our very own Trump Tower."

Matthias winced, worrying how Mrs. Poe would react to Sally's gaffe. To an architect like Matthias, to anyone with taste and an eye for line and beauty, Trump Tower was a gleaming, self-indulgent, egomaniacal grotesque. Sally knew that. Was she indulging in a little sniping? How well did he know Sally Phillips, beyond the altered images of reverie and nostalgia? What had she become?

Mrs. Poe was restrained: a flicker of a downward glance followed by the distraction of movement, as she went from the railing to a small chaise longue, not sitting so much as arranging herself on it, as if for a photograph. Either she admired the former billionaire's gleaming gaucherie on New York's Fifth Avenue or she disliked her husband's building just as much, and thought Sally's compliment ironic. Her real feelings would remain a mystery, like so much about her.

Poe arrived a few minutes later. To Matthias's surprise, he was not wearing a suit but was dressed much as Christian had been that afternoon, only the blue blazer he wore with his perfectly pressed gray flannels was double-breasted and emblazoned with a gold crest on the pocket that included a crimson "P." He wore an open-collared silk shirt and large gold-and-diamond cuff links that clashed with rather than complemented his huge gold watch.

"Sorry to be so late," he said, after greetings had been exchanged. "Busy, busy day." He looked to his watch with great display. "But we still have time for a tour."

Sally seemed delighted. Mrs. Poe, unlike most hostesses with something to show off, seemed unenthused. As Poe led his two guests inside, she remained on her chaise longue.

"Come on, Diandra," Poe said a little tersely.

"I'll just wait here. I want to watch the sky."

"Come on, I said!"

She rose, responding professionally, a model going to work.

What Poe had to show them was an outrageously immense amount of square footage for a city residence, extraordinary views of the city, and a lot of hard work by an expensive interior decorator with a flair for modern excess. He or she had probably done a few Los Angeles luxury hotels as well.

Poe conducted the tour much like an English nobleman wandering among ancient family heirlooms, though Poe likely had not owned the pieces he picked up and discussed for very long.

The paintings were much what Matthias had expected—contemporary works, mostly, some quite expensive. What nineteenth-century pieces there were tended to be flowers or still lifes. Hidden away in back corners or little-used rooms were a few that surprised Matthias. Some paintings from the early twentieth-century "ashcan school;" a Joseph Stella art deco pastel of New York harbor. Matthias wondered if Mrs. Poe had had anything to do with its acquisition.

He contributed little to the conversation, but did bring up the visit he'd been paid by the policeman from Michigan; and the extraordinary occurrence of a copy of one of his grandfather's paintings turning up in a murder across the lake.

"I'm sure it was done long ago. My grandfather used to give a lot of young artists access to his collection in the early days. He wanted American art of the future to have a German influence—thought there was too much French and English."

"Somebody got murdered over it, the painting?" Poe asked. He seemed fascinated.

"I'm not sure about that. But there was a murder."

"And it's a copy? Not an original?"

"Had to be. As I said, we went to my grandfather's museum. The original was still in the vault."

"That would be interesting to see. Do you still have the copy, so you can study them together?"

"Oh, no. He took it back with him. I just dropped him at the Days Inn over there."

Poe nodded, then moved on to another painting. Matthias was startled to see it was one by his brother—a rendering of the Chicago skyline at dusk as seen from the lake, the crimson-topped pinnacle of Poe's building prominent in the center.

"Your brother Christian did this for me."

"I hope it wasn't settlement of a gambling debt."

"Oh, no. I paid top dollar. I thought I'd get my money back, though. Christian's a pretty good customer of ours out in Michigan City. But he's done well at the tables. 'Mr. Lucky.' "

"He's done a lot better than anyone would expect."

"Nice guy, your brother."

Without returning to the terrace and their drinks, they went directly into dinner. The table was comparatively small. Matthias guessed that when the Poes threw dinner parties, they were usually very large, with many tables like this set up in many rooms.

"Diandra," Poe said, as they were served the first course—a light vichyssoise. "Did Bill Yeats call this afternoon?"

"I never answer your private phone, Peter. He didn't call the main number."

"He's buying me a sailboat," Poe said. "I was hoping to get a progress report before I talked to you, Mr. Curland. Excuse me, while I see if I can find out how he's doing."

As soon as he was gone, Mrs. Poe turned the conversation back to art.

"Mr. Curland," she said, her voice so cool and soft and sensual and directed totally at Matthias one might have thought Sally was no longer there. "Do you think this apartment could use a Dubuffet?"

As a matter of fact, he did—a great grinning, mocking skull-face, hung just at the entrance by the elevators, reminding the worthies who passed of their mortality.

"I don't suppose it would go with the decor."

"I suppose it would depend on your mood. Sometimes, when I'm here alone, I'm in a mood for a Dubuffet."

Returning, Poe seemed almost ebullient. He said his Mr. Yeats had located a perfect boat up at Traverse City, and would have photographs and specifications delivered in the morning. From that point on, the talk was exclusively about sailing. Poe wanted to know all about Matthias's experience, the races he had won— and lost. What the big prizes were in Great Lakes competition. He seemed surprised to learn that so many events involved smaller craft, and were won by enthusiasts, not rich men.

"Things have changed since J. P. Morgan's day," Matthias said.

"How do you mean?"

"J. P. Morgan, the financier?"

"I know who Morgan was," said Poe, a little testily. "What does he have to do with sailing?"

"He's the one who said 'You can do business with anyone. You sail only with gentlemen.' But it's not like that anymore. The big world-class events like the America's Cup are so expensive now they have to be financed by syndicates, or entire nations. Otherwise, sailing's become rather democratic. Here on the Great Lakes, all sorts of boats take part. The victories go to the best sailors, not the fellows dressed up like admirals."

"And you're a hell of a sailor, aren't you?"

Matthias didn't know how to respond to such a question. "I haven't done any serious sailing in a long time."

"But you're good. My pal Yeats says you're the best on the lake. Says you used to beat him all the time."

"If your Mr. Yeats is the gentleman I'm thinking of, I don't believe I ever raced against him much. I don't belong to his yacht club. I couldn't afford it."

Sally looked at him strangely.

Poe continued to pursue the subject relentlessly. He brought up his own considerable merits as a boatsman, noting the master mariner's certificate he had earned and that he'd become skilled enough to operate the *Queen P* single-handed, once he was away from the dock. But he admitted the regret he felt about having been too busy to learn sailing, that it was something he now wanted to do very much.

"There are a lot of good sailing schools around Chicago."

"I don't want to go to school. I want to learn on my own boat, from a top guy."

It was very clear what he was after. Matthias's disappointment was almost palpable. He had come to this dinner party expecting Poe to talk about his grand Cabrini Green real estate project. Yet Poe had not said a word about Cabrini Green. After dessert had been served, Matthias had pointedly tried to end the fixation on sailing by bringing up how much he thought the lakefront skyline had changed architectually since he had left, and how pleased he was with the sensible way he thought the gentrification of the area to the west of Lincoln Park had proceeded. Poe had asked if Matthias thought the park's Belmont Harbor was a better berthing for a sailboat than Monroe Street harbor downtown. Matthias replied that it made little difference, and stared down into his coffee, letting Sally push on with a description of an apartment close friends of hers had on Lake Shore Drive over-looking Belmont Harbor.

"Not to be old-fashioned," Poe said, pushing his chair back when Sally had finished. He struck Matthias as the least old-fashioned man he'd ever met. "But I think it's time for the gentlemen to retire for brandy and cigars."

The old-fashioned custom, of course, had been for the ladies to retire while the gentlemen indulged themselves with their manly tobacco pleasure at table. If Poe was unaware of that, his wife was not.

"Come on, Sally," she said. "I'll show you our kitchen. It's a little like the space center down in Houston."

Sally smiled politely and got up to follow her.

Poe didn't want to remain at the dining table. He led Matthias through several rooms and down a wide corridor to his study. Unlike the rest of the penthouse Matthias had seen, it was furnished archaically—an approximation of an old English library, with a strong admixture of state-of-the-art computer technology.

He poured two overlarge brandies. Matthias didn't want his, but accepted it, holding the glass uncomfortably. He was still bothered by the glass of wine he had had with lunch. Poe then offered him a cigar from a leatherbound humidor.

"No, thank you," Matthias said. "I don't really smoke. The occasional pipe."

"I love 'em," Poe said. He went to his desk, picked up a magazine with a large ketch on the cover, and handed it to Matthias after opening it to a page full of yacht sale advertisements. He pointed to a picture of a fifty- or sixty-foot sloop-rigged racing cruiser.

"It's just like this," Poe said. "The boat Yeats has a line on. You ever sailed anything like that?"

"Yes. My own boat is a lot smaller, though."

Poe seated himself in a large leather armchair, nodding to Matthias to do the same in an identical chair opposite. To their right, the windows gave out onto a view of the city to the west, long lines of streetlights converging in the far distance.

He lighted his cigar.

"Are you going to be around Chicago for a while?" he asked.

"I don't know. I came back because of a death in the family. There are some business affairs to attend to."

"Will you be around for the summer?"

"Probably. My father's firm has some problems I should help with."

"I know. I know pretty much everything about you. Had someone check you out this morning. Hope you don't mind. Always like to know who I'm dealing with. And, besides, like I said, I know your brother."

Matthias said nothing.

"Mr. Curland. Matthias. I'm going to call you Matthias. Call me Peter. I can't stand 'Pete,' but I like Peter."

"Peter."

"Matthias. I want you to teach me how to sail. I want to start as soon as I get delivery of this boat."

"I'm not a sailing instructor, Mr. Poe. Peter. I'm a painter, like my brother. And an architect."

"All right. So don't 'teach' me. 'Advise' me. I'll pay you a big retainer."

Matthias couldn't let this continue a second longer. "Mr. Poe. I thought you asked me here to talk about Cabrini Green."

"I did. And we're going to. But first things first. I haven't even decided what I'm going to put up there yet. The Chicago-Menominee race is in July. I want to know how to handle my new boat by the Chicago-Menominee. I intend to enter that race, and win."

"Mr. Poe, I can't teach you how to sail well enough to win a major Lake Michigan sailboat race. Not in that short a time. At best, I could get you to the point where you wouldn't embarrass yourself taking a boat out by yourself."

"That's good enough. I don't plan to be the skipper. I want you to do that."

"Me?"

"Yes. You be the skipper and I'll be aboard as the owner. I'll do some of the handling, when it won't interfere with anything, and put in some time at the helm. Like, maybe at the finish line."

Matthias simply stared at him.

"It's only a few weeks, Matthias. I'll pay you two thousand a week, with a big bonus if we win. What do you say, sporting proposition?"

"Do you always do things this way?"

"I like to move fast, Matthias. Like George S. Patton."

"My last Chicago-Menominee was six years ago."

"But you won."

"Yes."

"Say that again."

"Yes."

"Deal. Now come with me."

The room Poe took him to contained little more than a long table, upon which had been erected a scale model mockup of the central portions of the city and the downtown lakefront, including the full sweep of Grant Park. Poe turned on some overhead spotlights, then manipulated a control that directed a particularly bright one on a section that Matthias recognized as representing Cabrini Green, minus the notorious public housing projects. In their place stood block models of two tall nondescript high-rises, one nearly half again the height of the other—both painted a bright red.

"I had Cudahy, Brown work this up for me on spec," Poe said. "You know them? They designed the building we're in."

"I know them," said Matthias, without further comment.

"What do you think of the concept? The tall one's residential; the other, office. If it were closer to the Loop, I'd reverse it."

"Well . . ."

"Straight answer, Matthias. You're no fool."

"They're very predictable and uninteresting. It's a waste of all the open space you have there. You could do something very dramatic there that you couldn't get away with downtown."

"Exactly. Now what I'm about to show you is strictly between us. Gentleman to gentleman, like old J. P. Morgan. All right?"

"All right. Understood."

"I mean it, Matthias. I'm very fair with people who are fair with me. But people who aren't fair with me, I can be really unfair to them. You understand me?"

"That's not one of my faults."

"That's what they tell me. All right, Matthias. Take a look at this."

He picked up the smaller model, held it aloft for a tantalizing moment, then set it carefully atop the other.

Matthias was stunned. It was the very last thing he'd expected. Set apart from the downtown cluster, the tower the two sections formed gave an even greater impression of height—reach surrounded by space, as Frank Lloyd Wright had envisioned for the mile-high building he had suggested for the Southwest. Absolutely extraordinary, and in the midst of this great, sprawling city.

113

"What do you think?" Poe asked.

"I think you'll have the highest building in Chicago."

"Matthias, please. The highest building in the world. Like Trump the chump was going to put up, but never could. Higher than the one those new guys in New York are planning. We'd retire the title."

"Did Cudahy, Brown give you the idea?"

"Cudahy, Brown don't have ideas. They just try to please clients."

Matthias moved around the table, looking at the mockup from a different perspective.

"There are fantastic problems with a building this tall," he said finally, stooping down to squint at the model from what would be ground level. "The F.A.A., for one. You'd be encroaching on the O'Hare approach patterns."

"That didn't stop Sears Tower."

"You'd need all sorts of building permits and zoning variances."

"That can be taken care of."

"I'd fear for your occupancy rate. Especially for office space. Lawyers like to be near the courts and near other lawyers. Commodity traders near the Board of Trade."

"Vacant office space can be converted to residential, if necessary. This would be the prestige address in Chicago, in the country. We'd build an entire miniature city around it—stores, schools, theaters, a park. This would be like creating a brand-new suburb, like they're doing all the time out in DuPage County, only it would be right in the city, and it would go straight up."

"The structural problems would be tremendous. Your core columns would take up a lot of the interior. You'd need to devote a lot of space in the upper reaches to huge counterweights to deal with the wind stress. You'd need masses of elevators."

"Could it be done?"

"You couldn't run water up to the top stories. Not directly. At that height, the weight of the water in the pipes would break them. You'd need a succession of storage tanks and pumping stations."

"Could it be done?"

It was at that moment Matthias realized that all he wanted now was at hand, that his father need not go into an old folks' residence, that his brother might be spared ending up a derelict, that the family firm might not have to disappear into the files of the city archives.

"Yes."

"My favorite word."

"You'd need a fantastic engineer. Like Fazlur Kahn, who did Sears Tower. Unfortunately, he's gone now."

"An engineer, sure. And a doorman. But most of all, I need an artist. The whole world's going to be looking at this. It should be art. Great art. What do you think Cudahy, Brown would come up with if I asked them for art, for a real world-stopping dramatic statement?"

"A building like the one we're in. With a big red 'P' on top."

Poe knocked the two building blocks down, the effect as startling as when he'd put the one on top of the other.

He smiled. "These are just toys. I want art. I'm not offering you anything right now. I'm not promising you anything. But I'd sure as hell like to see what you might come up with. When I got clear of that storm on my way home today, I took my chopper up the lakefront to look at your building again. It's fucking terrific. The only thing wrong with it is that it's too small."

Matthias kept the irony to himself. The whole point of that building was that it managed to be something special in a relatively small space.

"My firm, my father's firm. There are just two employees. Cudahy, Brown has three hundred. You'd need the backup of a staff like that for a project of this magnitude."

"I'm not talking blueprints, specifications, stress estimates, all that bullshit. I just want a drawing. You do drawings. Do me one. I'll give you a week. Then we'll talk."

"Mr. Poe . . ."

"It's Peter. Like I say. I'm not offering you a thing, although I'll pay you for your time. And up or down, yes or no, the sailing deal still goes."

Matthias stared at the tabletop, his mind filled with a vision of the actual city. It might take no more than an hour or so to finish such a sketch. He was already getting an idea, something that had run through his mind years before, much as the image of Lake Point Tower must have run through Mies van der Rohe's decades before it was even a possibility.

"I'll try."

"And remember. Not a word to anyone. Not to that charming lady you brought tonight. Not even to your brother. He's a nice guy, but he talks too much."

Matthias paid no attention to this. "I can't believe how much has happened in the last few days."

"Move fast, Matthias. George S. Patton. You get where you're going with a lot fewer casualties."

In the Rolls, driving her home, Matthias asked Sally what she thought of the evening.

"They're not exactly North Shore, but he's really exciting."

That was what Matthias felt. Excited. For the first time in years.

Poe, another cigar in hand, went out onto his terrace and stood looking out over the lake. Diandra came to the doorway behind him.

"Do you want me to stay, Peter?"

"He liked you."

"I like him. He's very different from most of your business associates."

"He likes art."

"He's a painter."

"Diandra. Sometime this week, call him up and ask him to take you to a museum. The Art Institute, maybe."

"Why?"

"Just do it, Diandra. Be nice to him."

"All right, Peter. If that's what you want."

Upon returning to his hotel room, Zany called his wife, who told him that the dishwasher had broken and that her brother had called from Wyoming to say he'd be bringing his family out for a two-week visit again that August. A call to Sergeant Hejmal had produced the news that the radio had gone out in one of the police cars and that the State Police were going through some of the beach towns to the north and south looking for prospective fiends who might have killed the girl in the boat. Also, the district attorney had been on the phone three times asking if Zany had found out anything in Chicago.

"Tell him no arrests yet," Zany said, but Hejmal didn't get the sardonic humor.

After that, Zany took a shower and put on a clean shirt, then went out for a walk and dinner. The neighborhood was full of restaurants, but few he could afford. He settled on a pizza joint, ate more than he should have, had two beers instead of one, and then continued with his walk. Something was worming around in the back of his mind but he couldn't bring it forth. He wished he had his computer. He had come to use it in his work, feeding into it his thoughts and ideas and suspicions and mixing them up with evidence. He'd been able to locate and bust up that marijuana operation in Grand Pier that way.

Returning to his hotel, he found a message in his box from Detective Plotnik in Area Six Burglary. Zany went immediately to the pay phone in the hotel lobby.

"I think I may have something for you, Zany," Plotnik said, after another cop had fetched him from the men's room. "I thought it would be weeks before anything turned up, but sometimes you get lucky. You know, life is fucking strange."

It was Plotnik's favorite saying.

"How fucking strange this time?"

"Remember that weirdo burglary call I told you about? The broad in Old Town who thought one of her apartments might have been gone over by cops? Well, she called in a missing persons earlier tonight. Her tenant. Gone more than twenty-four hours. I mean, you know we wouldn't put something like this real high on the stack. I mean, shit. Gone twenty-four hours? A single broad? In Old Town? Wowee. But the description she filed. The tenant works for an art gallery, and she's supposed to be a looker. It made me think of the case you're working. I tried to get Mulroney and Stacek on it but they're out on this O'Rourke thing, looking for hookers." He laughed, a rumbling chuckle.

"Did you show her the photo I left you?" Zany asked. "The girl who turned in the missing persons?"

"Well, you know, it took awhile for the report to get over to us. I called the broad with the apartment as soon as I put it together, but there was no answer. I had a beat patrol stop at the residence address, but same thing. No one on the premises. Maybe she got spooked or something. Who the hell knows? You know, it's Old Town. Anyway, let me give it to you. Maybe you can stop by in the morning."

Zany wrote down the name, phone number, and address. Ruth Anne Mazureski. The missing girl's name was Jill Langley. She worked for the Laurence Train gallery on Michigan Avenue, and had been on her way there when the Mazureski woman had last seen her.

"You still have the photo, right?" Zany asked.

"Yeah, sure. Right here on my desk."

"I'm going to borrow it back," Zany said. "I'll be right over."

He drove his car fast, wondering if one of his former colleagues would dare hit him with a ticket. Not all Chicago cops were his friends. Plotnik had nothing more to report. He put the photo, embellished now with a small catsup smear, into a Chicago Police Department envelope, and handed it to his old pal.

"I'm off at midnight. You want to stop for a cold one?"

"Better not," Zany said. "I've got a lot to do and they want me back in Grand Pier tomorrow."

"Next time, maybe."

Mulroney and Stacek were still out on their big case. Zany used Mulroney's phone to try the Mazureski girl again, but got no answer. Speeding again, he went to the Old Town address, but got no response then, either. For a tempting moment, he thought of working the lock and taking a look inside, but decided against it. For all he knew, the Mazureski woman was sitting inside in the dark, scared shitless and holding a gun. Or she might come in and find him there, and he'd end up having to talk the Chicago P.D. out of breaking and entering charges.

Next he went over to the Curland house on Schiller Street, wanting the museum guy to take a good look at the photo, but no one answered and all the lights were out. As he headed back toward Lake Shore Drive, the half-formed thought at the back of his mind suddenly came to the fore. Stopping beneath a street light, he pulled the photograph out of the envelope.

It was her. The girl in the photo was the girl he had seen in the painting in the man's dining room. The nude. Painted by him. Matthias Curland.

He started to turn back toward the house, then stopped. He might end up waiting around outside Curland's door all night. Guys who painted nudes must pass their nights at all kinds of places. Instead, he drove over to the Train gallery, which upon arriving he realized was completely stupid. At this hour, it was of course closed. He stared at some of the paintings on display in the windows, then sighed in resignation and headed for his hotel. Everything would have to wait for morning, and why not?

None of these people were going anywhere, least of all Jill Langley, if that proved to be who was lying in his county morgue.

He was a very tired man by the time he swung open the door to his hotel room, but the longtime cop in him came instantly to life. Something was wrong. Things had been rearranged. His closet door was open. He recalled closing it before he left. One of the dresser drawers was open. His briefcase on top of the dresser was wide open.

His tape recorder and Polaroid camera had been taken. So had his pocket calculator and an expensive pen and pencil set his wife had given him as a birthday present but he always left in his briefcase unused for fear of losing them.

And the bloodstained painting—*Das Rot Turm*—was gone.

CHAPTER

4

SALLY HAD STAYED the night, having somehow persuaded her baby sitter to do the same at her place. She lay cozily in Matthias's arms and talked for a long time after their lovemaking about the future. She saw Peter Poe as a turn of fortune for the both of them. Matthias had not noticed, but sometime during the evening Poe had suggested to her that she might quit her little boutique and come to work for the foundation he had established earlier in the year. It was only in its formative stages, but he said he had great plans for it, and needed someone like Sally to help organize the various charity events he intended to hold under its auspices. He had mentioned a salary more than three times what she was earning at her shop. Matthias had drifted into sleep as she was going on about how they both could now resume their proper place in Chicago society.

His own visions were of buildings and, for a fleeting moment before total slumber, of Diandra Poe, walking, turning, her clothes flowing around her. Beauty in motion. Beauty as motion.

And that mind, thoughts as cool and clear as her words, thoughts shared only with the sky so splendidly reflected in her light-blue eyes.

Sally left him shortly after sunrise, waking him gently to say good-bye. Matthias was back to sleep before she closed the door behind her, not stirring until hours later. When he did get up, he was perspiring, and found the advancing day filled with heat. He was quite groggy and dizzy, having had two more brandies after the one he'd accepted at the Poes'. No crime in that, except that he had promised himself he'd have only one, and had gone to bed wanting yet one more.

Zany had to ring the bell of the Schiller Street house several times before someone finally came to the door. It was the fair-haired older brother he had talked to the day before, looking about as pleased as someone opening their door to a swarm of bees.

They stood staring at each other briefly, both of them blinking. The sunlight was intense.

"Sorry to bother you again, Mr. Curland," Zany said, "but I'm afraid I need to talk with you some more."

"I don't understand. I don't know what more I could possibly tell you."

"I think a lot, maybe. Could I come in?"

His eyes went from Matthias's unshaven face to his rumpled bathrobe to his bare feet.

"If it's that important." He opened the door fully and admitted Rawlings, gesturing for him to go on into the living room.

"Thank you."

"Let me get a little more presentable," Matthias said. "I'll be right down."

While he waited, Zany went into the dining room to look again at the nude on the wall. Curland joined him there, now clean shaven and wearing a white shirt and a pair of khaki shorts. His feet were in a well-worn pair of boating shoes. His legs and ankles were very tan, as tan as the dead woman's, what you'd expect from someone who did a lot of sailing.

Zany took a large white envelope out of the briefcase.

"That girl in the painting," Zany said. "Is her name by any chance Jill Langley?"

"Yes, it is. How did you know that?"

Rawlings took a photograph from the envelope, handing it to Matthias.

"Is this Jill Langley?" he said.

Curland stared at the picture. He seemed truly horrified.

"Yes," he said. There were tears in his eyes.

"I guess you get the idea, then. She's the girl we found in the boat."

Curland's hands were trembling. "Yesterday, after you said it was a young woman who'd been killed, I had this strange feeling that it might be her."

"Why's that?"

"I don't know. I called her. There was no answer. I told myself I was being ridiculous. I thought, if something had happened to her, we would have heard. She worked for a friend of my brother's. She used to work for us."

"You look kind of pale. Are you all right, Mr. Curland?"

121

"No."

"Maybe you should sit down."

Curland looked about, then went into the living room, still clutching the picture. He seated himself clumsily on the couch, then managed to put the photo down on the coffee table before him.

"You knew her pretty well?"

"Yes. Where—where is she?"

"In a morgue back in Michigan. It's part of the local hospital."

"Do you want me to come out and identify her? Officially?"

"You've kind of done that already, Mr. Curland. Anyway, I got a hold of her family this morning. Her father's coming out."

"They'll be devastated. Devastated. She was their only child. A very special girl. Very special. Lovely."

The last words were mumbled. Rawlings studied him with great seriousness.

"I've been pretty busy, Mr. Curland," he said finally. "I've learned that Miss Langley worked for an art gallery, owned by somebody named Laurence Train. Is that your brother's friend?"

"Yes."

"She apparently went there the night she was killed. Train doesn't know why she came in or where she went afterward. He said he doesn't know anything about any missing paintings, or copies of paintings. How long did she work for you?"

"More than five years."

"Did she have access to your vault, the one we were in yesterday?"

"Yes. When she worked for us."

"Do you own a sailboat, Mr. Curland?"

"Yes. Technically, that is. While I was in Europe, my brother leased it to someone—a lease with an option to buy. I had no control over it."

"The boat's named the *Hillary*?"

"Yes."

"We've got it over at Grand Pier. It's a little shot up, but it floats. Time of death we figure to be sometime after midnight on Friday. Were you in Chicago, Mr. Curland?"

"No, I wasn't. I was in New York. I stopped off to see my ex-wife. I didn't get here until early afternoon."

"You have a plane ticket receipt to show that?"

"Yes. I'll get it if you want."

"If you wouldn't mind."

Still shaky, Curland got to his feet and went into the library, digging the receipt out of a desk drawer.

Zany examined it carefully, then handed it back. "Your brother, Christian Curland. Do you know where he was that night?"

Matthias was staring at the photograph. "I'm not sure. Possibly with some friend—a woman, probably. Mr. Rawlings, please. We were the closest friends Jill had in Chicago."

"Right. Did Miss Langley have a key to the boat or something? The hatch cover was unlocked, not broken open."

"I used to keep a spare key in the bilge, in one of those plastic cases with a magnet. She knew about it. She had the use of the boat while I was gone—when I moved away, I left it here so she could use it—until my brother leased it."

"She was from Wisconsin?"

"Yes. Her father's a doctor. She studied art history here at Northwestern. She went to work with us after she got her master's. She could have done better. We were very grateful to have her, but she was wasting her life with us. She was wise to move on. It would have been better if she had left Chicago."

"So it would seem. Why did she go to work for Train?"

"I think for more money. My family has experienced some reverses."

"You seem real upset, Mr. Curland. How well did you know this girl?"

"Very well. As I said, we were very close."

"How close?"

Curland's eyes went back to the picture. "I should be honest with you. We had a love affair. If it had happened at a different time, a better time . . . I was fond of her. Very fond of her." He wiped at his eyes. "But I haven't talked to her in a long time. We wrote some letters, but that's not quite the same."

Zany took out a notebook and jotted down something. "Well, Mr. Curland, I'm a little curious about all this. We found her on your boat. She had one of your—she had that copy of one of your paintings, if that's what it is. Best we can determine, she had it wrapped around her body, like she was stealing it. Or hiding it."

"But it was only a copy. *The Red Tower*'s still in the museum vault. You saw for yourself."

"Yeah. Curious as hell. What's even more curious is that someone broke into my hotel room while I was out last night. They took a bunch of stuff, but they took the painting, too."

"Why would anyone want it?"

"I don't know. Usually when thieves work a hotel, they hit several rooms. Make the risk worth their while. But the hotel security guys told me they had no other incidents—and seldom do. Kind of strange. Where were you last night, Mr. Curland?"

"I went to dinner with some people. The Poes. Peter Poe."

"The billionaire?"

"I guess he's that."

"Who else was there?"

"Just Poe and his wife. And a friend of mine. Sally Phillips."

Zany wrote all this down. "Did you happen to mention to anyone that we'd talked? That I had the painting? Where I was staying?"

"As a matter of fact, I think I did."

"How long did you stay there?"

"I'm not sure. Until after midnight."

"No one left before that? While you were there?"

"No. Absolutely not."

Zany studied his notebook a moment, then put it away and stood up. "Thanks. I guess that's all for now. Is your brother coming back soon?"

"I've no idea where he is."

"I'd really like to talk to him."

"Is there somewhere he can reach you?"

"I'm kind of moving around. I'll call him later."

"Should I go back with you? To Michigan?"

"No need of that. Probably not a good idea. Her father, well, he didn't speak too highly of you people."

Curland stared at the floor a moment, then rose, following Rawlings to the door.

"It's funny," Zany said, glancing at Matthias again. "You're dressed exactly the same way she was, when we found her."

"I don't understand."

"It's nothing. Just an observation. I'm paid to notice things. You get in the habit. Well, thanks again, Mr. Curland. You really don't look too well. Maybe you ought to lie down or something."

* * *

124

When Rawlings had gone, Matthias did as the man suggested, falling back on his couch, but sleep did not come. His compulsion to do something—anything—agitated him. His overwhelming need was to talk to Christian, but there was little point trying to find him. He'd return soon enough from wherever his indulgence had taken him. This wrenching news was nothing he wanted to share with Sally. The myriad unanswered questions batting around his brain were beyond his capability of sane thought.

He needed escape, distraction. He considered a long, hard walk along the lake, but the heat was too forbidding. In the past, when he was upset, he would throw himself into work, but there wasn't any.

Or was there? Poe had written him a check for two thousand dollars—a week's wages for services as yet unrendered. He was still unsure that he wanted to be the man's sailing instructor. But the prospect of the new building had hooked him deep. His mind had been shaping lines and forms even as he had gone to the door to answer Rawlings's ring. He'd been given a week to produce a drawing. He had work—and then some.

He heaved himself off the couch and up the stairs, going to the small room that had been converted to a studio. After unearthing a sketch pad from the clutter on the drawing table, he flipped through to a clean sheet and picked up a pencil.

A square of emptiness before him, like the sky, like the rest of his life. Steadying his hand, he drew a line. He paused, then drew another.

Drinking coffee, forgetting food, smoking his pipe, trying to push away every thought and memory of Jill, Matthias worked well into the afternoon, but with increasingly desperate frustration. The idea he'd had looked marvelous, but he knew it wouldn't work. He tried others, with less success, then went back to the original. He got it so it made more sense, but it was far from satisfactory. And nothing he sketched could obscure the vision of death in the photograph, of Jill's eyes, staring blankly out at him. His lines became mad snarls. He tore out sheet after sheet, each attempt more ruinous than the other. The pad exhausted, he found another and tried again. And again and again.

Finally, after forcing himself to a long moment of absolute stillness, he set the pencil to paper with a gentler, much different stroke. At last he found solace. He began drawing sailboats.

* * *

Diandra Poe remained late in bed. She was normally an early riser—a habit from her modeling days, when mornings required so much elaborate preparation—but she wanted to be alone with her thoughts, without having her husband's break-of-day brainstorms intruded upon them. She had slept as usual in the nude, and lay after waking with the covers thrown back to enjoy the soft warmth of sunshine on her bare skin, examining her memories of the night before at leisure.

She had liked Matthias Curland—as much for his beautiful manners and the respect he had shown for her intelligence as anything. She had no objection to carrying out her husband's instructions to be nice to the man. Being Peter Poe's wife was her career now, and this sort of thing was just part of the job.

But he'd left how "nice" up to her interpretation and discretion, and she was intrigued by the prospect. She was very curious as to how and why Peter intended to use this well-bred, sensitive man, whether he had some immediate purpose or wanted Curland just to hold in reserve for one of his infinite number of future schemes. Peter was always thinking months ahead. None of his successes ever came as a surprise to him.

There had to be more to it than the office-apartment tower her husband was planning for his new development. Curland wasn't an active architect and hadn't been very successful when he was. The Peter Poe style was to hire the very best—the top. He already had one of the city's biggest and most prestigious architectual firms on retainer.

Rising finally, Diandra spent a long time in her bath, devoting the time as much to thought as ritual preparation. She dressed casually—for her—a summery lime-green dress with matching low-heeled shoes, just dressy enough should she decide to go shopping on the avenue, one of her several escapes from boredom. Then she went into her own study, which, though half the size of her husband's, contained considerably more books.

Among them was a copy of the *Social Register,* which Peter had given her but which she had rarely consulted. There was a listing for a Rudolph Curland in Lake Forest, with the names and addresses of three grown children following: Mrs. Annelise Blucher of Barrington; Matthias Curland of Cannes, France; Christian Curland of Schiller Street in Chicago.

The dark-haired brother had been in the Poes' penthouse twice, though never for dinner or any formal social occasion. He was extremely handsome, and had flirted with her. She supposed it was out of habit and, in any event, wasn't much interested. There was a snottiness about him. His glances were as mocking as they were suggestive, implying he knew very well she was not a fashionable lady at all, but merely the daughter of a factory foreman from Dearborn, Michigan, all dressed up like a lady. A factory foreman named Casimir Derwinski.

Diandra had few real friends in Chicago, though she'd been approached by many who wanted to be hers. They were more like Bitsie Symms and Sally Phillips than any of the old-line aristocrats to be found in the *Social Register.*

If she called Bitsie to ask about Matthias Curland, the woman would tell her everything she thought Diandra wanted to hear, even if she had to make up some of it. And afterward, she'd probably spread a lot of gossip about Diandra's inquiry. There was no telling how Sally Phillips would react to any questioning about her "beau"—the word she'd used when they'd been alone together after dinner. Probably she'd think Diandra was being predatory—though it should be obvious that the wife of Peter Poe had no more safe chance at infidelity than a wife of Henry VIII.

There were a number of small magazines published in Chicago, among them a failing but very social monthly that covered all the Gold Coast and North Shore parties. Peter had considered buying it, until his lawyer, Bill Yeats, had counseled against it with the warning that people would assume he was going to use it to assist him in social climbing—which was among the least of Peter's ambitions concerning Chicago.

The editor and chief reporter was a very nice if somewhat prim lady who'd been very pleasant and helpful to Diandra, keeping her company at not a few terrifying social affairs when no one else would approach, offering advice, asking no favors, and, in her reportage, treating the Poes at face value as major if newly arrived celebrities. She'd never once published any untoward gossip about them.

Diandra's call found her at work on a story about Bitsie's party. They talked about that for a few minutes until, hesitantly, Diandra got to her real purpose.

"We met a man at the party," she said. "An architect named Matthias Curland. My husband was quite taken with him. He's thinking of having him help with a project, but I don't know anything about him."

"Matthias Curland? He's one of the nicest men in town—or used to be, when he lived here. He went off the deep end a little after his divorce, *la vie bohème,* if you know what I mean. Is he moving back? I thought he'd just come home for his mother's funeral."

"I'm not sure. Are they old-time Chicagoans, the Curlands?"

"Well, not so much the Curlands; not on his father's side. But on his mother's side, he's an Albrecht—and they predate the Fields and the Potter Palmers, not to speak of all the farm tool and meat packing families. Very prominent indeed, in the old days. But, well, there are a lot of nice families who happen to be German-American. But the Albrechts were very German, if you know what I mean. They still are. And they have this streak. Not that they're demented or anything, but they're a little odd."

Diandra didn't want to explore this—not yet. Her husband hadn't acquired Curland because he was odd.

"But they're what you'd call Old Money?"

"Not just that. They've always been so very civic minded. Albrechts and Curlands have been on just about every important charity board there is. Plus the forest preserves and the Park District and God knows what else. They were going to name a park after Matthias's grandfather, but he refused to let them do it. I guess he thought they were only honoring his money. He should have been president of the Art Institute. Everyone said that. But he had this thing for German art, and he wouldn't give them anything from his collection. He kept it all for that little museum of theirs—you know, the Albrecht Collection?"

Diandra pretended she knew.

"He's part of the establishment, then," she said. "Matthias. Mr. Curland."

"Well, he could be. They all could. But . . . let me put it this way. Their name is still revered by the old families of Chicago, especially in Lake Forest. If they were to become active socially again, they could be right at the top. But, Diandra, they haven't a penny. All the money's in that museum, and they can't touch that. I really don't know how they've been surviving, although there are some stories about Matthias's brother, Christian. Well, I won't go into that."

"Matthias Curland came to Bitsie's party with someone named Sally Phillips."

"Sally's very nice. Not from a prominent family. I don't think she even made a debut, though her mother was quite a climber.

She has to work, you know. Runs a little boutique. Very nice, but . . . well, there are a lot of very available women around who could make Matthias much more comfortable. She threw him over for a truly awful man. If they're seeing each other again . . . well, I suppose some might say she was crawling back to him. She's very sweet, and it's very romantic to think of them together again. But I don't see how it could work—not unless he comes into some money. She—she likes nice things, if you know what I mean."

"Well, I was just curious," Diandra said.

"Can I print it that your husband's hired him to be his architect?"

Peter wouldn't like that. He liked to make all such announcements with a grand show.

"Why don't you just say that they talked about architecture?"

"I'll do just that. Diandra, are you going to be modeling in the hospital fashion show again?"

"I suppose, though they haven't asked me yet."

"Well, I'm sure they will. I'd like to see you more active, Diandra. Socially, I mean. Just remember what I said. Don't get involved with one of the diseases. Anyone can throw a ball for a disease. In Chicago, it's the institutions that count."

Institutions. The Establishment. What Matthias Curland, broke as he might be, thoroughly represented. No wonder Peter was so interested in him. He had enough trouble getting people like that to invite him to their clubs, let alone come to work for him.

But Peter's principal obsessions were money and political power. Curland didn't seem to represent that.

Diandra thanked the woman for her advice and information, saying she'd see her at the Gold Coast garden festival, if not before. After hanging up, she sat a moment at her desk, then took out one of her Art Institute note cards, one bearing a landscape by Monet. Her husband would prefer her using his household stationery, embossed with a great crimson "P," but she hated that.

She addressed him as "Mr. Curland," though she'd called him Matthias the night before. She wrote to ask if she might visit his museum, and invited him to lunch. At their penthouse. If she asked him to a restaurant, he'd probably insist on paying.

Would Peter like this? She was never sure.

* * *

129

Zany spent much of the day around Chicago's downtown water-front, showing his picture of the dead girl to the few boaters and fisherman he found there on this weekday, getting little that was helpful in response. He worked the place for several hours, as more and more boaters showed up—many of them obviously sneaking away early from work. None of them recognized Jill Langley, but one did say he'd seen a girl running along the dock the night of the murder. She'd been wearing shorts and a white blouse.

"She jumped into a sailboat and took off on the motor, without rigging the sails," the man said. "It seemed funny that she was in such a hurry."

"Was anyone chasing her?"

"No. Well, a few minutes later this guy came running up. He stood there looking at the empty berth and then went away. He sure seemed in a hurry. Was the boat stolen?"

"So to speak. Did you get a good look at him?"

"No, sir. Too far away. Except he was wearing a white shirt, a dress shirt, and it was unbuttoned. It wasn't that hot a night."

"No gunshots or anything?"

"Gunshots? No. Hey, does this have anything to do with . . . There was a story on the news . . . Is this the girl who was murdered?"

"Yes."

"Shit. Murder up in Lincoln Park. Murder here. Makes you afraid to come near the lakefront."

Zany took the man's name and address and thanked him, then walked over to the yacht club. The frowning maître d' in the dining room said he'd not seen anyone like the girl on the prem-ises. Neither had he seen either of the Curland brothers, quietly adding that they were not members.

Using a dockside pay phone, Zany tried reaching Christian Curland again, but without success. Matthias Curland, sounding a little distracted, promised to have his brother call Zany at his hotel.

Sure he would. Zany wondered what Peter Poe might have to say about the interesting dinner party in which the name of a Grand Pier, Michigan, cop's hotel came up in conversation. He got the number of Poe's office from information. The woman who answered transferred him to a secretary, who handed him off to another, who told him Poe was out of town in Indiana and wouldn't return until late.

Zany had a couple of beers in a Rush Street bar, deciding it was time to call it quits for the day. He'd make one last stop: Area Six homicide.

Baldessari was not happy to see him.

"As you might fucking notice," he said as Zany walked into his office, "we're up to our ass in whores here. I must have questioned two dozen of them myself."

The entire squad room was filled with short-skirted women, some of them looking very belligerent.

"The mayor wants an arrest," Baldessari continued. "I may have to book one of these broads just to say we're making progress—if we can find one that's a tall blonde with real good legs. One of the girls said she saw a hooker like that up on Broadway get into a station wagon with O'Rourke's plates. No one she knew. They came back a few minutes later and picked up the black chippie who got whacked with O'Rourke. For a guy his age, he must have been quite the stud."

"Can you give me five minutes?" Zany said. "I'm making a little progress in my own case."

Baldessari looked at his watch. "Okay, Zany. You got ten." The lieutenant took a sip of coffee and lighted up a Marlboro.

As quickly as possible, Zany told him all he'd learned.

"I've got a real itch about this guy Matthias Curland," he said. "There are just too many connections. He had something going with the Langley girl before he left town. He told me himself that he slept with her. Hell, he did a nude painting of her that he's got hanging over his dining-room table. That's an intense relationship. And he seemed scared when I talked to him. Real scared."

Baldessari stared at him through his cigarette smoke. "He showed you an airline ticket, you said."

"Yes, he did. But . . . This is more than I can handle on my own, Frank. You promised me Mulroney and Stacek, but you've got them working this Lincoln Park murder. I'd like to go through the gallery records. I'd like to talk to Peter Poe, and to the brother, Christian Curland. But I have no jurisdiction here, and I've got to get back to Grand Pier. I was hoping you might be willing . . ."

Baldessari suddenly leaned forward, his chair giving out a loud squeak. "Zany, do you know how high up I'd have to go to have people like the Curlands or Peter Poe brought in for questioning? Do you know how far they'd kick my ass when I told them that all I was going on was these weird suspicions of yours? I mean, what do you got, Zany? You've got shit. You haven't even established the scene of the crime. You've got no murder weapon. You've got no witnesses. The only crime we know was committed in Chicago was the girl's theft of the boat. Did you go over the boat for fingerprints?"

"The State Police did. Outside of this dentist's who was leasing it, the only match they made was with the girl's."

"Zany. I'm beginning to think you've spent too much time on the beach. What about the break-in of your room? There's a crime. Can't you get burglary to help you with that?"

"Plotnik sent some evidence technicians over. Everything was clean. No witnesses. A real pro. Or pros."

"Not your architect friend."

"Like I told you, he was with Poe. Along with Poe's wife and another woman."

"You think they all decided to waltz over to your hotel and lift your shit? Just for fun?" He was joking. Zany couldn't always tell.

"Frank, please."

"Zany, your ten is up and the clock's still running. If you could show me evidence that this homicide took place somewhere inside the Illinois line, I might get something going on it—after I produce something for City Hall on this O'Rourke case. But the way it is, I barely got time to call my wife. If you want to talk to Poe and the Curland brother, it's a free country. But I can't help you on that. Even if I could, I think you're way up the wrong fucking tree." He stood up. "Sorry, Zany."

"Okay, Frank. I understand your situation."

"You want to sit in while we chat with the rest of these chippies?"

"No, thanks. I'm dealing with a better class of people."

"They're all the same, Zany. That's the first thing you learn."

Poe owned seven hotels, four of them in Chicago. He was sitting in the lobby of one of the cheapest, reading a sailing magazine, glancing up whenever anyone entered.

The hotel, just north of the Loop, was marginally respectable, patronized by second-rate businessmen, tourists on bargain tours, and the occasional couple in for a quickie. The policy Poe had set for the management was to keep out the cheap whores from off the street, but to let higher-priced call girls work the place if they didn't make trouble. He'd been sitting in the lobby for less than an hour, and already three such ladies had come through. It was only a little past nine o'clock.

The staff thought he was just checking out the operation, and were unusually courteous and efficient as a consequence. They were paying far more attention to him than to the working girls who came in.

Another swung through the door. She was tall, beautifully built and nicely dressed, though the outfit was likely an inexpensive discount knock-off.

She was blond, or at least wearing a decent wig.

Poe felt lucky. He thought he'd have to spend several nights at this.

He watched her walk. "That one," he said.

The man next to him put down his newspaper. "Okay. You're sure she's a hooker?"

"She's not here for the Junior League. When she's done, follow her. Follow her until she goes home. I want to hear from you in the morning."

"That's all?"

"For now."

Deciding to make one more stop before heading home, Zany got Detective Plotnik from burglary to go with him to Jill Langley's apartment. They had no search warrant, but the young landlady remembered Plotnik and admitted them, after taking a look at Zany's badge and police I.D. She seemed to have taken the news of the Langley girl's murder as if someone had dropped a rock on her head. She'd been drinking wine, sloppily.

"I'm going to be in deep shit, Zany, if my lieutenant catches me working a homicide," Plotnik said, once they were inside the Langley girl's apartment with the door closed.

"You're not working a homicide. You're still investigating the burglary of this apartment. Also, my hotel room. Theft of one painting, or copy thereof, slightly damaged, previously in the possession of the occupant here."

"But my partner and I already went through here," Plotnik said, waving his hand at the tumbled disorder. "We didn't find zip. We couldn't even figure out what the burglars were after, the way they've torn the place apart. Look at this mess. And if they found what they were looking for, what could be left for us?"

"There's always something," Zany said.

What there was a shoebox full of letters in the closet. It

had been knocked over, but the contents were still on the closet floor, where they'd been spilled.

Some of the letters were old. Most were from her family. Two had foreign stamps on them. The name on the Cannes return address was M. Curland. Zany glanced over one of the letters.

"Look the other way, Maurice." He slipped both letters into a side coat pocket.

"I didn't see that."

"I know."

After stopping in a Clark Street drugstore, Zany made one more call to the Curland house. He decided not to mention the letters until he had thought about their contents some more, and had had a chance to talk to Christian Curland. Matthias Curland replied that his brother still had not returned and testily repeated his promise to have the man call. Then he paused, asking if Zany had learned anything more.

"Nothing very useful, Mr. Curland."

The other's hostility diminished. "Are you sure there's nothing I can do to help?"

"Not at the moment."

"Well, let me know."

After hanging up, Zany started walking back to his hotel, then changed his direction, heading to the Curlands' Schiller Street house. He was glad he left his car in the hotel garage. Otherwise, he'd be spending all his time looking for parking places.

No one answered, though there were lights on upstairs. He rang again. When there was still no response, Zany moved across the street, stepping back into the shadows of a narrow gangway just far enough to keep the house entrance in view. After waiting more than an hour, his hunger and bladder getting the better of him, Zany gave up. If Frank Baldessari had come into the case, Christian Curland could have been picked up.

There were three messages from Hejmal waiting for Zany when he got back to his hotel, plus another from District Attorney Moran and one from his wife. Zany went to use the bathroom but put off calling room service until he had returned the calls.

Hejmal sounded uncustomarily excited. "You better get back here, Chief. We've had an armed robbery."

"What?"

"The 7-Eleven out by the highway. They really shot up the place."

"Anyone hurt?"

"No. There were three people in the store. The counter guy and two customers. The perpetrators had them lie down, then started shooting. Took $127 U.S. currency and a couple of six-packs."

"Any description? Prints?"

"No, sir. They wore ski masks and gloves."

"Ski masks and gloves? To knock off a 7-Eleven?"

"Yep. We've got the State Police on the scene, but Moran wants you out here."

Zany swore. Grand Pier had never had an armed robbery, and he hadn't worked one in fifteen years.

Two six-packs. Must have been real thirsty.

Matthias had worked through the day, pausing only for a fitful nap, which had been interrupted by one of the Michigan policeman's persistent calls. He supposed the man was only doing his job, but he didn't seem very competent at it. There was little to be gained by such harassment, unless harassment was all he had in mind. Rawlings had even come around to the house again. Matthias had seen him from the upstairs window but refused to answer the bell, hoping the policeman would just go away, which eventually he did.

Matthias tried to put him out of his mind. After all the trauma and frustrations of this long day, he was finally on to something. His idle sketches of sailboats had brought him to the threshold of an idea.

His original concept for Poe's building was a magnificently simple one. A needle—a perfect needle—circular base and circular tapering sides rising 150 stories to a pinpoint top. Some might see in it a resemblance to the obelisk that was part of the symbol of the 1939 New York World's Fair, but with such extraordinary height it was much more than that, a departure from the architectual norm so radical it might dominate the skyline for decades to come. It would identify the city in the same dramatic way that its Mississippi River arch did St. Louis, especially set so far from the cluster of high-rises that had grown up around the Loop.

The uniqueness of its silhouette and statement ought to satisfy every craving of an egoist like Poe, yet the lines were so wondrously simple. No one with an aesthetic sense could quarrel with it. There was truth in such a structure—a spiritual truth, if anything that was to serve as Peter Poe's signature on the city could be so described.

The problem was that it would not work. To accommodate the stresses, the base would have to be too wide, but the upper reaches of the building would be too narrow. The very top floors would have space for only a small apartment or two each, crammed in around the core column and the elevators, piping, and internal machinery. It simply was not economical.

He'd done more than a dozen sketches, incrementally widening the base, shortening the tower, enlarging the structure—working desperately to bring design and capacity into balance. But it was of no use. They were antithetical.

Turning to sailboat sketches for relief and release, he'd let his mind relax. The images came so easily, the sweeping lines almost leaping from his pencil. The idea arrived almost as divine revelation. He had drawn the outline of a sail. He'd hesitated, his pencil poised, then stopped, leaning back in his chair. He'd stared at the simple connection of three lines, then propped up the sketch pad and stood up, backing away.

There it was—a building, one like no other ever built, ever imagined—a flowing, curving isosceles triangle, a building shaped like a sail. The right angle joining the base and the perpendicular would be its foot, the tapering end the tack. The entire structure would curve—providing increased stability against the stresses of wind—just like a sail billowing in a beam reach. If he used glass curtain walls for the two sides, the building would play with light more magically than Lake Point Tower.

He rubbed the side of his face, pondering. Poe would want a tower, a phallic erection piercing the sky. They all wanted something like that.

Well, he could have it. Matthias could add a cylindrical tower rather like his obelisk, affixing it to the sail's front, suggesting a mast. It would be less tapered. For most of its length, it would have to be perfectly straight, but the forward edge of its base could be flared, and the segment that rose above the head of the sail could narrow, sharply, to a point.

Matthias had gone back to the table in a rush, setting his hand to rapid effort. When he'd finished it in rough, he leaned back, his chair creaking.

It wasn't quite right. The creation looked too exactly like a mast and sail. Hunching forward, he made some quick erasures, then shifted the lines—making the line of sail at the head flare sharply upward, reaching to the top of the tower, softening the juncture of tower and sail to make it more flush.

Now he sat back again. It was far from a finished drawing. There were a multitude of details to be added, but he could think of no fundamental change to be made. The concept was complete. Out of the misery of this day, he had achieved a success. Would Jill have liked it? He used to show her everything he designed. As he thought upon that, he had little doubt. He recalled that she had once suggested something like this, on an evening sail at sunset, when they were on a course paralleling the lakeshore, gazing at the sails of other boats silhouetted against the Chicago skyline.

His mind kept working. If the design were to be kept intact and the desired superheight still reached, more land would be required—a long rectangular piece of property, extending farther than the boundaries of Cabrini Green.

But what was out there? Blocks of crumbling, low-rise slum dwellings. Poe was a billionaire. He could certainly afford the additional acquisition. That consideration could be brought up later. The first requirement was to sell him on the concept.

A sound downstairs startled him. It was followed by another, the slam of the front door, and then a loud crash. Something was knocked over.

It was Christian. Matthias heard him swear and continue swearing, shading into some mad, drunken, incomprehensible soliloquy, booming loud but intended solely for himself. Matthias ignored him, even when there was another loud collision. He rested his hands on the drafting table, held himself perfectly still, waiting for this crashing about to subside.

Finally it did. The following silence was eerie. Matthias toyed with his pencil, then set it aside. There was no point in trying to continue. The only choices left to him that night were going directly to bed, going downstairs to confront, even help his brother, or leaving the house, perhaps to spend the night with Sally. He might drive up to Lake Forest.

There was a loud, ringing explosion. Then another. Matthias knew at once they were gunshots. He'd no idea Christian had a firearm in the house.

He found his brother in the dining room. Matthias looked

about the room, wondering what his brother had shot. It wasn't himself. Christian looked dazed, but otherwise unharmed, standing by the long table, gripping a chair to steady himself, a revolver dangling from his right hand. He was staring at Matthias's painting of Jill. To his horror, Matthias saw that his brother had put two bullet holes in her chest.

"Couldn't leave her like you had her, big brother," said Christian, his speech slurred. "Picture perfect. Fullness of love. Killed her, Matt. Some bastard killed her. Shot her. Shot her in your boat. She's gone. Dead and gone. Dead and gone. You can't have her anymore, Matt. Not like you had her. Can't keep her all beautiful like that, perfect on your wall. No more, big brother. She's dead. Did you hear it on the radio? Killed her. Shot her up. Girl on your boat. It was Jill."

Christian pulled free when Matthias tried to grip his arm, but he got the pistol away. Christian seemed not to notice. He stumbled over to the opposite wall and wrenched the nude from it, hurling it across the floor.

"She's dead!" He stood there, shaking.

With that last, bellowed word, the nervous energy that had sustained him drained away. His head came forward. His arms hung limply at his sides. Matthias took him in hand and steered him to the living room and a couch. Christian slumped back. Beneath heavy lids, his eyes were red and wild and crazy, but his body seemed incapable of movement now.

"Drink, big brother," he muttered. "Whiskey. Gin. Something. Anything."

"I was going to make you some coffee."

"Drink! Been drinking all bloody day. Ever since I heard on the goddamn radio. She was so fucking lovely. First class. Classic and great. Better than us, big brother. Better than either of . . . Can't have her, you can't. Not like that. Nude after Ingres. Can't. Can't."

Matthias stood helplessly as his brother began to sob, tears flooding forth. He hadn't been witness to anything like this since they were children. He sighed, then went to the kitchen and poured them both stiff whiskeys, bringing the bottle. Christian was on the brink of unconsciousness. One more drink might end the agony of his day, bringing sleep. Matthias would join him in the drinking. It probably wouldn't help, but he was going to have to get through the night somehow.

Christian leaned forward to bring the glass dripping to his lips. Then he sank back again. "She loved you, Matt."

"I know."

"Shouldn't have gone off like that, big brother, off to fucking France. Shouldn't have. That's why she's dead. 'Cause you left her."

"Shut up, Christian."

"Fuck you, big brother."

Matthias took a deep breath. "I got the news from a policeman," he said calmly, quietly. "A policeman from Michigan, where they found her. They also found a painting, a copy of one in our museum."

Christian stared into his drink, then at once his eyes sought his brother's.

"Painting."

"Copy. The painting's still in the museum. I looked. The policeman asked me some questions. He wants to talk to you, too. He needs to know where we were."

"Where we were? Where were you?"

"In New York."

"In New York, with the stuck-up Hillary."

"I told him you'd call. He's at the Days Inn by the lake."

"Days Inn? Who would stay at a Days Inn?"

"A lot of people. It has one of the highest occupancy rates in the city. He wants to know where you were."

"I was sinning, big brother. In a gambling den. Sinning and winning. Peter Poe's gambling den. In Indiana. Later I was with a woman, a most charming woman. Very charming. But I can't reveal her name. Gentleman doesn't do that."

He lurched to his feet, sticking his hands in his coat pockets, then pulling them out again.

"I have receipts," he said. "Cash slips. Quite a few. 'Nother winning night. Must find them. What is this policeman's name?"

"Rawlings. Zane Rawlings. He's the chief of police out there."

"Chief Rawlings."

Glass in hand, Christian stumbled off down the hall. Matthias heard him rummaging in the study, then speaking on the phone. He was gone several minutes.

He reappeared, standing in the doorway. "He's checked out," he said. "Went back to godforsaken Michigan."

"Sit down, Christian."

Clumsily his brother obeyed. He gulped some whiskey. Instead of putting him under, the alcohol seemed to be reviving him.

"How could Jill have a copy of that painting?" Matthias asked. "It was Kirchner's *Red Tower* from down in the vault. We're not even supposed to look at those things. We've never allowed any copying. Grandfather forbid it."

Christian blinked, trying to focus better. "Jill had a key. She never turned it in."

"The vault has a combination lock."

"The numbers were in Grandfather's files."

"How could she make a copy? Rawlings showed it to me. It was perfect. Jill wasn't that much of a painter, not a professional painter. Not that good."

"Kirchner wasn't Rembrandt. He'd be easy. You could do some of his things from memory." The slurring had vanished from Christian's speech. His eyes were less wild.

"Why would she want a copy of a Kirchner? Jill had no love for German Expressionists. She liked Impressionists, John Singer Sargent, George Bellows, Winslow Homer."

"Perhaps that's a question we should ask Larry Train."

"Why Larry?"

"He sells a lot of paintings, big brother. He doesn't put them all in his front window. A lot of his clients wouldn't know a Kirchner copy from a real Norman Rockwell. He has clients in Fort Lauderdale, Palm Springs, all over—people we'd never run into."

"Are you suggesting Larry has some scheme going to sell counterfeit paintings? Copies? And Jill was part of it?"

Christian shrugged. "Larry might not have known the source, but Jill . . . We didn't part company very amicably—thanks to you."

"I think that's the most ridiculous thing I've ever heard," Matthias said. "I think it's disgusting of you to suggest it."

"She really came to hate you, Matt. Like some wonderful wine gone sour."

"You're drunk, Christian."

"Not that drunk, not drunk enough. I must attend to that."

He took a large swallow of whiskey. His face was very pale, but he seemed much steadier. He got to his feet again, finishing his drink.

"I'm going out, Matthias."

"You've been out. All day."

"Going to take a walk. Something. Got to work things out."
He started toward the door. "Don't wait up. May not be back
tonight."

The crime scene—the shot-up 7-Eleven out by the highway—was
closed and darkened when Zany drove by, yellow police tape
placed crisscross over the door, as Zany had ordered. He proceeded directly to the police station. Hejmal, one of Zany's lady
cops, and the night dispatcher were sitting in the outer office,
drinking coffee.

"Hell of a day, boss," said Hejmal. "Here's the report and the
victims' statements. The State Police have everything else."

"We got a witness on the perps' vehicle," said the lady cop, a
hefty blond named Barbara Vaclav. "A gray van. No markings.
Maybe Indiana plates. The state cops put out an all-points, but
there've been no stops."

Zany nodded, then went to pour himself some coffee.
"Where's Moran?"

"On television," Hejmal said. "He made the late news on the
local station. Said this is all the result of Washington cutting
back on Law Enforcement Assistance Administration grants."

"I didn't know there was an L.E.A.A. anymore," Zany said,
settling down at Hejmal's desk with the report.

"Some guy from Chicago called for you, chief," Barbara said.
"Christian Curland. Said you were looking for him."

Zany set down his coffee. "Did he leave a number?"

"Nope. Said he'd call back."

"I've been trying to get a hold of that guy all day." Zany
looked at his watch, then began reading the report. The coffee,
as usual, was terrible.

The younger Curland called again just as Zany was about to
leave for home. He spoke very slowly and carefully—as drunken
drivers often did trying to sound sober.

"My brother informs me you wish to know where I was Friday
night, the night when Miss Langley was—was murdered?"

"That's right."

"May I ask why?"

"I'm a policeman. This is what we do when people get murdered. She used to work for you. We found a painting on her, a
painting in your museum. Apparently a copy. So I'm a little
curious."

"I resent, sir, the implications of your question."

"Why don't you just answer it, so we can get this over with?"

"I was at a gambling casino, in Indiana. Poe's Palace. I have cash receipts to prove it."

"You were there all night?"

Curland paused. "No. Afterward, I came back to Chicago and spent the night with a friend."

"What friend?"

"A ladyfriend."

"And who was that?"

"Sir, you must realize that, I mean, this could be a considerable embarrassment for her, were it to become public."

"Mr. Curland, this isn't very helpful."

Curland said nothing. Zany leaned back in his chair, waving a good night to Hejmal and Barbara Vaclav.

"Wait a moment," Curland said. "I'll put her on."

Zany waited. He could hear them talking in the background.

"Hello?" The woman sounded nervous.

"This is Chief Rawlings of the Grand Pier Police Department. Mr. Curland said you can verify his . . . where he spent last Friday night."

"Yes, yes, I can."

"He spent the night with you."

A pause. "Yes, yes, he did."

"May I have your name, please?"

"Is that necessary?"

"Yes."

"Christian had absolutely nothing to do with what happened. He couldn't have been. He was with me."

"Yes, ma'am. But I need your name for the record. Otherwise this is kinda pointless."

"You promise you won't reveal it to anyone unless it's absolutely necessary?"

"I'm a policeman, not a newspaper reporter. We follow procedures here. In court, if it's pertinent, your name might be made public. I can't promise you it wouldn't. But, look, Mr. Curland isn't being charged with anything. If what you say is true, there's nothing to worry about. He's not a suspect. We don't have any suspects yet. I just have to check everything and everyone out. Now, please, what is your name?"

"Very well. It's Sally Phillips."

CHAPTER

5

POE HAD LET too much business pile up unattended because of his preoccupations. Concentrating on it, he let several days pass before getting around to his first sailing lesson from Matthias Curland. Mango was still in Indiana, so he had one of his other secretaries schedule the session, for eight A.M. the next morning.

Poe found Curland there at the appointed hour, on the dock and ready to go. He was dressed in khaki shorts, a navy-blue polo shirt, and boating shoes. Poe wore white trousers, a similar shirt, a pale-blue sport coat, and loafers—clothes he customarily wore aboard his motor yacht.

"Good morning," Curland said. He sounded cheerful, but looked a little drawn and haggard, as if he'd been ill.

"Morning. Where's the boat?"

"This is it."

Curland was standing in front of a small day sailor tied fore and aft to the dock. It couldn't have been twenty feet long.

Poe frowned. "I was expecting something bigger. What the hell is that?"

"It's a Rhodes nineteen. Made by the O'Day company. Very reliable. Broad in the beam. A first-rate boat to learn on."

"It's yours?"

"I rented it."

Poe glanced about the harbor area. What would people think, seeing Peter Poe in an overgrown dinghy?

"Let's get going then." Poe went to the edge of the dock and eased himself into the cockpit of the craft. His foot slipped and he landed on the seat with a thud, causing the boat to sway.

"Next time you might want to try better shoes," Curland said, undoing the aft line. "Something like mine. Or even tennis shoes. Something with purchase on wet surfaces."

"Right," Poe grumbled. He didn't like sitting there, being told what to do.

"You might also want to take off that jacket and stow it in the cuddy."

"Cuddy?"

"That compartment forward. You can stick it in one of the sail bags."

"I'll just keep it on."

"We could get some spray. The wind's more than fifteen knots out there."

"All right."

"Or are you too cold?"

"I'm not cold."

A storm front had passed through the city the night before but the rain clouds had blown out far across the lake. It was bright and clear in the wake of the line of bad weather, with cool, brisk winds out of the north. Poe could see flicks of whitecaps out beyond the breakwater. He felt unsure, even nervous. He hoped he could keep Curland from seeing that.

Taking a winch handle from his pocket, Matthias hoisted the mainsail, which immediately commenced snapping and flapping noisily. He had the jib up a moment later. With a quick flip, he freed the bow line from the cleat on the dock, and then clambered back to the helm just as the wind began turning the boat.

"I'll take it until we get out of the harbor," he said, pulling in the mainsail a little, the boat heeling over slightly as a consequence. Poe gripped the rail.

"It's kind of rough."

"Don't worry," Curland said. "We'll stay inside the outer breakwater today."

"Not too close to the harbor."

Curland studied him. "You'd rather people didn't see us?"

Poe glowered.

"Don't worry," Curland said. "We're just another boat. No one will notice who's aboard."

They zigzagged through the armada of craft moored in the harbor. Poe was annoyed at having to shift sides with every change of tack, but did as he was told. Curland maneuvered the boat effortlessly, seemingly without giving it any thought, working both mainsail and jib by himself, explaining that the ropes that held the sails were called sheets and that the others were lines. He kept talking throughout, giving Poe the reason for everything he did.

They passed the inner breakwater at some speed. The water beyond was choppy, causing the bow began to rise and fall sharply, the rocking making Poe feel a little queasy. On the *Queen P,* you hardly felt the bow pitch, even in rough weather. It had horizontal stabilizers just under the waterline.

"Maybe this is far enough," Poe said.

"I think so. There's plenty of sailing room. Not many other boats out."

Poe wondered if that was because of the weather. Fifteen knots didn't sound as bad as the water looked. He hoped he didn't look scared.

"I want to take the controls, I mean, the tiller," he said.

"Not quite yet. First you're going to have to master the points of sail. We'll start with a run."

He went on from that through a beam reach, close reach, and close haul, pulling the mainsail in closer with each change. The last maneuver brought them into what seemed the face of the wind, though Curland said they were at a forty-five-degree angle to it. The bow plunged and bucked, colliding with the oncoming waves with big slaps of spray. The craft heeled over sharply. Curland let the mainsail out a little, and they came back to a more level attitude.

"I really don't need to ease off on the mainsail like that," he said. "The rail's not exactly under water. But I think you'll be more comfortable."

"I don't want to be more comfortable. I want to learn."

"As you wish."

After the eleventh run-through, Curland let the boat fall off into a more gentle broad reach, then had Poe change places with him.

"Take the helm," Curland said. "You try it."

Poe was a quick learner. Though he was a little timid at coming up too close to the wind, he got so he could coordinate the sail and steering without any bungling. Curland was surprised, and pleased.

"Well played, Mr. Poe."

"What?"

"Well done. You're doing very nicely."

"So now I'm ready to go out myself?"

"Not quite, but you have an idea what it's about. Next time we'll practice some man-overboard drills."

"You're going to throw me overboard?"

Matthias smiled politely. "We'll use a lifejacket or something."

"Tomorrow morning."

"All right."

"I like this."

"Good."

"How are you doing with that drawing we talked about?"

"I'm done. They're in my car."

" 'They'?"

"I did a couple. I came up with two ideas. It's not a finished presentation, but you'll see what I have in mind."

"Let's go take a look."

Curland took the helm, brought the boat smartly about, and set it on a course for the harbor entrance.

Poe was surprised to see that Curland's car was a Rolls-Royce Corniche. He'd expected a nondescript American sedan of the sort so many Chicago Old Money people drove. They never seemed to care about this form of status.

"Nice car," he said.

"It's my father's. And it's very old." He unlocked the trunk, taking out a large, flat, slightly cracked leather briefcase. He removed the first of the drawings, the one showing the obelisk-like tower.

"Very interesting," Poe said finally.

"It's just a preliminary sketch," Curland said. "A rough. But the essential idea is there."

"I've never seen anything like it."

"It has some problems."

"I like the sharp point at the top. Like a sword point. It says 'Don't fuck with me.' "

"Well, that's not exactly what I had in mind."

"Sure it is. Because that's what I had in mind. You understood."

Curland looked away.

"So what's the problem?" Poe asked.

"It's not cost effective. You have too much structure for the inhabitable space. You'd have to charge too much for the apartments."

"Why? People would pay any amount to live here. If it's the world's tallest building."

"On the lakefront, perhaps, but not at Cabrini Green."

"Let me worry about that." Poe pulled out the second drawing, eyeing it with some puzzlement. "What's this? A sailboat?"

"It's supposed to make you think of one. It's a building. It has the extraordinary height you want, but a lot of ground-level frontage as well—without sacrificing a dramatic profile. The sides would be all glass. Depending on how you situated it, there'd be fantastic effects at sunrise and sunset."

"Hmmmm."

"It looks more complicated, but this design is much more efficient than the other. You'd have a lot of apartments—and office space. The problem here is the length of the base. You'd need more property, a more linear tract. You'd have to expand your Cabrini Green holdings by at least one more block. I made the calculations."

"It has that sharp point at the top, too—just like the other." Poe put the first sketch back on top, studying it some more. "You worked these up just in the last few days?"

"Yes."

"These aren't old ideas somebody else rejected?"

"No, sir."

"Amazing. I don't know why you got out of the architecture business."

"I'm afraid my ideas cost more money than most developers ever wanted to spend. And you couldn't put buildings like this up on Michigan Avenue."

"I don't want you worrying about money."

Matthias laughed, to himself.

"I'll let you know," Poe said, rolling up the drawings.

"Do you want me to work up some specifications? I'd need some help from Cudahy, Brown."

"I don't want you to do anything just yet. And I don't want you talking to Cudahy, Brown. If I decide to go with this, I'd want to announce it with a really big splash."

"Mr. Poe. You're paying me two thousand dollars a week. I should be doing something for it, aside from teaching you how to avoid capsizing."

"You're earning your money, and if I should decide to go with this, you'll be earning a hell of a lot more." He looked at his watch. "You want me to hire your friend Sally for my foundation? Handle the charity events? Is that Jake with you?"

"She's rather good at that sort of thing, I suppose."

"Say no more. Done deal." Poe hesitated. "There's something else I need your advice on. You were on the Park District board, weren't you?"

"No. I did some design work for them once on the new Lincoln Park yacht basin, but that's all. My grandfather was on the park board. My father was on the Forest Preserve advisory board."

"They're going to need a new president—with that O'Rourke guy getting killed. I've got a little influence downtown. Who do you think I ought to back?"

"I haven't the faintest idea. I'm afraid I don't have many political opinions."

"I just don't want to see it go to somebody's bought-and-paid-for hack. I think too much of this city. You know this guy Aaron Cooperman? He's already a member of the board."

"He's a fine architect. I went to school with him."

"He's a friend of yours?"

"He used to be a good friend, but I haven't kept in touch with him much in recent years."

"A real liberal, right? Friends of the Parks? Active in Jewish charities? Independent politics? Belongs to Temple Shalom?"

"As I recall."

"And a good guy, right? Straight, honest, can't be bought? Can't be influenced?"

"He's very much that way. But he's something of a zealot about some things. Once he gets hooked on a crusade, well, he doesn't stop to consider both sides of a lot of issues."

"You like him?"

"Yes."

"Good. I'll back him."

"Just like that?"

"I tend to do everything just like that, Matthias. Keep moving. George S. Patton."

"I see."

"Diandra says she's having you to lunch tomorrow."

"Yes. I meant to mention that. She wanted to see our museum."

"Take her to see all the museums. She doesn't have anybody

to do that with." Another pause. "Maybe you could paint her picture."

"Christian's the one to do that."

"No, thanks. I heard about his, er, brushwork. But I'm serious. You could do a nude. Christian says you do great nudes."

Matthias flushed.

"Diandra's a little skinny," Poe continued, "but you could do one like, who was that guy, Botticelli?"

"Sandro Botticelli. *The Birth of Venus.*"

"Broad in a seashell. Don't look so embarrassed. She's posed like that before. Top model, you know. Think about it. See you tomorrow."

Poe strode off briskly to his waiting red limousine, the rolled-up drawings under his arm. He was surprised that Curland had been such an easy buy. In a few weeks, he'd own every molecule of the man. And he really liked the designs—both the goddamn designs. That had surprised him. Curland was damned good. The top. He owed Bitsie Symms one for this guy. Maybe he'd let her become Diandra's best friend. She was really panting after that, though Diandra sure wasn't.

Poe was smiling as Krasowski opened the limo door for him. After he attended to a couple other items, he might even find himself having a wonderful day.

Matthias sat in his car without turning on the engine, contemplating the realization that he might soon be in business as an architect again, in a very big way. He had made copies of the drawings he had given Poe, but they were irrelevant. As a composer might carry every note of a work in progress around in his mind, Matthias had memorized virtually every line of his two designs. But they were exterior lines. Unlike a portrait painter, an architect had to provide the bones and sinew that supported the flesh, had to lay out the intricate network of nerves and blood vessels that would make his creation function. The more he could accomplish on his own, the less opportunity he'd give to the mediocrities at Cudahy to distort and diminish and corrupt his concept. He had much to do, presuming Poe said yes.

He didn't want to work at home, not with the possibility of Christian coming around to peer over his shoulder, and his father's office in that dingy old building depressed him. He decided he'd use the office in the family museum. Certainly no one else was. Christian had let the security guards go shortly after Jill had left. There hadn't been a request for a tour since he'd returned to Chicago. He turned the key in the ignition.

He pulled the Rolls up behind a rusty and dented sedan that had been stripped of its wheels. If he used this place on a regular basis, he'd either have to get himself a cheap car or rely on taxis. No one was on the street. He decided he could risk leaving the Corniche there for an hour or two on this bright and sunny day.

The work did not go well. Once settled into the museum's office, he tried concentrating on the blank page of the sketch pad before him, but his eyes kept drifting to the empty desk that had been Jill Langley's. She'd left two framed pictures on it. One was a print of a Winslow Homer seacoast scene that had been a favorite of hers. The other was a photograph of the three of them—Jill standing arm in arm with him and Christian on the deck of his boat. They were all smiling.

He wondered why she had left them there, but the answer occurred to him very quickly. The picture of the three of them was symbolic. By leaving it behind, she was rejecting them.

Matthias had already done that to her.

He swiveled his chair away and stared unhappily at the shuttered window behind him. He thought again about his brother's suspicion that Jill might have been involved in a complex form of art theft or a swindle involving copies of paintings in the vault. If nothing else, it offered an explanation for her violent death. But still it didn't seem possible. Jill had always been scrupulously honest.

Matthias put aside his work and descended to the vault, opening the heavy door. Nothing appeared to have been disturbed since he and the policeman had made their visit. The box containing *The Red Tower* was just as he had left it.

When he and the Michigan policeman first examined the Kirchner, a troubling thought had occurred to him. He hadn't given voice to it, but it plagued him now. What if the shot-up canvas the Michigan policeman had recovered had actually been the original, and this one was the copy? Locked away in the vault, who'd ever check?

Working carefully, he removed the work from its protective coverings, examining the canvas carefully. It looked and felt like the original. There seemed age enough in its texture and colors and fibers. Chemicals and a microscope should be able to determine that—at least they could show whether there was reason for suspicion.

He returned the painting to its coverings and case, but set it aside without putting it back in its place on the shelf. Instead, he began wandering through the collection, pulling out a few storage cases that looked suspicious, bearing scratches that might be fresh.

In the end, he settled on four—the Kirchner, two German Expressionist works from the "Blue Rider" school, and an Egon Schiele nude. After stacking them carefully on a work table, he went back upstairs and made a telephone call to a man he knew in the Art Institute repair and restoration section.

"Matthias? I thought you were in the south of France."

"Back for a visit. I need a favor, museum to museum," Matthias said. "Analysis. I've been checking inventory. Some questions have been raised about authenticity."

"I can't imagine Karl Albrecht buying something that wasn't authentic."

"I can't either, but the records are murky, and I've got to establish legitimacy for appraisal."

"Insurance company?"

"Something like that. Four paintings are involved."

"Pardon me for asking, but can you afford the fee?"

"The endowment can take care of that. It's provided for in the will."

"Well, of course, Matt, but it'll be awhile before I can get to them. We have some cleaning work on the new Italian show coming in, and we've had some new acquisitions that are in rather sorry shape."

" 'Awhile' means what?"

"A couple weeks, three, possibly more."

"I'll bring them over now, if you don't mind. You might find a free moment."

He stowed the four cases in the Rolls's trunk, then got into the driver's seat. For a long, unsettling moment, the car refused to start. He was about to panic when, finally, with the last few flickers of energy from the old battery, the engine caught. He gunned it several times, then pulled away from the curb.

Zany had taken to working late at his little police station, sometimes well into the midnight shift. This afternoon, however, he came home early, carrying a suitcase. He'd filled it with all the files and evidence from the Jill Langley case, including material from the State Police lab and the FBI field office in Detroit. His wife was still at her shop. She was tiring of this case. Mostly she was weary of District Attorney Moran's constant phone calls. When he wasn't trying to reach Zany, some newspaper or broadcast reporter was. The Chicago media had picked up the story, including the Chicago bureau of one of the news weeklies. Moran was carrying on like he was going to be on the cover of *Time.*

Zany dropped the suitcase on the couch in the small back bedroom he'd converted into a den, then went to the kitchen and poured himself a beer. He thought he'd give himself a few minutes in which to do absolutely nothing. He pulled out two of the kitchen table's chairs, dropping himself wearily into one and propping his feet up on the other. He'd had about three sips of beer when the phone rang.

It was Hejmal.

"Something wrong?" Zany asked.

"No, Chief. It's all quiet. Why?"

"I was just wondering why you called."

"Oh, yeah. I heard from that dentist. Meyerson? He said he doesn't want his boat back. He said he's getting out of his lease with the Curlands and we should give it to them."

"I'm not ready to give it back to anyone. We've got a court order impounding it."

"Should I call him back and tell him that?"

"No."

"Should I call the Curlands and tell them?"

"No."

"Shall I go home?"

"Give it a couple more hours, and run out to the highway and back on your way."

"Okay. Like I say, Chief, all quiet."

Zany went back to his beer, finishing it standing up. He fetched another from the refrigerator and went into his den, firing up his big computer.

It was an Omega 500, with a 2-megabyte RAM and 65-megabyte hard drive and 9,600-baud modem. It wasn't quite on a level with one of the Pentagon's CRAY units out in Cheyenne Mountain, but it could do some amazing things. Zany had added extra memory and an exotic array of special program packages, including a VCR hookup. He'd already used it to great advantage, entering videotape footage of the shot-up boat taken at several angles and using the computer to determine the bullet trajectories. The angles ranged from 40 degrees to 80 degrees, meaning that some of the shots were fired nearly straight down.

As if from an aircraft—possibly a helicopter.

He snapped open the suitcase, taking out a small square envelope containing a computer disk. It contained the texts of Matthias Curland's two letters to Jill Langley. He'd given the originals to Plotnik to return to the girl's family.

Zany had read them over several times, but still couldn't make up his mind about them.

> *My dearest Jill,*
> *Your letter causes me such pain. If I thought what you ask was possible, if I thought such a life as you suggest could ever be for us, I would [UNREADABLE] to make it so. I would beg, borrow, steal to obtain the money to bring you here, to make for us what you ask.*
> *But it is not possible, as I've told you many times. I barely survive here. My choice is to live on the generosity of a few wealthy friends or to paint near pornography for the fat pig of an Arab who is now my only client. When they tire of me—or I tire of them—I have nothing. For a little while last year, I actually lived on the beach. A vagabond. There is nothing in this for you.*
> *I paint now only for myself. This means that I paint for no one. I do not know why I continue. In the beginning, I thought that, as a man walking a road, I would arrive at some destination—success, truth, discovery. Something. But there is nothing. Absolutely nothing. I continue only because to stop would be the ultimate failure.*
> *I failed my family—father, mother, brother, grandfather. I failed the architecture [UNREADABLE]. I failed Sally Phillips. I failed my wife. I failed you. I don't want to do it again.*
> > *Adieu,*
> > *Matthias*

All very ardent and passionate, maybe even desperate. The second letter was more curt.

> *Dear Jill,*
> *I understand your anger. I do not understand your desire to cause trouble for people who have done you no harm. Your grievance is with me and me alone. I wish to*

make amends with you. I have thought for a very long time upon this. I have decided that the very best thing I can do for you is to persuade you to leave us, to free yourself from our family, to make for yourself a new life.

You say Larry Train has offered you a job. Do not take it. Leave the museum, yes, for God's sake do that, but do not stay in Chicago. Go to New York, to Washington, to someplace where your marvelous talent will be appreciated and rewarded and understood. Do not waste any more of your life with us. Find someone who deserves you. God knows, I do not.

Adieu,
Matthias

Zany sat staring at the screen for a long time, blinking almost in time with the cursor. Then he put fingers to keyboard and sent the file back into its special queue.

He'd acquired something else that day—a telephone number in Pleasantville, New York, up in Westchester County just north of the city. The party's name was a Mrs. Hillary Van Winkle. He'd tried her several times, but there'd been no answer. Finally her husband had answered, saying she wasn't at home. Zany told him what he wanted, emphasizing that he needed to ascertain Matthias Curland's whereabouts that Friday evening because it pertained to a homicide investigation, and asked the man to have his wife call him as soon as possible.

She hadn't. It was now ten-fifteen, New York time. He dialed the number one more time.

Her husband answered. She had returned. Her husband reluctantly summoned her. She picked up an extension.

She was not at all friendly. "It's a late hour to be calling, don't you think, or is this some kind of emergency?"

Zany got directly to the point. "Mrs. Van Winkle, your husband, uh, ex-husband, Matthias Curland, he said he was with you in New York last Friday night. It's pertinent to an investigation we're undertaking and I wonder if you can verify that."

There was silence. Zany heard breathing on the phone. He wasn't sure it was hers.

"What's this about? You told my husband there was a murder?"

"Yes, a homicide investigation. We're just trying to determine where a number of people were that night. The victim was known to your, to Mr. Curland."

"Who was it?"

"A former employee. A young woman named Jill Langley."

"Jill Langley?" She sounded quite shocked.

"Yes. Did you know her?"

There was another long silence. "Yes, I knew her. You might say she's the principal reason I'm no longer married to Mr. Curland."

"I see."

"What happened to her?"

"She was shot."

"God."

"Mr. Curland was with you then? That Friday?"

"No," she said finally. "He didn't come here."

"He wasn't in New York?"

"I don't know where he was. He called me a day or so before that and said he was in New York, so I suppose that's where he was. Are you telling me you think he killed Jill? In Michigan, did you say?"

"I'm not saying anything of the kind, Mrs. Van Winkle. I'm just trying to find out where Mr. Curland was last Friday night."

"Well, he wasn't with me. He called, I guess it was Wednesday, and said his mother had died and he'd just come back from France and he wanted to come up and see me. He was quite maudlin—very unhappy. I told him I didn't think it was a good idea. I'm afraid I put it quite strongly. That's the last time I talked to him. I hope I'm not getting him in any trouble telling you this, but that's the last I heard from him."

"You're sure?"

"Quite."

"Are you from Chicago, Mrs. Van Winkle?"

"I'm from here. I lived in Chicago for a few years, but I wish I hadn't. Is there anything else?"

"Well . . ."

"Good night, then."

Zany stared stupidly at the receiver in his hand, then slowly returned it to its place. The telephone instantly rang, like something ignited. Startled, Zany let it ring again, then picked up the receiver.

It was his dispatcher. "Got a call from Chicago homicide, Chief. A Lieutenant Baldessari. Wants you to get back to him right away."

"Okay. Thanks. Still quiet tonight?"

"Yeah. Well, there was a beach party kinda gettin' out a hand. Sent Zaluski and Meyer down to give 'em some words to the wise."

"Okay. Night."

Baldessari sounded very excited when Zany finally reached him. "We got our hooker in the O'Rourke case, Zany. A real looker. Tall blonde, name of Margaret Kozak."

"And you wanted me to be the first to know?"

"That's the good news. Guess what's the bad news."

"She didn't do it?"

"She did it, all right. We found a roll of U.S. currency and one of O'Rourke's business cards in a drawer in her apartment. Her prints were on both. So were O'Rourke's."

"How'd you find her?"

"On a tip. Anonymous caller. A woman. We figure it was another hooker. Turned her in to cool the heat on the street."

"What's the bad news?"

"Somebody whacked her before we got there. Made her a new mouth. Damn near cut her head off."

"Rough town you got there."

"It's a messy-looking crime scene."

"So all your troubles are over—except for the new homicide."

"We can take our time with this one—I mean, we can be real thorough. Downtown figures it was her pimp, or somebody's pimp. Icing her for picking on such a well-connected john stirring up too much trouble on the street."

"What do you think?"

"Sounds good to me."

"Well, congratulations, Frank. I was hoping you'd be calling with something that would be of help to me."

"Zany, I gotta tell you, there was some stuff in her place—hot stuff, I think. Polaroid camera, tape recorder, pen and pencil set. Stuff that fits a certain burglary report."

Zany's eyes were fixed on the blinking cursor of his computer screen. His brain was functioning much the same way.

"The pen and pencil set," he said. "Black and gold? Montblanc?"

"You got it."

"I didn't do it, Frank. My wife gave me that set. If it was me, I wouldn't have left that behind."

"Chrissake, Zany, nobody's made you on this. What we were

wondering, though—when you were here—you entertain any hookers in your hotel room?"

"Come on, Frank."

"Seriously."

"Seriously. I was working my case. I was up with you guys that night."

"And where else?"

"Walking around. Driving around."

Baldessari said nothing.

"I had nobody in my room, Frank. Not even room service," Zany said. "Just a burglar."

"I'm sure you're not bullshitting me, Zany, but we gotta wrap this one up real neat and tidy. Can you come out tomorrow and see if you can I.D. the dead chippie? Someone you might have seen somewhere around your hotel? I gotta get a sworn statement, too—before you can get your shit back."

"Thanks, Frank."

"I know how you are about stiffs, Zany. We'll cover up her throat or something."

"You didn't find a rolled-up painting there, did you? Couple bullet holes through it?"

"No such luck."

"I'll be out in the morning, Frank."

His wife came in just as he hung up the phone. She set a fresh cold beer on his desk, then stood with her hand on his shoulder.

"Something wrong?" she asked.

"It was Frank Baldessari. He wants me to come out tomorrow and look at a murder victim. They recovered the stuff from my briefcase. Including the pen you gave me."

"That's close to being a miracle."

"A real funny one." Zany put his hand on top of hers. "I'm going to have to go back there tomorrow. You don't mind, do you, Judy?"

"No, as long as you're not planning to make that a permanent arrangement. I like it out here."

"I'll be back as soon as I can."

CHAPTER 6

DIANDRA HAD LUNCH served out on the north terrace of Poe's penthouse, guiding Matthias to a chair with a view of Lake Michigan.

He kept his eyes on her. She was perfectly dressed—very proper but extremely fashionable and feminine in a chic white designer dress with a blue neck scarf and white-and-blue two-tone high-heeled pumps that made her an inch or two taller than he. As they seated themselves, Matthias caught a glimpse of a curve of small breast revealed by the deep neckline, looking away before she noticed.

Her menu included a cold soup and a shrimp salad. The butler brought a bottle of white Bourdeaux wine. Matthias took a small sip of his, then let it be. Diandra had a much larger sip of hers.

"Toxin," she said.

"Sorry?"

"Alcohol is a toxin. I have to remind myself of that. The body soaks up toxins the way it does water. I used to be more careful about such things."

"When you were a fashion model."

"I'm still a model, Mr. Curland. I just don't do it for money anymore."

He looked perplexed. She smiled, pausing to change the course of the conversation. This was not a direction she had intended.

"How was the sailing lesson?" she asked.

"The wind's light today. We had no problems. Your husband's a quick learner."

"He says you're a good teacher."

"I'm a better architect."

She smiled again, more sweetly. "You gave Peter some drawings—for his building."

"I'm not sure if he likes them. He was rather noncommittal."

"He hasn't talked to me about them. Not in any detail. He seldom talks to me about business. Usually I'm just as glad. But in your case—I wish I could give you some news. I know he's very excited about having this building put up."

"I'm afraid my designs are a little unorthodox—even outlandish."

"He said one looked like a sailboat."

Matthias studied her eyes for a sign of ridicule. "Yes. He'd probably prefer a building like this one, only taller."

"You might be surprised, Mr. Curland. Peter loves to surprise people." She turned in her chair. The light breeze blew a curl of hair against her cheek. "It's to go over there, up along the river?"

He nodded.

"I don't understand why he wants to put it up in a slum."

"It won't always be a slum. That's what this project is about."

"But wouldn't he make more money with something like that if it was closer to the lake?"

"Of course. But there are already too many buildings along the lake, including the one I put there. Just look at them all. They're a wall. If it wasn't for the park and the open shoreline, it would be horrible. Like Manhattan. No, your husband's building needs to be at Cabrini Green. It has to be by itself. It makes no sense, otherwise. It shouldn't be built, otherwise."

"You'd like to rearrange this city to suit yourself, wouldn't you?"

"I'd like to rearrange all cities."

"Peter thinks like that."

"With me, it's only fantasy. I'm not like your husband, Mrs. Poe."

"I know. I noticed that right off."

She only picked at her food, though she had a second glass of wine. He wasn't very hungry, either. He hadn't been since the policeman had brought the news about Jill.

"Would you like coffee, Mr. Curland? Or should we go now? I really want to see your museum. And I'd like to get out of here. I spend too much time in this place."

Something about her face had changed. The light-blue eyes were very somber.

"You're staring at me, Mr. Curland."

"Sorry." He rose and went to pull back her chair.

* * *

Matthias turned on all of the lights in the museum's main exhibition area, annoyed that so many of the fixtures needed new bulbs. Only a few of the paintings were left in shadow. He didn't suppose she wanted to study them all.

She walked on ahead of him. Again, he found himself transfixed by the beauty of her motion—her perfect poise and control and grace.

She stopped and turned, almost a dancer's turn.

"All these magnificent paintings," she said, "in this dark old building."

"It is a pity. The neighborhood was quite different when he acquired this place."

"Does anyone come to see them?"

"Not many. The ambience in this area is a little off-putting."

"Why don't you move the collection downtown?"

"Can't. My grandfather's will. Everything stays where it is. Exactly."

She moved on, glancing from painting to painting. "How much are all these worth?"

She reminded Matthias of her husband with that.

"It's hard to say," he said. "Someone made an estimate once, before I left Chicago. It could be between thirty and forty million—those that are on exhibition. The ones in the vault downstairs, perhaps half that much."

Diandra smiled. "You may be richer than my husband."

"He's a billionaire."

"Those are assets. I think he may have liabilities to match. But don't ever let him know I told you that. I'm not supposed to know about his finances."

Matthias shrugged. "The paintings don't belong to me, or any of us. They're the property of the family foundation. And they're art, not money. My grandfather wanted us to make our own way in life—not live off the genius and talent of others. Some of these painters died penniless."

"Your grandfather didn't."

"No."

"Then he could afford noble ideas like that."

"Yes, he could."

She looked away. "My father died broke," she said. "He was a foreman in an auto plant. He made good money, for a time. Enough to send my brother and me to college—a couple years for me, anyway. But there were layoffs and shutdowns and closings and he lost his job. He got another as a foreman for a parts manufacturer. One of those nonunion shops that sprang up when the auto industry began jobbing everything out. Most of the people there worked for little more than the minimum wage. There were no benefits, no health insurance. One woman worked a metal press. You know, you put a blank sheet of steel in, the press comes down, the press goes back up again, and you reach in and take out the stamped part. She did that all day, only once the press came down when it wasn't supposed to and cut off her hands. She had no money to pay for anything. There was no medical insurance, nothing. He decided he couldn't work at such a place, so he quit. His next job was in the service department of some car dealer—for about a third of what he'd been making at the auto plant."

She hesitated, taking in a deep breath. He sensed she hadn't meant to launch into this resentful diatribe.

"That was a noble thing to do, wasn't it?" she said. "Only he couldn't afford it."

"Your father sounds like a very honorable man."

"He was very Old Country. Polish. I'm part German and Polish, mostly Polish. He was from Krakow. He came here as a small boy. With his parents. His father was a factory worker."

She stepped close to one of the paintings.

" 'Hans von Aachen,' " she said, studying the name plate. "I never heard of him." She had pronounced the name perfectly.

"He was a sixteenth-century court painter for the Holy Roman Emperor, Rudolph the Second—the one whom some historians blame for the Thirty Years' War."

"I don't know about that, either."

"You're Catholic?"

"More or less."

"I'm Protestant. It was between us. Thousands and thousands were killed. A lot of them burned at the stake."

"Who is that naked woman? And why is she holding that sword? Did she stab that man lying on the ground?"

"Most of von Aachen's paintings were allegorical. She represents Truth, or Justice. Maybe Abundance. I've forgotten which. In any event, she symbolizes the empire. The wounded figure is discord. Rudolph the Second didn't like the war he helped cause. The painting was done on copper sheeting. That's why it's so jewellike, so well preserved."

"I think she must be Abundance. She's certainly abundant around the hips."

"Some think that was the womanly ideal of the time. Food was often scarce, so fatness was admired. People didn't live very long back then, didn't worry about health. I don't think they knew about health. You would have been quite an anomoly, for an aristocrat."

She gave him a smile with some slyness to it. "Do you think of me as an aristocrat, Mr. Curland?"

"In the best sense of the term, yes."

"Then I'm flattered."

"Your husband suggested I might paint you."

"I know. He told me."

"I wasn't sure he was serious." Matthias felt embarrassed, but completed his thought. "He said something about, well, a nude."

"I know." She said nothing more, moving on to the next painting.

They went through the three main exhibition rooms, her interest seeming to diminish with each.

"They're very pretty," she said, "but I think I prefer modern art."

"The twentieth-century works are all downstairs in the vault. We really shouldn't go down there."

"I trust you, Mr. Curland."

He flushed. "We're not supposed to go in there, unless there's a compelling reason, foundation business. But I broke the rule myself, yesterday."

"Whatever you say."

Matthias hesitated. "Well, why not? Just for a few minutes."

She kept several paces behind him as they descended the stairs, remaining in the doorway until he had turned on all the lights.

"It's like I imagine Fort Knox," she said.

"Not quite, but the vault walls are pretty impregnable—and absolutely fireproof. Is there any particular artist you'd like to see? We have a Kandinsky."

"Just something modern." She stepped up behind him as he opened the vault door.

"I'm afraid the 1930s are as modern as we get." He turned on the lights within the vault. "I'll see what I can find."

He glanced about the storage shelves, then pulled out a box. With some difficulty, he released its fastenings. A moment later he pulled forth a hideous painting. It showed a wild-eyed man crawling across a hellish, dark landscape. Half his face was in blood. Looking closer, she saw barbed wire, and a gun. The man seemed to be screaming.

"I'm sorry," Matthias said. "I seem to have picked an Otto Dix."

"I never heard of him."

"He was one of the 'degenerates,' what the Nazis called degenerates—artists they objected to because they were decadent or unpatriotic or Jewish, or because they glorified forbidden things like American culture, which Hitler thought too influenced by the Negro. Dix was considered unpatriotic. This is from his series *Der Krieg—The War*—World War One. As you can see, he didn't think much of it. Hitler thought it the most glorious time of his life. He liked to see it depicted in heroic, Wagnerian paintings." Matthias recovered the work with its protective cloth. "In 1937 the Nazis ordered a ban on 'degenerate art.' They burned some of it and confiscated the rest. They even staged an exhibition of it in Munich—'Entartete Kunst,' 'Degenerate Art,' to show the faithful how disgusting it was. Actually, I think Goering, who was quite a collector, kept some of it—pieces he liked."

Matthias closed up the box. Diandra was staring at him.

"Most of the artists, of course, fled the country, taking a lot of their stuff with them," he said. "Ernst Kirchner, one of my favorites, went to Switzerland. He couldn't take being called a degenerate and committed suicide. My grandfather was very troubled by all this. He hated the Nazis and bought up as many of these things as he could. We have quite a few pieces. I'm very proud to have them. But it's ironic. They're all locked up down here, and have to stay here, because of my grandfather's will. We might as well have left with them with the Nazis."

"You'd put something like that on display?"

"Oh, yes. It's truth, isn't it?"

He shouldered the packing case up into its place on a shelf, then turned to face her again. She was standing very close.

"I want to kiss you, Mr. Curland."

He was unable to move. This was something he realized he'd wanted to do since he first met her. But there was Sally. And there was Peter Poe. This was trouble—madness.

"Don't misunderstand," she said, her face gliding closer.

He tried thinking of Sally, of how much she represented his old life restored, but it was no good. Diandra's eyes closed. Their lips came together, softly, gently. His hand went to her back, but he did not pull her close.

She stepped back, looking at him with great seriousness.

"This is my way of embracing all this art, of thanking your grandfather for saving it. Does that sound crazy?"

"A little."

"Sometimes I get that way, Mr. Curland." She turned and went upstairs. She was waiting for him in the entrance foyer by the time he had closed up the vault and rejoined her.

"Don't tell my husband," she said.

"Of course not."

She smiled politely.

He switched off all the lights.

"Thank you very much, Mr. Curland," she said.

"I wish you'd call me Matthias. You did when we were at your place for dinner."

"Peter likes me to do that, call people by their first names. But it makes me feel a little uncomfortable." Her eyes held his for a moment. "I guess I don't feel so uncomfortable with you any-more—Matthias."

They drove back toward the lakefront along North Avenue, past small brick buildings with stores and bars on the ground floor and dark-windowed apartments above. The high-rises along the lake to the east seemed to beckon, like the towers of some distant, quite different city. But the real Chicago was here in these rough and gritty streets that stretched for miles and miles in every direction except east. Poe was in the business of destroying these old neighborhoods, replacing their raw, rough burly toughness with what in comparison was effete, ostentatious, and artificial. Matthias's great-grandfather had helped create some of these neighborhoods. If Poe built his new tower, they might disappear. And Matthias was helping him.

Diandra—he called her that now—was mostly silent on the drive back. Passing through the Gold Coast, they turned south onto the Inner Drive. At the next traffic light, she said something about finding Sally Phillips a very nice person. Matthias muttered something in response, but the conversation lapsed again until they reached the Michigan Avenue entrance to Poe Place.

"That was wonderful," she said. "I'd like to do it again."

"Anytime."

Diandra got out, closed the door, then leaned against it. "I think it may be some time before you hear from Peter, about that building."

"That's his prerogative."

"Would you like the answer to be yes?"

"I guess I would."

"Just make sure he learns how to sail." Another smile. "And make sure his boat wins that race."

Zany felt like a yo-yo, yanked on a string from one side of Lake Michigan to the other. He was now on the Chicago Skyway, thumping along past the old Indiana steel plants on his way back to the Michigan shore, wondering when he was going to be yanked back to Chicago again.

He'd identified his stolen property for Baldessari, and signed a statement reiterating that it had been taken from his hotel room in his absence and that he had never met or had any previous knowledge of the slain hooker who'd ended up with his possessions. A few of his former brother officers gave him some winks and a ribald hard time about that, but it didn't seem likely the Chicago P.D. was going to bother him about the matter any further. In fact, Baldessari didn't seem interested at all in the odd coincidence that his things were found in the woman's apartment. All that mattered to Frank was O'Rourke's business card, which he treated like some rare, priceless jewel—a ticket back to the peace and quiet of routine cases.

Zany had stopped once again at the Curland house on Schiller Street—as he half expected, finding no one home. He went up to Poe's business office, only to be told Poe was once more out of town.

A huge, chuffing semi caused him to brake sharply to avoid its swinging rear end as it pulled into his lane after passing him, a cloud of diesel smoke trailing in its wake. A sign overhead informed him he was entering Indiana. Poe's "out-of-town" destination could be nothing more than his casino up ahead in Michigan City.

He decided he'd stop on the odd chance Poe was there. As he thought upon it, a visit to the gambling palace might even be more productive if Poe wasn't. If Christian Curland had been out there before his rendezvous with Sally Phillips, Zany wanted to hear it from roulette croupiers and blackjack dealers and cocktail waitresses.

* * *

He got as far as the daytime pit boss. A squat, dark-haired, perspiring fat man in a mod double-breasted suit, he fingered Zany's police I.D. carefully. Zany had no more jurisdiction here than he did in Chicago, but the man raised no complaint about that.

"Sorry," he said, handing back Zany's I.D. "I wasn't working that shift that night."

"Is there anyone around who was?"

The man shrugged. "You'll have to ask them." He drifted away without another word.

Zany tried a couple of idle dice dealers and a cocktail waitress. She said she knew Christian Curland but wasn't on duty the night Zany mentioned. He moved on to a bartender, with the same result.

He ordered a beer, wondering what to do next. He had taken all of two sips when the pit boss reappeared at his side.

"Mr. Poe would like to speak to you," he said. "Come with me."

Zany took a large gulp of the beer then got up off his stool. "Come with me 'please.'"

"Yeah. Please."

The man led him back to the main lobby and then to a bank of elevators at the rear. They proceeded up to the top floor and an office suite as spacious as the one Poe had back in Chicago. The secretaries there studiously ignored him.

Poe, to Zany's surprise, greeted him at the door to the immense chamber that was his private office, shaking his hand and showing him to a long leather couch that faced a huge sweep of Lake Michigan out the wide, floor-to-ceiling window. One could probably see the lights of Chicago from it at night. Poe had no desk, but there was a long, glass-topped table at the far end of the room with two telephones and some papers on it. There were several modernistic paintings on the wall, but none remotely resembling the one that had turned up in the sailboat with the dead girl. A fireplace along one of the walls had some real logs with real flames curling around them, even though the temperature outside was in the eighties. Zany thought they only had offices like this in Hollywood.

"It's nice of you to drop by, Chief Rawlings," Poe said, seating himself carefully in an adjoining chair. "I meant to get back to you, but you know how it is—busy, busy, busy. I never seem to have a minute to myself."

"I'm investigating a homicide, as I told your people."

"So you did. I guess it's been pretty busy for you guys these days, too. Which homicide are you looking into? Something out here?"

"A Chicago girl. She turned up in my town up the shore, in a sailboat. It was in the papers."

"Oh, yeah. She worked for the Train gallery. I do some business with them. Nice girl, I guess. A real shame."

"Did you know her?"

"May have met her. I meet a million people. Usually I don't go into the Train gallery, though. Usually he comes to me. I was away that night, the night of the murder. Up with my wife at my place at Lake Geneva."

"That's not why I'm here, Mr. Poe. I'm checking on a customer of yours, Christian Curland. The dead girl used to work for him. He says he was here for part of that night."

"Chris Curland. Nice guy. A regular customer. I wish he wasn't. He's been on a hell of a lucky streak."

"Was he here?"

"If he says so, I'm sure he was. Like I say, I was up in Wisconsin. But let me call in somebody who was here." He got to his feet, as nimbly as an athlete coming off the bench, and went to a phone console, depressing a button.

"Have Mr. Mann come in here," he said. "And Miss Bellini, too."

Poe remained standing where he was. In a moment, a trim, well-dressed, mean-faced man entered, looking grimly unhappy, followed closely by the best-looking woman Zany had seen all day, if not all year. The man was dressed in the same kind of suit as the pit boss, but was much taller and handsomer, with a lean, muscular face. He had overlong, black curly hair that might have been a toupee.

The woman had hair as dark and curly, so long it fell down her back. She wore a tight-fitting knit dress that ended high on her thighs.

"Chief Rawlings," said Poe, "this is my executive secretary, Miss Bellini, and Mr. Mann, who manages my casino. Guys, Chief Rawlings wants to know if Chris Curland was here Friday night before last. A girl who used to work for him was murdered, and there may be some connection. Right, Chief?"

Zany nodded.

"He was here," said Mann, without changing his expression.

"We had a big crowd in that night, but I remember. He was here. Took a couple thou away from the roulette tables."

"I saw him, too," said the woman. Her eyes were locked hard on Zany's. There was nothing at all furtive about her, about either of them. "He had too much to drink. I was worried about his driving home."

There was something familiar about her—the voice, the build. Maybe it was the type.

"You work here at the casino?" Zany asked. "On Friday nights?"

"I work wherever Mr. Poe wants me to. I have an apartment here, in the hotel. I come out a lot on weekends."

Poe smiled, spreading his hands. "So there you are, Chief. You want to talk to anyone else? The night shift people'll be here in a couple of hours. I'm sure I can find someone who might have seen him."

"Does anyone remember when Mr. Curland left?"

"Maybe midnight," said the woman. "He said he had a date."

"Isn't that kinda late for a date?"

"Not for that guy."

"Anyone else, Chief Rawlings?" Poe said. "I can check with valet parking. They could probably tell you exactly when he left."

"I guess that's not necessary," Zany said. He knew he'd just be wasting his time.

"You want to hang around awhile anyway? Shoot some craps? Can I treat you to a drink? Cup of coffee?"

"No, thanks. I'd better get back to Grand Pier. For some reason, we're having a lot of trouble with lawbreakers this summer. Had an armed robbery the other day."

"No place is safe anymore. I'm thinking of increasing the security around here. But look, come on down whenever you want. Bring the wife and spend a weekend. I'll get you a suite. My treat. We've got a great beach."

Zany got up without responding. As Poe led him to the door, he dropped another question. "Curland has a brother, Matthias Curland. He wasn't around here that night, was he?"

The Bellini woman shook her head.

"I only met the guy the following Sunday," Poe said. "He's been away. In Europe. He's an artist like his brother, only not so good."

"I've seen his work," Zany said. "Thanks for your time."

"That's all I needed you for, Bobby," Poe said after Rawlings left.

"I need to talk to you," Mann said.

"We talked this morning."

"No, we didn't. I picked up my phone and listened to you talk. Now I've got something to say."

He sat down on a chair, leaning back, arms spread out. He might have been a dog pissing on another mutt's scent, he was so defiant about it. Poe went over to his glass-top table, making Mann turn sideways to look at him.

"So talk, Bobby," he said. "I'm always happy to hear what you have to say."

Mango was over by the window, staring at the lake. She didn't like the look in the casino manager's eyes. Mann glanced at her, then shifted farther in his chair to face Poe.

"I just heard from the investors again."

"You mean your friends in Atlantic City."

"I work for you, Mr. Poe, not them. If I was working for them, I wouldn't be telling you this."

"Tell me what, that they don't like the drop in the handle—the unofficial handle? This they have communicated to me, Bobby. Twice this week. I told them what I told you. The IRS is on my ass—sniffing around last year's records. They sent me a letter. I showed it to you. I sent your friends in Atlantic City a fax."

"The IRS has already looked at those records. They came up clean. Just like we figured. Anyway, the letter's from the U.S. Attorney's office."

"Same thing. What do you want me to do, tell them to go fuck themselves? We've got to fly straight and level for a while. I've got too much going for me now to risk it all getting hauled into tax court on a skim."

"The investors don't buy the letter, Mr. Poe. You got a lot of friends in interesting places. They think you got a friend with the feds. They think you're wringing the handle to get more money for your real estate deals. They asked me to check it out. Instead, I'm coming to you. You tell me what I should say to them."

"Tell them I'm not going to take a penny out of here that I'm not entitled to as dividends from shares. Tell them everything's going into the bottom line—the P and L, only more profit and less loss. All I'm trying to do is run a clean shop for a while, like it says to do in our casino license."

Mann glowered at him, then sighed in exasperation.

"You see all the receipts, Bobby, all the records. I'm not hiding anything. Check it out, just like they asked you to do."

"What I'm trying to tell you is that you've got a problem with them, Mr. Poe."

"I'll take care of it—the way I do all my problems. You just stick to your job and stop worrying." He gave Mann a smile that better belonged on someone doing a late-night television commercial.

Mann stood up, in a hurry now to leave. "I said my say, Mr. Poe. I expect you'll be hearing from them no matter what."

"Yeah, well, thanks."

The door closed silently.

"Goddamn gunsel," said Mango.

"You know what a gunsel is, Mango? It's Yiddish for prick."

"I know. That's him. Class A prick. You should never have agreed to take him on, Peter. You should have gotten your start-up money here."

"Do you know how much of the handle those Chicago guys wanted? It would have been like a juice loan."

"They wouldn't be giving you such a big hassle over this. They wouldn't stuff a bastard like Bobby down your throat. They're businessmen, like you."

"Right. I met one of their lawyers once. Big-time LaSalle Street guy who got hooked into them when he needed a little juice to feed the ponies he liked to watch stroll around the track at Hawthorne. He showed me his watch. A Rolex bigger than my Piaget. On the back, it was inscribed: 'To Bob from Sam, so that when they find you in a trunk they'll know I was your friend.' "

"Did they find him in a trunk?"

"No, he died of a heart attack—probably from looking at that watch too much."

"I think you ought to consider a switch in investors, Peter. It's not too late to go with the locals."

"That kind of affiliation wouldn't do much for my social standing here, babe. Not to speak of our Better Business Bureau rating. And Bobby's Atlantic City pals would have guys with baseball bats out here in an hour if they heard I was even thinking of such a thing. We shouldn't be talking about this in here."

"If it was a done deal, they wouldn't dream of messing with you. They're not big enough to take on the outfit in Chicago."

"I always appreciate your advice, Mango, but sometimes I wish you'd think about it a little longer."

"I'm just trying to help." She started to leave.

"Hold on, Mango," Poe said. "You and I have some other business to discuss."

She froze. She had been expecting this all day, of course, but he hadn't said a word about it, despite several opportunities to talk to her in private.

"Let's go out on the balcony," he said.

They went down to the end, away from the windows of Poe's office. Poe leaned against the railing and she did the same, standing very close to him, her perfume scenting the breeze.

"The boys were just supposed to make a drop in that hooker's apartment," Poe said. "The money and the business card, then phone the tip. Those were my orders. She was found with her throat cut."

"I talked to them. They said she walked in on them."

"I don't buy that. I told you they were to wait until she was turning a trick somewhere and then go make the drop. All very simple. That's how I laid it out."

"Things go wrong, Peter. She walked in."

"You told them to wait till she came back, didn't you? It was a setup. Another fucking murder."

She put her arm around his shoulders. He didn't pull away, a good sign. "It was necessary, Peter. It ties up all the loose ends. They'll close the case now and you and I can stop worrying. You didn't think it through enough. She might have turned up some John to testify he was with her the night O'Rourke got it. She might have been in the Chicago Avenue lockup that night. You didn't check any of that out."

"I'm a busy man."

"Yes, you sure are, which is why you shouldn't be worrying about little details like this."

"Little details? I'm told she bled over half the rug."

"It had to happen, Peter. I took care of it, the way Bill Yeats and I take care of dozens of things you want done or need done every day."

"Murder, Mango. I'm listed in fucking *Fortune* magazine and I've got Jacqueline the Ripper for an executive secretary."

"Does it really bother you that much, what happened? A couple of dead people?"

"O'Rourke, yes. The hooker, I don't know. If I'd seen her body it probably would bother the hell out of me."

"People get murdered in Chicago every day. You don't give a shit. Nobody does, unless it's a little kid or something. So who cares about some crooked old Mick pol who was about to kick anyway, or a bleached blond working girl who probably rolled Johns every night?"

"They were alive, babe. That's all anybody's got."

She took in a deep breath, letting go of his hand.

"You killed somebody once," she said. "You told me. In the Philippines."

"That was a long time ago," he said. "I was a kid in the navy. It was overseas, it was in a fight, and I didn't mean to do it."

"You got away with it, didn't you?"

"Yeah. I was lucky."

"You still losing sleep over it?"

"No. I didn't even know the guy. He was some slicki boy who pulled a knife."

"Well, don't lose any sleep over this."

Zany went to his office very early the next morning so he could get some paperwork done before a breakfast meeting with District Attorney Moran. He wasn't halfway through his first cup of coffee when his wife Judy came in, closing the door rather decisively behind her. Her souvenir shop was the first place in town to get the morning Chicago papers, and she had a copy of the *Tribune* folded under her arm.

She laid it out on his desk in front of him. A large front-page headline announced the discovery of a dead prostitute believed by police to be responsible for the murder of Park District President O'Rourke.

"This is the homicide victim you went over there to try to identify?"

"Yes."

Judy ran her finger, extended accusingly, down the long column of the story, coming to rest on a paragraph near the end. It stated that personal property belonging to Grand Pier, Michigan, Police Chief Zane Rawlings had been recovered from the dead woman's apartment. It quoted police as saying the property had been stolen from his hotel room earlier in the week.

Judy stepped back, her arms folded.

"This is true?" she said.

"Yep."

"You want to tell me about it?"

"Just as it says. They found my stuff. I told you about it night before last."

"You didn't say anything about any prostitute."

Zany stared at the newspaper page, blinking rapidly. "I can't figure out how the *Trib* got a hold of this. Frank Baldessari wouldn't have told them. None of the guys would."

"Every reporter has his sources. You used to be somebody's source."

"This is a leak. Very deliberate. I'm wondering who's got it in for me."

"What about the blond lady?"

Zany brought his thoughts back to present realities. "The blond lady. I never saw her before." He pushed back his chair to look more directly at his wife's face. "I had no hooker in my hotel room. I spent what little expense money I had on a couple of bad meals and some beers. I was burgled, plain and simple, and the painting they took is still missing."

His wife dropped her arms to her sides. "We've been married a long time, Zane. If we've got a problem here, we can work it out. I just need to know where we stand."

"We stand just fine, honey. The only problem we have is that someone is trying to put the screws to me. And they've been doing it ever since I started to work on this Jill Langley case."

"All right, I believe you," Judy said. "It's just that you look kind of guilty. Well, not guilty, but nervous."

"That's because I am nervous."

When he'd been a very young man working on a dynamite crew at that strip mine in Wyoming he hadn't been all that nervous because he learned the trade from an experienced old miner who wanted to get a lot older. He knew that if he did all the right things very slowly and carefully, nothing bad would happen. Even when making busts with the Chicago P.D. he'd been calm enough because he followed procedures very carefully, took no chances, and always knew what to expect when he went to a suspect's door because he expected the worst.

Now he had no idea what was going to happen to him next.

"In fact," he said, "I'm a little scared."

CHAPTER

7

ONE OF THE windows of Matthias's bedroom in the Schiller Street house looked west over rooftops and the low skyline of Old Town. If Poe used the obelisk design for his Cabrini Green project, its piercing needle would dominate this view. If Poe decided on the sail configuration to go with the tower, as Matthias allowed himself to hope, the view would contain little else. To fully see the sky, Matthias would have to go to the window. A small price for him to pay, perhaps, but he was fond of lying in his bed, contemplating the western horizon, especially at sunset.

He was doing so now. It was early evening, with the sun bright but low, filling the window with a glare of light. Sally was standing with her back to it, her naked body in sharp silhouette. Matthias squinted to see her more clearly, wondering why she wasn't returning to him. She had gotten up to go to the bathroom and been gone some time. Upon reentering the bedroom, she'd gone to the window.

She turned slightly, the sunlight catching the curves of her breasts. Her body was much the same as it had been when she was in her twenties. Slender and firm, but very womanly. He had never done a painting of her undressed. It would have been inappropriate, unseemly, when they were young. Her mother might have found out, and caused even more trouble for him than she had. Not much of a bohemian, Sally's mother.

He had done nudes of many of the women he had slept with, almost a courting ritual, though it was usually the women who suggested it. A sublimated form of the sex act, he supposed. Modigliani, Picasso, Goya—they had all painted their mistresses in the nude. Renaissance artists had included such women in their religious paintings—except those like Michelangelo, who favored boys, or Veronese, who didn't seem to know what a woman's naked form looked like. Veronese women were built like halfbacks.

"I start work for Peter Poe next week," Sally said.

"I seem already to have done that."

He was still employed merely as a sailing instructor. Poe had yet to say a single further word about the building project.

"I feel funny about it," Sally said.

"Because we'll both have the same master?"

"Because it's . . . I don't know, because it's a serious job, as if I were becoming a career woman. I never thought of myself like that. The job at the shop, it's always been just a temporary thing, a way to get by."

"The Poe position isn't all that serious, is it? Arranging parties?"

"The title is director of special events. I'll have a staff of three. He wants to throw a big ball—raise funds for the Holocaust Museum they're talking about building. I've never worked on anything like that."

Sally's mother had been a notorious anti-Semite. Was Sally?

"Jewish people? That bothers you?"

He couldn't quite make out her face in the glare of sunlight, but he sensed the remark displeased her.

"It's not that," she said. "Chicago's changed. Jewish women, black women, Catholics. They're on boards and committees now. They're part of society. I think it's fine."

"What then?"

"I'm not sure how I'll be accepted now. I feel like I've lost my place in the city, like I've become part of Poe's big machine. People will treat me like one of his little minions."

"Then don't take it. To thine own self be true, Sally."

"I don't have much choice, I don't think I could survive one more day in that shop, being nice to all those obnoxious people." She turned back toward him, folding her arms. "I'll be working with Mrs. Poe on that fashion show—quite a lot, I gather. Do you like her?"

He sat up. "She's all right. Rather too good for him, probably. Quite the lady. And very knowledgeable about art."

"Her father was a factory worker."

"A foreman, actually. And yours was a wallpaper salesman."

"In the beginning." She seemed to stiffen. This conversation was off course.

"What I mean to say is that such things aren't supposed to matter," he said.

"I guess they don't, anymore. She likes you. I saw her at a luncheon the other day. She asked about you."

"I'm sure that's all part of Mr. Poe's full press recruitment drive."

"If he accepts your design, will you do his building?"

"I haven't decided yet." Why did he lie? That building was the key to everything.

"If you do, it'll put your firm back in business."

"Certainly will."

"And when you're done, you can move on to other things. We both can. Though I suppose you might want to leave Chicago—again."

"That building will take two years at a minimum. It would take that if he started tomorrow."

"So this is for the long haul."

"Yes. If he goes for it. Long enough of a haul."

"I feel like we're at a point of no return. That it's our last chance to walk away from him."

The sun had touched the western horizon. Its light was turning to amber.

"Do you want to?"

"Matt. Are we going to get married?"

He wished he could better see her face. He felt so sorry for her, almost as sorry as he felt for Jill. Unlike Jill, he could do something about Sally, could undo what her wretched mother had done to her, to them both. Her happiness could now be assured with just a few words—his words.

"My darling Sally. I think the fates ordained that a long time ago. Your mother just got in their way."

She came toward him now, pausing at the foot of the bed. "You're sure?"

What about his happiness? What about Diandra Poe?

That was utterly impossible. He needed to remind himself of that now in a very firm way. He needed to make certain that what happened at the museum would never happen again.

"Yes." He said the word.

"Truly?"

"Sally, if I didn't feel this way, I'd be back on the Côte d'Azur at this moment, sketching people for drinks in some café."

176

She climbed onto the bed and crawled into his arms, pushing him back against the pillow. Her skin was very warm.

"I don't ever want you to have to do that again," she said.

"I don't either."

"No more sleeping on beaches."

"No."

"Matt?"

"Yes?"

"Are you over your wife?"

"Hillary? Yes. She's very happy with her new husband. I've no interest . . ."

"And Jill Langley?"

He hesitated. "I'm not over her murder."

"I don't suppose any of us is."

There was a sudden sound from the floor below, a door slamming.

"Christian," he said. "He disappears for two days and picks now to come back."

"He'll know I'm here. My purse is downstairs."

"I don't think he'll be exactly surprised."

"We should get dressed."

Matthias might have said that seeing Sally naked would be no shock to Christian, either. Instead he sighed in resignation. She began picking up her clothes.

They found Christian in the kitchen, mixing himself a martini.

"Big brother!" he said. "Sally! I've the most outrageous news."

He was smiling, the expression at once comical and cynical. Matthias simply stared, waiting for his brother to play out his game.

"Aaron Cooperman's been named president of the Park District," Christian said, barely restraining his mirth.

Another win for Peter Poe. "That's hardly outrageous. It was expected."

"Yes, but, big brother, guess who've they picked to fill the other vacancy."

"Why don't you tell us."

"Our father! They announced it this afternoon."

Matthias stared into his brother's wickedly glittering eyes. "Is this a joke? A little merriment to go with your gin?"

"I'm perfectly serious, Matthias. It's really true." Christian took a sip of his drink, then raised his glass in mock toast. "And why not? They've put judges on the Circuit Court who can't think as clearly as dear old dad. If he falls asleep on the job enough, they might just make him an alderman!"

Zany sat on his screened-in porch, enjoying a cold beer along with the sunset over the lake. He was waiting for a call, as he had been for several days. There was a New York cop he knew in the Manhattan burglary unit—a detective who specialized in art theft, a much bigger deal in that city than it was in Chicago. The detective, a friendly Italian guy like Baldessari, had been in his assignment for more than a dozen years and worked his beat like any other cop, relying on a network of friends and informants, most of them respectable art dealers but some of them crooks and snitches, to keep him apprised of any illicit traffic.

Using his computer, some art magazines, and out-of-town telephone books at the library, Zany had tried to work up a list of collectors and dealers who bought and sold the kind of art the Curlands kept locked up in their basement vault—pre–World War II German painters—but he didn't know enough. The New York burglary detective might be able to help him. The man might have heard about recent trade in Kirchner paintings. He'd promised to check his sources.

Zany had an Anne Murray recording on his CD player, but kept the volume low, so it wouldn't drown out the intermittent chatter on his police radio monitor, which he left on at all times now.

He was opening another beer when he heard the sudden sharpness of voice—Hejmal, almost shouting.

"Zane!" Judy called out. "Something's going on!"

Zany hurriedly got to his feet and went inside. He stood listening to the radio a moment, then went to the phone, not wanting to break into the conversation on the police two-way. Officer Vaclav answered his call, sounding even more excited than Hejmal.

"It's the St. Stanislaus Church, Chief!" she said. "They robbed it! Tied up Father Dubinin!"

"Men in ski masks again?"

"Yeah, I think so."

"Get everyone over there. Hejmal, too. You stay put. I'm on my way." He wondered where he had put his service revolver. He hadn't carried it in months—or was it years?

178

"Chief, don't you want me to call the state troopers?"
Zany swore. How could he forget that? "Yes."
"Well, I already did. Just before you called."
He could imagine a big smile on her broad face.
"Thanks," he said.

CHAPTER

POE'S BIG SLOOP—NEWLY rechristened *Lady P* and with the hull painted a bright crimson beneath the waterline—was one of twenty-seven boats in the Chicago-to-Menominee race, and probably the handsomest. Matthias had picked a good crew, most of them young—four men and a woman who had raced with him in the past. Poe had demanded the best crew, but Matthias had replied to that enigmatically, saying that such a crew would have to include Jill Langley, and that not even Peter Poe could raise the dead. Noting how disturbed Poe was by this, Matthias told him not to worry. The sailors were in good physical shape, enthusiastic, and worked well together. Yacht races were won by making the right decisions, and those came from the helm.

Poe didn't worry overmuch. The crews that *Tribune* sailing writer Bill Recktenwald had rated the best were aboard the commodore's boat and Bill Yeats's. The lawyer knew better than to win this contest. It would be up to Yeats to deal with the commodore as well—though Poe hadn't told Matthias that.

As a grand, attention-getting gesture, Poe had put up a $100,000 prize on the race, which traditionally had provided the winner only with a trophy. This unofficial side bet, which none of the other competitors had shown any interest in matching, had a considerable string attached: The victor had to give the money to his or her favorite charity. Poe would pay Matthias a bonus separate from that—if they won.

The ten-minute warning gun had fired, startling Poe as he was shifting into a more comfortable seat by the helm. Matthias had smiled, amused to see the mighty mogul caught unguarded, but said nothing. Poe was getting tired of that smile—pleasant and friendly but so irritatingly superior. A few days more, and Curland would be so much in his pocket that he could tell him to knock off the smiling as he might his maid or Krasowski—tell Curland to stand on his head if he wanted.

The boats were tacking and maneuvering into positions that would take them in a group over the start line at the next and last firing of the gun. Any bumping or fouling would be counted against them now, so the skippers were being very circumspect, slackening sail when necessary to keep clear of other craft.

Matthias was still at the wheel though he had promised Poe he could take and keep the helm until they were well away from the downtown waterfront. He was holding the *Lady P* back at the rear of the flotilla. Poe had objected to the time and distance they might lose, but Matthias countered that they'd be better able to judge the rival skippers' tactics and the play of the weather in this position, and plot their race plan accordingly. The wind was light, out of the west, but was expected to switch to the north and freshen by evening. Matthias planned to make his move for the lead while the wind was shifting.

There was a fair-size crowd lining the shore and the dock of the yacht club, Diandra Poe and Sally Phillips somewhere in it. Poe's man Krasowski was going to drive Diandra up to Menominee in one of Poe's red stretch limousines to await the end of the race. Poe had invited Sally to go along, but she'd declined, wanting to spend the weekend with her daughter, whom she feared she'd too much neglected. Matthias was just as happy. He wasn't sure how well Mrs. Poe and Sally were getting along.

Matthias glanced at his watch. "All right, Mr. Poe, let's trade places. Time to take the helm."

"I told you, Matt. Call me Peter."

"Very well, Peter. Take the helm."

Poe stood up, putting a hand on the wheel. There was a press boat full of photographers not too far distant. He turned toward it and waved, smiling broadly. They had telephoto lenses and would doubtless capture the vain moment.

"Don't you have the mainsail too far out?" Poe asked, trying not to be heard by the nearby crew members. "The wind's from the west. Shouldn't we be at a beam reach?"

"Correct, Peter. We'll trim it in when the starting gun goes off. If we do that now, we'll ride up on that boat on the port quarter. She's drifting to the right a little."

"You'll give the command?"

"I'll attend to the changes in sail. No one ashore is going to

181

hear us. You just keep the heading." He paused, adding "Skipper."

Poe grinned.

The gun caught him by surprise again, but he held the wheel fast. Matthias barked out an order and a husky young man on the main sheet smartly hauled the big sail in to proper trim. A blond-haired girl on the starboard winch simultaneously trimmed in the big Genoa jib accordingly. The sloop glided forward, spreading a wider wake, heeling at a steeper angle, gaining on the boat ahead.

"Fall off a little and we'll pass him," Matthias said. "I want a clearer view of the leaders."

"Fall off?"

"Turn it off the wind a little, Peter. To starboard. To the right. Remember?"

Poe nodded grimly, giving the wheel a shove.

"Too much, Peter," Matthias said. "Bring it back some."

Poe obeyed, clenching his teeth.

"Very good. Steady as she goes now."

"Aye aye," Poe muttered.

He looked over his shoulder. The press boat was following. He turned and gave its passengers a thumbs-up.

Grand Pier's Town Hall adjoined Zany's police station, so he hadn't far to go to the meeting he'd been summoned to—though it seemed a journey of a thousand miles. He'd always known his job carried the potential of ensnarement in local politics, but he'd heretofore managed to avoid that. Because of his status as a genuine former Chicago police detective, and the general lack of crime the community had enjoyed in his tenure, no one had ever bothered him—except for District Attorney Moran, who seemed to lust after as much crime as he could get the local newspapers and radio stations to cover.

Now everything had changed. Moran was getting crime heaped on his plate beyond his wildest fantasies, and Zany was over his head in political trouble. He was being called to account for himself and his little department. He wondered if he'd be able to walk away with his job.

The Town Hall contained a big outer room with a long counter at which the town clerk issued beach permits and dealt with tax matters and other municipal concerns. There were a couple of small offices behind the counter, and beyond them—

down a short corridor—a chamber used both as a courtroom and as a meeting place for the town board.

They were assembled there now, with Mayor Genevieve Braunmeister presiding. Moran was present also, as was the president of the local chamber of commerce. Braunmeister sat at the head of the table and the others along the sides. Zany, feeling very much in the dock, took a folding chair at the end. He nodded amiably at couple of the town board members, both of them his friends, but they looked away.

Mayor Braunmeister had a stack of newspapers in front of her. "You've seen these, Chief Rawlings?" She held up one of the front pages, as if it were a dirty thing.

"Yes, ma'am," said Zany. "Pretty lively reading, these days."

"It's a damned disgrace," said Moran.

Zany glanced at him with some amusement. Moran's picture had been featured on most of the front pages.

The chamber of commerce man cleared his throat. "The motels are reporting vacancies. In July."

"So where do we stand?" Braunmeister said. "Any arrests? Any suspects? Any idea as to what in the hell is going on?"

"No arrests, no suspects," Zany said. "But, yes, I have a real good idea what's going on."

This caught most of them by surprise. Moran frowned. Zany hadn't taken the prosecutor into his confidence about any of this.

"You want to share it with us?" Braunmeister said, leaning forward. She was a small, thin woman, with oversize eyeglasses. Her husband owned the local marina.

"I think the robberies are a response to my investigation of the Jill Langley murder. I think there are people who want me to lay off the case, and are trying to tie me up with these penny ante stickups."

"Penny ante?" said Moran. "They shot the 7-Eleven to smithereens. They assaulted a priest!"

"Why would a couple of stickup men care about your investigating a murder?" Braunmeister asked.

"I don't think they're professional stickup men. I think they're just goons who pulled these jobs on orders, orders from somebody who wants me to lay off the Langley case."

"And who might this somebody be?"

"I don't know."

They looked at one another.

"You haven't made any progress at all," Moran said. "You've

given me nothing to go on. In fact, you've hardly communicated with me at all except to ask for a subpoena to go rummaging in some art museum in Chicago."

"So what progress have you made, Chief?" the mayor asked.

"I've reason to believe that the dead girl was involved in some way with art theft, or art fraud, and that the two brothers who run that museum in Chicago may be involved—if not as perpetrators, at least as victims. Also, I think the art gallery she worked for could be part of it."

"You think these museum people and the art dealer are robbing 7-Elevens?"

"That's not what I'm saying."

"Do you have any evidence of their involvement?"

"No. What evidence I had was stolen from my hotel room."

"Yeah, we read about that," said another of the board members, a man who owned the biggest service station in town. He began to laugh. Soon everybody was laughing, except Zany.

He accepted the humiliation, glad of anything that might lighten their mood.

"And you don't have any suspects at all?" Braunmeister asked. Her levity hadn't lasted long.

"No suspects. Just suspicions."

The president of the chamber of commerce cleared his throat again. "You think these robberies will continue, as long as you're investigating the murder?"

Zany shrugged. "I hope not. The sheriff's office is helping us out with some extra patrols. And the State Police are watching over the interchange with the interstate."

The mayor's tiny fist came banging down on the table. "Goddamn it, Zane, that's the point! We're spending good taxpayers' dollars to maintain a police department, and we have to call in outside help to protect our convenience stores and churches? For God's sake, we've had to close the town swimming pool because of the recession. People aren't going to stand for this."

"How many trips you made to Chicago on that case, Zany?" the service station owner asked.

"A couple."

"Where'd you stay, the Ambassador East?"

"My expense reports are on file. I stayed at a Days Inn."

"That's some Days Inn."

"Look, I didn't ask for that sailboat to come bumping up on the breakwater."

184

"You know, Zany," said another board member, the town mortician. "It was just a twist of fate that it did. If the winds had been different, it might have come ashore at New Buffalo or Union Pier, or maybe St. Joe."

"We don't know where the homicide took place," Zany said. "The body came here. According to the law, we're stuck with the case."

"The State Police are on it, right? The criminal investigation unit?"

"As much as the district attorney here will let them. Their operating theory is that it was a robbery, that we may have pirates or something out here on Lake Michigan. They're not much interested in my theory. The Chicago police aren't either."

"What about drugs?"

"Not a trace of anything like that on the boat. No trace of anything but alcohol in her, according to the autopsy, and not much of that."

The chamber of commerce man cleared his throat yet again. "Haven't you come up with anything on the robberies, Zane? Not even a little clue?"

"No prints, but we recovered a lot of shell casings. We've got descriptions of the vehicle. There's an all-points out in four states."

"That's it?"

"We're working twenty-four hours a day."

"On the robberies or the homicide?"

"On everything."

"Not anymore," said the mayor. "We want you to drop this murder thing, let the state cops handle it. Mr. Moran agrees."

He could afford to, now that he'd gotten more publicity out of it than he'd received in his entire career.

"You took a vote?" Zany asked.

"We'll do it right now." Everyone at the table except Moran and the chamber of commerce man raised a hand.

"How the police department conducts its business is supposed to be up to me."

"Who holds your job is up to us," the mayor said. "We mean it, Zane. Forget this murder or we'll turn the police department over to George Hejmal. He at least doesn't think he's Sherlock Holmes." She lowered her eyes, and her voice. "I'm sorry. I know you're just trying to do your duty as you see it, but we see it different. We were going to ask you to back off anyway. What you say about the robberies, how they might be someone trying to tell you something—that only makes it all the more necessary."

"I guess there's nothing left to say." Zany started to get up.

"You know," said the chamber of commerce president, for once not clearing his throat. "It might help if you'd drop by the businesses in town. Reassure them. Tell them you've got everything in hand."

"No problem." Zany did that all the time anyway, excepting only the mortician.

This time it was Moran who cleared his throat. "I'd like to ride around with you a few nights—in one of the patrol cars."

"Sure thing. I'll arrange it with George. You can ride with him."

Zany went glumly back to the police station. Everyone there looked at him as he entered, but he said nothing, going directly into his office. There were some messages on his desk, one of them from the New York burglary detective. Zany crumpled it up and tossed it at his wastebasket. It missed and bounced back toward his feet. He stared at it for a long moment, then picked it up and spread it out on his desk, picking up his phone.

The New York guy had nothing really to tell him. He'd checked with every single one of his sources and snitches, but there had been no word of any trafficking in the kind of art Zany had mentioned, certainly no Kirchners. However, the detective said he'd worked up a list of the collectors he knew about who bought such things. He asked if he could fax it to Zany. The collectors were mostly in the New York area, though there was one in Baltimore, and a couple in Philadelphia.

"Don't have a fax," Zany said. "Just put it in the mail."

He gave the man his home address.

The wind had indeed brisked up, gusting now to twenty-five knots and more, but instead of shifting to the north, it kept swinging back and forth—west to northwest and back again—keeping Matthias busy with adjustments in sail. He had taken over the helm from Poe as soon as they were past Montrose Harbor. He and the rest of the crew had put on foul weather jackets against the spray that was kicking up and the weather front that was approaching. Matthias had invited Poe to go below, but Poe had elected to remain topside, sitting next to Curland and trying to keep out of the way. He'd poured himself a strong scotch and water, asking Matthias to join him, but his skipper had declined, saying that would have to wait until after the finish—if then. Curland didn't seem to drink much.

Poe's exhilaration had largely worn off, replaced by unspoken anger and frustration. Yeats had made one clumsy pass at trying to slow the commodore's boat, cutting across its bow but not hampering it much, and now he'd fallen behind, as if deliberately. The commodore's craft was in the lead, with Yeats second by several lengths. The *Lady P* was lying sixth—a good showing, considering their laidback start—but was losing ground on the leader. Matthias had changed course slightly to starboard, and the *Lady P* was pulling off to the right, slipping farther out into the lake. When this continued for more than a few minutes, Poe reached and pulled on Matthias's sleeve.

"What the hell are you doing?" he said.

"Taking what you'd call a gamble."

"A gamble? On what?"

"The wind. It hasn't shifted the way it was forecast. You see that line of clouds along the coast?"

Poe looked, then nodded.

"That's a weak storm front," Matthias said. "I don't think there's much heavy weather associated with it. May not even be any rain. It seems to have stalled for the time being, but when it passes, that's when the winds will shift for good, to northerly."

Poe's turquoise eyes were full of impatience.

"If the other boats stay close in like that, they'll have to start tacking to make headway. If we hang out here far enough, we'll be able to take a north wind on a close haul, without tacking. At least for a while. We should gain a lot of distance. Might even take the lead."

"I get the idea."

"When I say close hauled, I mean the absolute limit. It'll get rough, and it'll get wet. I really think you'll be happier below."

Poe drank some of his whiskey. "You keep saying that. I'll stick it out up here."

"At the least, put on some foul weather gear. You'll get soaked enough even with that."

Matthias was wearing khaki shorts, boating shoes, and a bright-red waterproof jacket. Poe was in white pants, red polo shirt, and deck shoes. He'd thought he'd looked natty.

"In a minute." Poe drank again. He really hated being told what to do.

He looked up at the huge straining sails, then over his shoulder, at the rest of the racing craft. "The other boats are pulling ahead."

"Don't worry. When they start tacking, you'll see them slow down in a hurry."

"The way we're moving off to the east, I'll need binoculars."

"That's the plan."

"What if the wind doesn't change?"

"As I said, Mr. Poe, it's a gamble."

They continued on their oblique course for nearly an hour—as best as Poe could determine at the increasing distance, falling back to twelfth or thirteenth. Another boat far back in the pack tried to emulate Matthias's gambit, but decided on it too tardily. When it finally gave up, turning back on a straight northerly course, it was much farther behind than when it had begun.

Poe watched another boat pass by on the western horizon.

"Maybe we ought to think about getting back with the others," he said.

"It's too late for that now. The wind's out of the northwest. We'd have to tack to get back among them. Probably end up last."

Poe stared into the west. The line of clouds seemed to be larger, nearer. "We could be out of business."

Diandra had told Matthias, "You'd better make sure he wins that race." He'd be out of business himself, for good.

"If there's one thing you can always count on with this lake," Matthias said, "it's a change in the weather."

The cloud line was moving, all right, and fast. The tops of the big cumulous billows were high, and in minutes they'd blotted out the sinking afternoon sun. The whitecaps were increasing. The mast stays hummed with the force of the wind.

"Cindy!" Matthias shouted above it. "Go below and fetch Mr. Poe some foul weather gear."

The blond darted through the hatch. Another hand took her place at the winch. Matthias had earlier exchanged the big Genoa jib for a smaller sail. Now he ordered the mainsail reefed a couple of turns.

The boat was heeling sharply. Poe had replenished his drink. He foolishly set down his cup to accept the gear from a speedily returning Cindy. The cup shot across the cockpit like something fired from a gun. A wave smacking against the hull doused Poe with spray before he quite got the waterproof jacket on. He swore. The clouds were tearing by overhead.

"Don't worry, Mr. Poe. This is hardly worth a small craft warning," Matthias said.

Poe swore again.

Matthias, gripping the wheel tightly, kept switching his gaze from aloft to abeam. To the west, there was a thin line of blue between the cloud base and the horizon. It ran uninterrupted from north to south. As they watched, it began to increase.

"Clear sky over there," Matthias said. "This'll be over very soon."

Poe hunkered down, gripping the railing behind him with both hands, wondering if he should put on a life jacket. One of the crew members forward had done so. Heaving folds of water foamed over the rail opposite. It looked as if the boom and billowing mainsail were about to dip into it.

Suddenly, with a wrenching lurch, the boat righted and the mainsail began to flap thunderously.

"We're in irons!" Matthias shouted. He looked up at the wind direction indicator on the little mast behind him. "Due north! Perfect!"

Poe was confused. The blond was back at her winch, looking expectantly at Matthias. Other crew members were scurrying forward.

"Ready about!" Matthias commanded.

"Ready!" came a chorus of responses.

"Helm's a lee!" Matthias spun the wheel.

Poe ducked as the big boom swung toward him. The girl and a crew member opposite her were cranking the winches furiously. The bow swung back toward the land. The sails cracked full of wind, which was coming now over the starboard side. Matthias had yanked himself over to the opposite seat. Poe followed, his shoes slipping on the Fiberglas deck, clambering furiously, pulling himself onto the seat. The heel now was worse than before, the mast tilted toward the coast. The bow thumped with each wave.

"Perfect!" Matthias shouted again.

Poe, wishing he were on his big motor yacht watching it all, pulled the hood of his jacket over his head.

They seemed to be sailing hellbent for the shore—though, glancing along the line of the bow, Poe could see their angle of approach was long and oblique. The other boats appeared to be milling about, sailing back and forth. As Matthias had predicted, the *Lady P* drew steadily abeam of them and then ahead.

"Son of a bitch," Poe said. "You're a genius."

"We've got to sail the entire coast of Wisconsin," Matthias said. "It's a long race to go."

"But we're gonna take the lead!"

"For a time. We have another twenty or thirty minutes of sailing on this bearing. Then we'll have to turn due north and tack into the wind like the rest of them."

Poe slapped him on the arm. "I've got great faith." He looked aft across the transom, the commodore's boat two or three football field lengths distant, the other craft zigzagging behind it. "I'm going below."

"Dry off?"

"No. I've got to make some calls over the radio. Business."

You can do business with anyone, but you sail only with gentleman, J. P. Morgan had said. What would that old man have made of Poe?

"This wind's going to stay northerly all night," Matthias said. "We'll have our hands full with the tacking."

"I'll be in my cabin. Just let me know if that son of a bitch gets ahead of us again."

"He will, eventually."

Poe was looking at Cindy. She was cute, with an upturned nose, long legs, and a terrific tan. If this was his motor yacht, he might ask her to come down below with him for a drink. Poe wondered if Curland had anything going with her. According to his brother Christian, he'd been fooling around with the Langley girl. Maybe both these guys were cocksmen.

"Just don't let things get fucked up, Captain," Poe said.

He groped his way to the hatch.

As promised, Zany spent the afternoon making his rounds of the Grand Pier, repeating the tour after dinner. Satisfied that everything was under control, he got onto the interstate and made the trip up to St. Joseph, pulling up at the county sheriff's office. The sheriff wasn't in, but his chief deputy was. He and Zany were fishing buddies. The deputy was a local man who had spent a few years with the Detroit police force, moving back home when he couldn't take the huge, nasty caseload any more.

"Coffee?" said the deputy, as Zany eased himself into an old wooden chair by the man's desk.

"Yes, please," Zany said. "It's going to be another long night."

"You still working that homicide?" the deputy said, bringing over two plastic cups.

Zany sipped. The coffee was worse than his own department's.

"Not officially," Zany said. "Got the word from the town fathers today. They want the State Police to take it over so I can deal with our little crime wave."

"We can't spare you any more men, not with all this drug shit in Benton Harbor."

Zany shuddered at the mention of St. Joe's decrepit neighboring city. Crime there was as bad as on the West Side of Chicago.

"Somebody made the observation today that, if the winds had been different, that boat with the dead girl might have washed up here. What would you guys have done?"

"Hell, that's easy. Notify the Chicago cops and try to figure out where the murder took place."

"I've done both. The Chicago guys weren't too helpful. Kinda busy these days. The coroner estimated she'd been killed around midnight. I had the Coast Guard work up a probable course for me, starting in Chicago. Calculating the winds and everything, they figured it traveled maybe twenty or twenty-five miles between that midnight and when it washed up in Grand Pier. That means she was killed pretty far out in the lake."

"Any idea where?"

"There are a lot of variables to consider, but probably one side or the other of the Illinois-Indiana line. Indiana's got a pretty good slice of the lake, you know."

"You going to call in the Indiana guys to help?"

"I'm not supposed to call anyone. Drop the case or else. And that could mean my job."

"What the hell, Zany. We've got a lot of unsolved homicides in our files. Nobody's sweating them."

Zany guessed they were mostly in Benton Harbor.

"Until this, I didn't have any. It isn't just that we're striking out that's chewing on me; it's that the perps are screwing around with me. They tried to link me with some murdered hooker."

"I read about that. I guess they whacked her pretty good. Throat job and all. Chicago cops turn up anything on that?"

"They're not looking very hard. They ID'd the woman as the perp in that big O'Rourke case of theirs. It tidied up things for them nicely. I don't think they're interested in poking around anything that'll mess up their happy ending."

"You know the investigating officer?"

"Yeah. Frank Baldessari. He's an old friend."

"Why not go over and see if you can get him off his ass? If what you say is true, it seems to me that if you solve the hooker thing you got a good lead on who waxed your lady of the lake."

Zany stared into his coffee. "To tell you the truth, I hadn't even thought about that."

"Police chiefs aren't the only guys who got smarts."

"Trouble is, I don't dare make another trip to Chicago. At least not an official one."

"Well, I wish I could help you, Zany. But I don't see how we can get involved."

"Actually, there is something you could do, though I hope it won't come to that."

"What's that? We can't spare you any more deputies."

"Depleting your manpower isn't exactly what I have in mind."

Bobby Mann had been on the floor of the Michigan City casino most of the evening, but, noting the time, returned to his office and turned on the television set. He had to wait twenty minutes before the 10 o'clock news got around to the sailboat race story, but there it was—a beautiful big picture of Lake Michigan in the bright sunshine, a crowd of sails against the Chicago skyline, people all along the shore. Poe's new boat figured largely in the story. They closed with a shot of Poe at the wheel, waving as the boats moved from the starting line.

Mann flicked his television off with a remote control switch, then swiveled his chair to look out his window at the blackness that was the lake, stretching off to the limitless north. Poe and his boat would be way up there by now, but it would be another day or more before he reached Menominee. It would be several days more before he returned to Michigan City. After the race, there was supposed to be a big party in Menominee. And Poe planned to sail his boat back to Chicago.

Mango Bellini had been in Chicago for the start of the race. If she'd come back to Michigan City, she hadn't looked in on him. Mann was running the casino on his own, as was often the case nowadays.

After glancing again at his watch, Mann pulled open a desk drawer and opened a metal cash box, scooping out a handful of change. He was going to use a pay phone to make his long distance calls, but didn't want anything showing up on his credit card.

He pocketed the coins, closed the box and the drawer, and left his office. After pausing at the downstairs bar for a drink and lighting a cigarette, he strolled out into the lobby.

"Leaving for the night, Mr. Mann?" said the doorman.

"Just going to get some air."

The wind was cool, coming straight down the lake. Mann turned onto the boardwalk. There was a couple necking at the railing, but they ignored him. Sauntering along, Mann came at length to some wooden steps leading to a parking lot. On the other side, near the street, was a public phone.

He knew the Atlantic City number by heart. The party on the other end answered quickly, and the conversation was over in less than a minute.

For his next call, he had to dig a folded piece of paper with the number on it out of his pocket. He let it ring six times, then hung up, immediately dialing it again.

"Yeah?"

"It's me. You guys in place?"

"Yes sir."

"I got the go. You're on."

"Gotcha."

"Do it right."

"Always do."

THERE HAD BEEN a weather advisory warning of a strong secondary front approaching that night behind the weak one that had swept across the lake in the afternoon. It struck shortly after midnight, kicking up a line of squalls and monstrous swells that set the *Lady P* to pitching violently, the bow slamming down after each crest with great thuds and smacks.

Poe rolled out of his bunk. He'd thrown up twice during the night and feared he'd do so again before he could reach the sink of his little bathroom. Fighting it, he pushed himself back against the side of the bunk, waiting until he felt confident enough of his stomach to move further.

The nausea passed, but with all the pitching and rolling, the best he could manage was a crouch when he got to his feet. Gripping handholds, he made his way into the main cabin, where three crew members, oblivious to the tumult, were sleeping peacefully. Poe lurched to the ladder and hauled himself up to the hatch. The doors had been closed against the storm. Opening one, he poked out his head, only to be drenched by a wave coming over the cabin.

Matthias was at the wheel, shouting commands to the crew members on deck. The girl named Cindy was stuffing sail into a huge bag. One of the young men was pulling frantically on a rope. They were all wearing life jackets over their foul weather gear.

More wave water sloshed down the back of Poe's neck.

Curland noticed him, but quickly returned his attention to his tasks.

"What's going on?" Poe shouted.

"We've got a storm on our hands! Better stay below!"

"We gonna make it?"

"I've switched to storm sails and reefed the main by half! We'll weather it! Don't worry! Get below!"

"Are we on course?"

"I'm a bit busy, Mr. Poe. Please, go back. I'll join you in a minute."

Poe wiped the water from his eyes. Feeling vulnerable, he dropped back into the cabin to strap on a life jacket himself, then hesitated. He didn't know if it would help or hurt his seasickness, but this certainly seemed time for another stiff drink. He managed to get a bottle of Cutty Sark out of the storage cabinet without breaking it. He tried pouring some into a plastic cup, but it spilled, so he drank straight from the bottle. He took two good slugs, then, steeling himself, started topside again. It wouldn't do to have one of the crew leak it to the papers that the mighty Peter Poe had ridden out a storm huddled in his cabin. He wasn't sure he wanted to be down there anyway, in case they capsized.

Before Poe could ascend the little ladder, Matthias suddenly came clambering down, easing past Poe and moving in remarkably graceful lunges to the little chart table. Hunching over it, he turned on a tiny lamp and pulled out a rolled-up plastic map.

"Are we lost?" Poe asked.

Curland ignored him. After returning the map to its place, he went back to the ladder and heaved himself back up to the hatch.

"Fall off more to starboard and ease the main!" he shouted to someone at the helm. "I want a heading of twenty degrees."

After snapping shut the doors, he slid back down and lowered himself onto a small stool mounted to the floorboards.

"You want a drink?" Poe asked.

Matthias gave him a not very indulgent look.

"Sorry," Poe said. "You're on duty. What's the situation?"

"The storm's a lot stronger than forecast," Matthias said, catching his breath. "I'm clocking winds of thirty-five knots, from the northwest."

"I thought the wind was out of the north."

"Lake Michigan, Mr. Poe. Things change, fast. We're holding our own, but I'm a little worried about the smaller class of boats. I'd hate to see this turn into another Fastnet Rock."

"What the hell's that?"

"They hold a race every year off the coast of England, to a little island called Fastnet Rock. There was a terrible storm back in the 1970s that hit them midway across. I think it wrecked a dozen boats. A lot of people drowned. Ted Turner ended up winning it. He lashed himself to his boat and clung to the helm. According to his crew, he hung on there all the way, shouting curses at the wind."

"Turner did that?"

"He got mixed reviews as a skipper, but no one ever doubted his courage."

"Are we still in the lead?"

"Before the storm blew up, the commodore's boat was about fifty yards astern and another fifty or so to port. The others I could see were well behind."

"How did he make up so much ground?"

Matthias smiled. "He's got people in his crew who competed in the Olympics."

"They're that much better than ours?"

"They're pretty damn good. He's also got a better boat."

"Shit. I could kill that Yeats."

"The *Lady P* is a fine sailboat. It's just that we've all had to tack back and forth all night and the commodore and his crew are hard to beat at that. If the wind changes again after this front passes—and I think it will soon—we can go back to steady sailing and back to skippering. The commodore's smart and very experienced, but not what you'd call devilishly clever. Much too conservative to take a lot of gambles."

"Hey," Poe said. "Who's sailing the boat?"

"Cindy's at the helm. Don't worry. She's our best crew member. Almost as good as Jill. They were friends, you know."

Poe frowned. "Maybe you should get back up there."

"I intend to, as soon as I use the head. You might as well get back in your bunk."

Poe shook his head, then lifted his bottle, taking a long pull. "You sure you don't want a drop?" he asked.

"No, thank you."

Poe returned the bottle to the cabinet, then moved to the ladder.

"Where are you going?" Matthias asked.

"Topside. I want to see all this."

"It's dangerous, you know."

Poe grinned. "I'll tie myself to something, like Ted Turner."

By dawn, the storm had blown itself out, leaving the sky crystalline clear, the distant Wisconsin shoreline sharply etched in the pale light, though it appeared to be miles away. The wind was no longer so ferocious, but still strong, and the *Lady P* was moving very fast, leaving a churned-up wake.

Poe was cold and stiff. When he turned his head to look back at the other boats in the race, it hurt his neck.

The commodore's craft must have run into some kind of trouble because, though still in second place, it had fallen far back. It was lying a good mile to the west of them as well. Squinting toward the south, Poe could make out five or six other sails.

"I hope nobody went down," he said. It sounded like the thing to say.

"I think everyone's all right," Matthias said. Cindy was sitting at his side, asleep despite the cold, her head on his shoulder. "We didn't pick up any distress calls. They're probably strung out back there all along the coast. Some of them might have hove to, to ride out the blow."

"How come the commodore's lagging back there?"

"He probably broke a halyard or a sheet, or maybe lost a sail. Don't worry. He'll be sticking with us. He's changed sails. Got his big main up again."

"What about us?" Poe looked at the straining canvas above him.

"I'll change sail in a few minutes. I want to wait a little longer on the wind. We've been making excellent time in all this, but the wind's dropping and shifting around to the southwest. If it keeps moving around behind us, I may put up the spinnaker."

"You mean that big balloon sail?"

"It's very pretty."

"You're sure the wind's not too strong? How soon before we reach Green Bay?"

"Late tomorrow. Relax, Mr. Poe."

They kept their lead throughout the long day, but the commodore's boat kept creeping up. At sunset, it was abreast of them, slowly but steadily pulling ahead.

"We're losing," Poe said.

"For the moment," Matthias said. He was sitting up on the transom, holding the wheel fast with his foot. "I don't know what else to do. We're on a run—the wind behind us. I've got up every inch of sail I can lay hands on. The spinnaker's set perfectly. That fact is, the gentleman has the best boat on the lake."

"If this were a car race, we could bump him off to the side."

"We'd have to catch him first. And it wouldn't be considered very sporting. You'd hear about it. Probably get yourself disqualified. If you won, they'd take back your trophy."

Poe stared down at the deck of the cockpit. His seasickness had vanished, and now he was hungry.

"You going to give that girl the watch again tonight?" he said finally.

"As I said, Cindy's the best we have."

"You like her?"

"Very much."

"She sure likes you."

"Mr. Poe, she's the daughter of an old friend of mine."

"I wish Diandra could see us. I don't think she believed I'd go through with this."

"I'm sure she has every confidence in you. I do. You handled yourself very well last night."

"The Cutty helped."

"I'd ease up on that. Clouds your judgment, Mr. Poe."

"It's your judgment that counts here. And it's Peter, damn it. Come on. Knock off the Mr. Poe."

Matthias looked off toward the setting sun and then sent a deckhand scurrying to put on the running lights. The commodore already had his on.

"You like Diandra, Matt?" Poe asked.

"You have a lovely wife."

"I'm serious about you doing her picture."

"I'd be happy to do her portrait, but my brother's much better."

"I want you, and I want a nude."

"I'm not sure that would be appropriate."

"She's a model. She's done nude shots with photographers. For body lotion ads."

"Mr. Poe. Peter. Sally and I are going to be married."

"Yeah? It's true?"

"We haven't set a date, but it's true."

The red light of a distant buoy was winking at them from near the shore.

"Depends on your financial situation, right?" Poe said.

"In part. But I don't think we're going to change our minds. It just a matter of the timing."

"You really want to do my building, don't you?"

"It's a fantastic opportunity. And it would be very good for the city, to have such a project in that neighborhood."

198

"I haven't made up my mind yet."

"So I gather."

Poe raised himself stiffly to get a better look at the commodore's boat. "He's probably laughing his ass off about us."

"I'm sure he's quite pleased with himself. He's won this race three years in a row—ever since he got that boat."

"And there's nothing we can do to slow him down?"

You paid a price for everything you took from life. Matthias had learned that much. But you never knew when the bill would come due, or how much it would be.

Matthias had just been presented with a big one. If he didn't pay it—if he didn't do now what he knew it would take for Poe to win this race—there would be no building, not for him. All of his newfound hopes and plans would slide irretrievably behind him, like the wake from this boat.

"Actually, there is something," Matthias said with a frown. "It's not illegal, but it's not the sort of thing I like to do."

"I'm down on the books as the skipper. What do you care?"

"I have a reputation, Peter. I have a lot of friends in this race."

"They didn't do you much good when you were living on that beach in France."

"I didn't ask them to."

"What's the deal? What do you have in mind?"

Matthias sighed. "He'll keep pulling ahead. When he's clear of our bow, we could slide in behind him and steal his wind. He'd have to fall off to get away from us, and we'd get the lead back. For a time."

"Do it."

"It's a little tricky. If we're not careful, we might ride up on his stern and cause a collision. Even if the boats weren't badly damaged, you'd be ruled out of race."

"Do it."

"He may never speak to me again."

"I will."

Matthias sighed again. "You're a hard master. Peter."

He waited another five minutes or more, until there was a fair breadth of water between the *Lady P*'s bow and the other's stern. Then Matthias turned the wheel, ordering hands to trim in the main and jib. The bow shifted to the left, and in short time the *Lady P* was in line behind the other craft. Matthias let out the boom again. The mainsail was soon pressing against the starboard mast stay.

Poe went forward to the cabin bulkhead, ducking his head to see under the jib. The commodore's boat was slowing. Though the light was fading, he thought he could see the other's big sail begin to slacken.

"We'll be coming up on him fast," Matthias warned.

"I don't care if you get close enough to kiss his ass."

"He'll be wanting to kick ours."

"Keep on coming, Matt."

They drew ever nearer, the commodore's boat increasing in size. Its helmsman was trying to maintain his heading. Poe could see crew moving hurriedly about the deck.

Suddenly the other craft's spinnaker fluttered a moment, billowed out again, then fell slack and collapsed.

"That's everything you could hope for," Matthias said. "He'll be a little while getting that up again."

Poe grinned. This was more like it. And it was his decision. He really was skippering this boat.

The *Lady P* plowed forward. They were seconds away from a collision when Matthias spun the helm and they veered away to the left. It seemed the *Lady P* might strike the other boat on its quarter, but she slid on by.

The two sailboats rode side by side, the *Lady P* pulling slowly past. The crewmen on the other boat were busy, but the commodore, standing at his helm, stood staring at them with raised fist. His voice came to them loud and raspy.

"You damned ruffian!"

Poe laughed uproariously. In a few minutes, they were well ahead.

In a moment, however, Poe's expression darkened. "Matt. What if he tries to do the same thing with us?"

Matthias hoped Poe would not be insulted by his answer.

"The commodore," he said, "is a gentleman."

The commodore was also stubborn. Twice during the night, he caught up to the *Lady P* and passed her, compelling Matthias to twice again repeat the wind-blocking maneuver. The commodore even extinguished his riding lights, daring Matthias to risk a collision, but the brilliant starlight was more than enough to delineate the commodore's huge sails and mast, and Matthias stuck to his guns, though he felt more than a little shameful doing so. Finally the commodore bore off on a tack that took him far to starboard, slipping farther and farther behind as he moved farther and farther out into the lake, where the *Lady P* wouldn't interfere with him.

"So much for him," Poe said.

"Don't count on it," Matthias said. "The shoreline curves eastward as you approach the Door County peninsula. We're going to have to steer to starboard ourselves. I'm sure we'll still have the commodore to contend with in the morning—not to speak of when we get to Menominee."

Both men were bone weary.

"I'll worry about that tomorrow," Poe said. "I'm going to turn in. How about you?"

"Not yet. I think I'll stay up through a little of Cindy's watch. Just in case the commodore tries to make another run past us."

"You're sure giving this your all, Matt. I wish I had more people like you working for me."

"If you're not going to give a sailboat race your all, you shouldn't be in it." He paused.

"Something else on your mind, Matt?"

"Yes. For days. I wasn't sure when to bring it up."

"Something about your brother, Chris? Something to do with Diandra?"

"No. I was wondering if you had anything to do with my father being put on the Park District board."

"Why, you don't think it's a good idea?"

"He's rather an old man, and not in the best of health."

"Vito Marzullo served on the City Council into his nineties."

"I'm just afraid my father isn't going to be a very energetic participant, or all that capable a one. I talked to him about it. I'm afraid to say he thought he was being reappointed to the Forest Preserve board."

"He's a distinguished man. After that business with O'Rourke, the Park District could use a little respectability. It helps to have your friend Cooperman as president, too. I don't understand what you're complaining about."

"I'm not complaining. I'm just wondering how much you had to do with it."

"I didn't pull any strings or anything. I suggested it to a guy is all. It was a very popular idea. The mayor even went for it. Your family's got a hell of a good reputation in Chicago."

"Good night, then, Peter."

"Good night, Matt. Happy sailing."

* * *

At sunrise, the commodore's boat was still off to the right, but no longer far behind. They were on converging courses, and another duel was likely, with the commodore the probable victor. The wind was blowing now from the west and had fallen to a fairly light breeze. Less heavy than the commodore's craft, the *Lady P* would have a more equal chance in gentle weather, but the rival boat still had an edge. What might make a decisive difference lay ahead—the turn around the tip of the Door County peninsula into Green Bay. If the *Lady P* was going to win the race, it would have to be there.

There were three sail visible on the southern horizon behind them, but, barring accident, they posed no threat.

Matthias had come back topside after only four hours' sleep. He let Cindy keep the helm, but took a seat beside her, having brought blueberry muffins and coffee for them both. The other crew members changed watch, the newcomers stretching and yawning. On their present course, they had little to do.

Poe didn't rise until midmorning. He'd washed, shaved, and changed clothes, but still looked haggard. Matthias guessed he'd had a nightcap or two before retiring. It seemed quite unlike the man to let his discipline go like that. Perhaps he was trying to be like Ted Turner, who'd mugged for the television cameras after winning the America's Cup with a bottle of whiskey in his hand.

"Shit," said Poe, looking to the east, "the bastard's still there."

"I expect he may even get ahead of us again," Matthias said. "But not by much. Anyway, my hope is to leave him behind for good when we make the turn to the west. I'm afraid we're going to have to take another gamble."

"What's that?"

Matthias called for one of the crew to fetch him a chart. When he had it spread out on his lap, he pointed out their present position, which was lying off the Door County town of Bailey's Harbor.

"Between the end of the peninsula here and this big island—Washington Island—is *le Strait des Mortes,* the gateway to Green Bay. Translated, it means 'the Strait of Death.' In English it's called 'Death's Door Passage.' Very dangerous water for big boats like these. Lots of rocks and shoals. There are a lot of shipwrecks on the bottom. Centuries ago hundreds of Indians were drowned there when their war canoes got caught in a storm."

"How dangerous?"

"It's fine if you stick to the middle and follow your chart, but that'll cost time. If you cut sharply southwest and run close in shore here by Gill's Rock, you can grab yourself a great big lead—unless, of course, you hit a shoal and founder. I can't envision the commodore trying to follow such a course. He has a somewhat deeper draft than we do, and he really loves that boat."

"You don't think I love the *Lady P?*"

"You hardly know her."

"I love my ass. I sure don't feel like joining all those dead Indians. How are you going to avoid those rocks and shoals?"

"I've sailed these waters. I've sailed this race five times. The chart's pretty well marked. Beyond that, I'll post a lookout in the bow pulpit and keep a close watch on the water ahead. And maybe it wouldn't be such a bad idea to pray, if that's something you do."

"Great."

"I've done it before," Cindy said. "Made the close run by Gill's Rock."

Poe stared at her. She wasn't giving him any choice. Peter Poe couldn't be shown to have less balls than some twenty-eight-year-old blond Yuppie.

"I want to win the fucking race, Captain," Poe said. "Let her rip."

Matthias wished he had chosen a better word.

The sun was sliding into its afternoon phase, dappling the waves ahead with shimmers of reflected light as Matthias smoothly turned the wheel and the gliding bow swung toward the broad expanse of water separating mainland from island. The commodore's boat, ahead and to the right, had made the course change just before, apparently headed for the middle of the passage. Matthias followed meekly along, doubtless making the commodore feel supremely confident. There were pine trees all along the shore, which was also marked by slate-gray cliffs. The wind had moved slightly to the northwest and freshened. Poe could see waves breaking beneath some of the rock outcroppings along the coast.

"When are you going to do this?" he asked.

Matthias pointed ahead. "As soon as we get by that headland. It won't be long."

Matthias had ordered everyone into life jackets, and Poe had put one on, as well. He wondered where to position himself through this ordeal, deciding to stand by the cabin bulkhead. There was a handhold to grip without too much obviousness, and he'd be near the rail in case they had to abandon the boat. The water up this far north would be cold, but it was hardly freezing.

His vantage spot gave him a clear view over the bow. He decided it couldn't be much worse than the times he'd flown through thunderstorms. He'd done that, all on his lonesome, and survived handily.

He heard Matthias call out the course change. The bow swung again, the mainsail and jib billowing farther out over the side. The young man in the pulpit was peering through binoculars. Other crew members were using binoculars as well.

Matthias was not. His eyes—temporarily, Poe hoped—were on the commodore's boat.

"He's holding steady to his course!" Matthias said. He was grinning. "He must think we're crazy."

Poe grinned back. He felt like having yet another drink, but pushed that idea away. He was very mad at himself for having such a rotten hangover on a day like this.

The *Lady P* sailed resolutely on. If it happened, Poe realized, it would be all of a sudden. Until then, everything would be as smooth as a Sunday cruise. Poe wondered if they should reduce sail and proceed more slowly and cautiously—but, hell, going fast was what this ballsy maneuver was all about.

He cursed himself for not having taken a video camera aboard. One way or another, this was going to be history.

The one jutting headland had given way to another, larger one. Matthias seemed to be steering directly for it. The shoreline was much nearer. Poe could hear the waves.

How fast were they going? Twelve, fifteen knots? As ordeals went, this one was taking painfully long. A dentist's drilling would seem a real zip after this.

How would Diandra stand up to something like this? How would Mango? He could see her standing on top of the cabin, hands on her hips, laughing her head off. That girl was completely nuts.

Sometimes.

Seagulls were circling overhead, as Poe thought upon it, like vultures. He'd seen the gulls picking over dead fish on the beach at his casino. Would they eat dead humans washed up on shore? They were scavengers. They'd eat anything.

For all his concentration, the lookout's cry caught Poe by surprise. He didn't understand what was happening. Nobody moved but Matthias, who jerked the wheel to starboard. The others stared to port. What did they see?

Poe heaved himself to the other side, gripping the rail. All he saw at first was water, then there it was, a long, dark gray shape just below the surface, like the back of a huge whale.

They passed the damn rock by no more than ten feet. Poe expected relief and exultation when they were clear of it, but the grim silence of the crew continued unabating. They still had a long way to go.

The lookout shouted again.

By the time they'd gotten around the second headland—the little fishing port of Gill's Rock appearing on their left—they had altered course half a dozen times, squeezing by obstructions to right and left, one rock so close Poe felt he could reach out and touch it. Twice the keel scraped bottom. Poe could feel the deck shudder beneath his feet. But the grating sound quickly diminished.

Fishing boats dotted the water ahead of them. The declining sun suffused everything with a bright and golden light. Now, at last, the crew began cheering.

Smiling, Matthias gave the helm over to Cindy. He stood up, stretching his back and arms.

"Well, Mr. Poe. You've won the race."

CHAPTER
10

THE *LADY P* CROSSED the finish more than seven minutes ahead of the commodore's boat. With Jill Langley in his crew, Matthias had once won this race by a margin of nearly half an hour, but he was just as pleased with the lesser showing. To Poe, that seven-minute separation was as good as beating the Russians to the moon.

Matthias had given him the helm as soon as they'd gotten through the cluster of fishing boats off the Gill's Rock wharf. The commodore had made one last desperate try, making a run down the west side of Chambers Island on a fast beam reach while the *Lady P* swept close-hauled along the island's east coast, but the effort came far too late. Poe steered his yacht into the Menominee River estuary looking like Columbus returning to Spain.

It wasn't as grand as an America's Cup finish. They were on the southern edge of the Upper Peninsula of Michigan, not at Newport or San Diego, but there were a number of small craft at anchor awaiting their arrival and a sizable number of spectators on the shore—even a small, five-piece band playing on the dock.

To Poe's greater satisfaction, there was a press boat crowded with photographers and TV cameramen—many of them presumably from Chicago—waiting at the river mouth. Poe became so preoccupied with posing for them at the wheel that Matthias had to warn him sharply to steer to port to avoid running aground.

They dropped anchor where an escort boat instructed, then Poe and Matthias went aboard for the trip to shore, leaving Cindy and the rest of the crew to stow the sails and follow later. The representatives of the race committee waiting on the dock greeted Poe warmly, but the trophy presentation and victory presentation would of course have to wait until the other boats finished and the official times were calculated.

This didn't prevent the reporters present from swarming around Poe, who obliged them with several conquering hero poses and a few quotes about the dangers of the voyage and the ease of his victory. He worked in the revelation that he had found sailing so much fun he'd lost interest in running a baseball team, and would probably abandon his plans to buy the White Sox. He said, however, that he was going to buy a larger boat and was thinking seriously of entering the next America's Cup race.

Diandra was hanging back at the edge of the crowd. Poe, annoyed that she hadn't rushed up to congratulate him, waved her forward with a curt gesture. She complied, moving gracefully through the spectators, giving Poe a kiss for the cameras and then standing with her arm around him. She was wearing a white, loose-fitting pants suit with a navy blouse and scarf, looking a little like a 1940s movie star.

She had taken off her sunglasses for the picture-taking. When Poe was done with her, she put them back on, then eased away and came over to Matthias.

"You did it," she said quietly.

"It wasn't easy. I'm quite amazed we pulled it off."

"Did Peter do anything at all?"

"You saw him take her out at the start. He stayed up top with me during a rather bad storm and had the helm for the last leg."

"After you had the race won."

"He acquitted himself well, given the circumstances. It's his boat. He's entitled to his moment of glory."

The commodore came ashore looking grim. He ignored the crowd that had gathered around Poe and went directly to the building adjoining the dock that the race committee was using for its headquarters. Poe watched him, then disengaged himself and joined Matthias and Diandra.

"What's that about?" he asked.

"I can guess."

"A protest?"

"Yes."

"Can you take care of it?" Poe asked. "I have some calls to make."

Matthias nodded.

"Can he make it stick?" Poe asked.

"No. We didn't come that close to him. But whatever he has to say is going to get into the newspapers."

"Maybe not. I've invited all the news guys over to the hotel for a little party. I've got a couple of suites, and rooms for you and the crew."

"Do you want me to come with you, Peter?" Diandra asked.

"I want you to play hostess to the newsies at the party." He looked to Matthias. "I want the crew over there, too. Maybe that Cindy of yours will keep the reporters' minds off of the commodore's beef."

Matthias nodded again. What the crew doubtless wanted most was a hot shower and some sleep. He desired precisely that himself.

"We'll see you in a little bit, Matthias," Diandra said.

Something about her was different—an edge to her voice, a sharpness in her glance. Matthias wondered if Poe was in for a fight that night. He wouldn't be expecting it.

Matthias watched them get into the big red limousine for the short drive to the hotel, then started over toward the race committee. He'd begun the race with friends in this group. Now he might not have so many.

Poe's first call was to Mango Bellini, who was waiting as instructed at his Chicago office.

"Everyone in the world has called you, Peter. I've got state legislators, aldermen, two banks, Bitsie Symms, and a guy from Cudahy, Brown."

Poe was in the bedroom of his suite, the door closed and locked. "Don't they know I've been on a goddamned sailboat for three days?"

"I guess they want to be at the top of the list for callbacks."

"Anything serious?"

"I don't think so."

"Is there anything else I have to worry about?"

"There sure as hell is. Bobby Mann."

"Mango. This call is going through a hotel switchboard."

"I understand, but listen to me good. Bobby had some visitors—three guys I really don't like the looks of. And he's been making some calls from pay phones. Pay phones! He goes out of his office and uses the pay phone by the boardwalk when he thinks no one's looking."

"How do you know that? You're in Chicago."

"I've had a couple of our guys keep an eye on him. He met with those three guys in some bum joint in Valparaiso—the kind of place he wouldn't be seen dead in, you know? Afraid he might get grease on his French cuffs or something."

"I'll talk to him when I get back. It'll be another three days on the boat, maybe more, since we won't be busting our hump."

"I wouldn't wait that long, Peter."

"I promised Diandra a sailboat trip back. You know, a little cruise. She's really looking forward to it."

"Bobby's acting spooky, Peter. One tipoff is how nice he's been to me. I was out there last night. He treated me like a lady, a real queen. Usually when you're gone he treats me like shit."

Poe had taken off his shoes and socks. He stared at his bare feet, thinking.

"What's your best idea of what's up, babe?" he said.

"I think your partners—Bobby's friends in Atlantic City—are fixing to do something quick about your new accounting procedures. Maybe even a change in management. I think these three mutts are their business representatives. Don't say I didn't warn you."

"You warned me, okay?"

"By the fucking way, those state legislators are getting kinda antsy, Peter. They extended the session to take up your museum bill, but they've got no one around to send in the signals. The House is taking the bill up on second reading tomorrow. You and Bill Yeats picked a hell of a time to go sailing."

Poe looked out the window. More sailboats were approaching the little port. He'd just won this race. Why was he allowing himself to be hectored like this?

"Lighten up, Mango. I'll charter a plane, all right? Fly it back myself. There's a big dinner here tonight. They're going to present the trophy. I'm not going to let Bobby Mann fuck that up for me."

"Congratulations, Peter. You must feel terrific, beating all those stuck-up bastards. But this is serious. You can't get back too soon. I'll meet you at Meigs in one of the limos. Radio ahead and give me some notice. I think we ought to have some friends around."

"Okay. Everything else is quiet?"

"Yeah. Quiet enough."

"Keep it that way. Don't go for any walks in the park, okay?"

"Love you, Peter."

"Me, too, babe."

"Are you bringing Diandra back with you?"

"We'll see."

"Maybe not, huh? We could have some fun."

"See you, Mango."

He sat a moment after hanging up. Krasowski had a couple of pistols in the stretch. Had it come to that? The biggest man in Chicago, sweating a few scumbags? Worrying about gunplay?

Once he was done with these bastards, that would be it. "You can do business with anyone, but you sail only with gentlemen," Curland had said. From now on, only gentlemen.

The commodore filed two protests—one against the *Lady P* and another against Yeats's boat. The race committee waited until most of the other skippers were in and took statements. Once that was done, they were quick to reach a decision. The complaint against Poe was dismissed. The *Lady P* had in no way interfered with the commodore's navigation, and stealing wind was a commonplace and permissible if ungentlemanly tactic. With Yeats they were harsh. Three other skippers had seen him steer toward the commodore. Yeats was disqualified and his fourth-place finish given to the next boat. The officials ignored the commodore's charge that Poe had put Yeats up to the underhanded tactic. He certainly had no proof of that, and the circumstance of his being Poe's lawyer was not unusual. Several of the yachtsmen in the race were on each other's corporate boards of directors. The commodore's own doctor had been in the race.

Furious, the commodore vowed to have Yeats ousted from his yacht club. Of Peter Poe's pending application for membership, he spoke most unkindly, indeed.

The commodore hoisted sail and started back for Chicago immediately, but all the other skippers and crews were at the dinner, as were a lot of yachtsmen from Door County across the bay, who had sailed or motored over to watch the finish of the race. The speeches and joking went on much longer than Poe, impatient, wanted, but finally they got around to presenting him with the trophy—a gold-plated cup much smaller than he had expected. He kept his remarks brief, but, to the surprise of many, gave Matthias a lot of credit for the victory—describing him as "my helmsman and navigator." He made a little ceremony about signing a check for $100,000 payable to his foundation, but did not elaborate on how it would be spent.

He'd already decided to hold another news conference in Chicago to do that. It would give him an opportunity to deal with the commodore's charges, making the old curmudgeon look like a bad sport. He might even suggest that the "favorite charity" the commodore would have given the $100,000 to had he won was the Republican Party. The mayor would appreciate that.

The dance band started up. Poe leaned over to speak to Diandra, but not to ask her for a turn on the floor.

"I called Chicago," he said. "I'm afraid I've got a lot of pressing business. I chartered a Lear out of Sturgeon Bay. I'm going back tonight—right now. You want to come?"

He knew very well she didn't.

"If you insist, Peter."

"I don't insist. You wanted to go back on the *Lady P*. Why don't you? Curland's got to sail it back anyway. There's a nice cabin. Some booze. You'll have a nice time."

She looked across the table at Matthias, who was talking to the blond girl from the crew.

"Whatever you say," Diandra said. She thought of something. "I'd like to stop at Door County on the way back. I've never seen it."

"Great. Whatever you want."

"I'll need a car there. I want to look around."

"I'll have Lenny drive the stretch over. Where do you want him to meet you?"

"I haven't the faintest idea."

"Make it Ephraim. It has a good harbor. Okay?"

"Have a nice trip, Peter."

He gave her a kiss on the cheek, then stood up, clutching his golden cup and patting her back.

"Matt," he said. "You'll have just one passenger tomorrow, okay? Mrs. Poe. I'm taking a plane back."

"You are?"

"Business."

"I'll try to make it as pleasurable a voyage as possible."

"I'm sure you will. She wants to stop over at Door County. I'll have a car waiting at Ephraim. Good-bye, everybody. Great job."

Poe waved to the crew members, then started walking quickly away. Abruptly he stopped and motioned to Matthias to join him. Curland, uncertain, rose and came forward.

"You got the job," Poe said. "I want you to do my building. That jake with you?"

"More than jake."

"Sure?"

"That building's becoming something of an obsession with me."

"Terrific." Poe slapped him on the shoulder. "Don't say a word to anyone, not even Sally. I still want to make the announcement in a very big way, okay?"

"Certainly."

"Your fee will run large, won't it? Like maybe a million when all is said and done."

"I've no idea."

"Well, I do."

Poe started off again.

"Excuse me, but which design do you want?" Matthias asked. "The tower, or the whole thing?"

"Haven't decided yet," Poe said, over his shoulder, and kept going.

Cindy asked Matthias to dance, and kept him out on the floor for two more numbers. When they returned, Diandra was sitting all alone, looking bored and unhappy. The music was a little faster than Matthias liked, but he went to her and asked if she'd like to dance. She accepted, but with a weary reluctance.

As he expected, she danced beautifully, if formally, keeping her body at some distance from his. In her high heels, she was again an inch or two taller than he.

"Having a good time?" he asked.

She turned her head to look into his eyes. "It's improving, but not enough."

"I'm sorry."

Diandra glanced around the room. "Can we go outside?"

"Whatever you like."

"I'd like to take a little walk. Maybe down to the river."

Despite the northern latitude, it was a warm night. Diandra maintained her distance from him, until they reached the walkway along the riverbank, when she slipped her arm in his.

"Peter seemed subdued," she said. "I thought he'd be doing cartwheels. Jumping up and down. Shouting."

"I guess he's preoccupied."

"He's always preoccupied. The only way to get his mind off business is with a lobotomy, and I'm not sure that would work."

They passed under some trees, and then came out into the clear again. Boat lights twinkled in the soft darkness.

"Why did you marry him?" Matthias asked.

She turned, her eyes meeting his.

"I'm sorry," Matthias said. "That was impertinent."

"It's not that. It's just that—it's funny, I was just now asking myself the same question. Though it's one I've asked myself many times, including on my wedding night."

"I was rude."

"Stop being so stuffy, Matthias. It grates on me after a while."

They moved on. The band music seemed to be floating in the air behind them.

"I married him mostly because I was curious, I guess," she said finally, her voice soft again. "I was doing very well as a model, making five hundred dollars an hour doing the New York shows. Modeling work is hard. You don't dare turn anything down. Your meter's running, if you know what I mean. What you turn down in your twenties you know you'll never get in your thirties, when you start to go old. But it was rewarding. I liked the life. I traveled. I had no interest in getting married, not then. Certainly not to an egomaniac like Peter. When he proposed, I said no. I think it threw him."

"But eventually you said yes."

"It wasn't his money, if that's what you're thinking, though I'll admit that was nice. I'd been proposed to by wealthy men before, most of them empty-headed fools, for all their business expertise. You know the type. That party of Bitsie Symms was full of them."

She slowed her pace. Their bodies bumped closer.

"They all wanted to buy a beauty. That was part of it with Peter. Be sure of that. But there was more. He found me capable, useful, not just a decoration. He was different in another way. He didn't just want to be rich and smiled upon. Peter's got a big game going on with the world, a contest, a war if you like, and he means to win. I was fascinated by the idea of being with him at the end, to see if he did. I was curious to know what it would be like to be Mrs. Peter Poe."

"And now you know."

"Yes."

"And?"

She turned to look at him in the dim light, her eyes seeking trust. "It isn't what I expected. There's no excitement, no challenge. He hasn't made me a part of things. I suppose I'd be appalled by what I discovered if he did, but it's hard being left out. I'm bored to tears most of the time, and my life is very lonely."

"I'm sorry."

"Don't be. We all have our sorrows. Mine aren't as bad as some."

"Do you love him?" His boldness surprised him. Something about pulling that dirty trick on the commodore had changed him, brought something long hidden deep within him to the surface.

"Do you love Sally Phillips?"

Boldness for boldness. He had no answer.

"Don't take this wrong, Matthias, but I used to hope I'd someday fall in love with someone like you—cultured, romantic, very intelligent. Someone who might write me poetry—or paint my portrait."

She took her hand from his arm. "That was when I was in college, a long time ago."

She halted suddenly, looking up. "What on earth is that?"

A long, iridescent, gauzy cloud was dancing overhead, far, far overhead. It was an astonishing thing, for the sky was otherwise clear, with bright stars everywhere.

"It's not on earth at all," Matthias said. "It's the aurora borealis. A plume of gases thousands of miles away. It's picking up the light of the sun."

"It's beautiful. I've never seen such a thing before."

"Normally you don't this far south, but sometimes the atmospheric conditions are just right."

"God, it's marvelous."

She leaned close to him again. They stood together, heads tilted back. She took a deep breath, then another, then closed her eyes, swaying slightly.

He couldn't help himself. He suspected he wasn't intended to.

Her lips parted slightly when they kissed. He gently pulled her closer. She yielded, then stiffened, finally pulling away.

"This is going to get us both into very big trouble."

"I'm sorry."

She took his hand. "No. Don't be. I'm just not thinking very clearly."

"Perhaps we should go back."

"Yes. You must be tired after all that sailing."

"Not really. Winning is always invigorating."

"That's what Peter always says. You can dance with your friend Cindy then. She certainly seems up tonight. I'm going to bed. I want to do some reading." She stopped and turned. "Across the bay there, that's Door County?"

"Yes. A little bit of Maine, here in the Midwest."

"Can we have lunch there?

"Sure. There's a Scandinavian place in Sister Bay with live goats on its roof."

"I hope it's a thick roof."

They walked back to the hotel. In the lobby, by the elevators, he kissed her hand and said good night, then paused.

"Your husband told me he wants me to do his building."

She smiled, a little cynically. "Matt, he decided that the instant he looked at your plans."

Matthias stayed at the party only long enough to chat with a few old friends and make sure that the crew were being treated hospitably and were enjoying themselves. He thought of checking the boat, but his fatigue from the race was beginning to catch up with him. Excusing himself, he went upstairs, hoping they wouldn't lose too much time making the side trip to Door County. He was anxious to start work on the project, as anxious as a child on Christmas Eve.

Matthias entered his room to find that a maid had turned down the bed, leaving the lights on. There was a bottle of gin and another of scotch on the dresser, along with ice and some mixers. Presents from Poe. He ignored these, but noticed an envelope left with them. It bore the words "Matthias Curland, Architect." Inside was a check from Poe made out for $25,000.

And more to come. A million dollars, the man had said. Enough to end all his worries for good, to fulfill his obligation to his ancestors, to buy the freedom that would enable him to set his life on course again, to strike for another, different horizon.

He sat down on the bed, staring at the check, then folded it and put it in his wallet. He turned on the television set. After the last few minutes of a situation comedy, the evening news from Green Bay came on. To his surprise, he didn't have to wait for the sports segment. The yacht race was the lead news story. It opened with a long shot of the *Lady P* crossing the finish, then cut to a much closer view of Poe at the helm, beaming—himself and Cindy in the background. There was more of Poe on the dock. Matthias had no idea how the Chicago TV stations would play the event, but here Poe was getting everything he could possibly have wanted. In closing the story, the news anchor made no mention at all of the commodore's protest. Matthias smiled. The man was blessed, or had made a pact with the devil.

The news program moved on to a story about a car wreck on the interstate. Matthias turned off the set and started for the bed, thinking how blissful would be this night's sleep, in contrast to so many he'd endured in recent weeks. It was then that he noticed that the red message light on the telephone was blinking.

The message was from Diandra, and brief. She'd left her suite number. It was just down the hall. Matthias picked up the phone, then set it down again. She hadn't said to call.

He sat quietly a moment, trying to think. All he needed to do was sink to his pillow and fall instantly asleep. He could talk to her in the morning. He could plead fatigue, or a late night. Or lie, and say he hadn't noticed the message.

He rapped on her door gently, half hoping that she'd be asleep and not hear. He was about to turn away when it opened. The room within was dark.

"Thank you for coming," she said. "I don't want to be alone tonight."

She closed the door behind him. She was wearing a silken robe. She tugged at its belt, opening it, then without hesitation came into his arms. Her kiss was hard and hungry, a glancing sharpness of teeth, the warmth of tongue. Heat was radiating from them, enveloping them. Her robe came off. His hands were everywhere over her. She was tugging at him. He stepped back. Together, clumsily, frantically, they pulled off his clothes. Then they were moving, spinning, falling into her bed. The sheets were cool, then warm, then forgotten. He felt her flesh moist against him—legs, stomach, breasts—her arms tight around his back, his face buried in her silken hair, his head swimming in the luxuriant scent of her neck. Then a sudden stiffness of her muscles, a brake swiftly and urgently applied.

She was breathing heavily. "Do you . . . have . . . something?"

He paused, poised awkwardly above her, then realized what she meant. He scrambled to his clothing, yanking forth his wallet.

When he returned, she was lying straight and still, but turned to him, her body curving, her legs rising and moving apart. The interruption had cost them little, except now he was thinking. Was he mad? What could have provoked this craziness, in him, in her? It was more than loneliness and attraction and passion. There was resentment. They were both the property of Peter Poe, and they were rebelling against him. The hell with you, Peter Poe. Fuck you, Peter Poe. He never talked like that, but he was saying it, over and over, in his mind, and now aloud.

She silenced him with another kiss, wrapping herself around him. The words vanished, were forgotten. An extraordinary giddy happiness swept over him, hushing all sound, all sense of movement, all else.

They fell asleep in each other's arms. Later, he awoke to find she had moved away to the other side of the bed. He thought he heard her crying, but there was only a vague sense of it. Sleep was hovering near. It returned.

When he awakened again, it was to a soft gray light from the windows. She lay with her back to him. He had wondered how she would look without clothing. He was surprised at the feminine roundness that softened the edges of her long and slender frame. Botticelli had indeed painted such women. Modigliani had. He would. This woman.

Matthias sat up, a pain throbbing at the back of his head. He was fully and sharply awake, feeling oddly cold. It was the next day. Whatever price was to be paid for this rash abandon, it would start soon.

He kissed her shoulder, but she did not stir, so he rose and quietly dressed. He looked at her one more time, sensing somehow that she was awake, but not wanting to speak to him. Then, still groggy, he returned to his room.

TO ZANY'S AND the town's relief, the crime rate in Grand Pier fell back to its normal, drunks-and-minor-nuisances level, making the added presence of sheriff's deputies and State Police troopers in town seem a little embarrassing. Nevertheless, Zany continued to make himself as visible as possible, dropping in at the stores, restaurants, and cafés throughout the day and patrolling the streets and main highway himself at least twice a night. As an added, pointed gesture, he had his officers increase their traffic stops. Anyone who drove a gray van into town was automatically pulled over.

He was wasting time, of course. He had come to the irrational, paranoid, but dead-certain conclusion that as long as he let the Langley case languish, this blissfully peaceful state would continue. He had no doubt that, the moment he should turn up on the snoop in Chicago again, Grand Pier would be hit once more—the deputies and troopers notwithstanding. It was like one of his more fiendish computer games, only for real.

His first stop this morning was at his wife's beach shop, where he picked up a copy of the day's *Chicago Tribune* and read it over coffee at her little lunch counter. As he turned to the sports section, the four-column picture on its front page jumped out at him. It was of Peter Poe's triumphant finish at the big Lake Michigan sailboat race, showing Poe, Matthias Curland, and some good-looking girl standing by the helm of Poe's boat, smiling at him in smug triumph from the newspaper page. He grinned back, then poured some of his coffee on them. His wife Judy looked at him as if he had gone nuts. In some ways, maybe his frustration was making him a little loopy.

He'd stayed out of Chicago, but he had called Frank Baldessari a couple of times—reiterating all the links between Jill Langley, the Curland brothers, Laurence Train, and Peter Poe; almost begging his old friend to treat them as leads and pursue them. But the lieutenant couldn't be budged from his disinterest. When Zany had suggested he try for a matchup of the prints taken from the seat of O'Rourke's car with those of the hooker who'd had her throat cut, Baldessari even got angry.

"Don't you think I did that?" he'd said. "They weren't hers. But so what? O'Rourke must have had half the whores in Chicago in that car."

"Did you run them through the FBI computer?"

"Let me do my job, all right, Zany? Seems to me you got enough stuff to worry about on your own turf."

Baldessari did help Zany to a small degree—having his detectives talk to as many of Jill Langley's friends and acquaintances as they could find. He'd also had his men canvass the boat owners at the harbor where Jill Langley had last been seen. He'd sent Zany a voluminous report, but none of it was of any use. He laughed at Zany's suggestion that he go for a wiretap on Train and the Curlands.

There were other ways of making progress. Zany leaked to an old reporter friend in Chicago all that he knew about the mystery of the paintings, along with the interesting fact that his copy of *The Red Tower* had been stolen along with all the personal items that had turned up in the apartment of the hooker presumed to have murdered Chairman O'Rourke. The newsman, Marty Killeen of the *Tribune,* at least sounded interested.

Zany also began calling police departments in cities other than New York that might have art theft or forgery details in their burglary units. Initially starting down the list of big cities, but then concentrating on those that had substantial German-American populations—Milwaukee, Baltimore, and, of course, Philadelphia. He got promises of assistance, a couple sounding quite genuine.

It then dawned on him, as it should have early on, that his own phone might in some way be tapped, and that all this long-distance sleuthing might invite another round of local crime. Thereafter, he started using pay phones and his A.T.&T. credit card, hoping Judy wouldn't scream too loudly at the bills.

After landing at Meigs Field, Poe and Mango went to his penthouse, where she laid out his casino predicament in grim detail and then gave him one of the finest nights of his life. The next morning they helicoptered out to the Michigan City casino. They found Bobby Mann working the floor, talking to the pit boss. He dropped his drink when he saw Poe and Mango come in. Poe was sure now that something seriously bad was up, and that Mango had in no way been exaggerating the problem. It surprised Poe to see Mann drinking at such an early hour. He almost never did that.

"Okay," said Poe, when he and Mango were alone back in his office. "I have no more doubts. What do we do about it?"

"I'm going to set up a meeting for you," she said. "With some prospective new partners who are gonna treat you a hell of lot nicer."

Diandra did not come down from her hotel suite until after breakfast, sending a message to Matthias that she'd join him on the boat. She arrived late in the morning, wearing white slacks, a designer T-shirt, sunglasses, and a large hat.

"I don't like to be in the sun too much," she said as he helped her aboard. "Do you mind if I stay below for a while?"

"Diandra, it's your boat," Matthias said. "Please stay wherever you like. Your cabin is aft, the one to the left of the ladder. The other one's mine."

"The one on the left. Thank you very much."

She turned from him as she might from a hotel desk clerk.

After getting under way, most of the crew went below as well, needing sleep. They had partied most of the night, including the young man he'd asked to check on the boat.

The sail across Green Bay was easy, with a steady following wind. Diandra didn't come up on deck again until they were nearing Ephraim's Eagle Harbor, marked on the horizon by a high church steeple rising above the town.

She sought what shade there was in the cockpit, pulling her hat down low, keeping her attention on the coastline stretching off to the south.

"It's no fun sailing when you're in that cabin," she said.

"Are you sure you want to make the trip to Chicago? You can always get a plane in Sturgeon Bay."

"I don't know. It would look funny if I rushed back like that. Peter would think something had gone wrong. Something between us."

"Has it? You seem unhappy."

"I don't want to talk about it."

Cindy was sitting by the starboard winch. She got up and went forward.

It was well into the afternoon when they dropped anchor, sounding the boat horn three times to summon a tender from the dock. Poe's chauffeur Krasowski was waiting with the ridiculously long red limousine. Matthias doubted the locals had ever seen a car that excessive in their town before.

The glass divider was up between the driver and the passenger compartment, but neither he nor Diandra spoke. It was a quick run up to Sister Bay. There was indeed a goat on the roof of the restaurant, quietly munching some of the thatch.

"Scandinavian custom," Matthias said. "For the benefit of the tourists."

She smiled, but that was all.

Krasowski stayed with the car. They took a table off in a corner of the main dining room. Diandra ordered wine and a salad. Matthias was hungry, and asked for Swedish meatballs. Feeling in considerable need, he also had a glass of wine.

"I'm sorry," he said finally, as they began eating.

"Sorry?"

"About last night."

"Why? Didn't you enjoy yourself?" Her voice was laced with sarcasm.

"It wasn't very wise, for either of us."

"Because of Peter? Are you afraid of him?"

"I'm afraid for you. What would he do if he found out?"

She sighed. "Anything from killing us to being immensely pleased."

"Pleased?"

"He likes you. He wants very much to have you keep working for him. He asked me to be nice to you."

"Not that nice."

"You never know with Peter. He's not what you'd call a moral man, is he? He fools around himself. He has a lot of women I don't know about, and some I do. He does whatever he wants. He thinks it's his right. He's Peter Poe, king of the world, top of the heap."

"That doesn't mean he'd be pleased." The idea of Diandra making love to him just to carry out her husband's wishes disturbed him deeply.

She looked at him darkly. "Don't worry, Matthias. He's not going to find out, and it's not going to happen again."

He looked down at his plate. She asked for another glass of wine.

"You seem very unhappy," he said.

"I'm just troubled."

"You just told me not to worry."

"I'm troubled about you, Matthias Curland. I wonder if you're a very moral person."

He was startled.

"Your brother's the kind of man who gives philandering a bad name," she said. "I don't like being in the same room with him. I'm just been wondering how much you might be like him."

"I'm not like him."

"Peter's told me about you both. He knows a lot about you. Your wife left you because you were screwing around with that girl who was murdered. You have a woman in France, but you're not back in Chicago two days and you take up with your old girlfriend. You ask her to marry you, and then you jump into bed with me."

He searched for words, but before anything useful came to mind, she went on.

"I don't know what you think of me," she said, "but I don't fool around. I've never cheated on Peter. It took a lot of courage and a lot of anger and not a little booze to leave that message for you, and to answer the door when you finally knocked. I did it because I wanted to, because I'm tired of never being able to do what I want to do. Because . . . I'm very attracted to you. I'll be honest about that. I was the first night we met. I thought you were special, special in a good way as Peter is special in what most people would consider a bad way. You're different from any man I ever met before. At least I thought you were. Now I'm not sure. I'm not sure at all, Matthias. When we were lying there, afterward, all I could think of is what woman you'd be sleeping with next. Probably that Cindy, judging by the way she keeps looking at you."

The waitress had brought a carafe. Matthias poured himself another glass of wine.

"I'm not like my brother," fearing he sounded like someone testifying in court. "He's addicted to women, the way he is to alcohol. They've always thrown themselves at him. Sex has been a part of his life since he was fifteen. He learned how to use it, to get what he wants, what he needs, early on. It's the only thing in his life that really works for him. I'm not like that. I don't know why we're talking about this. I'm quite embarrassed. But in all honesty, there have been very few women in my life. We just met at a complicated time."

"Complicated? It's very simple. You cheat."

He wanted to tell her that he wasn't cheating. He was searching—not for "the perfect woman," but for the woman for him, a woman much like one in a painting he'd seen long ago, a woman, as it happened, who looked much like her. But he didn't know how to say that without sounding idiotic.

He sipped his wine. She looked at him, her light-blue eyes troubled and sad.

"Leave that, please," she said quietly. "I want to go."

He put down money enough for the check. "Do you want to go back to the boat?"

"I want to drive around some more. I like this place, what I've seen so far."

There went up the coast all the way to Gill's Rock at the tip of the Door County peninsula, then across to Northport on Lake Michigan. The water was very blue up at Death's Door Passage. Here it was a brilliant green.

Bidding him to stay with the car, she walked out to the end of Northport's long concrete pier by herself. Matthias stood on shore and watched her, a solitary mysterious figure against the vastness of water and sky. It could have been a painting, though not one he could do, not with any success.

"It's very nice," she said, when she finally returned to him, brushing her windblown hair from her face. "I'd like to come up here again. I think I might like to have a place here someday." She glanced toward the car. "Peter would never stand for it, though. A place of my own, where I could come and be alone."

"I've sometimes thought of coming up here myself. One could make a living of sorts, painting beach pictures for people's summer homes."

"Some living."

"Do you want to go back to the boat? Or do you want to try to catch a plane from Sturgeon Bay?"

"I'll go back with you," she said matter-of-factly. "As I said, it would look funny, since I wanted to come so badly."

"We'll be on the water at least two nights."

"My cabin has a lock."

He said nothing more.

The crew was ready to hoist sail when he returned. Diandra let him take her arm as she got aboard.

"I don't want to stay below," she said. "In that cabin. It's like my life, riding along in a box, not knowing where I'm going."

"You can cover up. It's only a few hours until sundown. It'll cool off considerably once we get out in the lake."

"Is there booze aboard?"

"Quite a lot. Your husband must have thought we needed the ballast."

"Good."

Matthias sailed north out of the harbor, then, passing a big bluff to starboard, changed course to a northeasterly heading, wanting to stay as close to the shoreline as possible to make time. He really wanted to be back in Chicago.

They'd been under way only a few minutes more when it happened. Matthias was looking aloft at the trim of the mainsail when he heard a loud thump forward. He thought at first they had run aground on some rock, but a roiling cloud of oily smoke erupted from the bow hatch, curling back toward them and over the starboard side. An instant later there were flames. He saw one crew member leap backward into the water off the rail. Cindy was groping back toward the cockpit, clutching at the handholds on the bulkhead. Her blouse was on fire.

The wheel wrenched his hand. The bow was going down, taking water. The boat began to heel to starboard. Matthias let the mainsheet fly, then took the wheel with both hands, grunting as he turned it, lurching the burning bow back toward shore. They were a hundred yards or more from shallow water.

"Cindy!" he shouted. "Jump!"

She looked at him dumbly. Her blouse was still burning. Crew members were bolting up from below, frantic. He had to move. Quick!

"Everyone overboard!" Matthias yelled. "Hurry up! Go!"

He leapt across the canting cockpit to Diandra. "Can you swim?"

"Yes!"

He thrust a seat cushion into her hands. "Go! Quick!"

Lifting her up onto the rail, watching to make sure she got clear into the water, Matthias then lunged forward toward Cindy. The change of course put the fire at the bow and its choking smoke before the wind, fanning the flames and fumes ahead of them, but the orange curls, feasting on the paint, were licking inexorably toward the stern as well. He could see them reaching almost to Cindy's foot.

She was screaming.

Matthias pulled himself on. The boat was listing badly now to starboard and he was losing footing. Only his grip on the handholds kept him aboard. He felt the girl's screams as he might flashes of pain.

Jill, dead on a sailboat, his boat. Now Cindy. Hurry. Keep on.

Another reach, another grip. The wind shifted and he caught a gasping mouthful of smoke. He ducked low, another lunge. Close to her now. The cabin roof was on fire. Through one of the windows, he could see flames ripping along the inside of the main salon.

Finally he reached Cindy's outstretched hand. Pulling her to him with a wrenching effort, he caught his foot hard against a stanchion, then bent double to beat the flames out on her back, her flesh sticky against his skin, the palm and fingers of his left hand stinging, then numb.

Trying to pull her closer, he saw that her foot was caught. If he jumped to save himself, it would be the same as shooting her, except she'd die more slowly, more horribly, the most horrible way there was.

Another lunge. He flung himself on top of her, grasping at her thigh, then her shin. Reaching toward the nearing flames, he caught hold of her ankle and yanked it free of the rail line.

Somehow he was able to turn around. He put his arms around her chest. The boat was about to capsize. The steep list helped. Holding her tightly, he rolled. The lifeline scratched at his face, but they toppled clear. In an instant, they were in the cold, embracing water.

CHAPTER
12

MATTHIAS GOT CINDY onto the rocky beach and held her wrapped in his arms, oblivious to all else except the extraordinary fact that they were alive. She had lost consciousness but was breathing. He could feel each breath, though not her heartbeat. When she was a little girl and he a teenager, he used to carry her on his shoulders. He put his uninjured right hand on her bare leg. It was icy cold. Her father, though an old family friend, would hate him forever for letting this happen to her, just as Jill Langley's father seemed to hate him. Unlike Mr. Langley, he would have every right.

"Mr. Curland?"

Two of his crew were standing in front of him. "Is she all right, Mr. Curland?"

Matthias lifted his head slowly. The *Lady P* had foundered on the shallows, its stern sticking into the air at an angle, burning furiously. In a moment, the gasoline tanks in the bilge ignited in a huge, ugly ball of orange.

"Get a doctor. An ambulance," he said. He barely recognized his own voice.

"The people in the house are doing that," the youth said. "It's a long way to the hospital, but the guy said there's a doctor up the road. He'll be here soon."

"Did everyone make it?"

"Yes, sir."

"Mrs. Poe?"

"Yes. She's right here."

Matthias looked around him. Diandra was off to the left, sitting on a rock, staring at him starkly, transfixed.

"Is Cindy going to make it?"

"She has some bad burns," Matthias said.

"I don't understand what happened, Mr. Curland."

"Neither do I. But I'm damned well going to find out."

The minutes passed with dreadful slowness. Matthias refused to let go of Cindy until the doctor arrived, an older man with a nice, friendly but worried face. He said he was a gynecologist, but knew what to do. Matthias relaxed his grip. The doctor, helped by the two crew members, gently took Cindy away from him.

"We have to get her up to the house," the doctor said. "I need to treat her for shock. I brought blankets. We can rig a stretcher."

Matthias tried to get up, but his legs were weak and wobbly. He made the effort again, finally getting to his feet.

"How bad are the burns?" he asked.

The doctor was kneeling over the girl. "Pretty bad, in spots," he said. "It could have been a lot worse. I don't know how any of you made it."

They lifted her carefully onto a folded blanket, then the two crew members picked up the ends. Another ran up to assist them.

"I want to help," Matthias said.

"Let them do it," the doctor said. "They're not injured."

Matthias looked at his left hand. There were large gray blisters, ringed in red and black, on his palm and fingers. He turned the hand over. There was a blister there, too, and one on his forearm. He had ignored the throbbing pain. Looking at the ruined flesh, he could no longer. He clenched his teeth, waiting until he was master of himself again, then started after the others, up the wooden stairs from the beach to the house.

Diandra followed behind him. When they reached the top, finding themselves on a broad wooden deck, he stopped, catching his breath. A bald man in shorts, presumably the owner of the house, shoved a chair out of the way to make way for the stretcher bearers.

"Matthias."

Diandra was standing beside him. Her voice was soft and clear again. "Your hand," she said.

"I'll be all right."

"You should go to the hospital," she said.

"I will. With Cindy. I'm going to stay with her. You go back to Chicago, the fastest way you can."

She nodded. He could see tears in her eyes.

"Tell your husband I'm going to hold him answerable for this."

"God, Matt. It wasn't his fault."

"This wasn't an accident. There was nothing on the boat that could have caused an explosion like that."

Diandra shook her head. "I don't understand."

"It was a bomb."

"Meant for Peter?"

"That's a good bloody guess, isn't it?"

She looked off out over the water. "If we hadn't stopped over here today, we would have been miles out in Lake Michigan when it happened."

"Yes."

"We all would have drowned."

"Possibly. Cindy sure wouldn't have made it."

"If it hadn't been for you, she would have died."

He stared at her grimly. "Call your husband, Diandra. Go on home."

"When will you be back?"

"I don't know. I want to go in now and see to Cindy."

He wanted her to leave him. He had come aboard the boat that morning feeling, in a desperate, forlorn way, rather in love.

"All right. Call me when you can."

He said nothing.

"Please," she said.

"All right."

She took a step, then stopped. "I just want to say something to you, Matt. I take back what I said. You are special. Very special."

Poe hung up the phone, looking at it as if it were a contaminated thing. Then he set his elbows on the desk and buried his face in his hands.

"Is she all right?" Mango asked. There was concern in her voice, but he had no idea what answer she was hoping for.

"Yes. But it was goddamned close. Shit. The dirty fucking bastards."

He lowered his hands, then swiveled his chair to look at her.

"They tried to kill me, Mango. The fuckers tried to kill me. Blow me up in my own boat."

"Don't worry, Peter."

"Don't worry?"

"They'll all be dead in twenty-four hours. I got it all set up."

"What are you talking about?"

"That's what this meeting we're going to is about. To give them the git-go. Only they want to talk to you face to face first. Make sure they've got an understanding before they make it happen."

"I don't want to go to any goddamn meeting, especially with those guys."

"Too late to do anything else. And we've got to move quick."

"Move quick? What are they thinking of doing, flying over Atlantic City and dropping a nuke?"

"It's all arranged. Everything's in place. All they're waiting on is the word from you."

"How is it everything's in place? What are you talking about?"

"I set it all up. I called them as soon as I got spooked by Bobby Mann. I didn't want to take any chances."

"What if I say no?"

"It's your neck. But I'm not going to hang around and wait for them to come at you again. You say no and I'm going to walk out that door and get as far away from you as I can."

He swiveled back to face his desk. There was nothing there of any use to him in this.

"You want to build that building, Peter? You want to be Mr. Chicago? Be king of the heap? You gotta fight for it. Do or die. Come on. Let's go. They won't like it if we're late."

"Hold on, damn it. I've got to get a plane up to Wisconsin to pick up Diandra. She says Curland won't come with her. That girl he had on the boat is in the hospital. Burns."

"Make the call and then let's go. You've got bigger worries."

"What about Bobby?"

"We leave him alone for now."

"Why?"

"You don't want anything to happen that'll draw any more attention to you now. Especially when people start turning up dead in Atlantic City. What we've got to do now is give Bobby worries."

She was in charge. She had already made all the big decisions, running them by him almost as a formality. That would have to stop. But his own mind wouldn't work. Nothing, like it had a dead battery. Was this fear? He had never been like this in his life.

The restaurant chosen for the meeting was on the West Side of Chicago, near the University of Illinois campus, a cheap Italian joint with Formica-top tables. Poe's prospective business associates were waiting in a corner booth. Most of the restaurant's tables had people at them, but all of those around the booth were empty, no doubt according to instructions.

There were three of them, all middle aged, two in suits and one in a lumpy sport coat and purple polo shirt. They exchanged greetings and handshakes with exaggerated affability, but when everyone was seated it was the one in the polo shirt who spoke.

"Miss Bellini here's told you of our discussions? Facts and figures, all that shit?"

Poe nodded. He hoped desperately that his nervousness didn't show. He knew these men only by reputation. Looking at them face to face didn't contradict anything he had heard. "Yes," Poe said.

"Well?" said the polo shirt.

"What it comes down to is you want a third."

"Nothing more, nothing less."

"It's a lot."

"Your friends were getting half the skim."

"They put up money."

"We're putting up your life."

What the hell was wrong with him, haggling with them as if this were just another real estate deal? Like he was talking with bankers. He had even thought of bringing Bill Yeats with him. He could see now what a fucking colossal mistake that would be. Lawyering on top of dickering. These were up or down guys. Bet or get out.

Mango was looking at him impatiently. He was becoming impatient himself. Get this over with. Get it behind him. Get on with his plans. These guys couldn't possibly be any worse than the other bunch. And they were local. He wouldn't be the first major player in Chicago to do business with them. And that's all this would be. Just some business. They'd protect him. They'd have a stake.

"Okay," he said. "A third. But . . ."

"There's a 'but'?"

"This agreement can't go into force for a year. Did Mango make that clear? Everything's got to be on the up and up for a year. I need that time. The casino's a big part of the collateral I need for the loan on my new building. It's a very big deal I've got in the works. City Hall is part of it. No way to pull out. The bank'll have lawyers and auditors looking at the books. Everything's got to be squeaky clean."

230

"Miss Bellini explained that. It's jake with us. Absolutely. Give the place a clean bill of health. All the better for the future."

"And the casino is all that's involved. The Mississippi river-boats are a different setup. The hayheads out there are nervous enough about them as it is. And anyway, they don't bring in that much revenue. One of them lost money last year."

The man in the polo shirt looked at one of his colleagues, who nodded, then looked back. "Okay. But maybe we can talk about them later."

"Maybe."

The third member of the trio leaned forward. He had a narrow face and an oversized nose that made his dark eyes seem too close together.

"How's your wife?" he asked, surprising Poe.

"She's okay."

"You're not going to talk to the cops about that accident, right? It's all a big mystery to you. You don't know nothin'. Big men make enemies. Could be anyone tried to blow up your boat. But not nobody from Atlantic City, right? You don't know from Atlantic City."

"I'm not stupid," Poe said.

"Absolutely," said the man in the polo shirt. "So, everybody happy?" His colleagues nodded. "Let's drink on it."

He poured wine. They clinked glasses. It tasted sour to Poe, but that was probably his nerves. His mouth was dust dry.

"About what's going down tonight," Mango said. "Nothing happens to Bobby Mann."

The three looked startled. "What are you talkin'? He's the prick who tried to set you up."

"Nothing's to happen around Chicago," Mango said. "No connections. No coincidences. Nothing that could possibly involve Mr. Poe in any way. He doesn't need anything more in the papers."

"Okay, but how about like maybe Mann gets a friendly phone call, right after we—we make our down payment?

She thought on this a moment. "Okay. Yeah. He'll shit in his pants. I'd like that."

"He still worries me," Poe said. "You got somebody who can keep an eye on him? He knows all my people."

"Sure. I'll send a couple guys over in the morning. Some new waiters for you."

"Okay," said Poe. He itched to get out of there. "Miss Bellini and I are going out of town. Down to Springfield. Legislative business. We'll be back in a few days."

"Absolutely. You want a phone call when it's done?"

"No, thanks. You guys look like you know your business. I assume your street crew does. I'll find out about it when everybody else does."

There were more handshakes. Poe stood up.

"Pleasure doing business with you," said the man in the polo shirt.

J. P. Morgan. You can do business with anyone.

They took side streets back to downtown. Mango was sitting very close beside him in his limo. It was one he seldom used. The driver had forgotten to stock it with booze.

"Yeats is going to meet us in Springfield," she said. "We should leave pretty soon."

"I want to wait for Diandra."

"You said she wasn't hurt."

"She's probably shook up."

"She'll ask you questions you don't want to answer right now. Better you get scarce."

"I suppose you've already packed. You seem to have everything planned."

"Right down to where we're going to eat tonight. But I want to take care of something first. Larry Train called. He said some newspaper reporter's been asking around about a stolen painting."

"I thought the coppers were going to forget about that."

"The Chicago coppers. But not that bearded son of a bitch in Michigan."

"I told you to lay off of him. He's got that little beach town looking like a police convention. And anyway he's a nobody. No one's paying any attention to him."

"He doesn't give up. Don't worry. Just one more hit. Put him out of business for good."

The plane Poe had chartered to bring Diandra back from Door County was a small propellor craft that was cramped and uncomfortable and took hours to make the flight. Its course, due south, carried it over a wide swath of the open waters of Lake Michigan. It had only one engine and the pilot was very young. None of the crew members from the *Lady P* had accepted her

232

offer of a ride back, preferring to stay with the injured girl, so she was all alone. Sitting in the rear seat, she couldn't talk much with the pilot. She was tired, sad, lonely, and very nervous. By the time Meigs Field hove into view in the fading light of evening, she was ready to scream. When he lowered the flaps and landing gear with a sudden jolt, she actually did. He turned to look at her, though the runway was rapidly approaching.

"Fly the goddamn plane!" she said.

She must have rattled him. He made a bad landing, bouncing twice before the wheels finally settled.

One of Poe's red stretch limousines was waiting for her, the driver a man she didn't know. Peter wasn't there.

"Where's my husband?"

"Told me to tell you he had to go to Springfield, Mrs. Poe. Something about a vote on a bill. He'll be back tomorrow. He said you're not to go out tonight."

"That's an order?"

"I don't know, ma'am. I'm just telling you what he told me."

There were two armed security guards in the lobby of the Poe Place building on Michigan Avenue and another seated in one of the chairs in the elevator vestibule of the penthouse. There was a door she could close and lock on him, which she did.

The housekeeper was waiting, looking weary. "You want some dinner, Mrs. Poe?"

"No, thank you. I won't need you tonight."

Diandra knew where Poe usually stayed when in the state capital and thought of calling him, finally deciding against it. When she confronted him about what had happened, she wanted it to be face to face, and alone, in a situation where he couldn't get away from her.

She needed now to talk to someone, though—anyone, just to hear a friendly human voice. But who? She had no real friends in Chicago. She hadn't spoken with any of her old model friends in more than a year. Her mother wouldn't understand, would likely only become upset.

Pouring herself a glass of vodka over ice, she went into the huge living room and sat forlornly on one of the couches, staring out a window that looked over the buildings of the avenue and the lake—once again, the city going about its life without her.

Diandra wanted most to talk to Matthias, but feared he wouldn't come to the phone. She didn't even know the name of the hospital up there, or what town it was in. She should have stayed with him. She'd badly wanted to, but her husband had insisted on her coming back at once, and hanging around the hospital might only have made Matthias angry.

Come back at once. Then off he goes to Springfield.

She drank, the vodka cold and soothing, but not enough. She finished it hurriedly, then took a long, hot shower, thinking that would help, but it didn't. Putting on only a silk summer robe, she made herself another drink and went out onto one of the terraces. There were little lights visible on the darkening deep blue of the lake—boats. She looked over the railing, straight down, imagining herself spinning through the air to the concrete so far below. She'd been as close to death on that boat as she was now to such a fall.

Death. She'd found herself contemplating that implacable prospect more frequently after she'd turned thirty, but only at odd moments and only abstractly. Now it seemed an unseen but tangible presence, hovering near. She had no idea how badly injured the burned girl was. Could she die during this night?

She'd felt scornful of the professional beauties she'd known in New York who had married for money, thinking them essentially no better than whores, trading their looks and bodies for a grand, expensive life and the dubious privilege of having their names and pictures appear in the party coverage of *Women's Wear Daily* and *W* magazine. Somehow she thought she was different when she'd agreed to marry Peter. She'd told herself that it wasn't only his much-touted immense fortune that had attracted her, that had made her give in. She'd convinced herself she was genuinely fascinated by him—by his ego and drive and intelligence and what she took to be extraordinary courage, a man willing to take on the world, to kick it in the shins—as she'd told Matthias, fascinated by what life would be like married to such a man. A Polish man, just like her father.

She'd never for a moment felt anything like love for him. She liked Peter and enjoyed being with him when he was in one of his charming moods. But there was never any ardor, no depth or real warmth in their relationship. She'd come to dislike sleeping with him. The only pleasure came when it was over, because it was over.

That was the only price she'd expected to pay for marrying Chicago's richest man, if that he was—living with and being bound to someone she didn't love. His insensitivity and inconsideration and bullying aggressiveness were added, unexpected costs, but she'd learned to tolerate them.

Now the price seemed immensely great, more than she'd ever imagined. Marriage to Poe had proved dangerous—deadly dangerous—and she was scared.

Unless. If it was a bomb that had set fire to that boat—and she knew she was fooling herself if she tried to believe anything else—was it necessarily meant for Peter Poe? Nothing at all like that had ever intruded upon their life together before. The one thing she had always felt with Peter was safe.

But Matthias was another matter. A woman had been murdered on his boat, one of his loves. And now he'd almost been killed on the *Lady P*. She'd sensed early on that he was someone living on the edge of life, that for all his manners and calm demeanor and tradition-bound background, he probably lived a quite terrifying life. His brother was disturbingly strange.

Was the edge he walked that sharp? Was she wise to be anywhere near him?

"You've got it made," one of her model friends had told her the day of her wedding. "You're set forever."

God.

She forced herself to watch the late news. The TV station had a story about the "accident," though no footage from Wisconsin. They ran a videotape clip of Poe and Matthias crossing the start line of the Menominee race as the anchorwoman related sketchy details about the fire and the injured woman, noting how "fortunate" it was that Poe had returned to Chicago by plane. Nothing was said about any bomb. Her name was mentioned once, among the survivors.

Diandra turned off the set with the remote control, then sat for several minutes staring at the lake. Perhaps it would all seem better by morning. She went to the bar to pour herself one more drink, hesitating as she picked up the bottle, thinking how much she resented and hated Peter's not being at Meigs to welcome and comfort her. Then she took both glass and bottle, and went upstairs to her bedroom.

CHAPTER
13

THERE WERE FOUR hits to be made in Atlantic City and a fifth in Philadelphia. The target list had been debated, with some arguing for a smaller operation, some for larger, but it was finally agreed that this plan would take out all of Poe's principal problems, plus a couple of potential troublemakers for insurance. Consultations had to be made with certain important individuals in New York, Miami, and Las Vegas, but the situation was understood, and no one raised a beef. It was considered Chicago business, this job of work—and, besides, it would create new opportunities in Atlantic City.

This was a hurry-up job, but nothing they hadn't pulled off before. They had people in Atlantic City, in many useful places, and brought in some outside hires known for their ability at quick strikes. The ruse was a meeting call in Philly, ostensibly an inquiry into why a clumsy hit had been made on someone as big a deal and public a person as Peter Poe, as well as into why it had failed. The presumption was that all four of the Atlantic City marks would make the trip together, but one stayed behind complaining he was sick.

All he was was horny. After his colleagues left, he had a broad sent up to his suite—for an overnight, not just short time. He promised her a bonus, but, being in his bed when she could have been elsewhere, what she got was whacked along with him. Couldn't be helped.

The main hit was set up on the Atlantic City Expressway causeway that led from the gambling resort across the Intracoastal Waterway to the New Jersey mainland. It was an interstate highway, but not much traveled at night. The bomb was placed in a discarded tire left against the causeway railing. A hundred yards ahead, one of the hires posed as a motorist with a broken-down car—hood up, hazard lights flashing, stopped right in the middle of the fast lane. When the big white stretch with the three marks in it drove by the tire, veering into the right-hand lane to avoid the stalled car, the "stranded motorist" hit a button. The stretch turned into a junkyard. Hood down, hazard lights off, the hire was gone in a minute.

The man in Philadelphia, who in the ruse had supposedly called the meeting, was of course not informed of it. He elected to spend the night with a broad, too, which was a mistake. She was the hitter.

It was an expensive operation—counting the limousine driver and the unlucky hooker, seven bodies. But the payoff in the long run would be enormous. Like most businessmen in the Midwest, Poe's new associates in Chicago were fairly conservative. They played for the long run.

They were amazed that the five marks hadn't taken more precautions—indeed, that they hadn't made themselves real scarce as soon as they'd heard that their hit on Poe had gone awry. They probably took Poe for a chump civilian who could do them no harm and were counting on him being scared shitless, ready to come begging for forgiveness. They were probably putting their minds to when next to take a whack at him. The chumps.

Bunch of amateurs anyway. Everyone knew that, if you're gonna blow a boat, you put the charge in the bilge by the gas tanks.

Zany Rawlings heard the news about the burning and sinking of Poe's boat on the radio. He frequently turned on his favorite country and western station when he sat down at home to fiddle with his computer. The announcer read two sentences about the incident in the hourly news wrap-up. When there was no new information provided in the half-hourly update, he called his friend Killeen at his newspaper, working the late shift. Killeen pulled up the wire story on his newsroom computer terminal and read it to Zany—with some difficulty, as the reporter had apparently paused overlong at his dinner break.

"What was that about arson?" Zany asked.

"It says 'the cause of the fire is unknown but arson is being investigated.' "

"Who's on it?"

"Door County sheriff's office. And the Coast Guard, I guess."

"And there was only one injury?"

"Two. A woman named Cynthia Ellison, listed as serious but stable condition with burns, and the skipper, Matthias Curland. Minor burns."

"Son of a bitch."

"What?"

"Never mind. How are you coming on the O'Rourke story, the painting angle? Did Baldessari say he was investigating the connection?"

"Said he was looking into it. Otherwise, I'm getting mostly nowhere. I called the Laurence Train gallery and some others, but they acted like I was crazy. So did the burglary coppers."

"Which coppers?"

"Detective Plotnik."

"So are you going to do a story about it?"

"I talked to the city editor, but she said she wanted some more facts."

What was the newspaper business coming to?

"Okay, Marty. If I pick up anything more, I'll let you know. When this thing breaks, you can tell your editor she passed up a hot one."

"She'll still want the facts."

Zany stayed up long after his wife went to bed, drinking beer and going through his computer files on the case, over and over, pointlessly. He was confused as hell by the sailboat sinking. Curland and those people could have been killed—probably should have been. Poe might have gone to a watery grave, too, if he had stayed with them.

Zany had put both Curland and Poe in his file of possible bad guys. Now they were among the victims—or would be victims. Were they good guys? Or were there two sets of bad guys—or several? Did the incident have anything to do with the painting? Did anything have anything to do with anything? Was Zany Rawlings slowly losing his mind fooling around with this thing, imagining weird conspiracies and linking coincidences together like someone trying to solve the John F. Kennedy assassination?

He was groggy. Perhaps he'd been pushing this thing too hard, for too long. He probably would be wise to set it aside for a while, let everything settle, wait for some new development that would be more helpful, or for new evidence to turn up. When he was with Area Six burglary, he'd often let piles of cases languish that way—often solving them months later when a snitch passed something on or the perpetrators struck again. Everyone he knew, including most especially his wife, wanted him to step away from this investigation.

But this wasn't a burglary case, or some game he was playing on his computer. Two women were dead. Another had been burned. There could easily have been more victims in the two Grand Pier robberies. He couldn't walk away from any of that.

His wife stirred and wakened as he took off his clothes to go to bed, dropping his boots too loudly on the floor.

"It's past two A.M., Zane."

"Sorry. Been doing a little work."

"I think we should move," she said.

"What?"

"To Detroit, or maybe the South Bronx. Where we can get some peace and quiet."

Zany overslept the next morning, but took his time getting ready anyway, turning on the bathroom radio while he showered and shaved, taking more time to trim his beard.

There was a story on the news break about Poe's boat, but the information was exactly the same as the night before. Zany had read somewhere that most people now got their news from television and radio. They must not give much of a damn about what was going on in the world, let alone their own city.

He turned the dial to WBBM, an all-news station. They were interviewing some woman who'd written a book about lesbian parenthood.

In the car, he clicked on only his police radio, and got some news in a hurry. Hearing the call of a robbery in progress—his heart racing after the location was given—he pressed the accelerator to the floor and grabbed up the microphone.

"This is Rawlings. What's happening?"

"It's your wife's store, chief! A stickup! She just called it in!"

Then it was no long an "in progress." And she was probably okay.

"Got a description on a perpetrators' vehicle?" Zany was shouting into the mike.

"Negative, Chief."

"Call the sheriff's office and the state troopers! Get a road-block up by the interstate! Stop everybody."

"Ten four, Chief."

Two of his patrols and a sheriff's car had gone directly to the scene and beat him to it. They were in the store, talking with his wife. She was trembling, more with fury than with fear.

"They were in bathing suits!" she said. "Bathing suits and sweatshirts. Barefoot. They waited until I was done with a customer and when he left they pulled guns out of their beachbags and made me empty the cash register."

"What did they get, Judy?"

"It couldn't have been a hundred dollars, for God's sake."

"Describe them."

"One black. One white. They wore sunglasses. I don't know. They went out the back. Fast."

Officer Barbara Vaclav came in through the rear screen door, service revolver hanging in her hand.

"They got away clean, Chief."

There was a small dune behind Judy's beach shop, some vacation cottages and a hardtop road on the other side.

"They left footprints," Vaclav added.

"They touch anything in here?" Zany asked.

"Just the money," said his wife.

Zany went out through the screen door, the other policemen trailing. Two sets of foot marks, useless in the dry sand as far as recoverable impressions were concerned, led up through a narrow defile. Standing on top of the dune, Zany could see where they must have parked the car. They would have been taken for a couple of guys going for a morning swim.

"Canvass these houses," Zany said. "I want a description on that car."

He returned to the store. Judy was leaning back against the counter, arms folded, staring at the floor.

"Are you all right?" Zany asked.

Her gaze lifted like a deck gun being trained on an enemy ship. "This is it, Zane. No argument about it. You drop that goddamned case."

"Judy . . ."

"You drop it or I'm going back to Chicago. Or maybe Wyoming."

"There's been a new development. Somebody set fire to Poe's boat yesterday. Matthias Curland was on it—the dead girl's old boyfriend."

Her eyes were rejecting every word he uttered. "Now, Zany. Finito."

"Okay, okay. I'll let it go."

"Promise me."

"Promise."

"If you cheat on this I'm going to take an ax to your computer."

The phone rang. Zany had no doubt it was District Attorney Moran. If it wasn't, he was sure it would be the mayor.

Poe, Yeats, and Mango sat together in the front row of the public gallery that overlooked the floor of the Illinois State Senate. There were very few spectators in the old wooden seats—a couple of retirees with nothing more edifying to do with their time, a weirdo who haunted the legislature on behalf of some lunatic cause, and several lobbyists doing guard duty, keeping the lawmakers under observation until the last gavel fell on this extended summer session, lest someone try to put through a sneaker bill, or attach some odious amendment to the legislation under present consideration, which was the measure authorizing cities with more than two million population—i.e., Chicago—to issue general revenue bonds and impose a .025 percent tax on accommodations for the purpose of constructing new museums of public interest.

It was advertised as a "merely bill." As Poe's chief Senate spokesman had put it, "This bill merely authorizes the municipality in question to establish these institutions if it so wishes. Not a penny will come from the state treasury and not a penny can be spent without the approval of the city council and the park district. It's a local measure—no skin off anybody's back outside the Chicago city limits."

The mayor had agreed to support the measure early on, seeing it as a foothold in getting the lawmakers to allow an increase in the city's hotel tax in the next legislative session and knowing full well that the bill had become a holy crusade for the backers of the proposed Holocaust Museum. Chicago had only about a quarter of a million Jewish residents, but they spent a lot of money on public causes and exercised a political influence far out of proportion to their numbers. They made up the hard core of the "Lakefront Liberals" who had been such a sticky thorn in the side of the first Mayor Daley in the ideological turmoil of the early 1970s. In the modern era of consensus politics in the city, they were quiescent, but they enjoyed a good fight, and there was no point in stirring them up.

The Republicans were divided. Some were disposed to let the

city of Chicago tax itself to death if it wished. Others were opposed to tax increases of any kind in any form for any reason even if the tax was one levied on aliens from outer space. Most of the downstaters didn't much give a damn, though a few of them had used the opportunity for some log rolling, trading their votes in favor of the bill for future favors and commitments.

Poe's interest in it was widely known and considered highly curious. Most thought of him as a WASP. Some were aware of his Polish ancestry. In either case, his peg seemed to be in the wrong hole in the city's long-standing game of ethnic politics. The most common guess was that he was trying to get on the good side of the Jewish bankers he'd done so much business with, though the bank he was cutting his Cabrini Green project deal with had mostly Japanese connections. One House member, known for his wit, had introduced a spurious amendment calling for the bill to include authorization for a Pearl Harbor museum. It got one vote.

The House had approved the bill by a comfortable enough margin, but Poe was worried about the more conservative Senate. The voting that morning was to be on approval of a conference committee report that had merged the slightly differing House and Senate versions of the measure. Once the report was accepted, everything else was a formality. The governor had expressed no interest in a veto.

Still, as the Senate clerk called forth the measure from the calendar, Poe began to itch and sweat. He had laid down a lot of money. Nine key lawmakers had been bought and paid for in the Senate, more than twice that many in the House—each buyee carefully selected and romanced by Yeats and his lobbyists. But Poe was worried that they hadn't done enough, that he had too much allowed himself to be distracted by his yacht race and other business. The legislature could wreck his plans just as thoroughly as the bankers.

The vote was called. Instead of responding to a verbal call of the roll, as was still done in the United States Senate, the members simply turned a switch at their desks that was reflected by lights next to their names on huge electronic tally boards at the front of the chamber—green for aye, red for nay, yellow for abstention.

In all, delayed by the absence of two members who had gone to the men's room, the process took nine minutes. The final result was amazing. There were only six nay votes—five from conservative Republicans, one from a rabid ideologue who in public comment had expressed doubts that there had been a Holocaust.

"You win," said Yeats. "Again."

"It's a landslide. An avalanche. How'd you do that?"

"It was fairly easy to persuade the serious guys, those who like to be conscientious about their legislating. I convinced them it's for a good cause, it's Chicago only, and the city's really under-taxed when it comes to hotels. New York levies four different taxes on its hotel bills. Chicago's a piker in comparison. The guys who were bought were well paid. The others, well, it's July. It's hotter than hell down here. They hated the idea of an extended session. They just wanted to go home. Now, why don't we do the same?"

At the airport, waiting for their plane's gas tanks to be topped off, Mango took Poe aside.

"I've got the Philadelphia papers waiting for you when you get back to the penthouse. I think you'll enjoy reading them."

She'd waited until Yeats had gone off to make some phone calls before telling Poe this. Yeats knew nothing about Poe's deal with the West Side gentlemen and its payoff. He'd find out even-tually, but Poe had decided to tell him as little as possible. He and Mango could handle things on their own. All things considered, they were doing a hell of a job at it.

"The Atlantic City paper, too?"

"Let's not overdo it, Peter."

The housekeeper had put the out-of-town newspapers in Poe's study. He'd dropped Yeats off at the Hancock, but Mango stayed with him.

"Fix me a drink," he told her, settling down into his chair. "Scotch light. Help yourself, too."

The *Philadelphia Inquirer* had run the story inside, in the metro section. *Philadelphia Daily News* had splashed it on page one: "MOBSTER KILLED IN BED."

The secondary headline summed up the other killings. The story, carried on inside, was quite lurid. Finishing it quickly, Poe went back to the *Inquirer*. The facts there were the same.

He realized he'd crossed a line here. With O'Rourke, and the prostitute they'd stuck with his murder, he'd accepted what Mango had done, condoning—affirming—her actions. But he hadn't asked to have either of them killed, hadn't wanted it done. His former partners back East were something else. If he hadn't said yes in that West Side restaurant, they'd all still be alive. He might as well have pulled the trigger himself—clicked the switch that set off the bomb in the tire.

But he felt little remorse, less than he had over O'Rourke and the Chicago hooker. As he thought about it, none at all. It was good riddance. All of those guys must have killed people in their careers, or ordered it done. They were lowlifes, preying on every human weakness, in the business of screwing the public and cheating the government. It was good fucking riddance.

It was self-defense. They were out to kill him. They'd almost done in his wife and his architect, and they'd burned that pretty girl. It was justice. If he were ever tried for what he'd done, he'd probably stand a good chance of getting off.

And, of course, he never would be tried. Only a handful of people knew about his now thoroughly defunct Atlantic City partnership, and they all either worked for him or for them.

For the first time in days, he felt in command again, in full control. And, on top of everything, he'd won that yachting race. He was happy.

"Salut," he said, raising his glass. "To the future."

Mango lifted her drink in response, then froze. Diandra was in the doorway, wearing a bathrobe, looking terrible.

"Peter," she said, her voice a monotone. "I want to talk to you."

"In a minute," he said. "Okay, Miss Bellini. I want you to get back to work. I want to call a press conference for Thursday. And send a telegram to that girl's father. What's her name, Cindy Ellison? Tell him I'm real upset about what happened and that I'll pay all the hospital costs, everything. Tell him I intend to cooperate with the authorities in every way to get to the bottom of this."

Mango knocked back her drink in a few quick swallows. "I'll take care of it, Mr. Poe. See you at the office."

Diandra stepped out of her way to let her pass, not deferentially or courteously, but as if to avoid contact with something repulsive.

She seated herself in a chair by the window, compelling Poe to swivel away from his desk. He started to get up.

"Don't come near me, Peter. I'm not looking for a hug."

Her eyes were red, either from booze or crying or both. Her face was chalky white and her hair a tangle. He had never seen her looking like this.

"You had a close call up there, honey," he said. "You okay?"

"I can't think of a more inappropriate word for how I feel."

The robe was loose. She didn't seem to be wearing anything beneath. It was nearly five o'clock. Had she been in bed all this time?

"You don't look so good. You sure you're all right?"

"Am I supposed to believe that you care?"

"Of course I care. What do you think?"

"Then why weren't you there to meet me? Why did you go down to Springfield?"

"Had to, babe. My bill was up on final reading today. It was a special session, you know? They weren't going to sit there and wait on me. And Krasowski told me you were fine. Just got a little wet."

"Matthias said it was bomb. That it couldn't be anything else."

"Is that what he thinks? Well, maybe it was. I'm sorry you got mixed up in it. I should have taken you back with me."

"Most wives don't have to contend with bombs, Peter."

"Look, I'm sorry. I'm upset. I'm mad as hell about it. I'm going to make damn sure nothing like that ever happens again."

"Is someone trying to kill you, Peter? Why? What have you done?"

"I haven't done anything. I don't know who planted that bomb, if it was a bomb. Maybe it had something to do with Curland. He's the guy who had a dead girl turn up in his boat."

"I thought of that—for a very brief minute. But it's ridiculous. Matthias Curland doesn't even know the kind of people who use bombs. The only person he knows who might be mixed up in something like that is you."

"What do you mean, Diandra?"

She stood up, clenching her fists. "Goddamn it, what's going on, Peter? Tell me or I'll scream!"

"Ease up, babe. Ease up. Sit down, please. I'll tell you everything I know. You want a belt? You look like you could use one."

He could see her struggling with herself. Whichever side won, she sat down. "Pour me some vodka."

Poe filled a glass, adding ice from his machine.

"What I can tell you is this," he said, resuming his seat. He glanced down, arranging his thoughts, as if about to make a speech. "I have a lot of enemies, Diandra. You know that. There are guys who have lost out in deals, people I've pushed out of the way, *Social Register* types who think I'm an upstart, and I suppose a few weirdos who'd like to do something bad to me just because I'm in the newspapers and the magazines and on television all the time. You get as successful as I am and you find people who can't wait to see you take a fall—maybe hurry it along. Look at the way everybody piled on Trump."

She looked out the window. He couldn't tell how closely she was paying attention to him.

"But I think it could be more serious than that," he continued. "I don't remember how much I've told you, but I've had some mob guys interested in my Michigan City casino, the same East Coast guys I left Atlantic City to get away from. I've kept them at arm's length. I've done everything in my power to keep that place operating on the up and up—a strictly honest business. I don't think this sits too well with some elements. Casinos with them are like garbage to rats."

"Are you telling me I have to live in fear of being blown up just because you own a casino?"

"I can't get rid of it. I need it as collateral for my Cabrini Green loan. Everything else is in hock. I'm kinda overleveraged. But you don't have to worry. I've gone to, well, the authorities. I'm cooperating in every way. I think that, once there's some heat put on those pricks, they'll back off and leave me be. I'm sure of it."

"I can't stand this, Peter."

"I really don't think we have anything to worry about. I just can't let it get out, about the mob wanting to make a move on my casino. It would queer my new bank loan. And it sure as hell wouldn't do our social reputation any good. So, not a word about this to anyone. Absolutely no one. Including Matthias Curland."

"Matthias Curland."

"Yeah. How is he, by the way?"

"He wasn't hurt too badly."

"That isn't what I mean. How is he feeling? How is he disposed—toward me?"

"He's extremely angry."

"I shouldn't be surprised, should I? Well, he'll get over it. You can help."

"Me?"

"Sure. He likes you, doesn't he? Seems pretty obvious to me he does. A lot."

"That's what you wanted, isn't it?"

"Well, now I want something more. I want you to calm him down. I need to get back in his good graces."

"What are you suggesting?"

"I don't know. Whatever it takes. Be friendly. You were friendly with him up in Wisconsin, weren't you? After I left?"

"What do you mean?"

She really looked frazzled. He wondered what else.

"Did he make a pass at you? Did you fuck him?"

Her eyes widened. Her mouth was all twisted. He wished he had a picture of her like this. He'd have it enlarged and framed. For the next time she got out of line.

"I hate you, Peter."

"Fine. Hate me. Take a walk. File for divorce. Only remember, you signed a prenuptial. You walk away with nothing. I could keep your clothes, only I wouldn't do that."

"Look, you egomaniac son of a bitch, I went to my room after you left and stayed there. Matthias was dancing, with that Cindy. Why do you think he's still up there?"

He studied her. She looked ready to kill him. Instead of turning violent, though, she finished her drink.

"Look," he said, speaking softly now. "I wouldn't have minded. I'm an understanding guy. These are modern times. Hell, I don't want you to take a walk, Diandra. I'm glad you're my wife. I can't imagine myself married to anybody else. I don't doubt a thing you say. That broad made it real clear she has the hots for him. She's a hell of a looker. I'd be surprised if he didn't give her a poke. He's just like his brother, that guy. Doesn't matter he's engaged to that stuck-up Phillips lady. A good-looking piece of ass walks by, and bingo."

Diandra got up and refilled her glass.

"You're not going to turn into a lush on me, are you? That's a whole 'nother problem."

"Damn it, Peter, my nerves are shot. I drank myself silly last night, coming back to an empty home, when I needed you, and you off in Springfield with that she-devil secretary of yours. Now I've got the worst hangover of my life, all right? I'm trying to get back to normal. Leave me alone."

"Fine, babe, fine. All I'm asking is for you to be a good wife and help me out here. I need Curland. I need his ideas, his connections. It's the biggest goddamn deal of my life. I'm sorry those bastards tried to get rough, but that's all over and we're all out of it okay. But I don't want my plans knocked into a ditch just because my high-society architect has gone into a snit."

"He didn't say anything about derailing your plans. Your goddamned building is probably the farthest thing from his mind. He's just upset, angry. He wants to know what happened and who did it. And why."

"When the time comes, I'll give him a fill. Right now, I want you to calm him down, make him happy. Find out when he's coming back. Meet him at the airport. Go to his house. I don't care. Get him into a mood where I can talk to him. Tell him I'll do everything I can for that girl. I'll meet with him whenever he wants, wherever."

She collapsed back in her chair, staring down at her feet, part of her hair falling over her face.

"My bill was passed," he said. "Went through the Senate like a well-oiled cannonball."

"Hurray for you," she muttered.

He stood up. "You get well, whatever it takes. Then get your-self cleaned up. I'll take you to dinner tonight. Bice's. The Cape Cod Room. Whatever. I'm going over to the office. I've got five corporations to run. I haven't paid any attention to most of them for weeks."

He went up to her and put his hand on her shoulder. She didn't move.

"I love you, babe," he said.

She put her hand on his. It felt cold.

CHAPTER 1

MATTHIAS RETURNED HOME from Wisconsin as tired as if he'd walked instead of flown. He'd stayed up all night with Cindy, and haunted the hospital waiting room throughout the next day, though her father, upon arriving, had strongly suggested he leave. After spending the next night in a grubby motel, uselessly calling the burn unit for reports on her unchanging condition, he decided he might just as well be in Chicago. He wasn't doing Cindy any good, or himself. A sheriff's deputy had taken a statement from him, and he'd filled out a lengthy mariner's accident report for the Coast Guard. No one else seemed to have any interest in him.

A salvage crew had pulled the remains of the *Lady P* from the shallows, and some local divers had gone looking for bomb fragments at the request of the sheriff's office, but none had been recovered. The Transportation Department in Washington supposedly was going to investigate the incident, but it didn't appear that much was going to come of it.

His plane reached Chicago in late afternoon and he went directly to his Schiller Street house. As Matthias expected, Christian wasn't there. A number of messages were waiting by the kitchen phone, most of them two or more days old. He didn't even want to look at them.

He went up to his room and collapsed on his bed, fully clothed. The doctor had given him some painkillers for his hand, and he'd taken them—though, in the Prussian tradition of his family, he usually avoided such medication. You learn not to mind the hurt, his grandfather had told him when he was a little boy. Prussians don't cry.

It was dark when he awoke. He thought he'd simply reached the end of his sleep, that it was near dawn, but it was only a little past nine. He realized he'd been awakened by a sound. The damned doorbell.

He wasn't up to facing Sally. If it was Christian, he could just go find another harbor for the night. He had enough lady friends in the neighborhood.

Matthias sat up on the edge of the bed. With his luck, it might be that Michigan police chief again. Actually, that was one person he actually would like to see.

Swinging open the front door, he was surprised to find Diandra, an ethereal figure in a long white dress, hands clasped together, head slightly bowed.

"I called Door County. They told me you'd left today. I took a chance that you'd be home by now."

"And so I am."

"May I come in? I'd like to talk to you."

"Yes, of course. Excuse me. I didn't mean to be rude."

He led her into the living room. She looked around, curious. "It's just as I imagined your house would be."

"Please sit down. Would you like a drink?"

She hesitated. "Yes. Vodka and tonic. It will help."

He returned with two glasses, managing them clumsily with his bandaged fingers.

"How's your hand?"

"I certainly know it's there. The doctor said I should be fine in a couple of weeks. Cindy will be scarred for life—on her back and leg."

"They do wonders with plastic surgery now. Peter said to tell you he's going to get her the best."

"How nice."

She crossed her legs demurely, then sank back in the couch, lifting her glass and looking at him over the rim. "He's really upset."

"I'm sure he is. It was an expensive boat."

"You're being unfair. He wants to do everything he can."

"How about providing an explanation?"

She glanced away, to the painting of his mother, then back. "He'd like you to believe it was just an accident."

"I'd like to believe that myself. But it wasn't."

She sighed. "I'll tell you what he told me. And I believe him. He said he has some business rivals. I guess they're not very principled. He's not sure it was them, but he went to the authorities about them. He said he did, anyway. He doesn't think they'll try anything like that again."

"Sounds all very neat." He was angry, but not at her. He regretted his churlishness to her up in Wisconsin.

"I've heard of things like this before," she said. "A designer whose shows I used to work in had a showroom firebombed once, and never did find out why. In any event, Peter doesn't seem very worried, so it must be all right."

"Of course. Everything is all ticketyboo."

"What?"

"An upper-class English colloquialism. Sorry."

"Are you mad at me?"

"I'm just mad. I wish I knew at who."

They looked at each other. He had held her naked body just a few days before. He'd run his hands all over her. Somewhere in all that, he recalled that she'd told him she loved him—and he her. But that night was so far removed from their present circumstance that it seemed almost as if it had never happened.

"Where does this leave us, Matthias?"

He shrugged. "I wish I knew."

"Do you still want to do Peter's building?"

The truthful answer was yes. He couldn't get that out of his mind, either. When his plane was approaching Chicago, he'd looked off toward the slums along the north branch of the river, imagining the curving sail and soaring tower rising from there to the sky. He'd sternly told himself that he ought not have any part of the project now, then questioned why that was so. It wouldn't make any difference to Cindy whether the building was erected or not. Poe was going to put something up there. Why not his design?

"I haven't decided. I'd like to think about it some more, after I've managed a good night's sleep."

"Did I awaken you? I should have realized you'd be taking a rest."

"That's all right."

"Would you at least talk to Peter about it? He'd like you to."

"I don't suppose he's made up his mind on the design."

"As a matter of fact, I think he has—the full-blown one, with the sail. But don't tell him I told you. Please don't tell him anything I've said."

"Or done."

"Matt, please."

"You probably shouldn't have come."

"I had to. I couldn't leave things the way they were."

"Shall we just forget that night?"

"I don't want to answer that question."

He sought her eyes, but she kept them from him.

"All right. I'll call him. Perhaps tomorrow."

"You'll meet with him tomorrow?"

Had he sent her to arrange this? "No. I may call him tomorrow."

"He's holding a press conference Thursday, I think maybe about the building."

"I'll call him."

She finished her drink and set the glass on a coaster on the table next to her. Then she sat back primly, hands folded in her lap. "I probably ought to go."

"What about us?"

"I'd like to be your friend, Matthias."

"My friend."

The doorbell rang. As his father would say, people in polite society didn't come calling at this hour.

Another surprise. Sally. She rushed into his arms.

"Matt! I saw the lights and was hoping you'd be home. I was so worried about you, darling. I kept calling you. I couldn't find Christian. Are you all right? You gave me such a scare."

She pulled him tight and lifted her face to be kissed. He did as she wished, but stiffly, embarrassed.

"Oh, dear. Your hand. Did I hurt you?"

She stepped back, and then noticed the woman sitting in the living room.

Diandra gave her a weak smile. "Hello, Sally."

"Mrs. Poe." Sally's face darkened. "I didn't expect to find you here."

"I—I just dropped by. I wanted to make sure Mr. Curland was all right."

"Of course you did." She glanced at him unhappily and stepped back toward the door. "Well, I can see I've come at an inconvenient time. Good night, everybody."

"Sally, please stay."

She pulled open the door. "Perhaps we might talk tomorrow."

"Sally, for God's sake."

"Good-bye, Matthias."

Her heels clicked sharply on the walk.

Diandra got up.

"Now I really must go," she said.

"I don't know what to say."

She touched his arm, but only for a moment. "There's nothing to say. Just meet with Peter. We'll work things out from there."

Christian breezed in early in the morning, catching Matthias in the midst of fixing himself a bloody Mary.

"Home is the sailor, home from the sea, I see," he said cheerily. "Preparing to launch yourself again, big brother?"

"It's my hand. It hurts like hell. I'm afraid I've been using alcohol therapy."

"Grandfather would disapprove."

Christian put a kettle of water on and got a jar of instant coffee out of the cupboard.

"I don't mind," Christian said. "I enjoy a bit of role reversal now and then. I've got a busy day ahead of me. Larry Train's promised me my own one-man show and I've got to get some pictures together. Our friend Poe's already said he'll buy one. Sunshine everywhere, big brother."

"Do you have enough work at hand? I thought all you've been doing is portraits."

"May have to borrow a few of those back, just to flesh out the exhibition. We'll hang them as 'sold.' But I've got a few canvases here and there. I stashed some over at the museum, and there are a couple up at the house in Lake Forest. And of course Larry has some he hasn't sold. That's what sparked this. He thought we might as well make a big deal out of it."

"I wish you luck." He meant it sincerely.

Christian poured some hot water in the cup and then stirred the mixture vigorously with a spoon.

"Luck to you, too. Have you and Sally set a date?"

"That's not exactly been decided."

"I'll be happy to be best man. I am, don't you know."

He downed his coffee in quick gulps. "Must dash, big brother. Badly need a shower and shave. You want to come with me to the museum? Poke around a little? Look at my stuff?"

"I didn't know you had any of your paintings there."

"I put them away in the vault."

"I'm not really up to it. I have all these phone calls to answer."

"Well, suit yourself. You ought to watch that drinking, old fellow. It can get to you."

He started to leave, then stopped. "You haven't given Sally an engagement ring."

"No, I haven't."

"I know it's dreadfully middle class, big brother. But so is Sally. Why don't you give her Mother's? Sally would like that."

"Mother's ghost wouldn't."

"Mother wouldn't give a damn, Matt. It meant about as much to her as her marriage."

Among the telephone messages that had been waiting for Matthias was a surprising one. Douglas Gibson was one of his oldest friends, but they hadn't had much contact in recent years, the last time a chance encounter one evening on New York's Fifth Avenue. Now Gibson wanted to see him, rather urgently. When Matthias returned the call, he quickly suggested lunch at the Chicago Club. Matthias hadn't arrived at any sensible decision as to how to deal with Sally, and didn't want to wait around the house for another encounter with her until he'd made up his mind what to do. He accepted.

Gibson was a lawyer, quite possibly the smartest man Matthias knew in Chicago. They'd first met when they were beginning their careers, Gibson the attorney in a minor real estate project for which the Curland family firm had been hired as architects. Gibson was a country boy, the son of a well-to-do soybean and corn farmer out near Sycamore, the family holdings also including a small cannery and a fuel oil distributorship. A graduate of Northwestern and Yale Law, Gibson had switched from real estate to bonds, moving from law firm to law firm until now, at a remarkably young age, he was managing partner of one of Chicago's largest. His clients included a very major bank. Matthias had a fair idea of what he wanted to talk about, and why he was in such a hurry to meet.

At Gibson's request, they were given a table off to the side, out of earshot of the others in the dining room, which was fairly full.

"Martini," Gibson said to the waiter, then looked to Matthias. "Two?"

"Just a glass of white wine." Christian's talk about role reversal had unnerved him.

"Of course," Gibson said. "You're an artist now. Wine, bread, and cheese, right?"

"I'm just not drinking much anymore. Most of the time."

Gibson gave him an odd look. He always kept himself extremely well informed, about business, politics, scandals, people's personal problems. If he hadn't been so bent on making money, he would have been a superb journalist.

His appearance was deceiving. He had a farm boy's face. His suits were expensive now, but they always looked rumpled on him. The tie he wore was a little askew and the point of one of his shirt collars was bent. But Gibson masterminded deals that ran to a hundred million dollars or more. His personal income was probably close to three million dollars a year. He'd married a rich woman, but his own wealth now exceeded her family's. Ruth was a college professor much involved in civic causes, and served as chairman of one of the mayor's citizens commissions. They represented the new establishment that had taken over from the old families who had still been running the city when Matthias was a child. The Gibsons weren't *Social Register*—Ruth was Jewish, and the snooty *Register* seemed to frown upon that—but the Gibsons didn't care about such trivialities. They deeply loved the city in which they were so much involved. Some of the rougher political types considered them do-gooders, but that didn't bother them, either.

"I heard you were back in town," Gibson said, "but I thought it was just for your mother's funeral. Would have been there, but I was in Washington. Had some business with the Securities and Exchange Commission. Couldn't wait. I wish I'd been there. Sorry, Matt."

Matthias's mother had disapproved of Gibson. They'd been unable to disabuse her of the notion that his father drove a tractor for a living, though the man sometimes had done that, just for fun.

"I appreciate the thought, but you did well to skip it. An awkward business. We were glad to get it over."

"I hear you've been helping your father out, getting the firm back on its feet before going back to France."

"Something like that."

Gibson had very innocent brown eyes, the effect enhanced by large horn-rimmed glasses. Adversaries who took him for a naive rube, however, often found their back against the bottom of a ditch, as had once been said about another sharp Illinois corporate attorney of rustic mein—Abraham Lincoln.

"You've landed a pretty big client," Gibson said.

"Peter Poe."

"The very fellow."

The drinks came. Gibson lifted his in toast, then took a quick sip. "Saw your picture in the *Trib* at the wheel of his boat. Guess you're pretty good chums."

"Just a client."

Gibson grinned. He sipped again, then set the glass aside. As memory served, he probably wouldn't finish it.

"I really meant to call you," he continued, "even before I heard about you and Poe. Just been so damned busy. Out of town half the time. But when I read about that fire on his boat, I didn't want to wait any longer." He looked at the bandages on Matthias's left hand. "Maybe I waited too long."

Curland raised the hand and turned it, moving his fingers. "It's not as bad as it looks."

"People talk about getting their fingers burned in a business deal. This is the first time I've actually seen it happen."

They both smiled. Gibson sat back, blinking at Matthias. In a way, he reminded Curland of the Michigan police chief Rawlings.

"Matt," he said after a moment. "We think he has ties to the mob. That's why the bank I represent won't do business with him. I won't let them."

Matthias stared at his wine, then drank. He'd been harboring that same dark suspicion himself. As he sat all those hours in the waiting room of Cindy's hospital in Wisconsin, the thought had returned to him repeatedly as he'd sought a logical explanation for what had happened to Poe's boat.

But suspicions were not proof. Was his friend Douglas now providing that? If so, would it make a difference? Mob money was everywhere in Chicago. He could point to a dozen buildings that stood as monuments to it.

"My brother has become something of a friend of Poe's," he said finally. "He hasn't said a word about anything like that. I don't suppose you'd hold Christian up as a man of great virtue, but criminals aren't exactly his set. He'd drop Poe in an instant if he thought what you're saying might be true."

"Christian wouldn't know. Few people do. I'm not talking about the Chicago mob. It's an East Coast outfit. We don't have

256

any proof. Nothing I'd go to the government with. But enough to want to stay clear of him. When I heard what happened to his boat up there, I was scared to death about you."

"I talked to his wife about it. All she'd tell me is that he thinks it might have been the work of 'business rivals.' She said he isn't terribly worried about it."

"He wasn't on the boat."

"He might have been. If it was the crime syndicate, wouldn't he be afraid, wouldn't he get out of town, or whatever one does?"

"I didn't say the guy didn't have guts. He must, the way he throws other people's money around."

"He has a lot of respectable people associated with him."

"Including you. Are you going to stick with him?"

"Haven't decided." He kept saying that. Every time he did it seemed to have less meaning.

"Matt, I don't want to pry into your business, or intrude on a client relationship, if you still have one, but Poe plans to put up a monster high-rise on that Cabrini Green tract, isn't that right? That's the project you've been working on?"

"I haven't signed a contract, but I've done some drawings for him."

"I do deals, Matt. That's how I earn my living. I haven't gone near a courtroom in years. I've done big ones and small ones, winners and losers. But I've never seen as big a loser as this one shows every prospect of becoming. It makes no sense at all. I wouldn't put a dime into it."

"Poe's what you'd call a high roller. He likes to take risks."

"Standing on the edge of a cliff is taking a risk. This fellow is taking a running leap. No matter what he has in mind for that property, in that neighborhood, he'll be lucky to open with a ten percent occupancy rate, even if he gives space away. The location is insane. Townhouses maybe. Low-rise condos. But offices, luxury apartments. A monster tower. It's absolutely nuts."

"He views the project as a self-fulfilling prophesy. Put up the building, and the neighborhood changes. It's already beginning to. A project like this would be a fantastic anchor. Other developers would come running. Sandburg Village brought back the Near North Side that way. This would be much the same thing. Whatever you think of the man, he's certainly a visionary. It was people like him who built Chicago, people like my great-grandfather."

"Sandburg Village was residential, a lot of it low-rise, and right next to the Gold Coast. Arthur Rubloff was no fool. He was one of the most conservative developers this city's ever seen. He was dead sure Sandburg Village would work."

"I'm just an architect, Doug. My last big client here went bankrupt, but the building's still there. Anyway, imminent bankruptcy doesn't seem to be one of Mr. Poe's problems."

"We hear the money for this deal is coming from Japan."

Matthias shrugged.

"They're not fools, either," Gibson said. "Anything but. What the hell do they know that the rest of us don't?"

"They know that Peter Poe has made a lot of money with everything he's done."

Gibson always knew when to retreat from a point. He took another line of attack. "These aren't the most wonderful times for architects. A lot of the big firms have let people go. But you're one of the best I know—I say that friendship aside. We have clients who are still building, Matt. There are brand-new cities going up in the suburbs. They're part of that. I'd be happy to put you together with some of our people—if you decide to back away from Poe."

"Sterile office parks and sprawling shopping centers don't make cities, Douglas. Chicago's special."

"Well, consider it a standing offer. And, Matt, if you get into any more trouble with that guy, you call me at once, all right?"

As he expected, Zany was out of a job. After his short, unhappy talk with Mayor Braunmeister, he left his police car at the municipal building, parked with the keys in it, and walked home despite the hot summer day. His service revolver was his own property, and he had it in his briefcase, but he'd left his badge on his desk, which was now George Hejmal's. His former sergeant had offered to try to get Zany hired back as a detective, after things quieted down, but neither man knew when that might be. Zany didn't count that among his prospects.

His wife had closed the beach shop for a few days and was waiting for him at the house. She brought him a cold beer and one for herself. They sat on the screened-in porch and looked out at the lake. Around them was everything they thought they had wanted, or needed.

"Were they bastards about it, our town fathers?" she asked, when she got around to speaking.

"They were very generous. Six months' pay."

"Six months can come and go in a hurry."

"It could have been worse."

"What are you going to do?"

"Well, I suppose I could always go back to the Chicago P.D. Hang in long enough to get a pension. Then we could come back here."

"You'd hate that. So would I."

He took a swig. He was surprised at how content he felt, how confident. It might be delusion, but he felt wonderfully free.

"You know," his wife said. "There are things besides law enforcement. We have land enough to add a motel or something to the beach store. Maybe a real restaurant. Or marine supplies."

"That's a thought. Maybe a bar."

"Not a bar. But you're really willing to give up being a cop?"

"Not entirely."

"What does that mean?"

He shrugged.

"You're not still thinking about that damned murder case?" she asked.

"Just a little."

"Well, don't."

Zany smiled. "Anyway, I've got the day off. If I weren't so tired, I'd go fishing." He stood up, finishing his beer as he gazed off to the west.

"Why don't you take a nap?"

"Might. Right now, I think I'll fool around with my computer for a while."

Matthias went directly to Sally's apartment as soon as he guessed she might be home, not wanting to put things off any longer. She was fixing dinner for her daughter. While she busied herself with that, he played with her little girl in the living room, helping her cut out some paper dolls. The daughter was already as pretty as her mother, and very charming. She was one of the big pluses in the equation. Matthias's wife had not wanted any children. Jill Langley had, but that was another matter, another sorrow.

Sally took the little girl into the kitchen, then returned.

"I don't have a lot of time for you," she said. "I've a party to go to tonight."

"Do you want me to come with you?"

She seated herself in an armchair. She'd bought some new furniture recently. A few of the pieces looked to be valuable antiques.

Her steady, unhappy gaze was her answer.

"What's wrong, Sally?"

She looked away, her brow very furrowed. "I'll be blunt. Are you and Diandra Poe having an affair?"

"Sally, for God's sake. We were in a fire together. She just came by to see how I was doing."

"I'm not just talking about her being there last night. I'm talking about what I see in your face every time you look at her."

"She's very striking, very graceful. I'm fascinated by the way she moves."

"I'll bet."

"It has nothing to do with us, with what we have between us."

"Did you sleep with her up in Wisconsin? That was your first chance at her, right?"

"Sally . . ."

"Be honest with me, damn it! I was honest with you about Christian! You asked me that humiliating question and I answered you. All our lives we've told the truth to each other."

"All right," he said, looking down at his hands, hating himself for being such a coward. "The answer is yes. But it's not something that's going to happen again."

"Except for late-night visits to your pied à terre on Schiller Street."

"She was just about to leave when you came. She'd only been there a few minutes."

He was trying to give her every chance to stay with him. He didn't want to cast her back into her lonely misery. But he knew for certain that marriage to her would not and could never be what they had imagined. That he didn't want it. That he'd cruelly deluded himself—and her—in thinking that they could go back to what once was. But he didn't want any more guilt. There had to be something noble in all this, something selfless.

"I was worried sick about you, and you didn't even call. Not from Wisconsin, not when you got home."

"I was exhausted, a complete mess. I was very upset about Cindy Ellison. I didn't want to talk to anyone. I didn't invite her over. I was asleep."

"Matt, I know what Christian is. I chose him for my disastrous extramarital adventure because I knew it wouldn't mean anything to him, that there'd be no complications with him, that it was all the same to him as taking me out to dinner. But I can't be married to a man like that. I was once, and I hated it. I won't be made a fool of, Matt. Not in my city. I've been humiliated enough."

"I'm not like my brother." He'd said it again. He'd been telling himself that all day. In the same circumstance, Christian would leave Sally in a trice, on a whim. He never would have asked Sally to marry him in the first place, certainly not out of any feeling of obligation. Christian lived only for himself.

Sally folded her arms. "That's all I have to say."

"I was going to ask you if you'd like to have my mother's engagement ring."

"Under the circumstances, I think that would be very inappropriate."

"You're absolutely sure?"

"I'll be honest again. I'm not absolutely sure. I love you. I always have. In the fantasy world I've spent so much time in, I want to be married to you. I want us to have all the things we should have had in the beginning. But reality's different. I'm not sixteen anymore, am I? The truthful answer is that, yes, the possibility exists that I might change my mind, sometime. But it's a very slight possibility. The very large probability is that I won't. I'm not angry. I cried a lot last night, but I got over it. I should have known that what happened was going to happen, the way people who buy lottery tickets should know they're not going to win. What I feel is empty, deflated. Cheated by life again. The price I keep having to pay for caving in to my mother about you."

He rose, and started to come toward her.

"No, Matt, don't."

He stood awkwardly. "Do you want me to go?"

"Yes. I don't think we should see each other—not for a while, a damn long while—unless it's unavoidable. I'll explain it somehow to my friends."

"I think you're making a mistake. The same mistake you made when you turned me down the first time."

"You're not telling me the truth, Matt. I can face up to the truth. I'm a lot wiser than I used to be, when I let my mother always decide what was best. You learn a few things after a while. I know I'm not making a mistake."

"At least think about it." He'd give her every last chance. He'd leave the door open the tiniest inch. But he longed now for her to slam it shut, as he had slammed it shut on Jill, in what was probably the biggest mistake he'd ever made since leaving Chicago.

"I'll think about it. I'll be doing that the rest of my life." She got to her feet, the hostess preparing to see her guest to the door. "There's something else I want, Matthias. I want to keep this job with Peter Poe. I don't know where it will lead me. I'm certainly not in it for the long haul. But it got me out of that horrible pit I was in, and I don't want to fall back in. I don't want to go back to that store."

"I'm sure he'll be very glad to have you."

"Well, you just see to it. You and Diandra. You owe me that much."

BOBBY MANN LOOKED like a corpse. Poe had never seen skin that gray on a living human being. He stood up, gesturing Mann to a chair set squarely in front of his desk.

"Hiya, Bobby."

Mann sat down, his eyes looking like those of a rat caught in the light. He didn't say hiya back.

"I was surprised to find you still here, Bobby. I thought you might be taking a vacation, somewhere far away."

"I was told not to," he said, almost in a whisper. "Your friends."

"Nice to have friends, isn't it. Always looking out for you. And they're right. The middle of our busy season is no time to take off. You're needed here."

"I'm what?"

"Needed here. You've always done a good job of running this casino. Mango and I are going to be in Chicago most of the time now. At least for the rest of the summer. Got a lot going on. I'm going to depend on you to keep this place going—on the up and up. Every penny accounted for. Just like I ordered. I'd have been real pissed off if you had gone bye-bye."

Poe was trying to sound chummy. It didn't help that Mango was sitting on the other side of the office, staring at Mann like he really was a corpse.

"I don't understand what's going on, Mr. Poe."

"Sure you do. You're a sharp guy. I'm sure you get the picture. I think that, as things stand now, I can count on you to be my most loyal employee."

"Is that what you want?"

"Of course it's what I want. Look, Bobby, I don't hold any-thing against you. Honest. I know you were stuck in the middle of this thing. You came to me and warned me that those guys were going to get rough. I should have listened to you better. Live and learn, right?"

Mann said nothing. He looked like he wanted a cigarette, but was afraid to ask permission.

"Go ahead, Bobby. Light up. Mango over there's smoking like the Gary steel works."

Mann pulled a pack of Camels from his pocket, fumbling as he took one out.

A button on the phone console was flashing. Poe looked to Mango, who answered on the extension on her side of the room.

"It's Matthias Curland," she said. "He says he wants to meet with you."

Things were clicking. Poe's train was back on the track, gathering speed. He looked at his watch. He didn't want Bobby to budge from the chair, but he didn't want to talk to Curland in front of him.

"Tell him I'll meet him at two o'clock. I'll take a chopper back. Tell him I'll pick him up at his place."

Mango put the receiver back to her ear. Poe waited until she had hung up.

"Hell of a guy, that Curland," Poe said. "Got everybody off that boat alive. It really would have pissed me off if anyone had gotten killed. Innocent people like that—nothing to do with my business. And my wife, Bobby. If she had been at the other end of the boat . . . if that had happened, I'd spend every cent I've got making sure that everybody involved left this life in the most miserable fucking way possible. I've got a lot of money, Bobby. It would happen, believe me."

Mann simply stared. He looked like he knew he should say something, but didn't know what. "Yes, sir."

Just the right words. "If anything should ever happen to her again—if anything happens to Curland, to any of the people I'm associated with. If they're harmed in any way . . . Well, Bobby, if you went to Tibet for your vacation it wouldn't do you any fucking good. You understand?"

"Yes, sir."

"Like I say, I want you here. But you've got a lot of friends around the country. A few of them left, anyway. If you should be talking to them any time soon, you might pass that on. I've already made that clear to my friends."

"I understand."

"Of course you do. You're a sharp guy."

"Am I to understand you have new partners?"

Poe colored. This nice-guy crap was getting hard. "I've got two answers for you, Bobby. Number one is, none of your goddamn business. Number two is, absolutely not. Poe Enterprises is a one-man operation. I may have a lot of creditors. I've got a lot of assets. But I've got no partners. I didn't consider your friends my partners. Now I've got none."

Mann glanced over at Mango. She stared at him hard.

"So, Bobby, you got the picture? Everything crystal clear?"

"Yes, Mr. Poe."

"Okay. Get back to work. I want you to do something about the cocktail waitresses. They're not hustling enough drinks. Tell them to pick up the action or I'm going to start taking a cut of their tips."

Mann stood up. "I'll take care of it."

"And check out the rest rooms. I'm getting complaints that they're kinda untidy."

"You're fucking lucky we don't send you into the stalls with a toothbrush, Bobby," said Mango.

"Yes, sir," said Mann.

Curland was waiting on the curb outside his house when Poe pulled up in one of his red stretch limos. As Krasowski opened the door, Poe shifted to one of the rearward facing seats up by the glass divider, so he and Curland could look at each other while they talked.

"I thought we could go to my club," Matthias said, taking his place in the rear seat. "It'll be quiet at this time of day."

"I've had lunch," Poe said. "Let's just go for a drive."

They headed north along the lake. Curland looked quite haggard. He sat silently, waiting for Poe to speak.

"So, what's on your mind, Matt?"

"You know damn well what's on my mind. A burning sailboat."

"You're upset, aren't you? I don't blame you. Did Diandra tell you what it was all about? I know she went to see you."

"I'm sure she didn't break any confidences, but I'm not a stupid man, Mr. Poe. I have a fair idea of some of your troubles. What I want to know is whether there are going to be more of them."

"Absolutely not."

"I took what happened to Cindy very hard."

"So did I. I'll be perfectly honest with you, Matt. I'm pretty sure it was a mob hit. Thank God it wasn't a very well-executed one."

"I don't want to be associated with anyone who has to worry about mob hits, Mr. Poe. Cindy's going to be scarred for life."

"I'll do everything I can about that, but I want you to understand this, Matt. I have no dealings with organized crime. Absolutely none. People say a lot of things about me—think a lot of things—most of them wrong. They find it hard to believe that I could make so much money, be this successful, without cutting corners, without doing shady deals. It's a lot of crap. I wouldn't think of doing business with such people. If nothing else, it would get in the way of the things I want to accomplish, including our building. There isn't a penny going into that project that's in any way involved with criminals."

"I should tell you I've heard that might not be the case, from someone I trust."

"Well, your source is misinformed. I'm leveling with you, Matt. Everything about my project is on the up and up. The financing's going to come from the Japanese, some of the biggest and most respectable players in the world. I wouldn't go near anyone tainted in any way with something like this. Matt, if I was playing footsie with any of those mob guys, there wouldn't have been any bomb. It's the other way around. The outfit has been trying to muscle in on me since I opened that casino in Michigan City. I've told them to go to hell, that I planned to run a legitimate business. They threatened me with violence if I didn't give them a piece of the action. I guess I didn't take them seriously enough. They weren't Chicago people. They—"

"They're East Coast."

Poe studied the architect's gray eyes. They looked positively arctic. "Who told you that? This source of yours?"

"Is it true?"

"Yes. Atlantic City guys, with Las Vegas connections."

"They're the one who put a bomb on your boat?"

"It's a hell of a good bet. I can't think of who else would do it. I doubt it was our friend the commodore."

"Diandra said you'd gone to the authorities."

"That's right."

"And?"

"I'm not supposed to talk about it—to anyone. There's a big

266

investigation going on. The guys I think did it? They're dead. Someone got to them, those Atlantic City people. They were killed in gangland slayings out there."

"And who do you suppose did that?"

Poe shrugged. "Those are things we never find out. My theory is that it was probably the Chicago outfit. They got wind of what was going on and put a stop to it. I guess they didn't want any out-of-town thugs trying to move in here. If they couldn't get a piece of my Indiana action, they sure as hell weren't going to let out-of-town thugs try to muscle their way in."

Matthias looked out the window. They were passing Belmont Harbor, filled with small boats. "You know, Mr. Poe, until this summer, murder was something I only read about in the newspapers."

"Same here, Matt. Scares the hell out of me."

"Why don't you get out of the casino business?"

"I'm going to. Consider me properly spooked. But I can't yet. The casino's collateral. No casino, no building. But I think this 'unpleasantness' is all behind us now."

"You're sure about that?"

"That's what I'm told—by 'the authorities.' "

"Cindy's unpleasantness isn't behind her."

"She's going to be fine, Matt. She'll be sailing with us next summer. I'm going to get a new boat, maybe enter the Mackinac."

Curland looked at him as if he'd lost his mind.

They were approaching Montrose Harbor. Poe lowered the divider. "Turn off here, Lenny."

"Where are we going?" Curland asked.

"Out to the breakwater. I come out here a lot. Great view of the city."

Krasowski drove out to the end of the point, then parked and hurried out to open the door.

"We'll just take a little walk," Poe said. "Look at that view."

There was no finer prospect of the city skyline. The buildings marched down the coast to the grand assemblage of towers that marked downtown, the three highest rising like spires, Lake Point Tower standing alone, as if seated in the water—as no doubt its builders intended. Matthias's green pyramid was lost in all this, a shaded geometric shape, dwarfed by its neighbors, seeming to blend with the greenery of the park.

Poe leading, they went out onto the breakwater, walking past fishermen and grappling young lovers in bathing suits, none of them paying the two well-dressed strollers any mind. Did it bother Poe that he was not recognized? Perhaps no more, or no less, than it bothered Matthias that his own small creation was so unnoticeable.

They reached the end, blue-green water all around them. Poe leaned on the railing that ran along the center of the breakwater.

"Can you picture our building there?" Poe asked.

"Our building."

"Yes, 'our.' I want to do it, Matt. I want your design. The big one. The tower would be higher than any of the others, than any in the world, but Diandra's right. It would be just another needle. Like those in Seattle and Toronto. With the sail part, it would be unique—unmistakable. And big. You'd see it from O'Hare, from my casino in Indiana. From here. From the moon. It'll be fucking magnificent. And it'll be red. A beautiful, flaming red."

"The sunrise and sunset would do that for you. You wouldn't need to color it."

"It's what I want, Matt. Red's my color. It's my building. Hell, you made your building green. What's the difference? It doesn't have to be a bright red. Just a tint, like your Halsman Tower."

"There are people who still might object."

"Fuck 'em. The City Council isn't going to object. The Zoning Board won't. The Planning Commission won't. The Park District won't. The F.A.A. won't."

"What does the Park District have to do with it?"

"I told you, I want there to be a little park." He turned to look at Matthias directly. "There are going to be museums in this building—in the sail part. The entire main floor. Not just the Holocaust. I want a complex of museums that'll be devoted to all the city's ethnic groups. Irish, Polish, German, Hispanics, the whole garbanzo. Their histories, their cultures, their contributions. There'll be nothing like it in the country, not even the Smithsonian."

"Museums need staff, curators, directors, endowments, exhibits. Are you going to see to all that?"

"There are already some ethnic museums in the city—stuck away, here and there. A Lithuanian one, a Polish one. We'll start with those, and the Holocaust Museum. We'll have bond money and a new city tax on hotels. Don't worry about it. Everything's set. What I want to know now is, are you?" He gripped Curland's arm hard. "Are you with me on this? Will you do it? It's now or never, Matt. Bet or get out. What's your answer?"

Matthias's eyes lifted to the horizon again. He imagined the great, curving structure rising from the western reaches of the Near North Side—low end toward the Loop, the tower placed boldly to the north. He almost could see it, though he had difficulty envisioning it in even the palest red.

His gaze shifted, to the east, past the sailboats and cabin cruisers to the empty line where the deeper blue of the lake joined the pale sky. New York lay in that direction, as did the south of France. The emptiness was symbolic. His future—if he said no.

"All right."

"All right? A dinky answer like that to a question like this, to a project like this?"

"I'm not a demonstrative person."

"Okay. I'll take care of the demonstrative. From you I want pictures, not just drawings—paintings. A big architectural rendering. An aerial view. Exciting stuff. And I want floor plans. Use your imagination on the museums. On everything. But make it look good. I've got a press conference set up for Thursday. I was going to announce giving my hundred-grand victory prize to the Holocaust Museum fund, and maybe take care of questions about the commodore's challenge and what happened to the boat. But I'll do the whole thing. Unveil the works. Everything except how big it's going to be. Can you get me something by then?"

"Not easily."

"I'll give you until a week from Sunday. I'll switch the press conference to then. The Monday morning papers'll be wide open. Hell, it's summer. There's no news. All the TV will cover. They cover anything I do. Can you do it? A week from Sunday?"

"All right."

"One more thing, Matt. When you finish the stuff on the building, I want you to get started on that picture of Diandra. A full-length nude. I'll pay you for it, whatever you think is fair."

Matthias took a deep breath. "I told you before, I don't think that's a very good idea. I don't think she'd be very comfortable doing that."

"She'll do it. Don't worry. I want it. I want you to get started soon."

Matthias was deceiving himself with his reluctance. He wanted to do that painting, almost as much as he did the new tower. It would resolve whatever there was between them, one way or the other. But he wanted to give Poe every opportunity to change his mind, to say no to putting his wife in such a circumstance. He was going to be a gentleman in this, if nothing else.

"I'd really rather not."

"You want to do this building?"

"Yes."

"Then do Diandra. No painting, no building."

"Peter. If I paint your wife's portrait, it has nothing to do with the project. I'm not going to be bribed or threatened, about anything. Is that understood?"

Poe hesitated. The guy was insisting on standing on his own two feet. No Larrys, Curlys, or Moes in Lake Forest. So be it. Let him think what he wanted. "Okay. The building's a deal, painting or no painting."

"Very well." Why was Poe so bent on this picture?

"Will you do it? The painting?"

"That's entirely up to her."

"Okay."

Curland paused. "Are you going to keep Sally on, as your special events director, or whatever it is?"

So there was some wheelie-dealie in this guy after all. There was in absolutely everyone, wasn't there? Poe had built his entire career on that principle.

"Sure. Why shouldn't I?"

"What if I should back out?"

"You won't, but in any case, the job's hers for as long as she wants it. Shit, I need her." Poe extended his hand. Slowly Matthias reached out to take it. They shook hands firmly. Poe held on, keeping his grip.

"When they do a deal in City Hall," Poe said, "they have a way of saying it. 'I'm with you.' Only they say, 'I'm witcha.' Say it."

"I'm with you."

"No. Say it the other way."

Matthias wanted this colloquy to end. "All right. I'm witcha."

Poe shook his hand one more time, then let go. He started to walk back down the breakwater, more quickly now than when they come out here to the end. "Shall I drop you at your house?"

"If you don't mind, I'd like to go to the Art Institute."

"You going to look at some pictures?"

"A few."

"Just don't forget the ones you've got to do for me."

His friend in the Art Institute's restoration and repair department had his four paintings set against the wall, side by side. Kirchner's *Red Tower* made him sad, made him think of the picture the Michigan policeman had showed him of Jill Langley's dead face. There was death in the faces of the people hurrying along the street in the painting. Perhaps that was what it was all about. His grandfather had been a very old man when he made his decision to lock these works up in the vault.

"I'd be happy to go into detail, Matt, but I think all you need to know is that the experts' judgment is that they're all original. It's my conclusion, too."

"Including the Kirchner?"

"Definitely. You see these flecks in the gray of this building wall? Those aren't highlights that he added. He laid down a crimson base and then painted the buildings over it. They X-rayed it. There are at least three layers of paint there. A copyist wouldn't have done that."

"They're absolutely sure?"

"They were extremely thorough. The bill's in that envelope. I'm afraid you'll find it a bit dear."

"The museum can afford it, though I certainly can't."

"You don't seem particularly happy with the result."

"On the contrary. I'm quite delighted. I appreciate your taking the time."

"I'm sorry it took so long. As I say, we've been extremely busy. What made you doubt their authenticity in the first place?"

"Someone told me they'd seen *The Red Tower* in circulation."

"If so, it's fraudulent. A copy. This is a genuine Kirchner."

"What do you think it's worth? *The Red Tower*?"

His friend shrugged. "I read about a Kirchner going for $450,000 at Sotheby's in Geneva. That's not bad in today's art market."

Zany had been up in St. Joseph spending some time with the sheriff and was home late for dinner. He nodded at the casserole his wife had sitting on the stove, but took a beer from the refrigerator before sitting down at the table.

271

"You weren't doing cop work up there, were you?" his wife said, putting the casserole back in the oven. Zany could smell tuna fish and cheddar cheese.

"Not really. Just tying up a few loose ends. Filling him in on some old cases."

"Well, it's nice of you to do that, but you do have it firm in your mind now that you're no longer a cop?"

"Yes, ma'am."

They hadn't completely made up their minds about the future, but were seriously pursuing the idea of expanding the beach shop with an addition and selling marine supplies and fishing tackle. The local banker, doubtless feeling a little guilty about the price Zany had paid for simply doing his duty, had already agreed to lend them the money. The store wouldn't be ready until the next summer's tourist season, but the mayor had offered him a job at the marina for the interim. He hadn't yet given her an answer.

"You had a call, Zane. From Chicago. Matthias Curland. He said to tell you he had that painting checked for authenticity and that it's definitely the original. The one you found on the sailboat is a fake."

"Yes?"

"He said he had some others checked, too, and they're also originals. He said you don't need to call him back. He just thought you should know. I told him I'd pass on the message. I almost didn't."

"It's interesting news. If he's telling the truth." He started for the phone.

"Don't you call him back, Zane. Don't you dare."

"I'm not calling him. I'm going to call his ex-wife."

"What the hell for?"

"It's time I found out if the man does tell the truth.'"

"And then what?"

"I just want to satisfy my curiosity."

CHAPTER
16

EXCEPT FOR CINDY Ellison—whom he'd at last managed to talk to on the telephone and on whose improving condition he checked every day—Matthias shut everything else out of his life but the work before him. He didn't hear from Sally or Diandra— or Peter Poe—and didn't try to contact them. Often he let his phone ring on unanswered. Christian was seldom at the house, busying himself with his forthcoming gallery show, and Matthias was able to sketch and paint without distraction. He went at it all day every day and long into the night. It wasn't a matter of obsession. Not yet. He just wanted this phase of the job done and behind him, so he could move on to whatever was coming next. His injured hand was no impediment. Rather, the still-lingering pain seemed to goad him on.

He wasn't exactly producing masterpieces, but these illustrations didn't need to be. All that was required was bright color and mass and grandeur. All they needed to do was please Peter Poe.

But the developer wanted to make a big impact. The trouble with Matthias's pictures was that they were too small. To enhance the impression Poe was trying to make, Matthias was going to suggest that the principal rendering be photographed and that a huge enlargement of it be made and used as a backdrop for the announcement press conference. Usually when major development plans like this were unveiled, a scale model was presented, but Poe hadn't been interested in that. Perhaps it was just that he was in a hurry, or possibly because he wanted to avoid questions about how much land his building would take up. His Cabrini Green tract didn't quite accommodate their grand scheme.

To Matthias's surprise, he was finished in less than a week, but he held back from telling Poe he was done, except to arrange for the photographic enlargement of the principal illustration.

Matthias wanted someone whose judgment he valued to look at his design. This extraordinary building would likely be his major professional achievement as an architect. For all he knew, he'd muffed it. Some of the world's greatest architects had occasionally put up some truly awful buildings, full of the belief that anything they might do must perforce be brilliant.

Christian's eye and judgment were excellent. He might have made a national reputation for himself as a museum director had they been allowed to do more with the Albrecht Collection than carry out their grandfather's wishes.

He caught his brother early one morning when Christian, who was making a ritual of this, had dashed in to shower and change clothes. It disturbed Matthias that Christian was now back to begin-the-day bloody Marys, but he suppressed that. Matthias himself was content to drink coffee. Their roles were back to normal.

"I've finished the renderings," he said. "Have you a moment to look at them?"

"Always a moment for you, big brother. As many moments as you like."

Two of the watercolors were on easels. The others he propped on a table against the wall, facing the window light.

Christian smiled. "Poe will be ecstatic."

"I know what Poe thinks about this. What do you think?"

"I think it's bloody marvelous."

"The concept?"

"The concept, the depiction, *le tout ensemble.*"

"Really? You don't think the sail is too much?"

"If Chicago worried about 'too much,' Matt, there never would have been a Sears Tower, or a Merchandise Mart, or the first Louis Sullivan skyscraper. Big and bold, that's our toddlin' town, *n'est ce pas?*"

"Christian, a giant pig would be big and bold. What do you think of it as a building? Forget the scale."

"I think it's extraordinary, magnificent, unique, cleanly yet fully realized. No other architect could have done it. You've found yourself, Matthias. Forget art, forget the museum. This is indeed your true calling."

"You're sure?"

"I'm more than sure. I'm your brother."

274

"But don't you have any criticism? Don't you find anything wrong with it?"

Christian examined the aerial view of the building more thoughtfully.

"Well, I wouldn't want it here on Schiller Street. Ruin our lovely morning light, don't you know. Ruin everybody's. But out there in the city's sprawling nethers, it should be absolutely wondrous." He paused and squinted. "I don't like the base. I don't think it should bulge out like that. I'd rather it just came shooting out of the ground."

"Poe wants a ground floor with a grand entrance and big display windows, so I need some vertical facing delineated from the main structure—a façade, if you will, a storefront. He wants to put museums in there. The Holocaust Museum and the like, a lot of ethnic-oriented cultural and historical collections."

"Very civic-minded, our Mr. Poe. How appealing to the elected representatives of the people. How wonderfully ironic that we of the German Museum should involve ourselves with a Holocaust Museum."

"Christian!"

"Sorry, big brother. I forget your egalitarian sensibilities. At any rate, it's genius. I'm proud of you." He turned, looking at his watch. "I'm afraid I must be off. Larry Train's throwing a little brunch for me this morning. Some of his closest friends—and best customers."

They went downstairs. Christian stopped in the kitchen to finish the remains of his drink.

"You and Larry Train are rather close these days," Matthias said.

"He's been a prince—as good to me as Peter Poe has been to you."

"I didn't think he handled much contemporary representational art like yours. I thought he followed the norm—living abstract artists, long-dead representational ones."

"But I'm a local boy, in addition to being a fantastic talent. And besides, your relationship with Poe seems to have given the Curland name new cachet in this town. We're what you might call hot."

He emptied his glass and set it down. Matthias wasn't ready to let him go.

"I had Kirchner's *Red Tower* and a few other canvases checked for authenticity," he said.

275

"You went into the vault and took out paintings?"

"I had them cleaned in the process. It's allowed under the terms of the will. They're back in the vault, safe and sound."

"And?"

"They checked out. All authentic. All originals."

"Yes? So?"

"You had this theory about Jill, that she might have been involved in some kind of art fraud—selling counterfeit art on the underground market. I think you suggested that Train might be involved as well. That she might have been selling them to him."

"Drunken rambling, big brother. Nothing to it. I sounded out Larry on it—very discreetly. He positively *loathes* German Expressionists, especially all those dark, brooding, macabre fellows we have in the vault. Larry's a man for the pretty picture. Check his client list and you'll find his customers are, too. I really don't know what I was thinking. I was very upset. So were you."

"I still am, Christian."

"I presume that explains your recent resort to demon rum. We have to watch that in our family, Matt. Road to ruin, ha-ha-ha."

He took a step toward the door.

"We still have no answer to the question. Why Jill had a copy of *The Red Tower* with her when she was killed."

"That will likely haunt us the rest of our days, but I fear the answer has gone with her to her grave."

Matthias followed him to the front door. "Annelise and Paul are coming for dinner tonight," he said. "Can you join us?"

"Afraid not. Pressing previous engagements. I'm making all the social rounds with a vengeance these days. Stir up interest in my show."

"We're going to discuss family finances."

"How depressing. There's nothing more to discuss, is there? Thanks to you and me and Peter Poe."

After so many years in Area Six burglary, Zany had learned enough tricks of the trade to make a pretty good burglar himself. Back in the 1960s, a group of cops in what had been the old Summerdale District had given in to the temptation such expert knowledge presented. The exposure of their burglary ring and subsequent public outrage had resulted in a top-to-bottom reform of the entire police department.

This night, Zany would be following in the Summerdale ring's footsteps—not after goods or money, but simple knowledge.

Train had an expensive burglar alarm system at his gallery, but it was nothing that an expert thief—or a good burglary detective—couldn't master. Zany had examined the workings of hundreds of sophisticated alarms in his time—knew precisely how they functioned and how to disconnect them.

Chicago was blessed—cursed, as far as the police were concerned—with nearly as many alleys as it had streets. Zany waited until after nine o'clock—three hours after the gallery had closed—then turned into the one behind Train's gallery with no one noticing him and reached the back door undetected. It took about three minutes to disengage the alarm. He'd not be able to put it back together on his way out, so he'd have to make this look like a real burglary, which would mean he'd have to take something. He didn't mind. As far as he was concerned, this was tit for tat. The robbery of his wife's store outweighed any guilt he might have felt, and he didn't feel any.

As he had learned on his previous visit to the gallery, most of Train's inventory was kept in a basement storeroom. It was illuminated with overhead fluorescent fixtures. The storeroom had no windows, so he turned the lights on.

The room was full of paintings, some stored neatly in bins and racks, larger ones set against the walls. His search was far from easy. He had to look through more art than he'd ever had in a museum visit, but eventually found what he sought.

There was a wooden crate set to the side. It hadn't been sealed, but there was a hasp and a key lock. He picked it open in a matter of seconds.

He was enjoying wonderful luck. There they were—nine paintings—each confirming his suspicions. All German Expressionists, they were quite similar to *The Red Tower*. One, in fact, was identified as a Kirchner. It didn't need to be. The brazen woman in bright red who was its focal point was almost the double of woman in the *Tower* painting.

Each of the canvases looked genuine—either originals or copies done by the same expert hand, possibly treated with an aging chemical. That could be determined later.

What was not affixed to the paintings, or anywhere else Zany looked, was any paperwork—any hint of an eventual destination or prospective customer.

He started returning the paintings to the crate, then froze. There were voices upstairs—one flavored with an affected, almost English accent, the other, Christian Curland's.

Forcing himself to keep calm, he got the rest of the paintings back into the crate and set the lock back into position. He turned off the overhead lights and switched on the pocket flashlight he'd brought with him—like any good burglar—cursing himself for failing to replace its fading batteries.

They were coming downstairs. There were some very large canvases set against the wall in a corner. Zany hurried to them and crawled behind, wishing he was only five feet tall.

The two were carrying something, one of them grunting. He heard the sound of wood being set on the floor.

"These are the last?" said the voice Zany took to be Train's.

"I think it's enough," said Christian Curland. They both spoke with distinctive upper-class accents—Train's affected, Curland's sounding quite genuine.

"I wanted to get them out of the vault," Curland said. "I don't think Matthias appreciates my messing about in there."

"Let's have a good look at them."

There was more movement, scraping sounds. Then a silence.

"They're really quite good," Train said. "We should have done this a long time ago."

"When I wanted to, you weren't interested."

"What I told you back then, dear boy, was that they couldn't possibly bring you the kind of money you needed. Now that's quite moot."

"I daresay."

"Well, they're lovely. Simply lovely."

"Thank you."

"Lovely, Christian. Just like you."

Zany heard quiet, muffled sounds he couldn't quite fathom. Edging forward on his elbows, he cautiously peeked outside the other side of his shelter, then quickly pulled back.

He'd seen enough. The two men were embracing—and not simply in manly, comradely fashion. Train was kissing Christian on the lips. Zany found himself feeling acutely embarrassed.

"It's late," Train said. "Do you fancy dinner?"

"Dinner, and a stiff drink."

"We should celebrate. Shall we go to Les Nomads?"

"I think not, Larry. Somewhere more discreet."

"My place, then. We can listen to Vivaldi."

"Vivaldi."

It was the last word they uttered. The lights went out again. Zany lay there for a long time listening in the silence. Then he crawled out of his den. When he turned on his flashlight this time, its glow was dim indeed.

First he crept upstairs, making sure that Train and Curland had left the gallery. Then he returned to the crate.

He had to hurry. It was a long drive back to Michigan. He'd told his wife he was going to look up some marine supply wholesalers in Chicago to see what terms they might have to offer. He'd actually stopped by one to pick up some brochures as proof he'd done what he'd said. He'd left them in his car—on the front seat, so he wouldn't forget.

Zany had brought a large plastic shopping bag with him, carried rolled up. He decided he'd take two small paintings from the storage racks and one of those in the crate. If Train wanted to report its loss to the police with the others, well, that would be very interesting—if, as he had little doubt, it was an exact duplicate of one of the works in Curland's German Museum.

He stopped. Had Train and Christian Curland brought more such canvases? Curland had mentioned the vault.

The paintings they'd brought were by the stairs, set backward against the wall. Zany was sure that when he turned them face forward he find more German Expressionists. Using his handkerchief to prevent fingerprints, as he had done since he first entered the gallery, he turned the first one over, then the next, then another, finally all of them. He swore.

Something was damned wrong here. There wasn't a German Expressionist—real or ersatz—in the bunch. They were just paintings, Christian Curland's regular work. Two of them were portraits of women, very finely and almost photographically rendered, the kind society people hung above their mantels. The rest were street scenes of Chicago—extremely well done—and all very contemporary. Could Curland be an innocent in this? Just another artist peddling his wares? Was it only Train and Jill Langley who'd been doing this?

After taking the Kirchner from the crate and putting it in his bag, Zany went over the box again carefully. There was no label of any kind, but he noticed something he hadn't before. With a marker, someone had drawn the letters "P" on the side.

Standing for what? Poe? Pittsburgh? Philadelphia?

He had a big problem. He couldn't go to the police—not even his good friends in the department—with what he'd found without admitting that he himself had committed a crime: burglary one. There was no way to pass it off merely as an unauthorized search. And he was no longer police chief at Grand Pier, Michigan.

He needed some help. Fortunately, he now had someone he thought he might trust.

First things first. Zany had to get the hell out of the gallery. He picked out two other canvases—small, bad landscapes—and put them in the bag with the Kirchner.

His flashlight went out just as he was going out the back door.

Annelise and her husband were unusually circumspect at dinner, content to talk about trivial matters—Paul Blucher saying little at all. Over coffee afterward, however, they finally got around to the subject that had brought them together for the first time since his mother's funeral.

"So the family fortunes are improving," Annelise said.

"I think it's safe to say there's no longer a pressing emergency," Matthias said. "Father can stay on in the Lake Forest house for the immediate future, though we're not yet in the black. I'm working on that."

"You mean when Father isn't making a bloody fool of himself at Park District meetings."

"I had nothing to do with that."

"But you and Christian truly are taking care of everything? There's nothing more for us to worry about?"

"For now."

"Sounds too good to be true," Annelise said.

Her husband cleared his throat uncomfortably. "Would you mind if I looked at the books?"

"That's not necessary, Paul," said Annelise. "If we can't take Matt at his word, there's no point in being here. It's obvious the bills are being paid. Give it a rest."

Blucher looked away, in discomfort. For all the recurring rancor in the Curland family, he would never be as close to Annelise as her brothers were.

He brushed a few crumbs off his tie. The dressing for dinner ritual was not observed in the Schiller Street house. Annelise, a formidable, even elegant figure when in black evening gown, was wearing the kind of frumpy dress one might expect on a lady dog breeder from Barrington. Her husband was dressed in a drab blue banker's suit. Matthias was in his habitual old blazer.

"All this money is coming from Peter Poe?" Annelise asked.

"I'm on his retainer, for the time being. Yes. But Christian has been helping out, much more than you think. He's making a serious thing of his painting."

"You said 'for the time being.' Aren't you doing this monstrous new building of Poe's?"

"I've done some drawings. He likes the concept. Whether I stay on the project . . . we shook hands on it. I'd be going against my word if I turned him down. I suppose I'm ninety-nine percent sure I'll do it, if he keeps his word to me about a few things."

"Doesn't it bother you, that this is the only kind of work you can get as an architect?" Paul said.

Matthias colored. "This 'work' is probably the most extensive development project Chicago has ever seen—at least in a single structure. The building could become the most famous in the world. I'm not ashamed of it. The Civic Opera Building, I might remind you, was built by one of the country's leading swindlers. Poe's hardly that."

"I wouldn't be too quick with that assertion," Annelise responded. "Some say he's involved with crooks."

"I heard that, too. He broached the subject to me himself. He said people like that were trying to move into his casino business and he wouldn't let them. That's why they set fire to his boat, or so he thinks."

"Do you really believe that?"

"It's the most logical explanation for what happened—a rather compelling form of proof. He was supposed to come back with us on that boat."

"It's proof that you're stark, staring mad to be working for the man."

"In any event, I won't be sailing for him any more."

"Will you part company with him when the building's done?"

"It's a long way from that."

"I just don't know, Matt. I'm happy for you that you're back working again, but, this man . . . I feel it in my bones. He's bad. He's wrong. He's the sort of person Grandfather loathed, the sort he blamed for all the troubles in the world."

"A person very much like Great-Grandfather, whom we have to thank for most everything we have—including the Albrecht Collection. This great-families-of-Chicago nonsense gets a little sickening when you consider the greed and corruption and insensible cruelty that produced the money in the first place. Manfred Albrecht ruined hundreds of people. No one's ever accused Peter Poe of doing anything like that. He's put people to work."

They sat without speaking further, like three strangers in a public room.

"We have a long drive," Annelise said finally. "We'd better be going."

"I've a favor to ask first," said Matthias, looking directly at his sister, excluding her husband from his invitation. "I'd like you to look at my design—for Poe's building."

"After all I've said?"

"All I want is your honest opinion. You've never given me any less than that."

This wasn't entirely true. Annelise had always tended to gush over his paintings, even those Matthias knew painfully well were mediocre.

She looked about as pleased as if he'd asked her to do the dishes.

"It'll only take a minute," he promised. "The renderings are right upstairs."

"All right."

She looked at each of his depictions with intent and dutiful care, refraining from any comment until she'd pondered every one. He guessed that she'd made her judgment quickly, but was taking time to find the words to express it.

"I'll grant you this, Matt," she said at last. "It's very beautiful, very graceful—a wonderful and original idea. I can see what you see—how it would reflect the changing light. It's the kind of thing they'd be writing about in architectual textbook, long after we're dead. Maybe in a class with Frank Lloyd Wright, or Harry Weese."

She was gushing again. "And?"

"But I don't like it."

He was stung. "Why?"

"How high is that tower?"

"As proposed, a hundred and fifty stories. Though we're not making that public yet."

"And the sail part then would be, what—a hundred and fifty stories long?"

"Something like that."

"I find that grotesque, Matt. It would dwarf everything else in the city."

"But it's going up at Cabrini Green. There's nothing there."

"It's too damn big. It's Godzilla. It's a shameless, self-indulgent example of the worst kind of look-at-me ego gratification.

It's what you might expect to find in that godawful Houston—or Los Angeles. This is Chicago—like you always say, a very special place."

"Thank you." The words came out woodenly. "I appreciate your candor, but I think you're prejudiced because it's Poe's building."

"The ego I was talking about, Matt, is yours."

After they'd gone, he sat for a long while in the living room, searching his mind desperately for a rational way to discount her harsh verdict. Aside from her dislike of Poe, could it have anything to do with her being a woman? For all its grace, this would be a very powerful, manly structure. That was its appeal to Poe. Christian had thought it marvelous. Chicago was a masculine city. What had Carl Sandburg written?

"City of the big shoulders."

He'd taken that brawling strength and worked it into a thing of beauty, created a structure that would quiver with might and power and yet not present a single hard or ugly edge.

Glass in hand, Matthias got up and paced about the room, thinking about all he'd ever heard in his architecture classes, or read in any book on the subject. The world's cities were full of stark, square, forbidding Miesian boxes. Many of them had won awards and praise. He'd created something entirely different. That was the rub. Annelise, like so many of her background, was just too conservative, too worshipping of sameness, of the past.

He went into his study, full of sudden purpose. One bookcase was devoted to architectural works and texts. He plucked out one of his favorites, turning to a chapter about a building that had revolutionized architecture, transformed cities beyond the grandest plan of the venerated Daniel Burnham, excited the imagination of modern man far more than even the most ingenius works of the highly focused, rectangle-obsessed Frank Lloyd Wright.

Not Burnham's triangular Flatiron Building, as memorable a silhouette as that might be—a 1903 design that had in fact inspired his own concept for the pyramid of the Halsman Tower. Not the Empire State Building or the Chrysler Building or Chicago's similarly Art Deco Palmolive Building, which, with its revolving beacon and sentrylike position at the northern end of Michigan Avenue, had once been the principal wonderment of the Chicago skyline.

These were among his most enduring favorites, but what energized him now was a structure that few ever thought of any more in the modern era of sleek, sky-high towers—though it had presaged them.

It was New York's Woolworth Building, a Beaux-Arts masterpiece by Cass Gilbert. Completed in 1913, it still stood on its downtown lower Broadway site, commanding respect among all the latter-day giants that had sprung up around it. Twenty-nine stories and 792 feet tall, it had a broad, U-shaped base that consumed half its height, surmounted by a thrusting, slightly set-back tower with a Gothic peak. For a generation, it had been Manhattan's greatest building. It was massive even in modern-day terms, but despite its bulk, despite the then obligatory gargoyles that encrusted its peak and corners, it was the most profound vertical expression that any architect in that era had ever conceived, let alone achieved. Its shooting, fluted lines carried its majesty up to its very pinnacle. It was a true tower, expressing not merely height but greatness and grandeur and grace, as the cathedrals of Europe had done for so many centuries.

Many had derided it when it had gone up, calling it grotesque, and—like Annelise—too big. A newspaper cartoon of the time had ridiculed it by envisioning a future New York that was a convoluted, interlocking jungle of oversized, preposterous towers.

Not far off the mark, as prescient satire went, considering what eventually had happened to Manhattan, but it was an inappropriate criticism of Gilbert's achievement. For the time it was allowed to stand alone, to be appreciated as something unique and entire, the Woolworth Building was a symbol of triumph, of civilization at its most noble and reaching.

That is what Matthias intended for Chicago with his huge sailboat, and he would not be swayed—not by his family's notions of business respectability, not by his doubts about Peter Poe's character, not by the opinions of his friends and the Chicago establishment, not by any personal consideration, save his own creative urgings. He would see this thing done. The building was paramount. He had created it. Now he must see to it that it was given life. He'd let events and fears and his own confused emotions get in the way, almost to the point of his abandoning it. He must not let that happen again.

Whether as painter or architect, he truly was an artist. It didn't matter what went into a work of art—some of the greatest masterpieces in history had been born of the most sordid miseries and horrors. What mattered was the art. Only the art.

His phone rang. He was infuriated by the intrusion. There was no one he wanted to talk to at this extraordinary moment, when for the first time in years—perhaps all his life—he found himself utterly consumed and motivated by certainty and resolve.

"Yes?"

"Mr. Curland? This is Zane Rawlings, from Michigan?"

"Yes, what is it?" For days he had thought of calling this policeman, to enlist his aid in getting at whoever had put Cindy in the hospital. Now all that seemed completely irrelevant. If Poe was right, the persons responsible had more than paid the price. Beyond Cindy's recovery, he simply didn't care anymore.

"I need to see you, Mr. Curland. I have something that might be of interest to you. You said you determined that Kirchner in your vault is genuine? Well, I have reason to believe that more paintings from your museum—copies, maybe originals—can be found in Laurence Train's gallery. In fact, one of them has come to hand. So to speak."

That again. Jill Langley as art thief. Let that notion, as Christian had suggested, be buried with her in her grave.

"I've checked the paintings in my vault, Chief Rawlings. I had some of them examined by experts. Everything is in order. I've already told you that."

"But this is a Kirchner. Same kind of smiling woman. I'd like to show it to you."

"I don't care if it's a Michelangelo."

"Mr. Curland. This is a homicide investigation."

"You keep saying that. But you're not getting anywhere. All you do is make annoying phone calls."

"I think you should go over to Train's gallery and take a look."

"Why don't you do that? You're the policeman. I'm extremely busy now. I've no time for distractions. If you want to pursue your theories about art fraud, go see Larry Train; go to the Chicago police. There's nothing I can do for you."

"Well, think about it. If you change your mind, call me."

"Fine."

Matthias hung up. He stood perfectly still for a long moment, then started upstairs. He had an idea for one more rendering—a view of the new building much as Poe had described it out on the

Montrose breakwater, as Jill had envisioned such a creation that long-ago evening when they'd been sailing along the lakefront at sunset.

He'd show the new building as it might be seen from far out in the lake. There'd be a thin line of horizon, the three downtown supertowers rising pencillike above it. And there, just to the north, would be the magnificent sail, its glass curtain wall ablaze with reflected sunlight.

Then everyone might understand.

CHAPTER

17

AMONG THE MANY things Poe had neglected in all his travails were his household accounts. He was rudely reminded of them by a morning call from Yeats, who rang up just as Poe was finishing reading through the newspapers.

"A minor problem, Peter," he said, his voice full of lawyerly tact. "I just heard from the bank. They want some money."

"You told me all the debt service payments were made. A little late, but paid."

"And so they were. I'm not talking millions here; just thousands. It's your personal checking account. There have been some overdrafts, and you're twenty-eight thousand over your credit card line."

"That's ridiculous."

"Irritating, no doubt. But not ridiculous. The way you spend money, I wouldn't have been surprised if they'd said two hundred and eighty thousand. I've got the statements right in front of me. I meant to mention it to you some time ago, but it seemed kind of trivial, what with all your other concerns. Only now they're being very pointed about it."

Trivial? It was fucking bullshit. Poe wondered if someone in the banking establishment was trying to harass him.

"Well, transfer some funds from another account. You have my power of attorney to do that."

"Your other accounts are kinda close to red line this month, too. The only one that's flush is the casino's."

"I don't want to touch that."

"You want these guys to start dropping gossip about Chapter Eleven over lunch at their club?"

"That would be a load of crap."

"It wouldn't stop 'em."

Poe drummed his fingers on his desk top. "All right. Use the casino account. I'll make the amount good soon. A matter of days."

"May I ask with what?"

"I'll put some more paintings up for sale."

"You must have an inexhaustible supply."

"Just do as I say, Bill. I don't pay you a fucking fortune to make smart-ass remarks."

"Yassuh, boss."

Poe managed to hang up first. If the bastard didn't know so much about his business, he'd fire him.

There were in fact some household bills in a big manila envelope on his desk. As he did periodically, he'd had the office send them over so he could check on Diandra's spending. She'd been playing the nutsy shopper again—as she often did when she was unhappy about something.

The bill from Neiman Marcus alone was stratospheric. The crazy woman had been buying Bob Mackie gowns. They made her look terrific, but jeez.

Aping Donald Trump, he'd once told her she could buy all the dresses she wanted. He'd liked to brag about that at first, but this was getting painful. She wouldn't like it, but he was going to have to put on the brakes. He might even have to get her to sell some of her old things—stuff she'd worn only once or twice. Some of those clothes she hadn't worn at all. And shoes! A regular Imelda Marcos.

He looked through some of the other bills. His accounts-payable people had let quite a few of them slip. He was even in arrears on his goddamn newspaper subscriptions. What if the *Trib* put that in its gossip column—or let that fiendish columnist Mike Royko hear about it?

A shiver ran down his back. Had he been running this close to the edge? Why hadn't Yeats said something before this? Maybe he had, when he'd been asked to buy the sailboat.

Poe punched the button on his console that rang Larry Train. A girl at the gallery answered, though it was Train's private office line.

She said Train was down in the storeroom. He told her she had five seconds to get him to the phone.

"Yes, Peter. What is it?" Train sounded displeased, or at least bothered by something.

"I need some cash. I want you to dump some paintings. You

know that spaghetti thing I've got in my living room, the one you said was worth a hundred and fifty thousand? Start with that."

"I thought you liked that?"

"I hate the fucking thing. It's Diandra who likes it."

"Won't it bother her if you get rid of it?"

"I'll tell her it's out for cleaning or something. You can have a copy made."

"We're rather busy now, Peter. Christian Curland and I are working on his show."

Poe's voice got very low. "Larry. When I want something, nobody's busy."

A sigh. "I understand."

"And I want you to move that last shipment of Germans."

"Now? So soon?"

"Yes. As soon as possible. Go for top dollar, but I'll settle for almost any price—as long as it's quick."

"I'm not sure we can unload all eight right away. We have only the one prospective customer, and he's interested chiefly in Emil Nolde and Ernst Kirchner works. Half of what we have is Franz Marc."

"You're talking on the public telephone, Larry."

"Sorry."

"Anyway, that means we can sell five, right? Four Noldes and another Kirchner."

"Well . . ."

"You said 'eight.' There are supposed to be nine. Is something wrong, Larry? There hasn't been another fuckup, has there?"

"No, of course not."

"I told you what I'd do if anything like that happened again."

"You've nothing to worry about, Peter. I must have misspoken. I'm just a bit flustered today. Everything's in order. But really, I don't think you'll be able to sell more than four or five in anything like a hurry."

"Do your goddamn best."

"I always do."

"You had them all authenticated?"

"Yes. I have the certificates right here."

"And we're covered, right, as concerns the original, er, source?"

"We'll attend to that at the first propitious moment. There's that other party to worry about. He works at the museum sometimes. Movement's a little difficult just now."

"Don't worry about the other party. I'm going to see to it he's real preoccupied. There'll be a lot of propitious moments."

"Yes, sir."

"I'm holding my press conference on the Cabrini Green project Sunday at two o'clock. Everyone concerned will be there, including that other party."

"It would seem, then, that I'll be unable to attend."

"Get it done, Larry. If you can close a deal by the end of the month I'll raise your cut to fifteen percent."

"You're generous to a fault."

"But I'd like fifty thousand on account."

"Fifty thousand? Peter, you know what the art market's been like. I'm afraid I can't manage that amount."

"Why not? You'll have the goddamn spaghetti painting, won't you?"

"Art isn't money, Peter. Not until somebody's ready to pay for it."

"What can you manage?"

"Twenty?"

"Make it twenty-eight. And get a certified check over here by messenger today."

"I didn't think you worried about such paltry sums."

"Larry, I got where I am by worrying about all sums."

Poe hung up. He wondered if Train was screwing around with him. The fruitcake wouldn't dare try anything funny, would he? Not with bombs going off and bodies turning up in sailboats.

He looked at his calendar. He had thirty days to get everything ready for the Inland Empire Bank's Japanese money men. When that was a done deal, he'd be rolling in millions again.

Other people's money. It was the name of the game.

Zany knew there'd be hell to pay, but he'd stayed overnight in Chicago, in a cheap motel out by the Kennedy Expressway. He'd called Judy and told him he was going drinking with some cop friends and that if he got over his limit, he might sack out with one of them. She didn't sound as if she believed him, but it couldn't be helped. He certainly didn't want to come home toting three expensive paintings. They'd be a hell of a lot harder to explain than an overnight out.

He'd stop for a few beers on his way home. Maybe spill a little on his clothes.

Having forgotten to leave a wake-up call—and not at all sure that the drunken night desk clerk would have remembered it, in any event—Zany slept late. The long hours he'd been putting in these last weeks had been creeping up on him. He didn't bother showering—the better to convince Judy of a toot—but did stop for a greasy breakfast in the little café across the street from the motel. It reminded him of his Chicago cop days.

His first stop was the Curland house on Schiller Street. Matthias Curland would have to take some interest in the Kirchner he'd found if Zany thrust it into his hands.

When he opened the door, Curland looked as bad as Zany must. He appeared to have been up very late.

He clenched his teeth when he spoke. "Why do you persist in bothering me? There's nothing I can do for you now."

"May I come in?"

"No. Damn it, no! I was up working most of the night."

"I told you I'd come across a painting. In Train's gallery. A Kirchner."

"And I told you I didn't care."

Zany opened his plastic bag. He'd rolled up the canvas for protection. "Here," he said, "examine at your leisure. Just don't tell anybody where you got it, or where I got it."

Curland unrolled the painting. He looked at it as he might a piece of junk mail. "This is supposed to be from my museum?"

"That's what I hope you'll find out for me."

"And it came from Train's gallery?"

"Yes."

"How do you come to have it?"

"That I don't want you to find out."

A spark of interest came into Curland's bloodshot eyes, then vanished as the bleariness returned. "All right, I'll look at it. But not now. Later."

"Take your time. You have my number. I'll be waiting for your call. Just don't talk to anyone else about it. Not your brother, not Mr. Train. If you pardon the expression, you'll queer the deal."

"What?"

"Just an expression. I'm trusting you, Mr. Curland."

"How utterly kind of you."

He stepped back and started to close the door.

"I called your wife, your ex-wife."

Matthias hesitated. "You're bothering her, too, Chief Rawlings?"

291

"Official business. You told me you were with her in New York. The first time I talked to her, she said you weren't. I called her again. This time her husband wasn't on the line. He was out of town. She admitted she'd lied to me. She said she was with you that night, in a hotel in Manhattan."

Curland glanced down the street. He didn't appreciate having such conversations on his doorstep.

"She said you were in bad shape, that you'd been drinking. She said she'd stayed long enough to get you out of it, but her husband wouldn't understand."

"I was upset, about my mother's death, about having to come back."

"Doesn't bother me. I've gotten pretty shit-faced myself on occasion."

The architect seemed repelled by the remark.

"Look, Mr. Curland, do you want to get the people who killed Jill Langley? The people who are probably responsible for all the trouble that's been going on here?"

"Of course I do."

"Well, as things stand, that makes just two of us. Everybody else seems to be against me or just doesn't give a damn. So help me out. Check out this painting. Please."

Curland stared at the ground. "I'll see what I can do. When I have the time. Good day, Chief Rawlings."

"One more thing, Mr. Curland. Your boat. The Grand Pier police department is through with it. It's no longer impounded. You can come out and pick it up whenever you want. When you do, stop by my house. We can have a couple of cold ones—and talk. I trust that by then you'll have checked out this painting."

"I'll be out for the boat as soon as I can. Thank you, Chief Rawlings."

He closed the door politely.

Zany walked away feeling more confident. If nothing else, he had more proof that Matthias Curland was an honest man. He'd called him "Chief Rawlings." If he was one of the bad guys, he would have known Zany had been fired from the job.

Matthias stood there in the foyer, trying to think. He unrolled the canvas again, focusing his weary eyes as best he could. It was a Kirchner, that was clear. But, if Rawlings had found it in Train's gallery, it might only be because Jill had hidden it there.

He didn't want to think about any bad things Jill might have done. He didn't want to think about Jill at all now.

How did Rawlings get it out of the gallery? If it was official evidence, why had he given it to him? If he went to Larry Train about it, whether Rawlings was right or wrong, it would only stir up godawful trouble.

This was not the time for that. Matthias went to his front closet and put the painting up on the top shelf, among some hats and clutter.

Returning to the living room, he sat down on the couch and stared bleakly at the coffee table, where he'd spread out some sheets of paper from a sketch pad. They were covered with hasty drawings and floor plans.

He'd done something dumb. He'd left something out of his grand design, something simple, obvious, and altogether obligatory: a garage. There would be an extraordinary number of occupants in that building, and the garage would have to be huge. But he could think of no place to put it.

Zany really wanted to go home now, but he had one more visit to make—to the Art Institute.

As he expected, it being the height of the summer tourist season, the great museum was crowded. He queued up at the check room behind a couple of college kids carrying backpacks. When he handed the plastic shopping bag with the two purloined paintings in it to the attendant, she didn't even look at him—just slapped down a numbered tag on the counter. He pocketed it and drifted away into the throng, passing only about a half hour among the paintings, then wandering idly outside.

He'd been no more noticed than one of the pigeons on the steps. His shopping bag, he knew, would sit there a few days, then be turned over to the lost and found, where it might remain weeks or months before anyone seriously bothered with it.

And then? Well, he'd consider himself one of the Art Institute's benefactors.

He tossed the numbered tag into a trash can.

Nearing the Michigan line, Zany turned off at the next exit and then kept driving until he came to a bar—a country and western joint with a lot of old cars in front. The customers were staring transfixed at the television set, which was showing a soap opera.

He had four beers in fairly quick succession, went to the bathroom, and then drove on home.

Judy took one look at him and bought his story entire. "God, Zany, you smell."

"Sorry. I'll take a shower. After I get some sleep."

"Was this really necessary?"

He paused in thought, as if this were a truly profound question.

"Yeah," he said. "After what I've been through? It was."

"All right. I won't give you a hard time about it. This once. I'm going down to the store. I think I'll reopen tomorrow. I'm tired of sitting around. How'd it go with the outboard engines?"

He'd brought the stack of brochures in with him from the car. He showed them to her. "I'm not sure I want to be in marine supplies. Looks kinda dull. I think I'd like to open a bar."

"I'll bet you would."

When he heard her car drive away, he went to his phone. What did an art thief do after pulling off a successful job? He called the cops.

Detective Myron Plotnik, as he preferred to be, was at his desk. "Hiya, Zany. What's the word?"

"I was wondering if anything turned up on that missing painting of mine."

"Sorry. Not a fucking thing. I think it's long gone. You sure are hung up on that. I heard you lost your job out there. Are you still working the case?"

"Not really. Just wondering."

"Well, we got nothin'."

"You catch any other art theft cases? Anything that might be similar."

"Not a one."

"Nothing?"

"Blank sheet, Zany. No, wait a minute. Here's one came in last night."

Zany held his breath.

"Yeah," said Plotnik. "Woman on the Gold Coast. Said someone made off with a statue from her garden. *Aphrodite,* it says here. Seven-foot-high statue of a naked woman. What do you suppose anybody would want with that, when they could get one of those life-size inflatable dolls?"

CHAPTER
18

POE'S NEWS CONFERENCE, held in a ballroom of his grandest hotel, was as well attended as he possibly could have hoped. In addition to a small mob of local news media, there were correspondents there from two of the networks as well as from the Chicago bureaus of the news weeklies. There was even someone from *People* magazine. No foreign reporters had come—most noticeable to Poe, no reporters from Japan—but they'd be on hand soon enough.

Standing behind Poe when he took to the podium was as large an array of city fathers and other notables as he could pull together on short notice in the middle of summer. Aldermen Larry, Curly, and Moe were there, among a number of politicians. Poe had both Yeats and his establishment stuffed shirt of an attorney present, along with Matthias and Diandra, and a battery of architects from Cudahy, Brown. Most important of all, a beaming Aaron Cooperman was front and center, with Matthias's father standing uncomfortably behind him, looking a little dazed.

There was no one there from the Inland Empire Bank, but that was the last thing Poe would have wanted. They were to be involved later, after the project had become quite something else.

Poe began with a long paean to Chicago and its extraordinary architecture, and the leadership role it was taking in reviving America's old big cities from decades of decay. He painted a vivid verbal picture of what an urban paradise that end of the Near North Side would be ten years hence, and heaped embarrassingly gushing praise on Matthias for the genius he had shown in coming up with his unique design, calling him Chicago's greatest architect since Frank Lloyd Wright. Then Poe launched into a long personal testament to the deep and abiding love he had for the city of his birth, going on about how unhappy and frustrated he'd been trying to realize his dreams in such lesser, unvisionary cities as Philadelphia and New York.

When he could see the newsies begin to get itchy, he threw the floor open for questions. Park District President Cooperman had been promised an opportunity for a big spiel about the Holocaust Museum and the other ethnic installations, and was nearly beside himself with impatience. But Poe was going to hold him in reserve, for the strategic moment when he'd most be needed.

"Mr. Poe, you haven't said how tall this thing is going to be," a reporter had begun. "Isn't it true you plan to give Chicago the world's tallest building again? And beat out that guy in New York?"

"Chicago should always have the world's tallest building," Poe said. "But the dimensions of the project haven't been determined yet. This is just the concept, the design. I wanted to show it to you before we went another step further."

"You also haven't said how much it's going to cost."

"When we figure that out we'll know how high it's going to be."

There was a lot of laughter. Poe smiled. He was completely in control.

"Are you going to pay for it out of your own pocket?"

"I was going to, but then I looked at my wife's department store bills." He paused to wait for the next wave of laughter to subside. "Don't worry. This will be solidly financed. Like all my projects."

Then another reporter changed the subject. "Mr. Poe, can you tell us now why someone put a bomb on your yacht, and who you think did it?"

Poe frowned. "The Coast Guard and I think the Transportation Department are conducting an investigation into possible arson—local police, too—but no evidence of anything like that has been recovered. They sent divers down. Didn't find anything."

"What about reports that the crime syndicate is out to get you?"

"I've heard those reports, all that gossip. I've no idea if there's anything to them. I personally think the fire was just an unfortunate accident. I mean, I wasn't even on the boat. But I can tell you that I don't and won't do business with those scum. I think any businessman who does is no better than they are. And let me say something about my, er, first mate here, Matt Curland. Thanks to his seamanship and courage, everybody got off that boat alive. That fine young woman, Cindy Ellison—all the crew members, the best crew I've ever had—could have been killed. My wife could have been killed. Matt ought to get a medal."

"Do you think maybe someone was trying to send you a message?"

"What? To stay away from sailboats?"

"Mr. Poe, charges have been made that you might have cheated to win that sailboat race."

Now Poe let himself get angry. "You know, young man, that's absolutely disgusting. Yes, a protest was filed with the race committee and it was unanimously rejected. We were fair and square from start to finish. We won that race because we had the guts to take a few chances. Because we had real sailors like Matt here and Cindy Ellison aboard, not a bunch of high-society wimps who think sailing's just for aristocrats."

Matthias winced. Someone would duly note that both he and Cindy were in the *Social Register*.

"Anyway," Poe continued, relaxing again, "I think it was just sour grapes. I put up a hundred-thousand-dollar prize on that race, to be given to charity. I think the other guy is just pissed— excuse me, just miffed—because he's out the money. I think he was going to give it to the Republican Party."

The laughter this time was explosive. Moe almost doubled up.

"And while we're on the subject," Poe said, "I'd like to announce today that I'm contributing that hundred thousand— every cent—to the fund for the Holocaust Museum. And now I think I'd better turn the microphone over to President Cooperman so he can say a few words about that."

He stepped back, like an artist from a freshly completed masterpiece.

Cooperman spoke for a good fifteen minutes, giving what amounted to a history lesson wrapped in a sermon. When he was done, on cue, one of Poe's aides went to the mike to invite the press to refreshments in an adjoining reception room, cutting off any further questions.

As the newsies headed for the door, Poe drew Matthias and Diandra aside.

"What do you think?" he asked.

"A tour de force, Peter," said Diandra coolly. "I didn't expect anything less."

"I don't mean to sound impertinent," Matthias said, sounding exactly that, "but you said some things that aren't true."

"Salesmanship, Matt. Name of the game."

"But why can't we tell them about the building's height? That's the whole point of the thing."

"In time. In time. We do this step by step." He looked at his huge, glittering watch. "I've got to go over to the office. Meet with some people. Why don't you take Diandra home? I'll join you later. Probably this evening, after dinner."

"I think I'd better see to my father," Matthias said. "I fear he found this rather taxing."

"I'll have Lenny Krasowski drive him home in the limo. He can stretch out. He looks like he could use the nap."

At the penthouse, in Poe's living room, Diandra offered Matthias a drink, and he took it. She made herself one and seated herself at some distance from him on a couch facing away from the windows, putting her face in dark silhouette against the light. He couldn't tell what she was thinking, but perhaps that was just as well.

He looked at his watch, an old-fashioned sportsman's timepiece that had been in his family since the 1940s. "It's all of ten after three. Your husband said he won't join us until after dinner."

"This just dawned on you, Matthias?"

He felt himself blushing. "Would you like to do something? Go for a walk? Have dinner somewhere after?"

"Matt, you know why he had us come over here, why he's leaving us alone for so long. He wants his damned painting, his trophy painting of me."

"On a Sunday?"

"Would you rather go to church?"

"Why is he so obsessed with having this thing?"

"I don't think it's that. He's hung up on making us do it. It's his way of putting his brand on us, as if he hasn't done that already."

"You haven't told me what you think of my design."

"I haven't quite made up my mind. It's not beautiful, not like your other building, that Halsman Tower. Neither is it grotesque. What I'm trying to say is that I've never seen anything like it before. It's so different, so huge. If he gets to build it, if he gets the money, he'll change the city. There'll be all the other buildings, and there'll be this." She crossed her legs, leaning back. "That's what he's always wanted. I guess I have to say, Matthias, that it's a brilliant success."

"Tomorrow we'll start hearing from the critics."

"Don't worry about them. Peter won't."

Only a few minutes had gone by.

"Do you want to do this, Diandra?"

"Pose nude for you, for a painting? No. I don't particularly. But I don't mind. Do you?"

"I want to paint you. Very much."

Diandra rose. "He's prepared a room for this. Isn't that sweet?"

He followed her to an elevator. They stood close together, without touching, as it rose to the penthouse's third floor. He studied her skin, wondering how he would ever capture its softness and clarity. He looked for imperfections, finding only a few faint, tiny freckles. Her hands were beginning to show her age. He hadn't noticed that.

The door opened. She led him along a carpeted hall past several doors to a corner room at the end. Its windows faced north and east. Most of the furniture had been removed, but for two chairs, a plush, old-fashioned chaise longue, and an easel and work table covered with art materials, including a large wooden box filled with tubes of oil paint. There were three floor lamps in the room—a suggestion that there might be night work.

The canvas mounted on the easel was large, four feet by six feet. Matthias noted that a red drapery had been hung over the wall behind the chaise longue.

"He seems to have planned the whole damned picture."

"That's how he does things. You can work to order, can't you? You did it with the building."

"It isn't the same."

"I'm not going to undress in front of you, Matthias. Excuse me a moment."

She walked very slowly, leaving the room. Matthias looked at the paint and equipment Poe had provided. It was more than complete. There were a hundred or more tubes of oils, three different palette knives, and a dozen or more brushes. He picked up one and ran his fingers over it, deciding it must have cost twenty or thirty dollars. The palette itself was large, with rounded edges. He found he could hold it quite comfortably in his left hand, despite the burns and bandages.

He wanted to paint her lying down. She was a beautiful woman and Poe wanted her painted beautifully. As Matthias had learned in his life classes at art school in Philadelphia, models who had to stand for a long time tended to slump. Those put in a sitting position tended to sag—breasts slack, even flat stomachs bulging a little.

"All right, Matthias."

Diandra entered wearing a light-blue silken robe and nothing else. She went to a chair and, turning away from him, slipped off the garment and hung it over the back.

"Lie down," he said. "This will be a reclining nude. It will be easier for you."

She sat carefully on the edge of the chaise, then, in a single graceful movement, swung back, assuming a perfect pose.

"Should I be more decorous?" she asked. "Where do you want my hands?"

She was leaning on one elbow. Her other hand was resting on the curve of her hip. Her pubic hair was amply exposed.

"You're fine just as you are. The modesty should show in your face."

"Do you want me to be modest?"

"Yes. This will be a Dürer, not a Goltzius."

"Goltzius."

"He was a Dutch master, as was Albrecht Dürer. Goltzius is most famous for his Bacchanalian works—wanton smiles on everyone. Dürer went for the sublime. One of his models was probably the most brazen hussy in Amsterdam. She sometimes walked the streets naked—in the seventeenth century. But in Dürer's pictures, she was sublime."

"All right. Sublime it is."

"Don't force the expression. Just relax."

It was his practice to make a rough sketch first, getting all the proportions and perspective right—a lesson he had learned studying the figure studies of Thomas Eakins. Then he would concentrate on the details of the face, attending to the body last, working to make the body reflect the mood he found in the face.

He sketched, erased, and sketched for nearly an hour, but in the end, rubbed everything out again.

"What's wrong?"

"I can't get it right," he said. "Your face. All I see are your eyes. You're staring at me."

"Shouldn't I? Shouldn't I be looking out of the painting?"

"Yes, but . . ."

He put down his pencil. Her eyes were still fixed on him. When he kept standing there, she rose and walked slowly toward him. He thought she was going to look at the rough sketch on the canvas, but she ignored it.

"I think," she said, "that we'd better surrender to the inevitable."

She stood before him. His eyes fell from her face to her small, very round breasts. The nipples were erect.

Diandra leaned close and kissed him, softly, then more eagerly. His arms went around her. The skin was so soft—everywhere. He closed his eyes, feeling dizzy, trembly and tingly, and more.

Her lips left his. She stepped back, taking both his hands in hers.

"You're very warm," she said.

"Yes."

"Take off your clothes, Matthias, and come to the chaise."

Afterward, they lay facing each other, their arms around each other, each perfectly still. Finally he reached to stroke her face and hair. This had been so much more than their first encounter, more than making love had been for him in years. He knew it was over forever with Sally, with Marie-Claire in France, with any and all other women. He supposed he had known this the first moment he had looked upon her, but then she had represented nothing but impossibility. Now she was naked beside him. His. Not Poe's.

"I'm waiting for the earth to break open and the flames of hell to engulf us," he said.

"You weren't thinking of heaven, Matthias? I was. Actually, I was thinking that I was just now as far from death as I'll ever get."

She kissed his hand.

"And now?" he said.

"Now we should get on with the painting," she said, moving slightly away from him. "The light's changed. It's getting late."

Matthias sat up. "This is going to take many sessions."

"We'll let them take care of themselves."

His clothes were in a jumble. He began sorting them out.

"What if Peter had walked in?" he said, pulling on his trousers.

"I don't think he would do that. I don't think he's going to bother us until the painting's done."

"But doesn't he . . . ?"

"Peter Poe considers all possibilities. I'm sure he considered this one."

"I don't understand."

Her only response was to resume her pose.

Matthias worked steadily. The lines came easily. In a few minutes, the Diandra on the chaise began magically to appear on the canvas.

"Is it going better now?" she asked.

"Enormously."

"What do you see in my face?"

"Something sublime."

"What?"

"I'm embarrassed to say."

"You can't be embarrassed with me, Matt. Not anymore. Tell me."

"I see love."

She smiled.

"Peter will be pleased," she said. "He'll like that looking out at him."

Zany had spent most of the day fishing on a friend's boat with several buddies. The Grand Pier crime rate was remaining near zero, and George Hejmal finally took a day off to join them. All he had to tell Zany about the Langley case was that the State Police had taken over the investigation completely but had made no progress. Curland had come and retrieved his boat, blithely sailing it back by himself, despite some windy weather. He hadn't stopped to see Zany.

They got sunburned and drank too much beer, but Zany enjoyed himself thoroughly. His catch amounted to four far from huge perch and an undersized coho. He would have thrown them all back but wanted to come home with something to prove to Judy he hadn't been off somewhere playing policeman again.

She looked at him as if she darkly suspected he had.

"You got another call from Chicago," she said. "A woman."

"What woman?"

"She didn't leave her name. She wasn't very nice. She said you should return the paintings."

Zany froze. "I can't return the painting. It was stolen from me."

"She didn't say 'painting.' She said 'paintings.' Plural. What the hell is that about?"

He shrugged. "Beats the hell out of me. I don't have any paintings. She didn't leave a name and number?"

"No."

"Did she say she'd call back?"

"No. She just said to tell you that you'd made a mistake. A big mistake."

POE HAD A hit. The news stories and commentary about the project came in all week, and by anybody's measure, the response had to be considered a big cheer. There were a few minor complaints, mostly about the lack of details in his announcement, and a news commentator at the CBS TV station tossed in a jibe about the building being as big as Poe's ego, but Poe rather liked that.

He was less pleased with the *Tribune*'s architecture critic, who praised the design but said he hoped the rumors were not true that Poe planned to make the structure so outsized as to reclaim the tallest building title for Chicago. The critic thought this a dubious and extravagantly wasteful ambition at a time when Realtors were still in financial trouble because of the recession and past overbuilding.

But Poe had been expecting some really harsh attacks, and the architecture critic's mixed and politely worded review looked to be the worst he was going to get. Poe had been most afraid of the two newspapers' editorial boards, and had courted them assiduously. But both weighed in by the end of the week in support of the project, having bought his sales points in their entirety.

Why not? It was a hell of an exciting new building for Chicago. It would add generously to the city's tax base and, if built where promised, would make the reclamation of the Near North Side complete. Incorporating some park area and a museum complex in the project won a lot of applause—especially his inclusion of a Holocaust Museum.

He knew they sure as hell weren't going to applaud his real plans, but he'd certainly softened these people up. Whatever they might eventually think of his trying to put his project on the lakefront—when at last he dropped that megaton bomb—they were on record now at least as saying it was a wonderful building.

What he hadn't figured on was a racial problem. A local civil rights group that Poe had never heard of—that had probably been organized for this specific purpose—raised objections to the project, calling the building "a white man's monster" that was invading the African-American community and driving blacks out of the Near North Side. The group complained that if there was to be a Holocaust Museum it should go in a Jewish neighborhood. A few protesters staged a demonstration outside Poe's Michigan Avenue office building, but the news media largely ignored them. Poe didn't. They irritated him. He'd spent a lot of money helping the city relocate the remaining residents of Cabrini Green and could say without exaggeration that every one of them was going to be better off. He sent memos off to Cooperman and Matthias—with copies to the news media—saying there should be an African-American collection included in the ethnic museum complex as well. He'd announce that at his next news conference—once the protestors went away. He didn't want to seem to be bending to pressure. He cursed himself for not including African-Americans in the first place.

In any event, he was now ready for his next big step—his audience with the mayor, the invitation for which came with great swiftness.

The man was a little miffed that Poe hadn't come to him before his news conference, but seemed mollified by profuse apologies and by Poe's invitation for the mayor to stand beside him when he finally unveiled the scale model of the project and revealed its exact dimensions. Poe said he planned to do that very soon, but would be happy to hold everything in abeyance if the mayor was going on vacation or had some other reason for delay.

Poe brought Yeats, Aaron Cooperman, and Matthias along with him to the mayor's office, and it turned out to be Curland who made the clinching pitch. He showed the mayor a series of enlarged, mounted photos of other city skylines—New York, with its unique twin World Trade Center towers; San Francisco and its TransAmerica Pyramid and Golden Gate Bridge; Sydney, Australia, with its huge, exotic opera house overlooking the harbor; London with St. Paul's Cathedral and the Parliament buildings; Paris, and the Eiffel Tower.

He was about to turn to the District of Columbia and the Washington Monument, but the mayor waved his hand.

"I get the idea," he said.

"Chicago has several architectural signatures," Matthias said. "Aside from the three big high-rises, which really aren't all that distinctive except for their height, there's the Water Tower, the Wrigley Building, Tribune Tower, the Picasso statue at the Daley Civic Center. But they all rather blend into the general skyline and are comparatively small. I wouldn't diminish their importance for a moment, but when you look at the city from any distance, they're not visible—not like the Sydney Opera House, not like the World Trade Center, not like . . ."

"The Eiffel Tower," the mayor said. "Any estimate on the number of jobs this will mean?"

A man from the chamber of commerce who had also accompanied Poe quickly produced a suitably impressive figure.

"What's the area zoned for?" the mayor asked.

"Residential and commercial; also high-rises," said one of his aides.

"That's the first thing I checked before proceeding with this, Mr. Mayor," Poe said. "I've never asked for noncompatible use in any of my developments."

The mayor eyed him with that shrewd look of his, then let a little smile creep onto his face. "Do you really plan to put up what will be the world's tallest building?"

"I'd like to. If I get the F.A.A.'s approval and enough financing. A lot of the money's going to come from Japan. Is that all right with you, sir?"

"I don't mind the Japanese spending money in Chicago. You're going to have an Irish Museum?"

"Yes, sir. I can't think of a people who've contributed more to the city. I also want to have a Polish one. I don't know if I've ever told you, but I'm Polish-American. I was born here, grew up in Congressman Rostenkowski's district. My father was a precinct worker." That last bit was a lie, but he didn't think the man would bother to check it out.

The mayor picked up the painting Matthias had done of the proposed project as seen from the lake.

"Sailboat," he muttered, though not pejoratively.

"What better symbol for Queen City of the Great Lakes, Mr. Mayor?" said Yeats.

"The museums and the surrounding park land acquisition I envision will require City Council approval," Poe said, "and your approval, of course. We'll need authorization to issue bonds, and the city will have to levy that quarter percent hotel

306

tax the legislature just passed. I humbly submit that for your consideration, sir."

The "humbly" was a bit much. Poe regretted that; made him sound like some groveling office seeker. He could lose the man's respect if he kept that kind of bullshit up.

"No problem. We need a bigger hotel tax." The mayor set down the painting and pursed his lips. "I don't think I have any objection to this. But I want my office to be consulted every step of the way."

"Of course, Mr. Mayor. Bill Yeats will be my liaison. I think you know his uncle, Judge Yeats? In Chancery Court?"

"Fine man. Credit to the city. Let me know when you have that scale model ready. Make it soon, okay? I plan to spend as much of August as I can on the Upper Peninsula of Michigan. Get a little fishing in. But let's attend to this first."

"Thank you, Mr. Mayor. I think we're doing a great thing for the city here."

He stood up. They all shook hands. Poe hadn't asked for a building permit. He presumed that would be taken care of no questions asked. The people who had put up the First National Bank Building back in Mayor Daley's day had started construction without taking one out at all. Arrogant guys, bankers.

The next step was the City Council Committee on Finance. The ordinance Poe needed approved was simple enough. It authorized the bond issue and the tax for the museums and empowered the park district to establish them. With the mayor's support and Larry, Curly, and Moe among the committee members bought and paid for, the measure faced little ostensible opposition—unless someone took the time to read the fine print. Buried within the provisions was a single line: "the Chicago Park District is authorized to permit private commercial construction on Park District property to facilitate construction and maintenance of not-for-profit cultural institutions."

Poe had explained to the mayor's chief legislative aide that the language was necessary because the museums would belong to the Park District but occupy privately owned premises, and also because the park land Poe was deeding to the city would go over the underground parking garage he needed for the big building. Cooperman, no lawyer, went along with this.

The provision, of course, set an extraordinary precedent for Chicago by allowing commercial construction on park land.

Moreover, because the language was general and not specifically descriptive of the Cabrini Green site, it empowered the Park District to allow commercial construction on any park property in the city, provided cultural institutions were included in the deal.

In effect, if the ordinance became law and Poe wanted to put his building up in the middle of Lincoln or Grant Park, all it would take now was a simple majority vote of the park district board to make it happen.

No one had noticed or questioned this yet, but Poe feared some lawyer with the Friends of the Parks or some other do-gooding outfit might sniff it out. He was worried particularly about the newspapers' political and editorial writers, who in the past had been very clever about finding things buried in "merely" bills.

Larry and Curly took no chances. Instead of scheduling the proposed ordinance as a separate item on the committee agenda to be explained and debated individually, they put it in with a long list of ostensibly routine omnibus measures to be approved by a single voice vote. Any committee member could of course ask to have the ordinance explained and demand a roll call. There was a liberal independent alderman on the committee who might have done exactly that, but she, happily, was vacationing in France and unable to get back for the meeting.

The measure was adopted without a single eyebrow raised.

Poe had stayed clear of the committee session, not wanting to tip anyone to how concerned he was about that little provision, but afterward met with Larry, Curly, and Moe in Larry's City Hall office.

"You guys were terrific," Poe said.

He'd brought Yeats along with him—his aldermanic paymaster.

"Pleasure doin' business with you, Peter."

"How soon can it be brought to a vote before the entire City Council?"

"Technically," said Larry, "in five days. But I don't know if we can get a quorum together by then. Middle of the fucking summer, you know."

"Get it done. I don't care if you have to drag your people down from the Wisconsin lakes or haul them in off the beach, but get them here. The mayor wants this. He wants it all taken care of before he goes on vacation. That's all anybody needs to know."

"There's something we'd like to know. When are we—"

"Mr. Yeats here will take care of you. As promised. But not until I get a full council vote."

In the end, it took seven days, but a City Council meeting was held in which the enabling ordinance passed 39 to 0, with one abstention. That came from a black alderman who made a long-winded speech about African-Americans being dispossessed like the Israelites in the Bible, but it was intended mostly for his constituents and he sat down and stayed quiet once he got it in the record.

By the time the independent alderwoman returned, there'd be nothing she could do, if she even bothered to examine the ordinance carefully.

It was a stroke of genius, deciding to pull this thing together in the middle of summer. Yeats had thought he was crazy.

"Grab yourself a drink, Bill," Poe said to Yeats as the housekeeper ushered the lawyer into Poe's penthouse study several days later. "Thanks for coming over."

"You want me, Peter, and I come running."

"I thought you'd be off sailing."

"I've given that up for this summer," Yeats said, pouring some Glenlivet scotch into a glass. He added ice, then turned to look at Poe unhappily. "I get a lot of dark stares and glances when I walk into the yacht club now. The commodore's collecting signatures to have me bounced."

"Sorry about that."

"You won the race, right? That's all that matters. The trouble is, you would have won no matter what I did. I've incurred the wrath of my fellow yachtsmen kinda needlessly."

"I should have had more confidence in Curland. Hell of a sailor. The best. Anyway, you can always join another yacht club."

"Where, Grand Pier, Michigan?"

Poe studied Yeats, trying to keep his apprehension out of his expression. "Why do you say that, Bill?"

"Because the ramshackle yacht club out there is the kind of dump I'll probably end up in with what's happened to my reputation."

"Don't sweat it. When I'm finished with this project, I'll start a new yacht club of my own, right here in Chicago."

"And just where would you put that?"

"You know damn well where. Now, down to business. I want to talk a little strategy. Namely, do I move now to get a preliminary Park District vote on the project as it's set for Cabrini Green? Get their approval on the record? Or do I wait for the city to close Meigs Field and do it all with one swing of the bat when we make the switch?"

Yeats lowered himself into a comfortable chair, flicking a piece of lint off his highly polished loafers. "Where's Diandra?"

"What do you care where's Diandra? Don't worry about her. She's busy upstairs. Curland is painting her picture."

"Shouldn't he be working on the plans for your building?"

"That can wait a couple of weeks. This is a special order from me—a big nude for the living room."

Yeats stared, as Poe figured a Catholic priest might stare if told of such a thing. "You mean she's up there with him without any clothes on?"

"Nothing to worry about. They're both kinda married to me, aren't they? If he's enjoying himself, all the better. We need all the Curlands for this. So what do you think? Should I move now to get a Park District vote on the deal?"

Yeats sipped his drink, then swirled his ice cubes for an annoyingly long time. "I wouldn't do it, Peter. They're the ones with the ultimate authority now, thanks to the ordinance you got passed. If you push them on a vote now, then come back to them with all those interesting changes you have in mind, some of them might feel a little betrayed—especially Cooperman."

"He'll vote for anything with that Holocaust Museum in it."

"Maybe. Maybe not. But there's no reason to take chances. Even with his vote, you got a close margin. No, Peter. I'd do it all in one shot. In the meantime, you can sit back and let support build, which it certainly seems to be doing."

"I never got anywhere in this life sitting back, William."

"You asked my advice. That's what you pay me for."

"That's true. And I guess I'm getting my money's worth, because I think maybe you're right. Everything turns on Cooperman. If we put the park board on the record, then yank the rug, he'd feel foolish. We just want him to feel disappointed—crushed—when I let it get out that there can't be a building like this at Cabrini Green, that I can't get financing for such a long shot. That if he wants his Holocaust Museum it'll have to go somewhere else."

"That's right."

"But I can't sit and wait. We've got all this steam up, all this enthusiasm. I don't want that to dissipate. We've got to keep that working for us until the city announces it's going to close Meigs Field."

"Uh, Peter, I'm not so sure that's going to happen."

Time seemed to stop. The bomb that had wrecked his sailboat couldn't have stunned him as much as this if he'd been there sitting on top of it. "What did you say?"

"I said I'm not sure Meigs Field is going to be closed."

"What are you talking about? That's the deal! When they finish the new airport out south, Midway and Meigs are kaput. We've been counting on that since I first started this thing."

"Midway's out. That's for sure. But there are some second thoughts about Meigs. A lot of businessmen and politicians use the commuter airlines that operate out of there. You need a place for general aviation. Many, many reasons to keep it open."

"But people have been trying to shut it down for years. They almost did a couple of times. How come my guys on the City Council haven't said anything about this?"

"They probably don't know about it. My source is in the mayor's office."

"When did you find this out?"

"Yesterday."

Poe's turquoise eyes darkened with anger—and malice. His voice dropped low. "Why am I hearing about it now?"

"You've been in a real good mood. I didn't want to spoil it."

"Fuck the good mood! You should have got me on the horn instanter, goddamn it."

"It's not carved in stone, Peter. It's just a possibility. Just something to think about."

"Think about? Shit, Bill. My building has to go on Meigs. There's no other place."

"There's the suburbs. They're putting everything and anything up out there."

"Fuck the suburbs! This is for Chicago. We've gotta do something. Can we buy anybody?"

"You can buy most everybody, but not the mayor. And anyway, you're running a little low on the green stuff. I had to pay off our aldermen friends out of my own account. You won't get a penny out of Inland Empire and the Japanese until you've got something on paper that looks like an official go-ahead."

"Shit. Double shit."

"I'll work on it, Peter."

"You do that." Poe looked to the mantel of his study's fireplace. There was a scale model of one of his helicopters there—a large, gold-plated model that looked something like a trophy. "I just had an idea."

"You have one every five minutes."

"This is a good one. A closer. We could have a heliport next to the building. Provide commuter service to the big airports. In warm weather, maybe seaplanes. That might take care of the business flyer problem. Right? What do you think?"

Yeats shrugged. "Talk to your architect."

"Don't be stupid. He'd wonder how you'd have seaplanes at Cabrini Green. He'd wonder what the hell I was thinking—and why."

"He's got to find out sooner or later."

"We'll make it later. Get going, Bill. I want this taken care of."

When Yeats had gone, Poe realized how much he'd been shaking. His hands were still trembling. He had to do something, go somewhere, get out of this room, get out of the house. He called upstairs to Diandra—noting the inordinate amount of time it took for her to answer the house phone.

"Are you two finished up there—for the day?" he asked, hoping he sounded calm.

She took more time, then replied: "If that's what you want, Peter."

"No. That's all right. Enjoy yourselves. I'm going out for a while. Got to talk to someone about the project. Probably be back late."

"In time for dinner?"

"I don't think so. How much longer do you suppose Curland's going to take with this?"

"Why don't you ask him? He's standing right beside me."

Poe had no doubt. "That's all right. He can take as long as he wants. See you later. Don't wait up. Bye, babe."

He picked up his outside line, hitting the button that automatically dialed Mango. She sounded sleepy. How late had she been up the previous night?

"I need to talk to you," he said. "Big problem. I'm going over to my Michigan Avenue hotel. Meet me in the top-floor suite, and don't let any moss grow on that beautiful ass of yours getting over there."

"Do you want to talk or do you—"

"Be there."

She didn't take long, but by the time she arrived he was well into a big glass of scotch. She looked at him apprehensively at first, then recaptured her customary poise. "Big problem, you said."

"Yeah."

"Do you want to talk about it now or do you want to get out of those clothes?"

"I don't know. Can't make up my mind."

"You're looking kinda agitated." What he looked was a little crazy.

"I am agitated."

Her hand went to her zipper. The dress was very tight and she had to pull hard to get it down over her hips. Her large breasts popped up as they came free of the cloth. With the dress off, she was completely naked. She must have removed her underwear before coming over. Always ready, that Mango.

"Finish your drink," she said, heading for the bedroom. "I'll make things comfy. Maybe we can calm you down a little."

Mango knew about all the tricks there were to make a man feel really good, and she used them—at the end, almost desperately. Poe had tried to put on a good show, but his mind was in no way on sex. Somehow she managed to give him an erection and, somehow, got him to achieve fulfillment, but she almost failed, and that had never happened to her before. Whatever was troubling him was powerful stuff. When she was done, he just lay there, as limp as a dead man.

"You all right, Peter?"

There was a pause before he spoke.

"I'm all right."

She lifted her head to look at his face. He was staring straight up at the ceiling.

"You sure?"

"You were fine, Mango. Like always."

She sat up. She was covered with sweat. She felt cooler as it evaporated. "So now we talk. I'll get you another drink."

When she returned, he was still lying motionless. She set his

313

glass on the bed table, but took a big slug of the one she'd made for herself. She wanted a cigarette but feared that might irritate him.

"Okay, Peter," she said, seating herself against the headboard. "What's wrong? Are you still worried about that missing Kirchner painting Train had? I told you not to sweat that. I've got people working on it. We'll get it back."

"I'm not worried about that. It's a three-hundred-thousand-dollar problem. I've got a two-hundred-million-dollar problem. The mayor may want to keep Meigs Field open."

"He told you this?"

"Yeats did. He's got a guy in the mayor's office."

"Yeats doesn't know for sure half the things he tips you about. Sometimes he's just rolling dice."

"I don't like these particular dice. This could queer the whole fucking deal. Everything. This scares the hell out of me, Mango. It was supposed to be a certainty. They'd informed the F.A.A. they wanted to close Meigs. That's how I found out about it. That's when I got the idea for the building."

"Did someone get to the mayor? Or did he just change his mind?"

"I don't know." Poe sat up, reaching for his drink. "I just don't know. Worse thing is I don't have the faintest idea what to do about it."

"There's always something."

"No, there isn't. The guy's fucking incorruptible. And even if he wasn't, I don't have anything he wants."

She looked at his bare body. He was getting a little flabby. He probably hadn't worked out in weeks.

"It's not like you to give up."

"I'm not giving up. I'm just up against a wall. I didn't even know it was there!"

She sighed. "Peter, you've got plenty of time. You've got a lot of things you've got to do first. We're a long way from the sting. You've got the mayor to bite on your building idea. Now you've got to get him hooked. How soon are you going to hold the grand unveiling? The world's-tallest-building shit."

"Soon."

"Make it damn soon. Work up some local pride."

"I'm doing that."

"Get him hooked real deep, Peter. So that he'll be afraid of looking like a chump if he backs out."

314

"But how in the hell am going to I hook him on the Meigs Field site?"

"Maybe he's just afraid of losing jobs without the airport. Your building will mean a lot of jobs."

"You don't understand, Mango."

The hell she didn't. But there was no point trying to get Poe to think sensibly in his present state. He was scared shitless, and when that happened, he was paralyzed.

Mango would have to step in on her own, but she was ready for that. "Don't let it get to you, Peter. Not yet. We'll think of something. We always do."

"Yeah, right."

"There's always something."

Zany had gone for a late-night drive. He'd been staring at his computer screen to the point of going batty and needed to get away from it. Reflexively, almost as if he were still on patrol, he went through town on out to the interstate, then back again and up the beach road. A vehicle followed him out from the center of town, but disappeared onto a side road just before Zany entered the long curve that went around the huge dune that was Grand Pier's principal landmark.

With the help of the police departments out there, he'd been working that list of East Coast art dealers and art purchasers who had shown an interest in Expressionist art. When this was done, he'd try Europe. He was paying for the calls himself and Judy would raise a lot of hell when the bill came, but he wasn't going to worry about that now.

The trouble was that he was getting absolutely nowhere. No one had heard of any Kirchners being on the market. As one art dealer told him, all the world's great paintings were accounted for. When one changed hands, everyone knew. He'd had a hunch he might pick up a trail in Philadelphia, because of the letter "P" on that crate, because the town was full of Germans and nuts about art, but no one had seen a Kirchner on the market there in years.

He reached the small parking lot at the end of the road and sat a moment before turning around, looking at the lake with the car's lights off.

Zany was missing something. Whatever it was, he felt it looming large and obvious, something he should have figured out immediately, but had overlooked.

It suddenly hit him, and it was obvious, indeed.

If someone was knowingly buying stolen art under the table, Zany shouldn't be looking for purchasers who were actively collecting Expressionist paintings on the open market. He should be looking for someone who had been doing that but had suddenly stopped.

He clicked on his headlights and ground his car into reverse, scattering dry sand. There was no traffic on the road going back, and he stepped up his speed, slowing only for the long curve around the dune.

Just as he came out of it, he heard a muffled *bang,* followed almost simultaneously by a *thwack.*

He kept driving, hearing nothing more. The obvious explanation was a backfiring car; the *thwack* a rock kicked up by his tires.

But this was a sandy area, not a gravelly one. And there were no cars around to backfire. It wasn't his own automobile. His engine hadn't faltered for an instant.

Zany increased his speed further, not easing it until he was back in the bright lights of the town's main street. Then he pulled off into the parking lot of the bank. Leaving the engine running, he got out.

There was a hole in the trunk. Whatever had made it had entered diagonally, making a much larger hole when it emerged from the right fender just forward of the right rear wheel.

He backed into the shadows, looking around. There were some parked cars and loitering teenagers over by the Dairy Queen down the street; otherwise, nothing moved.

So there it was. A shot had been fired into his car. Nothing like this had ever happened to him before, though many of the burglary cases he'd caught had taken him into some of the worst neighborhoods in Chicago.

It wasn't a random shot. He couldn't think of anyone ever firing off a gun in Grand Pier, except for the armed robbers who had just cost him his job. It was a very deliberate shot. A single shot.

He'd been traveling fairly slowly around that curve. If whoever had been waiting there in the sand had wanted to kill him, it would have been easy. They had plenty of time to set up the shot. He'd been fully exposed to the patch of darkness from which it had come. Yet it hadn't even been a near miss. It had been fired low, and to the right, and in the rear. The aim was at the car, not him. There had been no follow-up shots, no attempt to correct the aim and get him.

The truth of it was plain and simple. He'd been given a message. They wanted their painting back. And Matthias Curland could have nothing to do with it, because he had the painting.

Zany hustled back to the car and, with tires screeching, spun it onto the street. He was home in five minutes.

Judy was back. She'd been down at the store, locking up. Zany tried to remember if he'd thought to turn off his computer. It wouldn't do to have her see the names of all those art dealers.

She seemed normal enough. "Want a beer, Zane? I was just going to get one."

He took her by the shoulders and gently eased her into a chair, leaning over her intently, his eyes on hers.

"We've got a serious problem," he said. "Remember how you threatened to go back to your mother in Wyoming? I want you to do that. Pack a couple of bags right now. I'm going to drive you to O'Hare. Tonight."

"Are you crazy, Zane?"

"Judy. I was out for a drive. On the beach road. Someone fired a bullet into the trunk of my car. I don't think it was an accident or someone fooling around. I don't know what it means, but it must have something to do with the Langley case. I know it means this: You've got to get out of here, and stay out until I think it's safe to come back."

"Zane. You said you'd get off this case."

"I did. All my cases."

"But what about the store?"

"I'll take care of the store. I'll get some kid to help me."

"What about you?"

He stood up straight. "I can take care of myself. I used to be a cop, remember?"

THE HEADLINES THIS time around were bigger and better—not only in the Chicago papers but on real estate section front pages in New York, Philadelphia, Washington, all over the country: "POE GOES FOR THE TOP," "CHICAGO DEVELOPER TO BUILD WORLD'S HIGHEST," "MONSTER SAILBOAT LAUNCHED IN CHICAGO."

As promised, the mayor had joined Poe for the "world's tallest" announcement. Like Poe, he was drawfed by the huge scale model that Cudahy, Brown had worked up in a rush from Matthias's drawings. The mayor, of course, got most of the ink and air time. The stories concentrated on the rivalry with New York, whose mayor, a Republican, capitulated immediately: "If they think they can afford it, let them do it. But I think they're crazy."

Despite all the news coverage, the Japanese and the money men at Inland Empire didn't budge from their original position. Not a cent without city authorization for the lakefront site—and Poe had better hurry the hell up about it.

He went hunting for Bill Yeats by phone, tracking him down eventually at his health club and summoning him forth from a squash game.

"Were you winning?" Poe asked.

"Yes. I was."

"It's only a game, William. I just got an idea. Call me back instanter from a safe phone."

Yeats was back to him in exactly four minutes.

"What is it, Peter?" he said, letting some impatience creep into his voice.

"How soon am I going to be issued that building permit for Cabrini Green?"

"Any day now. What difference does it make? You're not going to actually build the thing there."

"I want you to get another one, a blank one. I want it signed, sealed, all that shit, but with the location blank. Can do?"

"If you're thinking of doing what I think you are, there's a word for it. Forgery. Falsification of official documents."

"We're not going to do anything official with it. I just want it to circulate it in certain quarters—like maybe a bank on LaSalle Street and an office building in Tokyo."

"This is crazy, Peter."

"Just do what I say. Get a signed permit. Fill in the blank with the words 'Solidarity Drive.' Make a Xerox copy of it, and get it over to Inland Empire. Emphasize that it's for their eyes only—just to show them that City Hall is with us."

"What the hell is Solidarity Drive?"

"I'm ashamed of you, William. A lifelong Chicagoan, the best-connected lawyer in town, and you don't know Solidarity Drive?"

Yeats replied with silence.

"It's the roadway that goes out to the Planetarium and Meigs Field," Poe said. "They renamed it to honor Poland's Solidarity Movement a long time ago. It'll be the address of the new building. I kinda like that, don't you? Since we're going to have all those ethnic museums."

"Maybe we should rename it Holocaust Drive."

"Don't be a wiseass, Bill. Get it done."

"They still won't want to go ahead until you get approval from the Park District for building on the lakefront."

"Maybe they won't. But they might be willing to come up with a few million in up-front money. I'm getting a little close to Tap City."

"You're knocking on the gates, in fact."

"So get moving. You want your fees paid, don't you? Now, how are we coming on airport closure?"

"I've made discreet inquiries with our friends in the Transportation Department in Washington. They're neutral on Meigs, as long as general aviation is accommodated at one of the other fields."

"Anything else?"

"They tell me you should have no problem getting approval for a helicopter shuttle service."

"Have you figured out where this 'save Meigs Field' crap is coming from? Is it just the mayor's whim, or does he have some pilot friends?"

"He has friends with corporate jets. But there's some pressure coming from the commuter airline that serves Springfield. A lot of pols use it."

"So why can't they fly out of O'Hare or the new South Side airport?"

"They like Meigs."

"Is there anything we can do for that airline? To change their minds?"

"No."

"Is there anything we can do *to* them?"

"No."

"Yes, there is. The F.A.A. has application forms, right? That we'd have to submit for a helicopter shuttle?"

"Yes. I've got one at the office."

"Well, fill it out. Not for a helicopter shuttle, but for a commuter air service—to Springfield. Poe Airways. Direct competition."

"This is no time to go into the airline business, Peter."

"I've no more intention of doing that than I did of buying the White Sox. But I want them to think it's something I'm serious about. Make sure they see a copy. When they come back at you, tell them there's one thing that could make me back off—a transfer of their operations to another airport. Tell them I think it would be good for the city."

"I don't think it's going to work."

"Give it a try. Airlines are in a lot of trouble these days, especially the little guys. I don't think they'd want to go up against a billionaire with money to burn, do you?"

"Ha-ha-ha."

"No laughing matter, William."

"I read you loud and clear."

"Okay. You coming to Christian Curland's art show at Train's gallery?"

"I'm kind of busy, Peter. Especially with all these things you want me to get to work on."

"You've got time for fucking squash games, don't you? Be there. I want a big turnout."

"Yes, Peter."

"And bring your new girlfriend. What's her name?"

"You know her name. She works for you."

"That's right. Sally Phillips. Good-lookin' broad. Real class. I don't understand how Matthias Curland could pass her up."

"He's been distracted lately."

"What do you mean by that?"

"Nothing, Peter. He's just working hard, like all of us."

"Make sure you show up at Train's. With the money you're going to get out of this, you can afford to buy a few paintings."

Christian Curland's gallery show was to run a week. It began with an evening cocktail reception. Train had invited most of the city's notable art collectors. Few showed up, but, with all the people Poe had pressed into coming—and not a few of Christian's lady friends in attendance—the gallery was fairly crowded. Bitsie Symms was quite audibly present, her high-pitched laughter cutting through the jumbled noise of simultaneous conversations, reaching into every room.

Matthias came with Diandra. They had been working on his painting of her all afternoon. She was beginning to tire of these sessions. Their lovemaking made it all worthwhile, but prolonged the process, as did the frequent breaks they took—going for walks, visiting museums, taking time out for the occasional movie. She had a wonderful mind. In his company, her intelligence and intellectual curiosity about things had come forth like a prisoner being allowed out of some dungeon. Everything he had hoped and imagined about her was proving to be true. There were other revelations, some disturbing, like her passionate fondness for exquisite, beautiful, but painfully expensive objects—clothes, glass sculptures, pieces of jewelry. He couldn't imagine this woman the wife of a poor painter.

But maybe he was wrong. Perhaps it was just her habit, from having been married so long to Peter Poe. Matthias had underestimated her before, mistakenly. He put such worries from his mind. He lived totally in the present now. The building and his intimate hours with Diandra were about all there was to it.

They were close to being finished. Matthias wanted to do more work on the face and the body shadowing, but otherwise only the background remained undone, and that he could attend to in his little studio. The penthouse arrangement was making Matthias nervous. Diandra told him she'd discovered Poe had been at home on two occasions when they'd been making love. It bothered Matthias that Poe had so blithely accepted the situation, that he had never once come up to check on them. It was as if he had no objection to their intimacy, that he might even be encouraging it.

In any event, Matthias was miserable when apart from her, edgy and disconsolate when a day went by without her naked in his arms.

He was satisfied with the painting—or at least, confident that Poe would be satisfied with the final result. Were he doing it for himself, it would be quite different, but Poe wouldn't like it. That's why Matthias wanted to do more work on the face. He needed to take the love out of the eyes. Poe would know it wasn't for him.

In no way was the nude as accomplished a creation as the magical portraits by Christian of a variety of Chicago society ladies that now hung so glitteringly along one wall of the gallery. In the brochure for the show, Train had proclaimed Christian "the John Singer Sargent of our time," and it was true. Christian's portraits were the equal of that nineteenth-century master's commission work. Christian had imbued each woman subject, no matter of frumpy or aging in real life, with extraordinary grace and glamour and poise. He'd made each one of the women seem regal.

"I'm impressed," Diandra said.

"They're magnificent. I don't suppose he was paid anything like what they're worth."

"Maybe that doesn't matter to him."

"You don't know Christian."

"Who doesn't know me?" Christian had come up behind them, putting his arms around their waists. "Good evening, big brother. Delighted to see you, Mrs. Poe. Have you been gossiping about me?"

"Only in the most complimentary fashion," Matthias said. "These are truly fine, Chris. Extraordinary."

"Just like your building design."

"I've not seen them before."

"As I told you, I've been doing a lot of work at the museum."

"I see 'sold' stickers on quite a few of them," Diandra said.

"Of course they're sold," said Christian. "They were commissioned—sold before I started them. I just borrowed a few to flesh out the show. The stickers are an artifice—an inducement for people to buy the unsold ones, like salting the audience at an opera with clacques. When you think about it, the art business isn't really any different from the used car business."

"I'm sure they'll all sell," Diandra said.

"I hope so," Christian replied. "This is my finale, my farewell to Chicago—at least for a while."

"What do you mean?" asked Matthias.

"I'm going to move down to the Bahamas. I would have told you earlier, but I didn't make up my mind until tonight. Larry Train has a house down there and he's going to let me use it. Tropical breezes, tropical colors, tropical light. Just like Paul Gauguin in the Marquesas, only I think I'll skip the opium."

"Then you won't be doing any more portraits."

"Oh, yes. There's a resort nearby. I'll be doing portraits of guests and conducting a painting class."

"How on earth did you line that up?"

"Our mutual benefactor, big brother. Your charming companion's husband. Mr. Poe owns a piece of the resort."

Poe reached everywhere—even to the Caribbean.

"You're leaving soon?"

"By the end of summer; perhaps sooner. Don't begrudge me this, Matt. You had your years in the south of France. It's your turn to look after the noble Curland clan of Chicago. And I don't suppose you'll mind having the Schiller Street house all to yourself."

His wink at Diandra was quick, but she caught it and turned away.

"I'm really pleased you came, Matt," Christian said. "You'll have to excuse me now. I need to go flatter the very rich Mrs. Symms. Train said she's thinking of buying that huge skyline painting of mine. It's truly terrible, but she wouldn't know that."

He squeezed Matthias's shoulder, then hurried away.

"There's your friend Sally," Diandra said.

Matthias looked into the crowd. Sally saw him and nodded curtly, then moved away, a pained expression on her face.

"She's with your husband's lawyer," Matthias said.

"Quite a lot these days. Does that bother you?"

"No, not now. I suppose he's very rich."

"Peter helps keep him that way."

"I wonder if there's anyone here who isn't obligated to your husband."

"This talk is depressing me, Matt."

Matthias paused uncomfortably. "Sorry. I've just got too much Peter Poe in my life."

"Now you know how it feels."

"Let's leave."

"Can't. Peter will want to find me here when he arrives. You, too."

Poe arrived very late, with his buxom secretary in tow, if that was the right word for it. She gave Matthias and Diandra a speculative look, then smiled rather smugly.

"Good turnout," Poe said.

"I'm sure that doesn't come as a surprise to you, Peter," Diandra said.

"You finish the floor plans yet for the museums? They'll all fit in the building?"

"I'm afraid I haven't made much progress on that yet. I've been busy with the painting of Diandra."

"Maybe not busy enough. How much longer is it going to take?"

Matthias shrugged. "Not too long. Just a few more sittings."

Poe glanced at his watch, then, more quickly, at Diandra. "Maybe you ought to go back now and get some more work done on it."

"I'm really tired, Peter," said Diandra.

"Tired? From all that lying down? Come on, get it over with."

"Whatever you say, Peter. When are you coming home?"

"I won't be, tonight. When I leave here, Miss Bellini and I are going out to Michigan City. My guy out there, Bobby Mann, has been on his own too long. I'll be back tomorrow. Probably late."

Diandra and Matthias looked at each other.

"Good night, then," Diandra said. She kissed her husband on the cheek, then made her way to the door, Matthias following.

When they were gone, Train hurried up to Poe.

"The show's an absolutely brilliant success, Peter," he said, his eyes wandering across the room to Christian, who had his arm around Bitsie Symms.

"A nice way to handle the payoff. How much are you going to give him for the last batch of Germans?"

"Two hundred thousand. That's what was agreed upon for this bunch."

"We're a painting short."

"It's what we agreed upon, Peter. You said you didn't want him out at your casino anymore. This'll be his final payment."

"All right. I won't argue with you. We're getting enough out of it."

Train seemed twitchy. "Did Mango tell you about the painting? The missing Kirchner?"

"I told him we were taking care of it," she said.

"It was stolen, Peter," Train said. "Two other paintings are missing, from my gallery stock. Mango is sure it was that police person from Michigan. He used to be a burglary detective."

"And now he's a thief?"

"I'm taking care of it, Peter," Mango said tersely.

"The rest of the shipment was delivered?" Poe asked.

"Yes. The client is very satisfied. Paid in cash, as usual."

"And you sold my spaghetti picture?"

"Yes, sir. Not to him. Somebody in Fort Lauderdale. Sixty-five thousand. It's—it's not a good market."

"All right. Turn the money over to Yeats. I'm not going to sweat that Kirchner. After this, I don't want to hear anything more about any fucking paintings. I've got too many other things to worry about."

"Leave it to me, Peter."

"This Michigan guy, he hasn't gone to the Chicago coppers, has he?"

"We haven't heard from them."

"Okay. Thanks, Larry. Go enjoy yourself."

Train did as ordered, moving toward Christian and Bitsie Symms.

"Don't worry about the Michigan guy, Peter," Mango said. "He's a goof. A real hayhead. From Wyoming, y'know? We're sure he's got the Kirchner in his house. The people I have watching things out there said he brought a bunch of shit in from his car last time he came back from Chicago."

"Why haven't you gone after it?"

"You want more than the painting back, right? You want him to drop the case. We've got him on the run. He's got to be near the breaking point. He lost his job. His wife left him. Went back home to Wyoming. Can't take much longer." She hesitated, then lowered her voice. "We could take care of this real quick, you know. Just give the word."

"Not a chance. You kill a cop, any cop, and you've got trouble that'll never go away. I don't like these killings, Mango. None of them. Not even what went down in Atlantic City. No more."

"Don't worry. That's all behind us."

"Keep it that way."

Mango took his arm. "Let's go, Peter."

At Meigs, Poe got out of the limousine but just stood there, making no move toward his helicopter, though one of his pilots was sitting at the controls, waiting to start the engine. Poe stared for a moment at the skyline to the west, then shifted his gaze to the north, then out at the lake.

"What a view we're going to have," he said to Mango, who had gotten out to stand beside him. "There won't be anything like it in the whole goddamn world."

"I dream about it, Peter. You and me, up at the top."

"You don't dream about it the way I do," he said.

A small, twin-engine plane was approaching from the south, its landing lights looking like candles in the summer sky.

"I want you to go out to the casino by yourself," Poe said. "Give the books a once-over, but don't give Bobby too hard a time. Just enough to remind him we're still around."

"He'll know I'm there. Don't worry about it."

"Come back tomorrow."

She nodded. "Why aren't you coming?"

"I'm going back to the penthouse."

"You're going to drop in on them, unannounced, right?"

"It's time. Gotta move things along."

Matthias didn't even pick up a brush. Convinced it might be their last opportunity for some time—angry at Poe for his so curtly ordering them about—he and Diandra made love, leaving the lights off, barely pausing to take off their clothes. As with their first time in Wisconsin, it was more an act of defiance than ardor, frantically performed, swiftly concluded, bringing neither of them much pleasure. Afterward they lay in each other's arms, stroking each other in belated affection, Matthias feeling remorse, both of them unsatisfied.

"There are times when I feel like an animal in Peter Poe's private zoo," Matthias said. "Even now."

"Don't say that."

"But then I wonder what we'll do when the picture's finished."

"We'll find a way."

"I love you."

"Matt . . ."

"How many times have you told me you love me?"

"Many times."

"Always while we're making love."

"I love you, Matthias. Haven't I proved that to you? I don't know what more you could ask of me."

He pulled back, trying to see her face. "Would you leave him? For me?"

"Would you give up doing his building?"

"It won't take forever."

She said nothing. He caressed her breast, leaning to kiss her long neck, just beneath her ear.

The lights came on. Poe, looking perfectly calm, stood in the doorway.

"Hi, guys," he said with heavy sarcasm.

Diandra blinked against the light. Matthias could see tears in her eyes.

"Peter, what . . ."

"Changed my plans. Just in time, I see. Don't worry, I'm not shocked. I've looked in on you before."

Matthias glanced around the room. The outside terrace ran the full length of the penthouse. Anyone could have crept up to the window. Perhaps with a camera. He had never felt so helpless in his life.

"Look . . ."

Poe raised his hand, commanding silence. He ambled over to the easel, stepping back to improve his perspective.

"Very good," he said. "It's all done, except for the background. I guess maybe Larry Train can find someone to do that for me."

"It's not finished," Matthias said.

"Oh, yes it is. Perfect. You got everything there. Hair, face, tits, cunt. I like the look in her eyes. Yeah, you've really done her justice. Made me a nice souvenir."

Diandra stood up. "There are times, Peter, when I think you're a real creep."

"Shut up, Diandra. Get your clothes on. You, too, Curland. I think from now on our relationship is going to have to be strictly business."

"I don't think this is the time to—"

"I'll decide what's time for what. Get out of here, Curland. I'll call you when I need you."

Mango rolled over onto her back, exhausted. She was getting old. Two men in the same day shouldn't have knocked her out like this. Too much special treatment. Next time, she was just going to lie there like a twenty-dollar whore—no matter who it was who was screwing her.

"You're the best lay I ever had in my whole fucking life, Mango," said the man lying next to her.

"You're too sweet."

"What?"

"That's the way Poe's wife talks. 'You're too sweet.' 'That's just fine, darling.' I'm just trying it out for size."

"It sounds stupid."

"Your idea of being a gentleman, Bobby, is to tell a lady what a good fuck she is."

"Yeah, so? You want I should just pat you on the ass?"

"Forget it, Bobby."

Mann sat up and reached for a cigarette. "You want one?"

"Thanks."

He tossed her the pack. She made a face at him, then shook out a cigarette, lighting it herself.

"You sure you gotta go back tomorrow?" he said.

"That's what the man said. I do what he says."

"At least we've got the night together."

"No way, Bobby. When you finish that cigarette, you're outa here. I'm taking enough of a chance as it is."

"You made me wait a month."

"You almost waited for eternity. Anyway, I'm sure you had your pokes. You don't have to look far in this joint."

Mann exhaled, staring at her through the smoke. "You set me up, Mango."

"Set you up? I saved your fucking life."

"You help me arrange the hit, then you tip him off."

"I didn't tip him off. I just made sure he wasn't on that boat. Use your goddamn head, Bobby. It wasn't him I wanted you to hit. Hell, the way those greaseball chumps of yours fucked up the blow, he probably would have gotten off the boat alive and kicking like all the others. Then you really would have been in the shit. No way I could have stopped him from icing you."

"My friends in Atlantic City—"

"Friends? Those creeps would have whacked you first thing

they did. Just for fucking up the boat job. You got out of everything real lucky, Bobby. All thanks to me."

"He believed you when you told him I had nothing to do with it?"

"You're sitting here, aren't you?"

"You still want to take a whack at his wife?"

"No. That won't be necessary. He's going to dump her. Stuck-up bitch. Always treated me like shit."

Mango dragged on her cigarette, then brushed the hair out of her eyes. After all she'd done to make Bobby happy, it was a tangled mess.

"So what do you want me to do?" Mann asked.

"Just sit tight. Keep the handle out here honest, just like he said. We'll make our move on him after the Japanese money comes in for the building."

"Two hundred million?"

"When all is said and done. It'll go into escrow."

"And you think you can touch that?"

"I've got access to all the accounts, right? That fucking Yeats fought me all the way, but I got it."

"How much can we put our hands on?"

"A couple million. Maybe more. What Peter would consider walk-around money, but enough to keep us happy for a long time. The biggest score you ever made, Bobby."

He lay back against the pillow, still smoking, staring dreamy-eyed at the ceiling.

His brow furrowed. "What about his new partners, the outfit guys in Chicago?"

"All they care about is this casino. They'll be happy to have him out of the way."

"What about the Japanese?"

"Stop worrying, Bobby. Two or three million is like nothing to them. A write-off. It's Yeats I'm worried about."

"Maybe he and Poe can be together, when it goes down."

"That was the first thing I thought of. It'll be no sweat."

He reached and touched her back, then ran his hand down to her bottom. "When can we do this again? Will you be out here any time soon? Without him?"

"You'll have to come out to Chicago."

"Chicago? Are you nuts?"

"I can't be making a lot of solo trips here. He's going to New York in a few days, to do some television shows. We can use the boat for fucking. The harbor's right near downtown. I'll give the crew some shore leave. You can take a chopper out; be back here in time for the night shift."

"I'm not supposed to touch the choppers, not for personal use."

"You can catch a ride on one bringing the happy gamblers home."

"In a few days, you say."

She put out her cigarette, then got up. "I'm going to take a bath now, Bobby. You get the hell out of here. Don't worry. It'll all work out fine. I know what I'm doing."

CHAPTER
21

FOR THE NEXT few days, Matthias stayed close to his own house, as much a prisoner of his humiliation as his dilemma. The loneliness was nearly unbearable, but he didn't want to talk to his family or friends, as he was sure they would ask him about the Poe project, a subject that now afflicted him with almost as much bitterness as it did uncertainty. Poe had his drawings. He'd accepted Poe's money. Any court of law would consider the design Poe's property now, certainly any court in Cook County. Poe could leave it to Cudahy, Brown to finish the project. They'd do a shoddy job, but Poe would have his building. There'd be little Matthias could do to stop him, except denounce him, and that wouldn't accomplish much. Disgruntled employee. Adulterer.

He could see Poe putting down Cudahy, Brown as principal architects. Matthias still wanted that building to be his. It was.

Christian had vanished after his gallery show, doubtless taking up residence with some new amour. The prospect of comparing notes with his brother on the pitfalls of adultery was in any event appalling.

Poe didn't call. Neither did Diandra. In fact, Matthias's telephone didn't ring at all. He was glad enough about that at first, but in time the silence became oppressive.

He read. He played music—Carl Orff's *Carmina Burana,* Ravel's *Pelias and Melisande,* Erik Satie's *Trois Gymnopédies,* and, in the hopes of a more joyful mood, Leon Redbone. He drew endless sketches of sailboats and smoked his pipe constantly. In the dark of evening, he went for walks through the neighborhood. He drank, one night so heavily that he called his ex-wife, but she sensed his mauldlin mood and cut the conversation short.

He also opened his mail. Saturday's brought a letter that bore Doug Gibson's law firm as a return address.

"Matt," it said, simply, "this came my way. You ought to ponder it."

Attached was a Xerox copy of a building permit, made out to Poe Enterprises, Inc. Matthias read over it twice, but all that caught his eye was the site location: "Solidarity Drive." He presumed that was the name Poe had chosen for the address of his development, as other Chicago builders had adorned their creations with such vanity addresses as "One Magnificent Mile." "Solidarity" served as an allusion to the ethnic museums, but still seemed peculiar.

But Peter Poe was a most peculiar man.

Why had Doug Gibson made a point of this? His friend was not at all the sort of man to jibe at people because of their ethnic backgrounds.

Matthias also read the newspapers. A column in the business section of the Sunday *Tribune* leapt out at him as if it were a page-one story. Its quite small headline asked: "POE PROJECT IN TROUBLE?"

The columnist, sounding much like Doug Gibson, devoted a lot of space to reasons why a super building on the Cabrini Green site could not possibly repay its investment. More jarringly, it contained the line: "The financial backers of the project, a Japanese consortium represented by the Inland Empire Bank, have reportedly told Poe they will not invest in the Cabrini Green location and that he must find a more viable alternative site."

Matthias went to his telephone. The housekeeper answered, saying Poe was out of town. Instead of asking for Diandra, he left a message for Poe to call him as soon as possible.

Matthias had Yeats's number. It didn't really surprise him that Sally answered—early on a Sunday morning.

"I need to speak to . . . to Mr. Yeats," he said as politely as possible.

She hesitated. If she was about to talk to him herself, she thought better of it. "Just a moment, Matt. I'll get him."

"Sally?"

"Yes?"

"Are you all right?"

"I have everything I need, Matt. And he's a very nice man. Hold on."

Yeats came grudgingly to the phone. "Is this something that can wait till Monday, Curland?"

"Did you read the *Tribune* this morning? The column in the business section?"

A pause. "Yes."

"Is it true?"

"Some of it."

"Would you mind telling me which part?"

Yeats went from grumpy to solicitous. "We're having to re-think the Cabrini Green site, Matt. But don't worry. There's going to be a building. Your job is secure, despite, uh, recent complications."

"Complications?"

"Mrs. Poe." Yeats cleared his throat.

So Poe was letting people know about his cuckoldry. It was logical that he might talk to his lawyer about such a thing, but what did this mean for Diandra?

Yeats had probably told Sally.

"Anyway, we're going ahead with the project," the lawyer said. "The money will be there. We have your plan. All we have to do is find a new site."

"That's a pretty big *all.*"

"Peter Poe is a pretty big man."

"Please have him call me. As soon as possible."

"Matt, I don't *have* Poe do anything. But I'm sure you'll be hearing from him—sooner than later."

After hanging up, Matthias went looking for a map of Chicago that he remembered having in the desk in his study, then took it to his upstairs studio, where he was keeping all his specifications on the new building. He spread the map out on his drawing board and leaned over it, examining the city center, block by block.

It was impossible. There was simply no room for a structure that big within the Loop, or among the new high-rises that had been built on the periphery of downtown. Certainly there was no place for it along the North Michigan Avenue corridor, or in Streeterville to the east or in the Gold Coast to the north.

Where then? In the newly gentrified River North section next to the Michigan Avenue corridor? The building would obliterate acres of art galleries and studios, chic restaurants and boutiques. It would ruin a reclaimed neighborhood that had given the city considerable pleasure and pride. The mayor wouldn't stand for it. And the real estate would cost Poe a fortune.

Matthias sat back in his swivel chair, pondering the map as he might the actual city from an aircraft. Yeats had sounded extremely confident. Poe must feel the same. But why?

He went downstairs and made himself a drink. His aerial painting of the building was still propped up on a bookcase. It almost seemed a living thing—haunting him, taunting him.

His long-silent telephone now rang. He thought it must be Poe, that Yeats had quickly reached him.

It was Diandra.

"Matthias? You called here for Peter. The housekeeper just told me."

"Yes."

"What were you going to say to him?"

"It was about the building. There's an article in the *Tribune*."

"Matt, I need to talk to you."

"Do you think that's wise?"

"I don't give a damn. Peter's in New York. He'll be there all week, bragging about his building on television shows."

"I can't go to your place."

"No. And I shouldn't go to yours. But we have to meet. I need to see you—in person."

He had an overpowering need for that himself. "Does he have you chained to the furniture?"

"He's left me perfectly alone. Free to do what I please. He doesn't even talk to me. It's creepy. I begin to wish he'd rant and rave, that he'd do something. I don't know what he's thinking."

"I have an idea," he said. "Let's go sailing."

"Sailing. Isn't that a little frivolous, under the circumstances?"

"We'll be alone."

She thought upon it. "All right. I'll change clothes."

"Meet me on the embankment of the Monroe Street harbor, by Buckingham Fountain. In an hour. I'll tie up there."

She reached the rendezvous before he did. Sailing the *Hillary* across the harbor from the rental dock, he saw Diandra's tall figure standing on the edge of the shore, her hair blowing out behind her in the breeze. She was dressed in white shorts and Reeboks and a navy-blue top, looking marvelous. Easing the sailboat off the easterly wind to glide obliquely toward the embankment, he glanced about at the people in the park. No one seemed to be watching her.

After getting aboard, one hand to the rail, she leaned close and kissed him, quickly but warmly.

"Do you get the message?"

"I think so. I hope so."

"Know so."

She gave him a small smile, then seated herself forward, allowing him room to work the boat. With the wind out of the east, he had to tack back and forth almost constantly to clear the many craft moored in the harbor and beat his way to the opening in the breakwater.

Once past it, turning abeam to the wind, he could sail up and down the lakefront on the same point of sail. He headed south, motioning Diandra to move nearer. He put his arm around her. The flesh of her back was warm beneath her thin blouse.

"You wanted to talk," he said.

"First tell me what you were going to say to Peter."

"There's a column in the *Tribune* today. It says his backers won't let him put up the building on Cabrini Green. It made it sound as if there never will be a Poe tower in Chicago."

"Don't think that for a moment. If there was anything like that in the wind, I'd have known it. Peter would have shot himself. He's obsessed with the building, Matt. It's as if nothing else he's done in his life matters any more."

"But where's it to go?"

"It's a big city."

"Cities get very small when you start looking for desirable real estate. Most of Chicago's is along the lake, and that's overbuilt as it is."

"He must have someplace in mind."

"I'm going to sail down past McCormick Place," he said, referring to the huge, rectangular exhibition hall that sat like a beached aircraft carrier just to the south of Meigs Field. "Something occurred to me. There's some open space over and around the railroad tracks behind Burnham Park and the lakefront. It would cost a lot, if they agreed to cede the air rights, but it could be done."

"Not a very prestigious address."

"Neither was Cabrini Green. The idea is to make it one. And it's a lot closer to the Loop."

She stretched her long legs out over the centerboard housing. "I'm not sure what he has in mind."

"Let's take a look down there anyway."

Though it was not a business day, Meigs was busy with small aircraft. A single-engined Cessna entered the landing pattern overhead at such a low altitude it seemed they could reach up and touch it.

"The day is so beautiful," she said, once the plane's noise had abated. "You and I haven't had many of those, lately."

"What did you want to say to me?" he asked.

She took his hand in both of hers. "I don't have a lot to say. I love you. I don't want to spend the rest of my life with him. I want to spend it with you. I've been miserable these last few days."

"You'd really leave him?"

"Matthias, if you and I just kept on sailing toward the horizon now and never came back, I'd be perfectly happy."

She released his hand.

"But it would be better if you finished the building project," she said.

"What do you mean?"

"He's not going to just let me go—'Good-bye, Diandra; have a nice life.' He'll want to bargain, cut a deal. He does that with everything. It's in his rotten nature. If we were both to walk out on him, just like that—he'd go crazy. He can make it hard for us, Matt. He has a long reach. You could end up being very sorry you ever met me."

"But the building will take at least two years. We can't go on like this, not for two years. Not for another goddamn day."

"I'm not talking about me staying with him. But if something could be arranged—if he thought he was having his way." She turned to him, her knees touching his. "It would make a world of difference for you, getting this building up. You've been drifting through your life—not very happily, as far as I can tell. Now you've got hold of something. You've found yourself. You're an architect, a wonderful architect. With this building, you'd be one of the most important architects in the world. I don't want you to throw that away—not just for me."

He adjusted the tiller. The drift was taking them too close to the seawall that bordered the airport.

"I want to be with you no matter what," she said, "but please think hard about this."

336

"I haven't heard a word from him since I so disgracefully departed your premises."

"He'll want to talk to you when he gets back from New York. I've no doubt about that."

"And in the meantime?"

She took his hand and placed it on the inside of her thigh. "We have several days of meantime, don't we?"

There was a distant clatter coming from the southeast, the sound more insistent and intrusive than the dull buzz of the airplanes. Matthias looked in its direction. There was a speck in the sky, growing larger.

"Helicopter," he said. "A big one."

She turned to watch. As it came nearer, bright in the light of the high western sun, they could see it was red.

"It's one of Peter's," she said, "coming in from Michigan City."

"Are you sure?"

"Who else has helicopters painted like fire engines? Not even the fire department."

"Everywhere you look, Peter Poe."

"Don't worry. He's not aboard. He called our housekeeper from New York this morning. This is one of his big shuttles. They ferry the gamblers back and forth from the casino. The rich ones, anyway. The winners. The others take the bus."

The thudding chatter became a din. The big machine—a huge white "P" painted on the side—cast them in shadow as it thundered overhead, turning toward the airport. The runway was clear and there was no traffic in the pattern. The helicopter was going straight in, descending rapidly for a landing on the apron in front of the terminal building.

Mango watched the approaching helicopter from the bridge wing of the *Queen P,* which was moored in the harbor just behind the airport. She had thought of taking the big motor yacht out onto the lake, where she'd have a clearer view, but it would stick out like the fucking *Queen Elizabeth* on the open water. She hated operating the big tub on her own, anyway, no matter how much of a thrill that seemed to give Peter, and it wouldn't do to have crew members aboard.

She'd given them the whole week off, for as long as Poe was in New York. They'd had little to do that summer anyway. Peter was so distracted by his big project, he hadn't thrown a single party aboard the boat—and that was the ostensible reason for buying the oversize craft in the first place. The crew was grateful for the liberty, but seemed suspicious—especially the captain. Maybe they were worried this might be a harbinger of being laid off. There were a lot of rumors going around among Poe's army of employees about his financial state.

The hell with them. She'd explained that she'd wanted privacy to do some work for Poe—true, enough. They'd done as they were told. They damn well knew that if she wasn't *the* boss, she usually spoke for him.

Mango knew for certain Bobby Mann was on the chopper. She'd called him in the morning, to confirm that the way was still clear for their cozy get-together, and then called again at the scheduled departure time of the chopper shuttle—just missing him, as the man at the casino helipad had put it.

She wasn't missing him.

After pausing to take a sip of her drink and a last drag of her cigarette, Mango picked up the little black box she'd set on the navigation console, amused at how much it looked like the controller of those remote control cars that kids played with. The outfit guy in Chicago who'd set this up for her had explained its operation. Simple enough. You aimed the antenna, activated the device with the metal switch, and, when the light turned green, pushed the red button. He said it would work within a mile range, and she figured it wasn't as much as half a mile to the terminal building.

The trick would be in the timing. The idea wasn't to blow up the whole damned chopper, as Bobby's people had so clumsily tried with Poe's boat. The explosive charge was very small and had been placed in the main rotor housing. When the charge went off, the rotor blade was supposed to come flying off the machine, leaving it to screw a big hole in the ground. The helicopter had to be high enough off the ground to give its passengers more than a bad bump, but at the same time she had to make sure it was over the runway, and not just open water. It had to impact on airport property and do as much damage as possible. Gauging that would be hard at this distance, but she was concentrating. The man said the puff of smoke and flame at the rotor head would be barely noticeable. People might take it for an engine backfire.

Mango clicked the switch and smiled when the green light

came on almost immediately. She had the antenna leveled at the point in the sky where the chopper was changing from a small speck to a big red blob. She glanced down at the dock. There were a few people there, but no one was looking at her. What was she? Just a woman trying to work a portable radio.

The red blob became more defined. She could even see the flare of reflected sunlight on the pilots' window. It would probably help to have the sun in their eyes.

The aircraft came toward the airport at an oblique angle, turning midway along the runway and seeming to pause, though it was coming right at the terminal. She watched it descend, counting to herself, remembering how long it took Peter to make a landing with this kind of approach in his private chopper. When the machine was about four or five stories above the terminal roof, she hit the button.

At first, nothing seemed to happen, but then the helicopter suddenly darted down, a long black shape spinning crazily off to the side above it. Mango reached for her drink.

Matthias had the sail out at a beam reach, and they could see past it to where the helicopter was heading for its landing. There was a *pop,* barely audible above the sound of the turbo engine, but Matthias thought nothing of it. Then at once he grabbed Diandra's arm, gripping her tightly. The aircraft was plummeting, lunging forward as it fell, colliding with a great crash against the terminal's huge floor-to-ceiling windows and bursting inside, exploding in a monstrous ball of crimson and orange flame. The wreckage carried far. In a moment, a thick, boiling, oily cloud of smoke rose from the other side of the building.

Diandra was in his arms, holding him tightly, saying the same thing over and over: "Oh, God, oh, God, oh, God."

When Zany had become a suit assigned to Area Six Burglary, the old-timers liked to tell him about how cop work was done in the days before the reformers had taken over the department. There'd been a six-foot-six mustache Pete of a patrolman over on the West Side who'd killed eight people in the line of duty and carried a sawed-off, pistol-grip shotgun in his belt that he reprehensibly referred to as his "nigger chaser." A homicide dick down in the Central District was called "Yellow Pages" because of his penchant for extracting confessions from suspects during interrogations by coming up on them from behind and whacking them on the top of the head with a telephone book. It compressed the vertebrae in a very painful way but left no mark.

A more contemporary legend had to do with two veteran burglary detectives who set out to nail some perps who were among the most sought after felons in the department case files, even though they'd never shed a drop of blood.

Vietnam was in full swing then and body bags were coming back to Chicago in regular succession. The papers ran funeral notices for them, noting that the deceased had died in the war. Nothing like a funeral to get an entire family out of the house. When the bereaved were off at the memorial service, the burglars would hit the residence, having an easy time of it because the neighbors usually went to the funeral, too—as was to be expected with kids from the block getting wasted in the war. The bad guys chose their marks carefully, going for addresses in solid, respectable neighborhoods.

When they'd ripped off half a dozen houses this way, the two detectives decided to put a stop to it for good. Using the house of one of their brothers-in-law, they placed a phony notice in the paper, giving the brother-in-law's address as that of the deceased's. As the family, looking suitably mournful, went out the front and got into their cars, the two detectives came in the back and, with the house lights out and two big service revolvers cradled in their laps, took seats in the living room and waited for company.

The perps showed up right on schedule. When the homicide guys arrived on the scene in response to the subsequent "gunshots—men down" call, they found both burglars lying just inside the vestibule, each with big holes in him. The two detectives claimed they were fired on first. The perps had guns, but no bullet hole or anything was found in the walls. The investigators from Internal briefly looked into the matter, but nothing was ever done about it. No one wanted to hassle the detectives about it. You didn't prey on people in mourning. Not during a war. Not in a family town like Chicago.

Zany had been happy he'd joined the department in modern, more enlightened times, but now he found himself thinking about those two long-ago detectives real hard. He was sitting in an armchair in his darkened living room, holding his own service revolver in his hand. The front door was locked, and he'd set a wastebasket full of empty beer cans up against it. The back door was double-locked with a deadbolt, and all the downstairs windows were shut tight and locked as well—except for one, the living-room window he'd been sitting there staring at for more than an hour.

The mysterious people who'd been after him about the paintings had stepped up their efforts, making threatening phone calls at all hours, and one night firing off a shot through a window that had almost taken out his computer. He figured they wouldn't try to kill him until they got their hands on the canvas. They'd already broken into his car, to make sure he didn't have the painting in the trunk they'd put a bullet through. But folks were known to change their minds—especially when they began to lose patience—and Zany didn't want to take any chances.

He'd asked George Hejmal for some protection, and such was promised, but Zany knew from his own experience as police chief what that would mean with such a small force—hourly drive-bys, the occasional window check.

So he'd decided on his ruse. There was a bar four blocks away on the main street that he'd from time to time patronized in the past. With Judy off in Wyoming, he'd taken to making nightly visits. He did this for real at first, but this week turned to using the place for subterfuge. He'd drive over, parking his car prominently in front, have a beer or two, then get up to go to the men's room, slipping out the back, returning to his unlit house to sit until near the tavern's closing time.

He'd clued the bartender in to what he was doing. The bar was crowded in the summer, and no one seemed to notice his sudden absences. If someone did say something about it, he could always make out that he was courting a lady on the sneak. He had no doubt local gossip was running in that direction anyway.

Zany had never fired a gun at a human being. He'd killed a deer once in Wyoming, as a teenager, hunting, and regretted it forever after—the death in the poor animal's eyes haunting him still.

But there'd been death in the eyes of the girl on that boat, and fear in the eyes of the 7-Eleven clerks and the priest. And Judy's. Enough was enough.

Unlike the two old-time burglary detectives, he wasn't planning on whacking these bastards. He just wanted to lay hands on a live human being who might be able to tell him just what in the hell was going on—and testify to it in court.

The sky was overcast that night, shutting out the moon that had been providing romantic enhancement for the boys and girls down on the beach for much of the week. Tired of sitting in the shadows doing nothing, Zany had fetched himself a couple of beers. It was a mistake. Now he had to go to the bathroom.

But he didn't budge. They were coming. They had had their way with the little beach town all right, but that didn't mean they weren't klutzes. He heard their car or van pass slowly, then, a few minutes later, come by again—same engine sound, same slow drive-by.

Zany sat up straighter in the chair, getting a tighter grip on the pistol and resting it on his knee, pointed at the window screen. He'd rigged up a hand switch that connected via an extension cord to the lamp in the far corner. It would keep him in shadow but light the intruders up bright and clear.

The first noises came at the back door, a muffled rattle of the lock. He feared they might break the glass or otherwise bust their way in, compelling him to make a quick change in tactics, but they proved more subtle than that.

Now there was more noise along the side of the house. Then, at long last, came the creak of a floorboard on the porch. A long silence followed, after which he heard a long, ripping scrape. They were cutting the window screen. Garden-variety burglars. Zany had caught a hundred cases with entry like that.

He raised the pistol. There were more ripping, cutting sounds, then the first of them lifted the severed screen and stepped inside. He looked around a moment, listening, then turned to help the other. When both were inside and standing—in the process crossing a legal threshold as concerned lawful home protection shootings—Zany hit the light.

"Don't you motherfuckers move!" he shouted.

He hoped the vehemence of his shout and words would freeze them, but instead they panicked. The black man of the pair went for something in his belt that Zany, as he squeezed his trigger, fervently hoped was a firearm.

Zany's bullet hit him in the lower chest, knocking him back against the window. The other guy started to leap to the side, going for his belt, too. This time Zany could see it was a gun.

He fired two shots, the last one going high, hitting the man in the head. He dropped like a piece of furniture.

The black man was moaning and crying, clutching his middle, profanities burbling and gurgling out of his mouth. Dogs were barking. Blood was spreading on the carpet.

Zany came just close enough to them to make sure they posed no further threat, then went to his phone.

"Grand Pier police," said Vaclav.

"Barbara, this is Zane. I've had a burglary at my house. There was gunplay. Two suspects hit. Get someone over here in a hurry. And get an ambulance."

George Hejmal pulled up in minutes, a patrolman with him—a young officer, who was a nice guy but something of a yo-yo. Looking at the two gunshot victims, he kept saying "God Almighty."

"Do you have an ambulance coming?" Zany asked. "The one guy's hurt pretty bad. I don't think the other's moving."

"Never gonna move again," Hejmal said.

"Well, watch them both good, anyway," Zany said. "I've got to take a leak." He put his hand to his stomach. Urination wasn't all he had to attend to in the bathroom.

When he returned, having flushed an odd mixture of used beer down the toilet and washed his perspiring face, he found the two policemen standing with their backs to the perps, staring at him.

"We won't need an ambulance, Zane," Hejmal said. "The black guy's expired."

"Shit," said Zany. "I was counting on that not happening. Do they have weapons?" He didn't want to take another look at the bodies.

"Yes, sir," said the young officer. "Two great big goddamn automatics."

"Don't touch anything," Zany said, going for his phone. "I'm calling in the State Police. I want these two individuals identified real good."

Hejmal glanced at the bodies, then back at Rawlings.

"We've got a problem here, Zane. You're just a civilian now, and you've shot and killed two men. I'm going to have to make out a report. I mean, hell, Zane, I think I'm supposed to take you in for questioning."

Zany shook his head. "You're not talking to a civilian, George." He reached into his back pocket and pulled out a shiny new leather case, dropping it open to reveal an even shinier silver badge. "You're talking to a deputy sheriff. I was sworn in three weeks ago."

"Why in hell didn't you tell me?"

"Didn't want Judy to find out."

"Well, I guess she will now."

POE CANCELLED HIS television interviews and took the next available flight back to Chicago. He had Mango get the word out to the newsies when he'd be arriving, and there was a mob of them at O'Hare. The airport manager turned an unoccupied waiting area over to them for an impromptu news conference.

Poe, eyeing the group warily, stepped to the microphones and made a brief statement relating his shock, grief, and concern for the victims' families. Then, directing his words to the television cameras, he made a detailed announcement. He was halting all helicopter operations at Meigs immediately and switching them to Midway instead. This was easy enough, as the city, at the request of the National Transportation Safety Board, had temporarily closed Meigs, but Poe said he meant his abandonment of the field to be for good.

Then he announced he was forming a committee to work for the permanent closure of Meigs and the transfer of the property to the Park District, noting that the city had informed the F.A.A. more than a year before that it was contemplating taking exactly that action.

Finally, he said, he would ask the Park District's approval to erect his ethnic museum complex not at Cabrini Green but on the Meigs Field site, which he said he hoped would be named Immigrant Park.

A reporter jumped in with a question. Weren't the museums a key part of his Cabrini Green complex? What did this mean for the rest of the project?

"Everything's changed. I don't know what I'm going to do now."

"You mean you're not going to go ahead with the world's tallest building?"

"I didn't say that."

"There are reports that you're running short of money."

"If you're talking about the piece in the *Trib,* it didn't say I was going broke. It said the Cabrini Green site might not produce as much revenue as we'd like. We might have to find another location."

"Like Meigs Field, Mr. Poe?"

Poe colored. "Look! I just told you! I don't know what I'm going to do yet! The first thing is to take care of the people who were injured in that crash. And the families. Then I want to make sure that no aircraft flies into Meigs Field again. This could have been a major disaster. There were boaters and picnickers and all kinds of people all around there. People have been telling me for a long time that Meigs should be closed. I didn't listen to them. Now I am. So should you. Loud and clear."

"Have you talked to the mayor about this?"

"Yes." It was true. Poe had called him as soon as he'd heard about the crash, though that was all they'd talked about in their brief conversation.

"You told him you wanted to put your building on Meigs Field?"

"No, damn it! I just said I thought Meigs should be closed, and all I'm saying now is that the museums should go there. The Field Museum is near there. So are the planetarium and the aquarium. It just makes good sense."

A news commentator from one of the TV stations was waving his hand. Poe recognized him before he could stop himself, wishing he hadn't.

"Mr. Poe, what would you say to those who might accuse you of exploiting this terrible tragedy to further your own agenda?"

Poe's voice got very deep. "You son of a bitch," he said, slowly, hoping this would make the newscast sound bite. "How can you be so damn cynical at a time like this? My employees were on that helicopter! People who have been with me for years! One of my closest associates, one of my closest friends, Bobby Mann, my casino manager, was killed. I could have been on that chopper. And you're accusing me of exploiting? For God's sake, I'm just trying to do what's right."

He wiped his eyes, stepping back. Yeats moved to the microphones.

"Mr. Poe has to leave now," he said. "He's going to the

hospital to meet with some of the survivors. Thank you for your time, ladies and gentlemen."

Poe and his entourage were already moving swiftly down the concourse.

Poe took only Mango with him in the limo. He trusted Krasowski with his life—for good reason—but put up the glass divider anyway.

"You're just hell on wheels, aren't you, Mango?"

She saw something in his eyes she hadn't expected. His grief was genuine. What the hell next?

"It was an accident, Peter. The rotor blade came off. That's what everybody's saying."

"Sixteen people on that chopper. Old ladies. Honeymooners. Three people killed in the terminal. Eleven in the hospital. A real slaughter this time, Mango."

She lighted a cigarette. "Can't take it back."

"I don't believe this."

"Had to be done, Peter. Bobby was fixing to have you taken out. He was scared you were going to kill him."

They were speeding along the Kennedy Expressway, Krasowski steering the big stretch—license plate "Poe 1"—in and out of the traffic.

"How do you know that?" Poe asked.

"He was making more phone calls again—to Philly. I decided the time had come to ice him. I got some help from our Chicago friends."

"You iced him and eighteen other people."

"Had to do it. Saved your life, Peter."

"And maybe got me involved in a murder rap. The worst fucking murder in Chicago history."

"An accident. There've been a lot worse airplane crashes. For God's sake, Peter, nobody's going to accuse you of blowing up your own helicopter. If they figure out what happened—and that could take them weeks, if they ever scrape together all the bits and pieces of metal—the first thing anyone will think is that somebody tried a hit on you, like with your boat."

"Wonderful."

"Don't be a wimp about this. You're ahead of the game now. You've just got to keep moving. Everything's lined up, right? Just like you wanted."

"Not the mayor."

"I don't think he knows what to do, what to think. But I'll bet he won't reopen that airport."

He rubbed his chin. "Any word from Inland Empire about some up front money yet?"

She shook her head. "Yeats said they're still waiting to hear from Tokyo. Mr. Yamaguchi is taking a real serious interest in this."

Two hundred million dollars was serious money, but Yamaguchi was worth billions. Poe wondered what it would be like to actually own a billion dollars, not owing a penny.

"So what's next?"

"Matthias Curland is waiting for you at the penthouse."

"Oh, boy."

"I told him to be there. Don't worry. He's the least of your problems. You just gotta lean on him hard now. The guy's a cream puff. Some fucking German. Cold as steel on the outside, but soft and gooey inside. He's not like his brother. Christian may be a high-society lush, but he's got guts."

"What about that Kirchner?"

"I'm afraid it's goners, Peter. I don't know what that dumb cop did with it, but if he was going to make serious trouble about it, we would have heard by now. Anyway, they can't touch you."

"They might get to Larry Train."

"They won't."

He wasn't going to ask what she meant by that.

"We took a couple of casualties in Michigan," she said. "Going after that painting. That hayhead cop got trigger-happy."

"Mango . . ."

"They were outside hires, remember, Peter? Nothing to worry about. Like those Purple Gang guys Capone used in the St. Valentine's Day Massacre."

He shook his head. "Now I'm Al Capone."

"You're sitting pretty, Peter. Lighten up."

Matthias was waiting in the penthouse living room. Poe was expecting a fight, but the architect seemed strangely calm, if darkly serious.

"Your wife is upstairs," he said coldly.

"You two have a tiring day?

347

"The helicopter crash made her sick."

"Me, too. I was just at the hospital. Those poor bastards. I need a drink. You want one?"

"No, thank you."

"You look like you need one. Brandy?"

"All right."

Poe returned with two snifters and a bottle of Courvoisier, then took a seat opposite Curland. They stared at each other—the mongoose and the cobra.

"Let's get to the bottom line, Matthias," Poe said, leaning forward, resting his arms on his knees. "I still want you to do my building. No matter what."

"What does that mean, 'no matter what'?"

"It means that I don't want anything to interfere with that. Not what's between you and Diandra, not anything."

"She wants to leave you."

"Maybe she does. But let's put that aside for the moment. There's been a change in plan. It'll be on the news, so I might as well tell you now. Because of the accident, I think Meigs Field is going to be closed. So I want to put the building up on Meigs."

The statement was a lob. Poe waited calmly for Curland's return shot, but he just sat there, though some of the color drained from his face.

"Solidarity Drive," Curland said finally. "The road that goes to Meigs is Solidarity Drive."

"I guess it is."

"You've been planning to put the building there from the beginning. You lied to me. You lied to everyone."

"You lied to yourself, Curland. Did you really think rich people would want to live at Cabrini Green? It was never a go. It was just a way to get things started. I don't understand how you could be so dumb not figure that out."

"If you're equating intelligence with dishonesty, I suppose I am dumb."

"Well, it's time to smarten up."

"And so I have. I want nothing more to do with you." Matthias got up.

"Sit down," Poe commanded. Matthias ignored him, heading for the door.

"If you ever want to see Diandra again, pal, you'd better freeze in your tracks."

Matthias halted. "Diandra has nothing to do with this," he said, turning.

"The hell she doesn't. Look, just hear me out. Then you can make your decision. All right? Five minutes?"

"I don't know what you could possibly have to say that would change my opinion of you and your plans for this building."

"You'd be amazed."

"I'm not even sure there's going to be a building, Mr. Poe. There was an article in the *Tribune* this morning that said your investors were backing out."

"There's going to be a building. And the investors aren't backing out, not if I put it up on the lakefront. That's the deal."

"Fine. Go get another architect. I'm not going to be part of construction on the shoreline."

"It's not a crime, pal. And you're already part of it." Poe rose, brandy snifter in hand. "Come with me, Matt. I want to show you something. Five minutes."

Reluctantly Matthias followed him out to the big windowed room that contained the tabletop mock-up of the city. Poe turned on the overhead spotlights. The model of Matthias's building, the mastlike tower painted a brilliant crimson, glittered brightly.

"This is how it's going to be, Matt. We'll have to move it out into the lake a little. Make an impoundment—devote as much of that peninsula as we can to park land, to please the tree and grass lovers, not to speak of the Park District. It will cost more money, but my Japanese friends have plenty of that."

"It's monstrous. It overwhelms Grant Park. It dominates the city. It's too big. It can't go there. The city has kept the lakefront open for more than a century. You can't come along and change that."

"That's bullshit. What do you have here? Lake Point Tower, right on the lake. What's this, overlooking Grant Park? The Standard Oil Building, over a hundred stories tall. What's this big fucking thing? McCormick Place. I'm not doing anything different than these developers did."

"You're putting up a wall between the downtown of Chicago and the lake. For God's sake, Poe, is your ego that big? If you need a new site, why not down here, over the Illinois Central tracks?"

"The tallest building in the world—the greatest building in the world—my building, is not going to go over any goddamn South Side railroad tracks. It goes here. Nowhere else."

"People died there today—in one of your helicopters. No one's going to let you put this up on their blood."

"Yes, they are. Everything's rolling."

"And so am I. Good night, Mr. Poe. I wish you'd move to another city."

Poe let him get as far as the doorway this time. "You want Diandra?"

"She wants to leave you. She's not your property. You can't stop her."

"Sure I can. You, too. Hear me out. I'm going to make you an offer."

Matthias stopped. Here it came, just as Diandra had predicted.

"I'm going to give you a choice, Curland. If you walk out of here and Diandra goes running after you, I'm going to make the both of you real fucking sorry you ever even heard my name. She won't get a penny. She signed a prenuptial agreement—ironclad. If she files for divorce, I'll contest it. I'll drag you both through the courts, and I've got a lot of friends on the bench. I'll give interviews to the newspapers, to the magazines, to TV—along with some fascinating snapshots I had taken. I'll give your society friends the biggest scandal they've had to giggle about in years. I'll go to the cops—and I've got a lot of friends with the cops—and tell them they ought to look into your relationship with that murdered girl, Jill Langley—how you were screwing her on the side and ditched her. How that might have something to do with her turning up dead in your sailboat. That'll get into the papers, too. Your name—your family's name—won't be worth shit when I'm through."

"You're despicable, Mr. Poe."

"And what are you? You fucked Diandra, a married woman. My wife. You cheated on your wife with Jill Langley."

"Will you stop this?"

"Shut up. That's not all. I'll also see to it that you never work as an architect again. I'll tell them all that you screwed up the design, that I had to get Cudahy, Brown to straighten it out, that you sold me a bill of goods about how it would work at Cabrini Green. That you were bilking me for money to pay off your family's debts."

He paused to sip his brandy, as if this were idle dinner table

350

conversation. "And that's just for starters, Curland. I'll think up lots more stuff. I'll put my secretary, Mango, on it. She's a real whiz at dreaming up ways to make people feel bad. You doubt that I'll do it?"

"Not for a moment."

"Your other choice is to play ball with me. If you do, I'll make you a happy man. You'll get full credit for the building. You'll be the most famous architect in the world. And you can have Diandra. She's damaged goods, as far as I'm concerned. But she's expensive, Mr. Curland. You'll need dough. I'm willing to settle a couple million on her—make it five million. When the building's done, you can go wherever you want. South of France? I'll get you a villa. I'll get you a new sailboat. You'll live happily ever after."

"You're so generous."

"My middle name. But you gotta play ball. There's something else."

"There's always something else with you."

"Not that much. Look, the building's a go. I've got everything lined up. The Meigs Field site will be a hard sell, but we can do it. The newspapers will be against it, but I can take some wind out of their sails—especially the *Tribune,* with the way they lobbied for McCormick Place back in the old days. The public will be for it—not the tree lovers, maybe, but the real people who live out in the neighborhoods. Especially the ethnic groups. I'm one of them, remember? I've got the votes in the City Council. I've already got what I need from the state legislature. I've got only two problems: I've got to sell the mayor on it, and I need a vote of approval from the Park District board."

Matthias was shaking his head.

"Hear me out, I said. You can help with the mayor—that stuff about an Eiffel Tower for Chicago. He likes that. You can also help with the Park District. I think I've got the votes, but it'll be close. A one-vote margin maybe. I think I can count on Cooperman. This is the only way he's going to get his Holocaust museum, but there's one other vote I absolutely have to count on."

"My father's."

"You got it."

"Mr. Poe. I'm afraid you can't even count on my father staying awake through a Park District board meeting."

"Yes I can, if you see to it."

"So that's it."

"That's it, Matt. A simple choice. You can have fame, riches, success, and the love of your life—if that's what she is—as your wife. Or you can have ruin, misery, poverty, disgrace, and more legal trouble than you ever dreamed of. And all I'm asking you to do is help me put up one of the man-made wonders of the world."

Matthias stared, first at Poe, then at the model on the table.

"Think about it hard," Poe said. "I'm pretty sure I can get Cooperman to call a meeting of the park board in the next couple of weeks. It's only authorization, but I need it to move ahead on the money end. I'll give you until then. I'll consider your father's vote your answer."

"I gave you my answer."

"No, you didn't. Two weeks, Matt. Whatever you're thinking now, you've got two weeks to think again."

"I want to talk to Diandra."

"Oh, no. No Diandra. Not until that vote."

"We'll see."

"Indeed we will."

Poe let Curland go to the elevator by himself. He was sure he had the guy hooked. He might run out the line a little, but Poe would reel him in soon enough. He sipped his brandy. The big building looked almost as magnificent on the table as it would out there on the lakefront.

Matthias walked home, but had dispelled little of the confusion in his mind by the time he got there. He turned his watercolor of the new building to the wall, paced his living room for several minutes, then turned the picture facing outward again.

It looked so wrong now—the great sailboat rising out of the slums of the Near North Side. It didn't belong there anymore. What was never intended to be couldn't be. His notion that such a grand, monumental creation could be erected in such place was a foolish mistake; his rendering, a wasted effort—like so many of his notions and efforts throughout his wasted, mistaken life. He'd been swindled, exploited; left empty, deflated, and despoiled—and he had no one to blame but himself. As Poe had said, he'd lied to himself. That was how men like Poe succeeded, persuading other people to lie to themselves.

Poe could go on with this without him. Cudahy, Brown would make changes, of course—add embellishments, corrupt the line, pervert the beauty to make it more commercial and profitable.

They might dispense with the sail altogether and simply put up the tower—a tower of their own conception. That was all Poe was really interested in—the height. He wanted to own the top. He wanted his name on it.

Matthias pondered the picture sadly, then began to reexamine it, putting the foreground and background out of his mind, imagining instead a pure field of blue.

Why not on the lake? If it was true that Chicago's long and devout belief in an open shoreline had kept the city from becoming another Cleveland or Milwaukee, there was no great danger of that happening now. No one would seize upon Poe's building as a precedent for establishing factories and glue works in Lincoln Park. No one could duplicate Poe's creation, his creation. There would never be another occasion for such a monstrous construction.

Or was that conceit? In the 1950s, who would have conceived of a Chicago spiked with all the monster towers it now possessed? Who would have envisioned the vast, hundred-mile sprawl of sterile suburbs? Ages hence, billions of people more, there might be a city full of monster buildings, reaching all around the lake. Whatever he and Poe might or might not do could ultimately be nothing more than an irrelevant footnote in the architecture books, like so many of Louis Sullivan's once-dazzling creations in the Loop.

Conceit, indeed. Goethe, his grandfather's hero, had called architecture "frozen music." It was something else, man's pitiful attempt at frozen time, at immortality.

What else had Goethe written? "The fate of the architect is the strangest of all. How often he expends his whole soul, his whole heart and passion, to produce buildings into which he himself may never enter."

Goethe. There was also Shelley: " 'My name is Ozymandias, king of kings: /Look on my works, ye Mighty, and despair!' /Nothing beside remains. Round the decay, /of that colossal wreck, boundless and bare, /The long and level sands stretch far away."

The wisdom of writers. Paltry stuff compared to the wisdom of the artist. Matthias had always thought that. Now he wondered.

He went to his study, not simply for the brandy decanter that was there. With Sally no longer a concern in his life, he'd put his print of Egon Schiele's whore back in its place.

The whore looked down at him now, recumbent and weary,

her nakedness worn like old, disheveled clothes. Why do you bother me? her pained and tired eyes said. You're looking for wisdom, and surely I have none for you. All I know is that life is pain and then there is death. If love is as far as we ever get from death, I've had love, every kind of love, and it isn't very far away at all. Don't bother me. Don't bother yourself. Have another drink, *liebchen.*

Matthias poured himself a half glass of brandy. He took a swallow, and then another.

Another pair of eyes were staring down on him, from another portrait. White hair. A large, gray mustache. Icy blue-gray eyes. People always remarked on the cold dignity of his grandfather in that picture. Now Matthias realized the true nature of the stern old gentleman's expression. It was scorn.

What could he do to please that long-dead man? What had he ever done that could?

He drank again from the brandy, his eyes fixed on the patriarch's. Then he set down his glass and went to the front closet, where he had left the rolled-up painting the Michigan policeman had brought him.

It was still there—Kirchner's ubiquitous woman in red with her garish, mocking smile; the stream of people rushing along the street toward a flaming horizon. It was almost the same painting as the one with which Jill had died, except that, in that one, Kirchner had them streaming toward a crimson tower.

Rolling up the picture, Matthias put on his jacket and went out the front door. The old Rolls started. He steered it west.

The museum office looked different from when he'd last seen it. Christian had been working there and had cleaned up thoroughly afterward, compulsively neatening everything. How had he left the vault?

It took Matthias awhile to find the right bin, but there it was. The wooden case opened easily to reveal the same woman in red, the same people, the same street.

He didn't bother putting it back. He went directly to the phone and called Zane Rawlings.

23

L<small>IEUTENANT</small> F<small>RANK</small> B<small>ALDESSARI</small> was having an easy morning. His section had caught only a couple of cases the night before. A homeless person, as they now called winos, had been found beaten to death in an alley near Old Town and the district coppers had reported an apparent suicide in a high-rise on Lincoln Park West—the victim a rich guy with a history of alcohol abuse and emotional problems, as they now described nut-case drunks. The mope had hanged himself from a hook in his closet with drapery cord. Divorced guy. No one home. Cleaning woman found the body. Close the book.

As neither case was in any way pressing, and everything was quiet on all other fronts, Baldessari took himself a long break—coffee, Marlboro, and idle thoughts.

But they were of a sunny day at the beach, which made him think of Zany Rawlings's little town across the lake, which reminded him of Zany's case, which brought him right back to his job. He'd shared his unit's amazement and amusement at the news that Zany Rawlings had popped a couple of perps out there in the dunes—in his capacity as a deputy sheriff, no less. Mulroney said he must have whacked the bastards by accident, while pulling out his revolver.

"Maybe old Zany mistook 'em for electric typewriters," another detective had said, recalling the enormous hole Rawlings had inadvertently put into one of those machines downstairs in burglary getting his weapon out of a drawer one night.

Baldessari had joined in the laughter, but his mind came back to the matter now with more seriousness. Zany had clocked the two in a burglary attempt on his house, which he said was related to stolen property involved in the Langley murder.

Which Zany had insisted was inextricably linked to a certain burglary and two homicides in Chicago, including what had been the number-one homicide case in the department, now closed. O'Rourke, Robert.

The lieutenant was not about to reopen that investigation and stir up downtown all over again. But a little look-see might be in order. The dead perps were a couple of out-of-town hired hands—last known addresses in Newark, New Jersey—but hired help had bosses, and Baldessari didn't want somebody else coming at his old friend. The dead guys had been carrying heavy-duty weaponry.

It occurred to Baldessari that maybe there was something he had passed over in his rush to get City Hall off his back, something that could help Zany work this out. If ever there was a cop who needed help at his job, it was old Zany.

He called for the case file.

Baldessari had finally done the professional thing about the prints taken from O'Rourke's station wagon. Run every one of them through the FBI computer out in Washington, just as Zany had asked, and those from the murdered hooker's apartment as well.

Those from the murdered blonde's apartment and the black chippie who got wasted with O'Rourke naturally enough produced arrest records—multiple busts for prostitution and soliciting. The set taken from beneath O'Rourke's car seat turned up a rap sheet, too. As they didn't match those of the dead blonde, Margaret Kozak, who everyone now agreed was O'Rourke's killer, Baldessari hadn't paid too much attention to them. The record attached to these mystery car seat prints had a name—Rose Scalzetti—and listed three busts, also for prostitution—two in Miami and one in Atlantic City. The lieutenant had attached no significance to the far remove. Hookers moved around. Miami, Atlantic City, Chicago, Vegas, Los Angeles. Some hookers stuck with their turf and pimps; others drifted around, always looking for a better score.

The only thing that really grabbed Baldessari about this was how the hell anyone could be arrested for turning tricks in Atlantic City. It was like getting pinched for double parking in New York.

Still, he thought he'd better check her out now. You never knew.

Rose Scalzetti. A nice Italian girl shouldn't have to be doing that kind of work.

He called in Mulroney.

"Get on the horn with the coppers in Atlantic City," he said. "I want to find out more about this lady."

Rawlings and Matthias Curland had phoned five art collectors who, according to the calculations of Zany's computer, were the most avid buyers of Ernst Kirchner works and German Expressionist art in the city. And they'd abruptly stopped buying art the previous year.

They got nowhere with four of them. Two had very good reasons indeed for so mysteriously halting their collecting. They'd gone Chapter 11. Two others were worried they might soon share such a fate.

The other collector on the "hot" list was in Philadelphia, and they were unable to get him on the phone. Matthias recognized the name, Herman Franck, noting that the man had once been associated with his grandfather. Franck was nowhere near Chapter 11. He was one of the richest men on the East Coast.

They decided to visit him in person. Matthias made the arrangements over the phone with Franck's butler, identifying himself as Karl Albrecht's grandson, and saying he had a painting to sell—discreetly. He said he'd bring it with him. The butler called back, saying Franck had agreed to see him.

Discreetly.

Franck was an older man, well into his seventies. He had been both a friend and a rival of Matthias's grandfather, having amassed one of the country's great collections of German and pre-World War I Russian Expressionists paintings. Unlike Karl Albrecht, he had freely loaned them to museums, and had talked to the Museum of Modern Art about making a gift to the institution of the larger part of them, provided they'd be installed permanently in a display chamber bearing his name. When the museum had balked at keeping them all on permanent view, he'd withdrawn his offer. He'd allowed the Philadelphia Museum of Art to stage a huge exhibition of all his holdings, declared it his last show, and then returned all the works to the galleries in his huge house out on the Philadelphia Main Line.

Franck had kept collecting, however. The previous summer, he'd paid a world record price for an Emil Nolde.

Then, the previous October, he'd ceased his acquisitions and even dismissed his New York agent. This had taken people quite by surprise. Franck had vowed to go to his grave with a greater collection than Albrecht's.

Though his computer had put Franck on the "hot" list, Zany had known nothing about the rivalry with Matthias's grandfather. If he had been aware of that, he would have gone to the old man first before bothering with all the other collectors.

They took a cab from the suburban railroad station. After being admitted to the house by the elderly butler, they were ushered into a library, and asked to wait.

"Makes your place in Chicago look like a shack," Zany said, eyeing the endless shelves of leather-bound books.

"No one should live like this anymore," Matthias said. "This house ought to be a museum. It probably will be someday."

Franck entered, moving haltingly, and made his way to a large mahogany desk without stopping to introduce himself or shake hands. With a gesture, he invited them to take chairs. Glancing at Zany with some disapproval, he turned to Matthias.

"I knew your grandfather well," he said.

"I know."

"I worked with him on the 'Save German Art' committee in the thirties, when I was in college. He was an opponent of the Nazis when many German Americans were cheering Hitler on. He contributed a great deal of money to get Jews out of Germany. Did you know that? A fine and considerable man, Karl Albrecht. Too bad he was so stupid and narrow-minded about art."

"He had his eccentricities," Matthias said.

"Locking all those wonderful paintings away like that. I no longer exhibit mine, as you may know, but I allow students and scholars to come and see them by appointment. Would you like to look at my collection?"

"Perhaps later," Matthias said.

The old man coughed. He had fewer years than Matthias's father, but seemed older. Too much time spent indoors.

"You said you had a painting for sale," Franck said. "A German Expressionist."

Matthias snapped open the big briefcase they had brought, but moved no further, letting Franck's eyes linger on the lid.

"You're not allowed to sell paintings from your museum," Franck said.

"That's correct. This one isn't part of my grandfather's collection. I came by it oddly."

"Well, let's see it."

"I'm told you have one of the most extensive collections of Ernst Kirchner paintings in the country."

"Possibly the world. Let me see it!"

Matthias still hesitated, letting the old man's eagerness and impatience build to the maximum. Much depended on how dramatically his expression changed—if it did at all.

Curland opened the lid, unrolled the painting, and held it up. "A very rare work, you'll agree," he said.

Franck looked as stunned as if Matthias had held up a blank piece of paper. His left hand began trembling. His pale-blue eyes blinked, uncomprehending. They had their man.

"That's *Street Scene, Leipzig,*" Franck said. "Completed in 1919."

An expert, indeed. Matthias nodded.

"It's part of your grandfather's collection. I can't buy that."

"But you ordered it, sir. Didn't you? From a collector in Chicago?"

The old man's face had gone pale, but now began to color. He coughed, continuing to do so in violent spasms. Zany was afraid he might keel over on them.

"Are you all right, Mr. Franck?"

"No." They all sat waiting for the coughing to subside.

"Mr. Curland," he said, "I'm afraid I have no business to conduct with you."

"On the contrary. I said this wasn't from my grandfather's museum. And it's not." He reached into the briefcase again, handing another rolled painting to Zany, who unfurled it and held it up.

"That's the *Street Scene, Leipzig* from my grandfather's vault," Matthias said. "The one I'm holding is a copy. A wonderful copy, don't you think? Done by a real expert. Only an art historian or a restoration technician could tell them apart."

Franck had now gone so pale it seemed to Zany someone had pulled a plug on his blood.

"But I have certificates of authentication," Franck sputtered.

"You have what? On these?"

"No. I know nothing about these paintings of yours. On my own. I never buy a painting unless it's examined by an expert and certified as authentic. That's true of every painting in my collection."

Matthias set the painting in his hands on the desk. Zany did the same.

"Let's put it this way, Mr. Franck," Rawlings said. "Suppose someone had an original Kirchner in his possession and agreed to sell it to you. Suppose he had a recognized expert examine it and make out an affidavit attesting to its authenticity, as you demanded. But suppose that, when it came time for shipment, he replaced the original with an excellent copy like this and sent it along with the certificate."

"Suppose he did this to you with a lot of paintings," Matthias said.

"You'd have a whole bunch of phonies on your hands and be out a lot of money, but you'd never know it," Zany said. "Unless a couple of guys turned up with evidence to prove it beyond a doubt. And we've checked. The paintings in the Albrecht vault, right now, as we speak, are authentic. Anything that might have been sold is guaranteed fake."

"Completely spurious, however perfect the likeness," Matthias said.

"Anyone who bought them has been had. A nice, neat con job."

Franck sank back into his chair, looking very small and frail. "My God," he said weakly.

Anger came into his face, strengthening him.

"Matthias Curland," he said. "Do you know who was a party to these sales?"

Matthias nodded gravely. "I'm afraid so."

"Your own brother. And you knew nothing about it?"

"I've been living in France, for several years."

"Who else was a party to these sales?" Zany said. "Who was the middleman?"

"I don't think I should say anything more," Franck said.

"Was it Laurence Train?"

The old man simply stared.

"There won't be any charges placed against you," Zany said. He pulled out his deputy's badge. "I say that with some authority. We'll presume you didn't know these were paintings covered by covenants of Karl Albrecht's will, that you bought them in good faith. As far as I'm concerned, you're not part of a criminal conspiracy. You're just the victim of an art swindle."

"Were you trying to buy another Kirchner this summer?"

Matthias said. 'A work called *The Red Tower*? A companion work to this one."

"Yes," said Franck, barely audible. "It was never delivered."

"Was there another party involved in these transactions?" Zany asked. "Besides Laurence Train?"

"Yes. Another collector. Someone I'd bought paintings from before."

"You want to tell us his name?"

"It's Peter Poe."

CHAPTER
24

WHEN THEY ARRIVED back at O'Hare, Rawlings went to collect their bags while Matthias hurried to a pay phone and called Poe's penthouse, trying once again to reach Diandra. He'd been calling her for several days, always with the same frustrating result. The housekeeper answered and said, "Mrs. Poe is not home," never telling him anything more.

This time, the phone rang unanswered.

Matthias rejoined Rawlings in the concourse. "No one home," he said. "I don't know where she is."

"We'll find her." Zany looked at his watch. "I've got to get over to Area Six and get the paperwork started on this case."

"Paperwork?"

"That's where you start."

"You didn't do paperwork before you shot those two men."

"That's a cheap shot, if you'll pardon the expression. They were in my house. With guns. We're going after some big people here. You start with warrants."

"Don't take too bloody long."

"Where are you going?"

"I want to find Christian. I'll start with the house in Lake Forest. I want to check on my father, too."

"What will you do when you find him?"

Matthias took a deep breath. He didn't want to lie. There'd been enough of that. "I'm going to tell him about our visit to Mr. Franck."

Zany scratched his head. "You know, Matt. What I have to do could take a real long time. They may want to go to a grand jury first. The Chicago cops will want to be real careful how they go about this, not to speak of the state's attorney, who—may I remind you—is a politician. If you tell your brother what's up now, he might get scarce before the authorities are ready to move."

"Christian told me he was planning to move to the Bahamas. I wish he'd already done that."

"I'm not sure what he'll be charged with. They might even offer him an out—unindicted coconspirator, or cop some kind of plea. It's Poe and Train who are the main bad guys."

"I'm not asking for any favors. I'll leave all that up to Christian. He knew the consequences of what he was doing. I just want to give him a chance to face up to them on his own."

"But I can count on you to go through with this with me, right?"

"All the damned way."

"Okay. I'll meet you back at your place as soon as I can. Don't go off and do something crazy. Wait for me."

The old Rolls-Royce was still in the O'Hare garage where Matthias had left it—too old, apparently, for anyone to want to steal. The engine started, but with some complaint, and made odd noises once he got it onto the expressway. He nursed it as best he could. It took much longer to reach Lake Forest than he had counted on.

Annelise was there, but Christian was not. A maid told Matthias he could find his sister upstairs, in the guest room Christian used when he stayed there.

"Matt!" his sister said as he came through the door. "Where have you been? I was just trying to reach you."

"I had to go out of town. Where's Christian?"

"He went off somewhere with Father. Look what I've found, Matt. All these paintings. None of them finished."

Matthias glanced at them. Half-finished copies. German Expressionists. A bloody factory going here. "Did he say where he was going with Father?"

"Downtown. There's an emergency meeting of the park board. Something like that. Christian said he'd drive him. Look at these things. I can't believe Christian did them. They're so ugly, like the paintings in the basement of the museum."

On one, a skull-like face in torment. Otto Dix. On another, a cruel-looking man in military uniform, his arms tightly holding a terrified, nearly nude woman. Ernst Kirchner.

"Throw them away," Matthias said. "How long ago did Christian and Father leave?"

"At least two hours. Is something wrong?"

"Yes, but I'll take care of it." He stepped forward and gave his sister a brief hug and a kiss on the cheek. "Nothing for you to worry about, Annelise. If Christian calls, tell him I want him to bring Father back here at once. And I'd appreciate it if you'd wait here until he does."

"What's the matter, Matt? What the hell's wrong?"

"Nothing. I just don't like Father attending these meetings. I don't like him being on the park board. I should have gotten him to resign his seat before I left."

"It's only a board meeting. All he has to do is sit there."

"There's more to it than that. I'll call you as soon as I can."

"Where are you going?"

"To the city. Please do as I say."

He thought he might yet get to the board meeting in time, to stop the vote, to extricate his father, but the old Rolls finally failed him. When he reached the off ramp from the Kennedy Expressway at Division Street, in full view of downtown Chicago, the engine commenced a continuous sputtering, then died. He coasted to a stop on the shoulder by the embankment wall, the exhaust belching oily smoke. A Volkswagen convertible full of teenagers rumbled by, its passengers laughing at him.

As well they might. By the time he walked to a gas station and got a tow, he'd lost half an hour. It was another twenty minutes before the cab he called came. He reached Park District headquarters just in time to find Poe and his secretary about to get into one of Poe's red limousines.

"Matthias," said Poe, surprised but looking cheerful. "I thought you were out of town."

"I came back, but not soon enough, apparently. Where's my father?"

"On his way home, with your brother. He sure as hell came in handy. We got it by just one vote."

"You bastard."

"Knock it off, Curland. What's wrong with you? We're all set. We're rolling. You're going to be the world's greatest architect."

People were streaming out of the building, some of them possibly reporters. Matthias didn't care. He felt in no way restrained. "You couldn't wait, could you? Ram everything through, no matter what."

"Wait? Why wait? Come on, Matthias. Everything's set. I meet with the mayor tomorrow morning, and then it's a go. I'd take you along, but the way you're acting, I don't think you'd be a lot of help."

"I'll see the mayor on my own, Mr. Poe. I'm going to stop you. You're not going to have your building. Not where you want it."

"What are you going to do, threaten to have your Republican friends vote against him?"

Matthias stepped close. He'd forgotten how much he towered over Poe. "I'm going to tell him he'll be doing business with a crook, Mr. Poe. A common thief."

"What the hell are you talking about?"

"An art thief, Mr. Poe. You and Larry Train and my brother, selling pictures from our museum."

"You're crazy. Go to your museum and take a look. I'll bet you there's not a fleck of paint missing."

"Art swindler, then."

"You're nuts. Now get out of my way. I'm a busy man." He started to push past.

"Herman Franck," Matthias said.

Poe stopped, worry in his look. "What about him? I sell him paintings. So what?"

"You've sold him fraudulent copies of pictures in our collection. I have a signed statement from him. I'm going to show it to the mayor."

Matthias now saw something in Poe's eyes he'd never encountered there before—fear.

"You'd sell out your own brother, because I want to put a building on the lakefront?"

The secretary had been staring at Matthias with icy fury from the moment he'd first spoken. Now she stepped between them, pushing close to Matthias, her eyes blazing, her lips curled back. "You're not going to the mayor, to the cops, to anyone y'understand? You're going to take that signed statement and shove it up your ass!"

The other people on the sidewalk had looked at them, but none had lingered within earshot. Matthias stepped back. Mango moved close again.

"Listen to me, Curland," she said. "You want Peter's wife, don't you? You're in love with that well-dressed set of bones, right? That's what you told Peter."

"She's leaving him."

"Not just yet she isn't, sweetheart. We've got her stashed, where you can't get to her. You say one word to anyone about this art shit and the next time you'll see her will be at her funeral. A little accident, y'know? A swim in Lake Michigan with no place to go. People swell up in the water. They swell up like sausages. That's how she'll look next time you see her. I mean it. That's what'll happen."

Matthias stared at her. He had never looked into such a hateful face in his life. Only in paintings.

"You think I'm bullshitting? Think about that helicopter that went down at Meigs. Think about Park District Chairman O'Rourke. Think about the bomb that went off in your boat."

Matthias turned to Poe. "Your own wife? You'd let this happen?"

"Listen to her, Curland. She means business."

"You get out of this town, Curland," Mango said. "You be outa here tomorrow. And you don't say anything to anyone about nothing!"

"And Diandra?" He was ashamed at how rattled he must seem.

"Play ball, and she'll be all right," Poe said, his confidence returning. "I guarantee it."

"If you don't, you'll find her with the fishes," Mango said. "And I guarantee that."

"First thing you do," said Poe, "you hand over that fucking statement."

"I don't have it," Matthias said. "I left it with someone for safekeeping."

"Get it back," Poe said. "I want you at my penthouse with it in your hand tonight."

"It may take longer."

"Tonight."

"It could take all night, damn it! I don't know where this person is at the moment."

"All right. I'll give you till tomorrow morning. I'm not a hard guy to get along with. You be at my place with that thing by the time I come back from meeting with the mayor. Say, ten o'clock. Then we'll work it out about Diandra."

Matthias wondered why Poe was being so generous. Was he going to use the time to try to get to Franck?

"Don't fuck this up, Curland," Mango said. "Death's a long time."

He stood there motionless, watching helplessly as they got into the rear of the limousine. Mango made an obscene gesture as the long car roared away from the curb.

"They've all got to go, Peter," Mango said, as they turned up Michigan Avenue. "Train, Curland, all of them."

"No, Mango."

"And you have to do something about your wife."

"Diandra doesn't know anything." Poe was pouring himself a big drink.

"How can you be so sure? She was screwing him, wasn't she?"

"No more of this. Not now."

"Now's when it counts."

"I mean it. All they have is the word of that old fossil in Philadelphia. I can talk him out of it. Buy back the paintings. Something. And anyway, I've got friends in the courts. This'll go nowhere."

"You're wrong, Peter. This could go to the mayor's office. He's not exactly a sure thing, you know. Anything could turn him the other way."

"More murders sure would."

Mango stretched out her legs. She was staring forward, thinking.

Poe drank, then added more whiskey to his glass.

"Did you have to tell Curland about all those killings?" he said.

"He got the message, didn't he?"

"You left out the Langley girl. How come?"

She gave him a weird smile. "That wouldn't have been honest, Peter. I didn't lift a finger against that little bitch."

"Who did?"

"One of Train's friends maybe."

"I'm not looking forward to this thing with the mayor tomorrow. It won't be like cutting another deal. I've nothing to offer him. I'll just be begging."

"Buck up, Peter. Play your hand. It's a good one. In fact, I just thought up a new hole card for you. What were you planning to do with that Cabrini Green land of yours?"

"Sell it. Maybe put up some townhouses."

"I've got a better idea. You're going to give it away."

"Oh, yeah? Who to?"

"To a worthy charity. To the mother church. I think you ought to go calling on the cardinal tonight."

"The cardinal?"

"The mayor's a very religious guy, Peter. What do you want with a bunch of slum property anyway?"

Matthias took a cab and went directly to his Schiller Street house. He hoped somehow Christian and his father might have gone there, but the residence was empty. He hurriedly called Annelise. Without offering any useful explanation, he told her to take their father to her place in Barrington as soon as he arrived, and to keep him there indefinitely.

"And have Christian call me immediately."

"Won't you please tell me what this is all about? You have me frightened."

"It's all very complicated. All you have to know is that I've taken on Peter Poe."

"What does that mean?"

"It means that I want you to do as I ask. Trust me, Annelise, please. It's all for the family."

"All right, Matt. Call me tonight. Please."

"As soon as I can."

It took him awhile to track down Rawlings through the Chicago Police Department phone system, but he finally got transferred to the burglary section and Zany was summoned to the phone.

"They had a meeting of the Park District board today," Matthias said. "My car broke down and I got there too late to stop things. They voted Poe's way—thanks to my father."

"There's still time. He's not putting up that building tomorrow."

"I caught up with Poe on the street, Zane. He made a threat. If I don't drop this and give Franck's statement to him and get out of town, he'll have Diandra killed. He has her hidden away somewhere. I'm to meet with him tomorrow morning."

"His wife?"

"That Mango woman made the threat. She talked about some other murders—O'Rourke, the people in the helicopter."

"This is playing kinda rough for a civic-minded businessman."

"I believe them, Zane. I don't doubt this for a minute."

There was a long silence on the other end. "Son of a bitch," Zany said finally.

"I wasn't to go to the police."

"Well, it's sure as hell too late for that. I've already talked to my friends in burglary and some guys in homicide. Things are rolling."

"God."

"Maybe we can figure out a way to stall Poe."

"He's going to kill her, Zane. Make it look like a drowning accident. That's what that Mango woman said. 'She'll be with the fishes.' Those were her words."

"That must mean they have her on a boat. Probably that big motor yacht of his. Ought to be easy enough to find."

"We have to do something. Quick."

"I'll call the Coast Guard. It'll be awhile before I can get out of here. They're kicking this up to the top brass. I can't just walk out on them."

"Zane, I said he threatened to kill her!"

"I understand. You have until tomorrow morning, you said."

"I'm to go to his penthouse with what he wants and wait until after he gets back from meeting with the mayor."

"Are you at your house?"

"Yes."

"Well, sit tight until I get there. I'm doing everything I can."

"Zane, remember what you said about your wife? How you almost dropped this case because you were afraid for her?"

"Yes."

"That's how I feel about Diandra. Only if I'd been you, I would have dropped the case."

Matthias watched the minutes pass by on the mantel clock in his living room until they accumulated to an hour, then two. He accepted this ridiculous waste of time at first. Rawlings was a longtime policeman. He had to trust the man as Zane had trusted him. But the minute hand kept moving, well into the third hour. Matthias became worried, then frantic. Diandra could be dead.

Annelise called to say his father was safe at her house. Matthias tried to reach Franck in Philadelphia, but the old man wouldn't come to the phone. He left a message that he was not to be disturbed with the butler, who treated Matthias as if he were selling magazine subscriptions.

He tried to reach Rawlings at Area Six burglary again, but was told Zany had gone downtown with two other detectives. Matthias started to phone Poe's penthouse, with no clear sense of what he would say, then hung up. All Poe would want to hear from him was that he had Franck's statement—and Rawlings had that. The Chicago police had that.

At last he heard someone at his door, a rattling sound. What in hell was Rawlings doing, picking the lock?

To his amazement, it was Christian. He staggered into the foyer, lurched against the doorway, then took a few unsteady steps into the living room. He stood swaying, his eyes wild. He was as drunk as Matthias had ever seen him. How had he accomplished this in so short a time? Had he been drinking all day again? Had he gone to the Park District meeting like this?

There was a bottle of vodka in his hand—almost empty.

"Goddamn you!" Matthias bellowed, all his fury boiling forth. "You sold us out! You used Father like a bloody puppet. I could kill you for what you've done."

"Probably should, big brother. Probably should. But it's much too late for that." He collapsed into a chair.

"We know about the paintings, Christian. We talked to Herman Franck."

"So I've been informed. My smarter, older brother. Too smart for his own good. Ruined everything. Ruin, ruin, all is ruin."

"I know everything. And so do the police."

"My high-and-mighty brother. Always doing the right thing."

"You ought to rot in jail, Christian. But you can probably avoid that. If you get out of town now. Out of the country. And never come back. My God, you can barely walk. Did you drink all that vodka driving back down here?"

Christian waved the bottle at him, then drank again. "Know everything, big brother? You don't know everything."

He became oddly calm, glancing about the paintings on the walls of the room, then settling his unfocused eyes on Matthias, as best he could.

"Do you want to know who murdered Jill, Matthias? Who shot her through the back and left her like a piece of garbage? Well, you should know. You loved her. She loved you. You have to know. You might as well, since everything's finished. All gone. *Alles kaput.*"

He sat up, then leaned forward, staring down at the floor, his dark hair falling over his face. "I killed her, Matt. I shot her. I listened to her screams. Right there in your boat, out in the middle of the goddamned lake."

Matthias went numb. He sat paralyzed, unable even to speak.

Christian was weeping. He wiped his eyes, trying to regain control of himself. He pushed himself back erect in the chair. Another big swallow of vodka.

Matthias sat and waited. He had to hear every word.

"You'll never understand, big brother, but it was all for the family. For the goddamned family. We were going broke fast, Matt. Headed for the junk heap. I started going out to Poe's casino. Had to get some money somehow. Won a little, at first. A lot, actually—first few times. Then I started losing. Got terribly behind. Poe cut me off when my debt went over a hundred thousand. Didn't know what to do. Bloody desperate. You've no idea. How could you, indulging yourself on the Côte d'Azur. Expatriate painter. Selfish bastard."

He closed his eyes, then opened them again. His face had become a macabre mask.

"I had this brilliant idea. Way to get out of the hole. Take a painting from the vault. Make a copy. Put the copy in the vault. Sell the painting on the black market. You'd never look in the vault. In all those years we almost never went down there. Never disturbed anything. And if you did take a look, there'd be the copy. Damn fine copy. You'd never notice the difference. Smart fellow, I am. Almost as smart as you."

He put his hand to his eyes again. "I went to Larry Train. Poor old Larry. Totally unscrupulous, but a dear fellow in his way. I knew he'd traded under the table. Sold fakes. Sold stolen paintings. He liked my idea—thought I was quite clever.

"But then I thought about it. I felt guilty. You don't think I have a moral bone in my body, but I couldn't bring myself to do it. Couldn't sell the original. Grandfather's legacy. All we have left. Grandfather's hand on me, reaching from the grave. So I tried to back out. But Larry would have none of it. He came up with this scheme. Use the original to get a statement of authentication, then make a switch and send the buyer the copy. It was so good, you couldn't tell the difference. But he wanted to use a third party to sell it, another collector, someone who'd been selling things under the table to avoid paying taxes." He sighed. "Unfortunately, that someone turned out to be Peter Poe."

Christian looked up at Matthias wearily.

"You killed Jill? This isn't just drunken raving?"

"I killed her." The words came out like heavy, rolling stones.

"How could you do that? I can't believe it."

"Hear my mournful tale, big brother. I'm only going to tell it once."

"There's a policeman on his way here. I want you to tell him."

"Oh, no. No policeman. Just family. Just you."

Christian seemed on the verge of passing out. Matthias fervently hoped he would. Then they could just take him away. Lock him up in a prison hospital ward—the mental ward. Christian had to have lost his mind. There was no other explanation.

"Larry's scheme worked brilliantly," Christian said. "The buyer—Herman Franck—bought the fake and never questioned it. I'm that good, Matthias. That damned good. Master forger. He wanted more paintings. Poe found a couple of other buyers. I did a lot of copies. Poe made a lot of money. My fees were very generous. I paid off my gambling debts, the family's debts—a lot of them, anyway. Gambling. That's how I was paid. I'd give the copies to Train as fast as I could turn them out and then went out to Michigan City and won big at the tables. Every time. All wonderfully neat. No one ever questioned anything."

More vodka. The bottle had little left.

"But Jill got suspicious. She was a very bright young lady, as you always said. I spent too much time at the museum. Went down too often to the vault. She began asking me about it. Followed me down there once. I had to get her out of the museum.

"I couldn't fire her. She'd just complain to you, and then you might come back. I told her you were still in love with her. Offered her money to go to you in France. At once. But she wrote you instead. And you refused her. Upset her terribly. She was terribly angry, terribly sad.

"But that worked out. She became quite miserable, working there in the museum. Everything reminded her of you. I had Larry offer her this fabulous salary to come to work for him. She accepted."

Now the bottle was empty.

"But it was a stupid idea, as Poe said. Larry came to the museum a lot. Packages arrived at the gallery from me. She became as suspicious of him as she was of me. I half wonder if she didn't take the gallery job just to find out what was going on."

He looked down at his hands. "And, eventually, she did."

"And so you killed her?"

"Poe's secretary," Christian said. "Mango. Ridiculous name. Extraordinary woman. She took a liking to me. It got to be more than that. I went to bed with her. I thought she could help me. Keep me out of trouble with Poe. But it became more than that. When Poe was away, we'd go to his boat. Pretending it was business, don't you know. That's where Train had the paintings delivered.

"He had one in a crate with some others at the gallery, all marked and ready for Poe. Jill took it to the boat. She opened it for some reason. Maybe it came undone. Pandora's box, yes? She opened it. She recognized the painting.

"Jill didn't know Mango and I were aboard. She went through the cabins—I guess looking for more paintings. I don't know. She found us together. In bed. I threw on some clothes and went after her. Chased her across the docks. But she made it to your boat. Got away. Out into the lake. She had the painting. A copy of a Kirchner. It seemed like the end of the world to me. She knew about the painting scheme. She knew about Mango and me. It would all come out. I didn't know what Poe might do. Kill us?

"It was Mango's idea to go after Jill in the big yacht. There was nothing else we could do. There was no crew aboard. Mango took it out herself. Amazing woman. I couldn't pilot that big boat. You probably couldn't either.

"Took awhile to find her. Tried to get her to heave to. Mango tried to run her down, but Jill was too good a sailor. Finally, we got alongside her. Mango gave me this gun. I'd been drinking a lot. I only meant to frighten her. I didn't know what we were going to do with her, but I didn't want to kill her. But she began screaming at me. And Mango was screaming at me. There was a helicopter out there. Thought it was coming toward us. I panicked, Matt. I went crazy. Had to stop the screaming. Had to stop Jill. Had to stop everything that was happening."

He began sobbing, showing no sign of lapsing into unconsciousness. "And I never found the painting. I looked all over the boat. She had it under her blouse, didn't she? Never thought to look there. Didn't want to touch her body. She was, she was still alive."

More crying. Matthias stood up. He had to keep Christian there, but how? Hit him? He was so full of rage he probably would kill his brother if he picked up a weapon. The fireplace poker was close at hand.

"You need another drink," Matthias said.

"Yes."

"I'll bring a bottle."

"Please."

He hurried to the kitchen. The gin bottle on the counter had less than an inch in the bottom. There was a case of liquor in the pantry. Matthias went to it, retrieving a liter of vodka.

When he returned to the living room, Christian was standing. He'd gone into the study and now had the revolver in his hand.

"What are you doing?" Matthias asked.

"Open the bottle for me."

Matthias did so.

"Give it to me."

He did. Christian drank, almost losing his balance.

"Larry Train's dead," he said. "Strangled. I did that, too, Matthias. Just a few minutes ago. Busy goddamn day, Matthias. Mango insisted. He knew everything—a lot about Poe. Mango thought he would talk if they gave him a reduced sentence or something. Poor bastard. I went to his house and he hopped into bed and lay there waiting for me and a minute later he was choking to death. I'm supposed to kill you, too."

Matthias blanched. He was across the room from the fireplace and the poker. Christian could barely stand, but he had a firm grip on the pistol. If Matthias moved, he might fire.

"Don't worry, big brother. Won't do it. Couldn't do that. Not family. Never family. Mango doesn't understand that."

He turned and started toward the doorway.

"Where are you going?" Matthias said.

"Going to solve everything, Matt. Going to solve everything."

"Stay here!"

Christian brought the gun to bear, aimed waveringly at Matthias's chest. "Get back, Matt. Let me do what I have to do."

Christian backed across the room, knocking over a chair but remaining erect. At the front door, he paused.

"Good-bye, big brother. I love you. It's true."

Then he was gone.

Matthias rushed to the phone to call the police, then stayed his hand. It would take forever to explain this to them, and another forever to persuade them to do something about it. Where was Rawlings?

He went to the door, flinging himself outside. Christian was nowhere to be seen. Nothing moved in the street. Matthias turned right and ran to the corner. There was a couple walking hand in hand toward him. No one else.

He went the other way down the block. Again no sign of Christian. Turning the corner, he ran along that street. Nothing at that intersection. Running again, he went east, then south, zigzagging through the neighborhood, ultimately to no point.

At length he stopped and leaned back against a building wall, catching his breath. Where had Christian gone? To shoot Poe? The tycoon's bodyguards would cut him down. How could someone go wandering the streets of Chicago with a gun in one hand and a bottle in the other? Wouldn't the police stop him, pick him up? Would there be a gun fight? Would they shoot him down in the street?

Christian might have gone to his car. It would amaze Matthias if his brother could drive one block without hitting something in his condition, but he'd heard nothing.

Defeated, Matthias walked slowly back to his house. As he approached, he saw a police car double parked in the street. A man got out—Zane Rawlings—and the police car pulled away.

Rawlings saw him. "What are you doing out here?"

"I was looking for my brother." Matthias stopped in front of the big bearded man. "I've very sad news. I've solved your sailboat murder for you. It was Christian. He just told me. He killed Jill."

"Son of a bitch." Rawlings had his small suitcase with him. He picked it up. "Let's go inside. I'd better use your phone."

Rawlings hung up and gave Matthias an unhappy look. "They have a citywide out on your brother. Give them a man with a gun report and they get pretty excited." He sighed. "There's a meeting tomorrow morning with the state's attorney about Poe and Train. They won't issue a warrant until then."

"Train's dead. If what my brother told me is true, and I'm afraid it is."

"I'd better report that, too."

"What about Diandra?"

"I called the Coast Guard. They had a helicopter patrol out. Spotted Poe's yacht on the south end of the lake, a few miles northeast of Gary. Hard to tell what state it's in—maybe Indiana, maybe Michigan, maybe Illinois. They said it wasn't moving. No wake."

"And?"

"That's all we have working for us—a location."

"No one's going after her?"

"Matt, this isn't like the movies, where a hundred squad cars show up magically at the end. In real life, you need paperwork and justifiable cause. All Chicago P.D. has is a man with a gun report and the statement from Franck indicating a possible art swindle. No one's even made out a complaint. They want Franck to do that. Somehow, I don't think he's going to jump up and fly out here. Even if he did, he couldn't get here until tomorrow. I argued like hell, all the way up to the top, but that's where it stands. A sheriff's deputy from another state doesn't have a lot of clout with the police superintendent, and that's who made the draw."

"What about the Coast Guard? One of the other police departments? The FBI?"

Rawlings shrugged. "If we had evidence of a kidnapping, but we don't. I have a couple guys from my department coming out in a boat, but they're just going to sit on what they figure is the state line and monitor the situation. That's all they can do, Matt. They have no jurisdiction in Indiana. It's not hot pursuit. They have a possible threat, relayed hearsay by me from you. No one's about to go boarding that boat with drawn weapons on the basis of that. Not without a warrant. This is Peter Poe we're talking about. This is the man's wife. There's no record of previous assaults on her. No complaints. Not even a domestic dispute. My pals up at Area Six just checked."

"So what do we do?"

"If you want, we go out there and try to get her. I don't mind breaking regulations. I'm not exactly planning on a career with the county sheriff's department."

"I do want, very much."

"We'll need a boat."

"There's mine."

"A sailboat? That'll be a first in police work. It'll take half the night to get out there."

"I don't know what else we could get at this hour. I have an auxiliary engine and a full tank of gas."

Rawlings pondered this. "Maybe we should go after Poe."

"He has all sorts of bodyguards. And doing that wouldn't help Diandra."

Zany rubbed his beard. "I guess that's what's at the top of the agenda, then." He rose. "You ever fire a weapon?"

"Yes. I was in the army."

"In the army? An artist?"

"Family tradition, military service. It was only two years. R.O.T.C. I was a lieutenant. I qualified with an automatic pistol."

Rawlings went to his bag and took out two revolvers, sticking the larger one in his belt and handing the smaller one to Matthias. "Was your brother in the service, too?

"No. But I taught him to shoot. He's good. He seemed to enjoy it. Sense of power, I suppose. He never had much of that in my family."

"For the sake of my brother officers, let's hope he's as drunk as you say."

Christian could now add armed robbery to his crimes, at least technically. The night attendant at the gas station on LaSalle Street where he stopped refused to sell him the cans of gasoline he asked for, arguing that Christian was drunk. So he'd pulled his revolver on the youth, and within minutes he had four gallon cans in his trunk. He gave the fellow a hundred-dollar bill before he left. If this was robbery, the attendant seemed happy about it.

Train had paid Christian his final fee before he was killed. Christian hadn't counted the money, but he guessed he had many, many thousands of dollars in his pockets. It could take him out of the country, take him far. But it was too late, too late.

There were a number of black youths on the street near the museum. When Christian parked the Jaguar, hitting a lamp post in the process, they started walking toward him. He took out the revolver and fired a shot in the air. They scattered. When Christian had the gasoline inside, he locked the museum door. If they were brave enough to go back and fool with the Jaguar, they were welcome to it.

He went into the office and turned on the lights. He still had the vodka with him. He drank some, then went to the main desk and sat, staring stupidly at the table where Jill had customarily worked.

Foolish, foolish girl. Imbecilic Matthias. After Sally had ditched him for the wealthy lout, he'd spent the rest of his life looking for the perfect woman, and there she'd been all the time. If he had married her instead of the selfish Hillary—if he'd welcomed Jill to France when she'd ask to come—they all would have lived happily ever after.

Instead, she died. Everybody died. What difference did anything make, once you were dead?

Immortality was such conceit. How many artists had there been in Paris at the time of Delacroix, or Degas? Thousands. What remained of their work now? Those ancient Japanese screens in the Art Institute. Who even knew the names of their makers? All the wall texts said were "Circa 1600," or "Daimyo Culture." Immortality. Ha-ha-ha.

Christian got up and turned on the lights in the exhibition rooms, wandering through them, looking at the paintings. He paused by a still life—peeled fruit, a dead fish, a dead fowl, a human skull. Sixteenth-century German, done in the Dutch manner. Always the same message. Mortality. Always. Even in the midst of plenty.

He was feeling woozy and wobbly. Barely able to stand. Had to hurry. Much to do. Couldn't pass out. That would ruin everything.

Christian grinned back at the skull and gave it a small salute.

He splashed the gasoline against the walls and along the floors. It didn't go as far as he thought, but he supposed it would do. The structure was stone, but the walls were plaster and wood, covered with ancient wallpaper. The paintings would burn wonderfully.

When he was done, he stood a moment. Should he go back to the office? Sit there and keep drinking until the end? Wouldn't do. Had to hurry. How fast did gasoline evaporate?

He took out a lighter, one he'd bought to light Mango's endless cigarettes. He probably should have found a way to kill her, too. She was as much at fault as Jill Langley. Bloody Lady Macbeth. It would have been a wonderful irony if she were to perish with all the rest of them. He should have an irony.

Looking around at all the paintings, he thought of something marvelously ironic. Their grandfather had made his great decision. All the pretty things were to be kept on permanent display. The ugly paintings—the Expressionist and Modernist—to be locked away forever in the vault.

But the vault was fireproof. Art as beauty would perish. Art as truth would survive. Better than that, all those pieces would be given to the Art Institute, for all to see.

At long last, he was defying his grandfather, defeating him, subverting his grand design.

He took another drink, a long swallow, then dropped the

bottle. He was perfectly calm, his nerves all numb, his brain barely working. He needed some paper. Where to get paper? But, of course, he had pocketsful—wads of green, useless paper.

Christian pulled forth a hundred-dollar bill, crumpled it up, then set it on fire with the lighter, holding the edge gingerly. When it was fully aflame, he staggered to a wall and neatly dropped it onto a still moist pool.

The suddenness of the ignition startled him, its heat and force sending him reeling. He caught his balance, standing in the center of the room, watching the bright flames dance all about him.

Now. No use waiting. Here at last was the end of time. Matthias always said that one's last thoughts ought to be of someone you loved. Christian could think of no one. No one at all.

Good-bye then. He put the barrel of his gun to his temple and pulled the trigger.

Matthias had used his auxiliary engine to get out of the harbor, but, once clear of the breakwater, had killed it and hoisted sail, taking a heading to the southeast. The sky was hazy and the moon low. There were dots of lights here and there in the murk ahead, anyone of which could be Poe's boat. The wind was from the north, a steady breeze around ten knots, fine for a leisurely Sunday afternoon sail but frustratingly weak for their present task.

"Hot pursuit," said Zany. "At least Poe's boat isn't going anywhere. We hope."

"I want to save the engine for when we might need it most."

"Fair enough. I just wonder if it might be faster swimming."

"Jill made it across the lake in a single night."

"Yeah. Dead."

Matthias lighted his pipe. He rubbed at his eyes, but not because of the smoke.

"Maybe we should have taken someone else's boat," Zany said. "Like cops do with people's cars in the movies."

"I wish we weren't on this one."

"Just be careful how you handle it when we get near them, or you may get your wish."

"We could be making a big mistake."

"All part of making decisions."

"I'm not talking about whether she's on that yacht. I'm sure she's there. They wouldn't have it sitting out there for any other reason. I was just wondering . . . I hate to say it. I hate to even think of it, but what if she's there willingly, sitting there watching television or reading, going along with this just because Poe asked her to?"

"If you can't trust the love of your life, Matt, then where are you?"

"The love of my life, Zane, washed up on your breakwater in this boat."

Matthias had chosen some twinkling riding lights on the southeastern horizon as a bearing, but, as they neared them, they discovered they belonged to a smaller, different cabin cruiser. Matthias fell away, steering the *Hillary* in a wide circle, changing tack as they crossed the wind.

"Sky's beginning to get light in the east," Zany said. "We may have a big problem."

"Keep looking."

They made another slow circle, each man searching a different quarter of the horizon as the boat moved. As they came about again, Zany ducked under the boom, peering aft.

"There! That's it. Gotta be it. Looks as big as a ship."

"Perhaps it is a ship, an ore carrier or something."

"What? Lying off Michigan City? Its running lights are off. No ship's captain would do that." Zany settled back in his seat. "At the least, we can get them for a marine violation. Does this sailboat of yours have a radio? I'd like to check on my boys on the boat out of St. Joe."

"I did have a radio, but it was stolen, I think while you had the boat impounded."

"Well, you know Grand Pier. Hotbed of crime."

Matthias centered the steering, gazing due south. "She's a couple miles or so off. I wonder if they see us."

Zany looked up. "We're making it kind of easy for them, aren't we?"

"Let's attend to that." Matthias went forward, and began to lower sail.

The auxiliary engine on the *Hillary* was thirty-five horsepower, and they closed with the motionless motor yacht with surprising speed. When they were near enough to see the clear outlines of the *Queen P*'s superstructure, Matthias cut the motor back to near idle.

"We'll approach from the stern," he said. "I think the only

people at all alert at this hour will be forward on the bridge. I think there's a swimming ladder at the back. It will make things easier."

Zany checked the load in his revolver. "God only knows what weaponry they have on board."

"Take the tiller," Matthias said. "I'm going below."

He emerged from the cabin hatch carrying what looked to be pistol-size cannons.

"Back up," he said. "Flare guns. You wouldn't want to get hit by one."

Matthias worked his way astern of the big yacht, then headed slowly toward its fantail, inching closer and closer. Nothing moved on the deck, though they could see cabin lights.

As they neared the big boat, its bulk looming above them, the swimming ladder visible against the white breadth of the stern, Matthias cut the engine and let the *Hillary* drift the rest of the way on its own momentum. Zany went forward, taking bow line in hand, and leapt to the little diving platform next to the ladder, making the bow line fast to the metalwork.

"Let's go," he said softly.

Creeping along the main deck, they heard voices and a clatter of noise coming from a porthole just below them. From the sounds and smells, they judged it to be the galley.

They reached the stairs leading up to the bridge deck without encountering a single crew member, but shrank back against the bulkhead at a sudden swath of light appearing above.

Footsteps on the metal. Someone was coming down.

Zany pressed back flat against the wall, then raised his pistol. As the man, small but very sturdy looking, came by, Zany stepped out behind him and brought the butt of the gun down sharply on his head. He gave a grunt and toppled forward.

"Come on," Zany said, his revolver in his other hand, and started up the stairs.

They burst through the door to the bridge one after the other, guns to the fore. A man standing by the steering whirled around, startled and frightened. Another man sitting in a chair by the opposite windows had been drinking coffee. He froze, cup midway to his lips, and stared at them, stupified.

"Which one of you is the captain?" Zany asked.

"He's in the head," the man with the coffee cup said. He gestured at a door.

Zany glanced at Matthias to make sure he was being serious

about the way he held his weapon, then went to the door, turning the knob and shoving. From the toilet seat, the skipper looked up.

"What the hell is this?"

Zany held up his deputy sheriff's badge. "Police," he said. "Where's Mrs. Poe?"

"In the main cabin, below. Directly aft. You're really police?"

"Really am."

"Well, look. I don't know what's going on here. I think Mr. Poe's having a fight or something with his wife. Locked her up down there. Told us to take the vessel out here and heave to until further notice. We're just crew, just following orders. We don't know anything about trouble with the police."

"Nowadays husbands don't get to lock up their wives," Zany said. "Get your pants on and get out here."

They got the captain's keys from him and put him and his two mates in an adjoining chart room. Just as Zany was about to close and lock the door, the captain said, "Poe's got two men aboard. I think they're armed. Mean-looking bastards. One should be sitting by her cabin. I don't know where the other one is."

"Thanks for being so informative. Where's the rest of the crew?"

"Off watch, asleep. Except for the guys in the galley."

"Okay, see you later." He turned the latch. At the main stairs leading to the cabins below, Zany paused to look back at Matthias. "Okay, Matt, here's where it gets to be like the movies."

There was only one man to be seen, in a chair by a door at the end of the main corridor. He was awake, but not very alert. Zany and Matthias were within a dozen feet of him before he realized they weren't part of the crew—and saw their guns. He went for his belt.

Zany didn't want to do this again. "Hold it!" he said.

The man's hand kept moving. There was a sudden bark of a sound, followed by a whizzing *phhhhhht*. The man's upper chest exploded in sputtering, multicolored flame and he fell back, screaming, writhing on the floor.

Zany jerked his head back. Matthias was looking at the smoking flare gun in his hand, his expression mournful.

A door behind him opened. Another man emerged, a pistol in hand. He took in Zany and Matthias and his pitiful comrade in a second's glance. Zany had a gun on him. He dropped his pistol.

They all stood watching as the stricken man died, helpless to do anything about it. Zany made a strange sound. Turning away, he threw up. Stepping back finally, he wiped his mouth with his handkerchief and took the empty flare pistol from Matthias.

"Save problems later," Zany said. "I did it, okay? Having three of these guys on my sheet's the same as two."

"The keys," Matthias said.

Diandra was standing in the center of the cabin, her eyes wide with fear. She had a bed sheet wrapped around her, bare feet and shoulders showing. Matthias glanced about the cabin. The wretches had taken her clothes.

She came into his arms and clung to him tightly, the sheet dropping slightly, the bare skin of her back clammy and cold.

She spoke his name over and over.

If you can't trust the love of your life, Zany had said.

Matthias told her he loved her.

CHAPTER
25

LIEUTENANT BALDESSARI BROUGHT his breakfast to work in a paper bag—two chocolate doughnuts, a large coffee black. He had two packs of Marlboros in his pockets.

Mulroney was in Baldessari's office, in one of the side chairs, looking through a file folder. He stood up. "You're in early, boss."

"Meeting with the fucking brass on this Poe thing. Is that the morning report?"

"You want the good news or the bad news first?"

Baldessari sighed. Why did people still do this? "Give me the bad."

"Someone clocked Laurence Train. In his townhouse. Looks like a fag job, but you never know, especially with him being under investigation and all."

"He isn't—wasn't—under investigation yet. Not officially. What else you got?"

"You heard about that four-eleven alarm at the German Museum?"

Baldessari nodded. "WGN radio had it."

"Everybody has it. But now we got a positive ID on the crisp one they recovered. From his watch. Engraved. Christian Curland. Firearm recovered, too. Thirty-eight special. Gunshot. Big hole in the skull. Probably self-inflicted."

"Never take that for granted, Mulroney." The lieutenant took a big bite out of his doughnut. They'd want him to know all about this at the meeting in the state's attorney's office.

"The museum doors were locked, boss."

"Let's just leave it up to the medical examiner. Is there good news? Or are you just yanking my chain?"

"Got a report back from the Atlantic City P.D. Rose Scalzetti?

She changed her name and left the life. Went legit. Singer, something like that. She got a job in a lounge at a casino out there. New name's Mango Bellini."

It was familiar, but Baldessari couldn't remember why.

"The casino was owned by Peter Poe," Mulroney said. "The lady still works for him, here in Chicago. Executive assistant or something. Hooker days behind her."

Baldessari pushed away the doughnuts and took a burning swig of coffee, then lighted a Marlboro, thinking. "This is the same broad? You're sure?"

"We rechecked the fingerprint match," Mulroney said. "It's exact."

"Okay," said Baldessari. "Pick her up."

"Is this going to screw up the O'Rourke case?"

"Not if I can help it. But don't charge her with that. Make it the killing of that blond hooker for now."

"We'll need a warrant."

"Judge Cohen's over in the coffeeshop. Let's go ruin his breakfast."

Poe hesitated before getting into his limousine, turning to look up at the windows of City Hall.

"Come on, Peter," said Mango. "What are you afraid of, he's going to change his mind?"

"He just seemed so uneasy about everything."

"Look, he gave you the go-ahead, okay? Now let's get over to the cardinal's house and turn over the deed, as promised. Everything else will take care of itself."

"He asked me if I knew anything about what happened to Train and Christian Curland."

"He probably asked his staff that, too. Now relax. We're out of the picture on those. My bet is Curland took care of Train and then killed himself."

"Why would he go after Train?"

"Running scared, maybe."

"You said he had guts."

"He was a drunk, Peter. A loser. Now let's go."

Krasowski headed up LaSalle Street, moving slowly in the heavy morning traffic.

"When we've signed the deal with Inland Empire, Mango, I want to get out of here for a while. Out of the country."

"A little Bahamas?"

"A lot of Bahamas."

"You gotta take care of Diandra first."

"What do you mean, 'take care of'?"

"Your divorce."

"That'll take some time."

"It doesn't need to. You've got friends in the courts, remember? You don't have to worry about Curland's brother now. What can he do? Train's dead. Christian's dead. That girl's dead. It's just that old man Franck's word against yours, and you can say you didn't know the paintings were fakes, that you bought them from Train the way Franck bought them from you. You're all right on this score."

"Maybe."

"So get rid of Diandra. Give her some money so she'll agree to an uncontested divorce and let her and Curland go on their way. And you and me on ours."

"I need him for the building."

"The hell you do. Those other guys of yours can figure out the numbers and blueprints."

"If Inland Empire and the Japanese don't hurry up, I'm not going to have any money to give her."

"Relax, Peter. Come on. You've taken care of everything they asked for. All you have to do now is turn over title on Cabrini Green to the cardinal."

A beeping sound interrupted them. Krasowski picked up the front seat car phone. "It's Mr. Yeats, Mr. Poe."

Poe wiped his palms on his trousers, then lifted the rear seat receiver, waiting for Krasowski to hang up.

"I needed you with me this morning, William," Poe said. "It was hard doing this solo. His honor can be real scary sometimes."

"Sorry, Peter, but I told you the bank wanted to see me this morning, that it was important. It was."

Poe waited. "Yeah? And?"

"Well, I don't know, how to tell you this, but I'm afraid the building deal is off."

"Off? What the hell are you talking about? I just left the mayor! I'm going to get a building permit, a real one this time. It's all set!"

"A call came in from Mr. Yamaguchi late last night. I don't know what time it was, Tokyo time. but real late here."

"Yeah, so what's his problem?"

"Mr. Yamaguchi has been looking at the drawings real hard. I'm sorry to say this, but he's changed his mind."

"You mean he doesn't like the design? We'll change the fucking design! We'll do it in a week, sooner, if he wants. Today!"

"That's not it, Peter. He loves the design. He thinks it's the greatest he's ever seen. He doesn't want to put his money into your building anymore. He wants to put up the world's tallest building in Tokyo. He wants Curland's design for himself."

"Curland works for me. He can't do that."

"You can't copyright a building, Peter."

"This is crazy! Call Inland Empire back. Tell them I'll fly to Tokyo!"

"It's too late, Peter. Believe me, it's an undone deal. Mr. Yamaguchi seems to have his heart set on this. He's an old guy. He wants to leave a monument. For the greater glory of Japan, the emperor, and Yamaguchi, Inc."

Poe sat there, holding tightly to the phone, trying to forestall the moment when he'd hang it up. That would be finality. That would be the end. There had to be something.

"What about other investors?" he said weakly.

"No one in Japan will want to lend an American money to undercut Mr. Yamaguchi."

"Fuck the Japanese. What about American?"

"In this recession? I'm afraid that kind of money for a single structure would be looked upon as a dubious enterprise. These are conservative times, Peter. Everyone's thinking retrenchment. We've talked about this."

"There's got to be somebody! What about Germans!"

"Please, Peter. You're going to have to think about retrenchment yourself. Consolidation. I'm afraid you've got Chapter Eleven breathing down your neck now. I'd better start drawing up some papers."

"No."

"Peter—"

"No!"

"Listen to me, Peter. You have $4.5 million outstanding with three different banks from when you bought the Cabrini Green tract from the city. I was asked about it this morning. You'd better think about dumping that property real fast."

"You're no damn good, Yeats! You're a lousy fucking lawyer! All you've got are connections, and they're not worth a shit!"

"Why don't you call me back later, Peter, when you've had a chance to calm down. Collect your thoughts."

"I'll collect your ass, you mick bastard! Fuck you! You're fired!"

Yeats hung up. Poe lowered the phone slowly to his lap, but moved no further.

Mango was staring at him, studying him, her face impassive.

"You want to tell me?" she said finally, her voice as expressionless as her face.

Poe stayed silent. Mango had seen corpses who looked better than he did now.

"Never mind," she said. "I heard enough. It's all down the fucking toilet, isn't it?"

"Yes."

Mango lighted a cigarette, then looked to Krasowski. "Forget the cardinal's house, Lenny. Make it the penthouse."

"No," said Poe. He still hadn't let go of the phone. "Not there. I don't want to go there."

"Where then, Peter? You just want to drive around? You want a drink?"

"Cabrini Green."

"What?"

"I want to go to Cabrini Green. It's still mine."

Zany had used the *Queen P*'s radio to contact the sheriff's men from Michigan. When they were aboard and everything was under control, he made a patch call to the Chicago office of the FBI. He had a bona fide interstate kidnapping here. The yacht had crossed two state lines.

The agent in charge sounded a little confused by what Zany told him, but told him to bring the yacht back to Chicago's Monroe Street harbor, where he'd be met by field agents. Then they could sort everything out.

Sorting everything out was going to take a long time, maybe longer than Zany planned to stay a policeman.

Curland's *Hillary* and the sheriff's boat were taken under tow—the sailboat given the longer line. Matthias went aboard his craft to handle the tiller, to make sure the sailboat didn't become fouled on the other.

Diandra, who'd found some sailor's clothes that fit her, went into the *Hillary* with him. She said she didn't want to spend another minute on the *Queen P*.

It was chilly in the open cockpit, but Matthias put his arm around her and the rising sun began to warm them. She yawned, then apologized. The lifting and falling motion of the boat once they were underway was very lulling.

"Did you get any sleep?" he asked.

"Not much. I was really afraid they were going to kill me."

"So was I."

"Gallant knight to the rescue." She patted his knee.

"Why don't you get some sleep," he said. "It's a long way back."

"What about you? You didn't get any."

"I'll be all right."

"Superman."

"Just a sailboat skipper."

Diandra shifted on the seat, then lay back with her head in his lap. She took his hand and held it to her chest. "I don't ever want to let go of you."

"Just rest."

The Chicago skyline was fully in view by the time Diandra awoke. She sat up and stretched, then nestled close to him. "It's warm now."

"Getting there."

"Summer's almost over. It was the longest one of my life."

The *Hillary* was riding up close to the smaller boat again. Matthias pulled the tiller toward him, making the bow turn away and the line swing taut. "We're nearly there."

"How much longer?"

"A half hour."

"Matt, there'll be policemen there, won't there? I'll have to make a statement and fill out forms or something, won't I?"

"We all will."

"I'm not up to that. Not now."

He smiled. "Neither am I."

Taking his arm from her, he went forward, pulling on the bow line, bringing the *Hillary* closer to the big motor yacht. When the line was slack enough, he untied it at the *Hillary*'s end, letting it slip into the blue-green water. The sailboat began to fall back. After returning to the helm, he opened the lid of the control compartment and started the boat's engine.

"It's so noisy," she said. "Why don't we use the sails?"

"It's a bit of work."

"I'll help. I'll have to get used to that."

The breeze was light, but filled the sails. Someone on the bridge of the *Queen P,* probably Zany, sounded the yacht's thundering horn as Matthias turned the *Hillary* away. Matthias couldn't tell if it was farewell or warning. He waved, and kept on his course, heading northwest toward Navy Pier.

Diandra moved close to him again. "The city's so beautiful from here."

"It's the best place to see it. I used to come out here often, just to do that, look at the city, with . . ."

"With Jill Langley."

"Yes."

"I'm sorry you lost her."

He didn't speak.

"But I'm glad I found you," she said.

"Me, too."

Some seagulls wheeled overhead. Diandra looked up at them. "That's how I feel now. Free."

"We paid a price for that."

"Now we can be whatever we want. Do what we want. What do you want to do, Matt?"

"Clean up the mess my brother made. Then, I don't know."

"Sure you do."

"Well, I know one thing. You said you married to find out what it would be like to be Mrs. Peter Poe. Would you like to find out what it would be like to be Mrs. Matthias Curland?"

"I already know what that would be like."

"And?"

"The answer is yes, Matt. A thousand times yes. I can get that divorce now. On my terms. We beat him, Matt. You did. You and that funny policeman. He'll go to jail, won't he? Because of the paintings? Imagine Peter in jail. Pushed around by everyone."

"I just want him out of Chicago."

"I want him out of my life. Far, far away."

The wind dropped. The sailboat glided on, straightening, then creaking over into a heel once more as the breeze revived.

"We can get a place in Door County," she said. "On the water."

"All right."

"For weekends." She cuddled closer. "What do you want to do, Matt, aside from marry me?"

He only smiled.

"You don't want to go back to painting, do you? Be an artist?"

"I want to do another picture of you. With your clothes on. A formal portrait, just for me."

"Do you still want to be an architect?"

"Of a sort."

"A sort? How many sorts are there?"

"I don't want to do buildings anymore. I don't want to have to deal with people like your husband again. I think I'd like to do sailboats. I've been thinking about it all night."

"Architects do sailboats?"

"Marine architects. Sailboat designers. Yes, I think I'd like to do that very much. Buildings are static. Great lumps that just stand there. Sailboats are motion. Beauty and motion, all in one. I'd like to create that."

Her eyes were on Lake Point Tower. Its curving glass sides sparkled in the sunlight.

"I've never heard of any marine architects," she said.

"They don't get to be very famous. Or very rich."

"You're sure that's what you want?"

"Yes."

"I want what you want, Matt."

"I love you." It was true. Love is an ever-diminishing quantity, but there remained enough. Just enough.

"I want you," she said. She kissed him, then leaned her head against his shoulder. Navy Pier, the city, their future, was getting near.

"We'll live in Lake Forest," she said.

He stared ahead.

"Is that all right? Can you afford that?"

"It's all right."

You awoke every morning, and you looked for what was left. He patted her leg. "It's all right."

Poe poured more whiskey into his glass. Mango looked at him disgustedly.

"We've been sitting here for fifteen goddamned minutes, Peter. What's the point?"

The limousine was parked on the cracked pavement of a Cabrini Green sidewalk, in a vast empty space in the midst of the abandoned high-rises. Demolition work had been started and there were piles of broken concrete rising from the sparse grass, looking like ancient burial mounds. Poe was staring out the window, as if in a trance.

"Come on, Peter. We've got things to do. You've got big problems."

Poe sipped his whiskey. "Shut up, Mango."

She folded her arms and snorted, her expression very dark. Poe got out of the car.

"Now what?" she said.

"Just wait."

Glass in hand, he walked slowly across the grass, pausing to look up at the ruined buildings, then moving on. Coming to one of the mounds of broken concrete, he stopped, then began making his way to the top.

Mango watched him. "What the hell's he doing, Lenny?"

"Let him be, Mango."

"I think he's lost his fucking mind."

She waited, smoked a cigarette, then waited more. Poe was just sitting there, a little man on his little hill, gazing off to the southeast, toward the downtown towers.

"Enough's enough, Lenny." She snapped open the door.

"What're you going to do?"

"Just wait here. Have yourself a belt."

It was a hard climb up the pile of concrete. Mango ripped her stockings on the sharp edges and cut her hand. She swore, but Poe paid her no attention at all.

She knelt on a flat slab just behind him, leaning close. "What are you looking at, Peter?"

"I'm looking at nothing. Nothing at all."

"You looking at where your building was going to be?"

He didn't speak, didn't move.

"It's gone, Peter. All gone."

"I know."

"You can't just sit here."

"Nowhere to go."

She looked back to the car. Krasowski was still behind the wheel.

Mango shook her head, then pulled her purse around and reached inside. She carefully took out the pistol and raised it to the back of Poe's head. Pathetic bastard.

"Keep looking, Peter."

The shot stung the air with ringing echoes.

She clambered back down the pile quickly. Krasowski was out

of the limousine but just standing there, looking stupid. Mango took off her shoes and began running, heading for the nearest of the empty buildings. Once safe inside its darkness, she glanced back through the doorway. Krasowski was heading toward the mound.

There was a back way out, an old metal door, half off its hinges. Mango put her shoes back on and walked out through it, hurrying out of the project and across the street, into the old neighborhood. She had a pair of sunglasses in her purse and put them on.

Black faces stared at her as she walked by. She had a lot of cash with her, more money than any of these people would likely see in any one place in all their lives. She'd taken that precaution weeks before. If anyone messed with her, she had the gun.

Her high heels clicking on the worn sidewalk, she kept on, heading north, then turning east, disappearing into the big sprawling city. Once again she'd have to move on, as she'd been doing all her life. Find another place, find another name, find someone else—only this time, for once, not a loser. That was the trouble with the fucking world. So many losers. There were so many, there wasn't any room for the winners. A winner didn't stand a fucking chance.